Sick Love

A Shadow's Legacy Novel

Book Two

Sick Love

LONNIE DAVIDSON

SICK LOVE

Published by LDA

Library of Congress Control Number: 2024900272

ISBN: 979-8-9895644-1-5 (Softcover)
ISBN: 979-8-9895644-2-2 (Hardcover)
ISBN: 979-8-9895644-3-9 (E-book)

Visit the publisher/author:
www.lonniedavidson.com

To love lost and that yet to be found

Sick Love

Chapter 1

My fists, my legs, my body ache, heavy from the fatigue of battle. With deep breaths, I do my best to slow my breathing, but my mind and heart are racing a mile a minute, and I cannot calm down. Especially, not with him in front of me.

The Messenger. A herald of the long since defeated Demon army. A parasite that has taken the lives of countless people in his mission to resurrect his fallen leaders. Including my parents.

He glares at me with decayed eyes, riddled with splotches of white, black, and yellow. The withered skin on his human vessel's half rotted face twists and stretches as he smiles. "You can't stop it boy." He says as he proceeds to peel away the flesh hanging from his arms. His blood: a mixture of pus and bile pour from his wounds with his every breath, but he is unfazed. "The Generals will rise and with their resurgence you will fall, and New Birth will be theirs." He continues, his voice like rocks in a blender. I look down to the pool of blood that blanketed the whole floor, beneath my feet. It was beginning to shine with a low glow. "Look, even now they stir."

Statuettes, made from varied materials rise out of the blood. They shine with an ominous light that makes my skin crawl. *I gotta stop this.* My body tenses as energy surges through and around me, cloaking me in a shroud of darkness. It condenses over my skin until it forms into the armor and bone claws of the betrayer, 5th general of the demon army, Shadow. In a burst of power and speed, I propel myself towards him.

Within arms-reach, The Messenger swings a fast and powerful right haymaker aimed at my face. Shards of bone protruding through the skin of his fist. At the last second, I drop under it and drive my shoulder deep into his already wounded abdomen. His feet fly out from under him, and we slam onto the ground, splashing into the blood.

Before he can react, I hop up to my feet. My claw poised high, ready to pierce his chest and destroy his heart, ending him and his plan. He stares up at me with a twisted smile and starts to laugh. "It's too late." His body melts into a putrid puddle of brown slime right from under me.

"NO!" I yell.

The statuettes explode in a show of light, turning the world around me white.

I fall to my knees looking for the blood, or what remained of The Messenger, but everything was gone. I slam my fist into the ground frustrated. "Not again."

"Easy Kyle." Someone says next to me. I snap around, hopping to my feet, prepared to fight. But as I notice and recognize the tall, muscular man standing next to me, all the fight leaves me. "Leo."

His clothes are dusty and torn like the last time I had seen him. Bond to that chair. He looks at me, his eyes dull, grey and devoid of life. "It's okay Kyle. You tried." He says softly.

Panicked, I step away from him. The armor and claws melt away in a cloud of smoke. "Leo...I...I'm sorry. I couldn't save you."

He puts his hands up, to stop me from talking. "It's okay. You tried." He continues. To my horror, the flesh on his neck starts to tear from one side to the other across his throat. Blood pours down his chest as he smiles kindly. "You tried." He says again.

I reach out to him, but he vanishes before I can touch him. "Leo, I'm sorry."

The sound of applause echoes from behind me. As I turn to face it, the scene changes and I'm standing on a grassy plain that stretches as far as the eye can see. The sky is grey, with huge storm clouds quickly rolling in. The applause gets louder as three shadowy figures appear around me, clapping and laughing as if I'd done something funny. "You tried. You failed. We are amongst you." Their voices speak in unison.

The sound of thunder draws my attention to the sky. Red lightning dances within the clouds as they swirl above me. "We couldn't have failed."

A hand takes me by the throat and lifts me off the ground. Looking at my attacker, I see his arm stretched out from within a cloak of flowing darkness. He looks at me with gleaming crimson eyes that danced with amusement and power. "But you have. Now, sweet dreams." He says his voice like a distant whisper.

There's a flash and everything goes red. For a second my body, my mind, my soul is on fire. Then it all goes black.

A hand caresses my cheek. "Hero...Hero...Kyle wake-up!" I hear Valene yelling.

"Va...Valene?" I manage.

"Kyle, look at me. Look at me!" she demands, gripping both sides of my face, her hands; hard and hot. The sound of a crackling fire is right in my ears and the smell of burning flesh in my nose. I open my eyes and gasp at the sight of her. She's not staring at me with her golden eyes, but with empty pockets of smoldering embers. Her once bronze skin, blackened from the flames now raging around us and within her. "It's your fault." She says.

"Valene?"

"How could you fail?"

"We tried. I..."

Her hands cover my mouth. The heat of the fire coming from her moves down my throat into my chest. "No excuses Hero. We're burning. Everyone. And so will you."

I try to fight her, but I can't move. The burning quickly spreads throughout my body. When my hand burst into flames. I try to scream, but her hand is like a vice, and she just holds me. The flames creep up my arm and I start to panic. *Valene, please let me go. Please help me. Somebody, help me!*

Something soft, but heavy lands on my chest. I look up through tears to see a cat standing on me. "Little brother. Little brother! Wake up!"

I snap awake, sitting up gasping for air. Frantically, I look around in the darkness surrounding me. After a second my eyes adjust and I see the nightstand next to me. The desk across the room. And the windows with light from the streetlamps shining through. *I'm in my room. I think.* I rub my eyes taking a deep breath, trying to calm myself.

"Kyle?" A voice says cautiously next to me.

I jump, looking towards the voice. "Who's there?" I ask sharply.

From out of the darkness a grey cat with black stripes leaps up onto my bed. Her head cocks to the side as she looks at me with concern in her greenish yellow eyes. I take a deep breath and manage to calm myself bit. "...Mayra?"

"Yes, it's me. Little brother, are you okay? You were crying out in your sleep."

"Oh, yeah...um ...It was just a... a really bad nightmare."

She looks at me and sighs in relief. "Yeah, I have those too. What did you see?"

Images of the dream run through my mind, and I can feel my eyes beginning to sting with tears. "Can we not, right now, please."

She walks up to me putting head to mine. "No, of course." I take hold of her and clutch in my arms. She wraps her tail around my arm and snuggles into my chest, as she purrs.

Minutes pass and I feel better. I relax my hold on Mayra, letting her go. She spins around and sits on my legs. "Ready to talk? What's bothering you?" she asks.

"Mayra. I... I feel so helpless. So weak. Like a failure."

"Why is that?"

"In my dreams, I keep fighting the Messenger and I fail to stop him and the ritual. I keep trying to save... save Leo, but I can't. And then...everyone is burning and Valene she...hurts me. All because I failed. Because I'm weak."

Mayra groans, before she lets out a little laugh "Little brother, losing is hard. Be it a fight. A family member. Or... the person you love. It's frustrating. But you needn't worry about what you have already lost. You should be focusing on what you have. You have me, Serena, your friends, The Kirs and Valene. We all understand the situation that you were in. Beyond what you've accomplished there is nothing more you could have done. You do understand that don't you?"

"I do. It's just."

"Now if you feel that you need to get stronger to protect that which you have. Then by all means. But the type of strength that you're looking for takes time. Do you understand?"

"Yeah. Thank you. I am sorry."

She licks my hand. "I know and you're welcome. Now, go to sleep. I'll be here with you."

I lay back. Mayra curls up onto my chest. 'Focus on what you have...' I feel myself drifting to sleep when the smell and the sound of a crackling fire appear. I open my eyes and just stare at the ceiling. Until everything just goes dark.

Chapter 2

Valene stands over me. Her flesh charred and blackened. "Kyle, it hurts." She reaches down to me. I try to move, try to get away but my body won't budge. Her flame torn hands caress my face. The smell of smoke and burning flesh makes my eyes water, and my stomach churn. "It burns." She says her voice crackling like wood in a fire. Her fingers begin to dig into my skin, as her grip tightens. "The burning, burning...we're all burning!" She screams, getting into my face. She looks me in the eyes, hers empty and smoldering. "You failed."

"I..." The chime of my phone goes off in my ear. Like smoke in the wind, Valene vanishes from on top of me. Instantly, feeling returns to my body and I take a shaky breath covering my eyes. "I'm sorry."

Between my fingers, I see the light of the sun cast on ceiling through the blinds. My hands move to my stomach, so I can run my fingers through Mayra's fur and calm my nerves. When I grab nothing, I remember that she's not here. She hasn't been here for about a month now and It's been hard without her.

The phone chimes again. I pop it off the charger, to look at it. I can't help but chuckle at the notification. A text from Valene. 'Hey Hero. Call me.'

I stare at the screen for a long time before clicking her photo. It was her, normal, beautiful. Her long curly hair up in ponytail. Her bronze skin gleaming in the light and her gold eyes shining like em...embers. 'It burns.' Her voice rings in my ears. The phone grows hot in my hand, and I put it down next to me. Minutes pass as I stare up at the ceiling. "Come on Kyle, get a grip. It's just Valene. The real Valene." I pick up the phone and dial her.

"Good morning, Hero."

I sit up, my mouth becoming dry at the sound of her voice. "G...good morning. Is everything okay?"

She sighs, "Not really?"

"What's wrong?"

"Well, I haven't seen my boyfriend in a while. That's what's wrong."

"Yeah, I'm sorry. You know school, finals, and everything."

"Yeah, sure. Mother wants to see you. Will you be gracing us with your presence today?"

I rub my face and neck. The feeling of her hands is still fresh on my skin. "Valene..."

"Kyle, please." She says softly.

"Okay." I say through a sigh. "I'll be there in a half hour or so."

"Okay, see you soon." She hangs up.

With a deep breath I fall back onto the bed. *My nerves are shot. And with this dream I never know what to expect. Except that Valene will be there. Come on, you can't keep avoiding her. The real her.*

I roll out of bed, grabbing a pair of shorts, and t-shirt before heading to the bathroom. As the light turns on, I get a good look at the mess that is me. Bags under my eyes, my hair is unkempt, and my skin is pale brown. Well, I haven't really been outside too much lately either. *This will be good for me.*

I splash water on my face, brush my hair, and brush my teeth. *There we are, fresh and clean.* There's a knock at the door. "Kyle sweetie. Is that you?" says an older voice I haven't heard in a while.

"Yeah, it's me. Can I help you with something Serena?"

She gasps so dramatically that I can imagine her leaning on the door, exacerbated by the notion of my question. "I haven't seen my dear nephew in ages. And you spurn me with such a nonchalant and unenthusiastic answer. I am hurt."

Opening the door, there's a teenage girl no taller than me, with a big grin across her face. Her deep brown eyes shining with excitement. "You may sound like my aunt, but this face." I palm her face, pushing her out of the way. "Belongs to my slightly annoying and immature sister."

"Immature?! I'll have you know young man that I am a thousand years your senior and your legal guardian. I am the pinnacle of maturity."

"Oh yeah? Who was it that drew on my face with a permanent marker? Covered me from head to toe in shaving cream? Then dripped ghost pepper hot sauce in my mouth. All while I was asleep." I say looking at her over my shoulder.

To my surprise it's not the young face of my sister, but the older face of the aunt that has raised me most of my life. "Me and that sister of yours are going to have a talk."

"You're annoying."

There's a cold burst of wind as her body shifts back to her young form. "Oh, come on Kyle. Lighten up. It was all in good fun. You've been a bit of a sourpuss lately. Especially since Mayra left."

"Where is Mayra?"

She shrugs, "Who knows. I would like to say that she's on some secret mission but honestly, she's like any other wild cat. She just moves from place to place. And she's going through some things. She'll back though."

"I know." Looking at Serena, I see that her smile has drooped, and her eyes were down to the floor. "Hey." She looks at me as I hold my arms open. Happily, she rushes up to me, and squeezes me tight. "Thank you for trying to cheer me up."

"It's no problem sweetie. I just wanted to help a little. Like I used to when you were young."

"You have."

"So, where are you off to so early?

"The Kir's for morning training. Want to come?"

Serena quickly backs away from me. "Oh, yeah. See I have a few errands to run. You know, gotta get that stuff together for your graduation party."

"That's a month and some change away."

"Better to get things now than later. Tell everyone I said hi. Bye." Serena shadow walks away, vanishing in a cloud of black smoke.

She keeps dodging going over there. I'm sure she's avoiding being put through the ringer of a workout like we all have. But I can't talk. I've been avoiding going over there too. *Better get going before I change my mind.*

In front of my room, I grab the handle of the door with my right hand. Energy courses through me and into it. An intricate symbol etches itself into the wood door with an orange light. The crest of the of the Kir family. "Zelaport. Fiend of the Kir home. With Key in hand, I command thee to open."

Flames burst out from around the edges of the door, and it starts turning to stone. The face of a horrifying gargoyle slowly protrudes out, locking its lifeless eyes on me. It smiles revealing its jagged teeth. "Master Kyle. How may I be of service?" It asks so properly and distinguished.

"Wow, it worked."

"Indeed. The house of Kir and Ross have been connected. From this point on, all you must do now is take hold of this handle and speak where you would like to go within the Kir estate."

"Cool. The training room please."

"As you Command." Zel says, bowing his head. He sinks back into the door, and it turns back white. The handle twists in my hand and opens to the training room. Valene and Jason stand in the middle of the wooden floor at attention. With a deep breath I step through the threshold. The door shuts behind me, drawing everyone's attention.

Jason's golden eyes light up with excitement. "Bro!" he yells as he breaks rank. He rushes over to me and wraps his arms around me, nearly knocking me off my feet. "Where've you been?"

I run my hand through his curly hair. "I missed you too Jase. Just been working through some things."

"Mon chou." A voice, thick with a French accent says from behind me. "What have I said about breaking rank?"

"Sorry mother." Jason gives me a good squeeze before rushing back over next to Valene.

I spin around. His mother, Selene, stands tall with her arms crossed. Her dark skin gleaming with sweat as she stares at me with her emerald eyes.

She smiles, nodding at me to follow him. "Yes ma'am."

I rush over next to Valene. I look at her for and she doesn't budge. She doesn't even crack a smile. *She's probably mad at me.*

Selene walks in front of us. "Kyle." With a deep breath I step forward. "What is the first stance of the demon art *Nigi?*"

"*Toralu* - Fortress."

"Begin!"

I widen my stance and bring my fists back to my rib cage. Without hesitation my hands and feet move in unison. Shifting my guard from front to back, left to right. My base is solid. My arms are strong but fluid, always moving in a circular motion to protect my center. Until I end where I began.

"What is the second stance?"

"Lokar – Blooded."

"Begin!"

Bringing my hands up, to my face I stagger my feet, getting into a boxer's stance. With as much power I can muster I throw the first punch, a hard left jab. Followed by a right hook. From there I unleashed a flurry of kicks and punches doing my best to keep up the intensity. With a whipping roundhouse kick I ended where I began.

"Very good Cheri. You've done them both perfectly as expected. I'm happy to see that your absence hasn't dulled you. Now do them both ten more times. Valene, you will watch him. If he misses even one step, he will have twenty pushups for each miss. Am I clear?"

"Yes ma'am." We both say.

"Welcome back Cheri. We missed you." She says walking over to Jason.

I look over to Valene, who is just staring at me. *It has been a few months since we've seen one another. I don't know what to say.* "Valene."

"Yes?" She says taking a step towards me.

"I'm..." A flash of her flame ravaged self appears with her hands stretched out to grab me. I look away from her and take a step back.

"Kyle?"

I take a deep breath, trying to quell the panic building in my chest. "We should get started." I say looking forward and getting into the *Toralu* stance.

From my peripheral, I can see that she's back to normal. A confused look on her face. Until it scrunches into annoyance. She crosses her arms and stares at me. "Yeah, you're right." She positions herself in front of me. "Begin."

The first three sets are smooth. Getting back into my stance I lock eyes with Valene. My heart is already racing, but it becomes wild with fear as her form changes right before my eyes. "What's the matter Hero? Begin." She says her voice crackling.

I close my eyes and take a couple deep breaths. *It's not real. It's not real.* A hand lightly grips my shoulder. My eyes snap open to the burned Valene in my face. "Hero?"

Every fiber of me tenses, as panic fills my body. I knock her hand off me. "Don't touch me!" I yell as I push her away from me with all of my strength.

Valene slides back a couple of feet. Shock in her burning eyes. "Kyle?"

My hands are trembling, and I can't catch my breath. My eyes blur from the tears welling in them. "I...I'm sorry...I need a minute." I rush out of the door and into the long stone corridor that leads back to the house.

Placing my head onto the cold stone, everything slows down and I can breathe. "Kyle?" Valene says from behind me.

At the sound of her voice everything tenses back up. My stomach churns. "Yeah?"

"Are you okay?" she asks softly.

"As I okay as I can be." I say looking at the wall. "Are you okay?" I ask looking over my shoulder.

Her face is contorted with worry, but I can tell how angry she is due to her eyes flickering back and forth between black and gold. "Yeah. Now are you going to tell me what really has been going on with you?"

"I don't know what you're talking about. Everything is fine."

Her hand takes my shoulder, and she spins me around, facing her. She slams me against the wall. Her eyes pure black now, "Don't you **dare** lie to me!"

I can't help but cower and look away from her as her face changes again. "Please Valene, let me go."

She exhales sharply in disbelief. Her hands soften their grip, and she slides them around me, holding me. "Hero, talk to me. Let me help."

I hold her back, putting my face onto her shoulder. "I don't know if you can."

"Hero spill it."

"For the past year, I've been having a reoccurring nightmare. About The Messenger, Leo, The Generals and..."

"And what?"

"At the end of it all, I see everyone burning. And you...you blame me for it all."

"What?" She pushes me back to look at me. Her eyes are golden, but I do my best not to meet her gaze. "Kyle I would never."

I touch my neck where the flame torn Valene has grabbed me so many times. "Well, maybe not you, exactly."

She sighs and caresses my face. "You should have come to me about this earlier."

"I was afraid."

"Afraid of what?"

"That you would hurt me. Like you do in my dreams."

Her eyes flicker black as she narrows them at me, growling under her breath. "How dar..." She stops biting her lip. Valene takes a deep breath. Her eyes swirling between black and gold. "Kyle, what was the first thing that I told you when we met?"

"That, I was safe with you."

She stares at me for a long second. With a sigh, her eyes settle on gold again. She kisses me on the forehead. "Go home Hero. We'll talk later." She walks away and back to the door leading to the combat room.

"Valene." I call out. She stops at the door just staring forward. "I'm sorry." Without even a glance back she opens and walks through. It slams shut behind her, the echoing sound rattling me a bit.

I lean against the wall for minute trying to pull myself together. "Well, that could've gone better." I get up and make my way to the door. Taking the handle, I consider just sucking it up and going back in there. But when I think of Valene all I see is her burning and then attacking me. "Zel, to my room at Serena's please." The door warps and opens to my room. "Thanks." I walk through and flop onto my bed, face first.

Chapter 3

Laying on my bed, I stare up at the darkness of my ceiling. Images of the flame torn Valene slowly edging closer to me cloud my vision. Her crackling voice, echoing, calling out to me. I roll over onto my stomach, putting my face into my pillow. *Leave me alone.*

Fingers grip my shoulders from behind, and I hold my breath. "We're burning." She whispers. "I'm burning Hero. It hurts...IT HURTS!"

I pull my pillow closer. *Go away. Go away. GO AWAY!*

The alarm on my nightstand blares to life and her hands vanish. Slowly, I look up from the pillow and over my shoulder. There's nothing there. Just the dark of my room. The digital display on the clock reads four o'clock A.M. "When did I fall asleep?" My phone chimes with a reminder that I have school today. *Great.*

I roll out of bed. Throw on a pair of sweats, shoes, and a shirt, before heading downstairs to the kitchen. It's still dark and the lights are still off. There was no pot of tea on the stove yet. Meaning Serena is still asleep. I go through the sliding doors out onto the deck. It's still dark and a little chilly but once I start my workout, I won't feel it.

Dropping to the ground I start my warm-up set. One hundred push-ups, sit-ups, and squats. It takes no time to get through it. Honestly, I don't even break a sweat from it anymore. *Maybe I'll push it to two hundred next time.*

I walk out onto the grass and get into the *Toralu* stance. With a few deep breaths my mind grows silent. My skin crawls as I feel the energy swirling though out my body. I focus it around, my hands and legs. Black smoke, the manifestation of my energy, erupts around my fists. It swirls, condensing down until they take the shape of claws and leg armor made of bone. Exhaling, I move into the first movement of Toralu. Then I go through Lokar.

Finishing the forms, everything starts to spin. My legs feel like gelatin as they give out and I fall to my hands and knees, barely able to catch my breath. Holding up my claw, I can feel its weight. Feel it slowly draining my strength away. *For the past year I've worked with them, they've never felt like this. I wonder what's causing it.*

They vanish and the strain on my body with them. "Kyle?" Serena call out from the deck. I look up to see her leaning against the rail in her bath robe, sipping at a cup looking down to me. "Are you okay?"

With a deep breath I push myself up to my feet. Steadily fighting fatigue. "I could be better." I say standing tall. "What are you doing up? I thought you didn't have any meetings today?"

"There was an emergency meeting called by the head of the school board. Apparently, something just happened between one of the members and their wife. They've been having troubles lately and it must have come to a head. You want the whole tea?"

"No thanks. I'm having my own relationship problems."

"Oh. Do tell."

"Valene is mad at me."

"Oh, is that all?" She says unamused. "I've known her my whole life. That girl has always had a short fuse. What'd you do?"

'What was the first thing that I ever said to you?' I hear Valene say.

"I think I offended her."

"Ah. Don't worry about it too much. She'll get over it in time."

Yeah, tell that to Michael. She nearly threw Jason through a wall when he asked about him a while ago. "If you say so." I say as I walk by her and into the house.

Upstairs, I get into the shower. I'm not in there long. Just enough to alleviate the ache starting to set in. In my room, I get dressed, grab my bookbag and head back downstairs. "Hey, I'm about head out. I'll catch you later." I yell out into the kitchen.

I focus on my energy, letting it pour into the air around me. I picture a spot I frequent near the school that's secluded and put energy into the thought as well. There's a pull at my being as the air in front of me slightly tears open to Limbo, the realm of the dead. Which I'll be slung across to the spot I've thought of. "Wait!" Serena yells rushing up to me. "You're going to shadow-walk?"

"I was. What's up?"

"Let me drive you to school, since I'm going that way anyway."

"You don't have to..."

"Come on please. It'll be one of the last times that I'll be able to do it since you'll be graduating. Pleeeaassse?" she asks with big puppy dog eyes.

"Okay. You can take me."

"Yes, let me go get ready." She rushes upstairs. Twenty minutes later she appears in a gray pantsuit, heels, and a gray clutch. "How do I look?" She asks coming down the steps.

"Professional. But I don't think they'll let you in looking like you."

She looks at me confused, before she pulls out a compact mirror. She notices her younger face. "Oh yeah." With an inhale the air grows cold around her. The features of her face warp and shift until they solidify. Serena's face is now rounder with a few more wrinkles and more mature. "Better?" she asks, her voice older as well.

"Hi aunt Serena."

"Oh, shut up. Let's go."

We pile into her little red sedan. And she takes off like a bat out of hell out of the driveway and down the street towards the highway and downtown Roc.

The bell rings as I sit at my desk. Mrs. Jay, my homeroom teacher starts talking about the finals prep happening this week and the preparation for graduation after that. I pull out my phone to set it to vibrate, but stare at the screen for a second. The only notifications on it are a random news article and a couple of e-mails. But they're not what I'm looking for. It's been a week since I had my little episode over at the Kir's and I haven't heard from Valene since. I've called, left messages, and texted her but she hasn't answered. "Mr. Ross." *I know she's mad, but she would normally say something by now even when I didn't go over there she would call or send a text. Something.* "Mr. Ross!" I look up from my screen to my teacher waiting patiently at the whiteboard. "Now, I know that you'll be graduating and leaving out of here soon. But would it hurt you to put the phone away and pay attention. This stuff will be on the finale this week."

"Sorry Mrs. jay." I put my phone away and listen to her prattle on about history, until the bell rings for second period.

"Kyle!" some yells out from the crowd, as we head to the next class.

Scanning the hall, my eye falls on a hand waving above the crowd along the wall, near some lockers. Walking around a bunch of people, I come up on a girl wearing black tights, a white T-shirt and a jean vest that had been mangled from a jacket. "Hey Page."

She looks over her shoulder. "Hey, big boy. Where have you been? We didn't see you all spring break, or at prom last week."

"At home. Going through somethings."

"Ooo, demony things?"

"Yes?"

"So, you gonna talk or are you going to make me pull teeth?"

"It's been a lot. Reoccurring nightmares, sleepless nights.

"You mean like what you were going through last year?"

"Kind of, but a little more aggressive." The smell of fire starts to fill the air, and the frayed edge of her vest starts to singe. I tap my cheek hard, and everything clears up. I sigh. "Anyway, how was Prom?"

"It was a blast. The food was good, there was a band. Ah, you would have flipped your top at I and my date's dresses. We were hot and thick, with two C's." She says snapping her finger. "Rica and Airca were there too." Says blandly. "They weren't too keen on being there, but you know." She closes her locker and turns to me. "Why weren't you there with that hottie of a girlfriend you got? She was the talk after you brought her to homecoming."

"We're going through some things. Stuck my whole foot in my mouth. Now she's mad at me. I think."

She pats me on the head. "Yeah, that sounds about right. Poor baby.

I swat her away. "Come on the bells about to ring." We make our way through the hall into our class.

In the classroom Rica sits at a desk next to the window, flipping through her notes. "What up mama?" Page asks sitting in the seat next to her.

"Good morning, Page." She looks up to me. Rica breathes in sharply before she vigorously pats her freshly braided hair. The air around her becomes sour as she tenses up. She clears her throat. "Kyle." She says touching the golden crucifix on the chain around her neck.

"Hey. Your hair looks good. Did you do it yourself?" I ask.

A smile touches the corner of her mouth, breaking the obvious nervousness on her face. "Yeah, took forever."

"It is really nice."

The tension melts away from her shoulders as she takes a true breath. "Thanks."

Page snaps her fingers grabbing our attention. "Hey, if you're going to flirt with anyone." She points at herself.

"Not flirting." I say getting to my seat behind Rica.

Rica laughs. "Besides, if he was going to flirt with anyone besides Valene. It would be Airca."

I sit back in my chair. "I don't know about that. Ever since last year, she's been cold towards me."

"Can you blame her? Not only did you shoot her down, but then you bring this around." Page says holding up her phone, with a picture on the screen. It's a picture of Valene in the purple dress she wore for homecoming.

"One, I did not shoot her down. Two, why do you have a picture of Valene?"

She quickly puts her phone down on the desk. "Mind your business."

"You first." She sticks her tongue out at me. "Where is Airca? The bells already rung."

"She's been doing a lot to keep herself busy. I think she's working with the student council for graduation and everything. I mean she is officially the valedictorian." Rica explains.

"I figured that it would be you." I tell her.

"Yeah, this year was a little rough. But it's just high school, there's always college."

The class starts and we all just sit there listening. Except Rica, who is the only person taking notes.

The next couple of classes pass so slowly. Nothing interesting happens. Just a lot of talking. Which is aggravating because I'm tired. It's never been such a chore to stay awake. I've never had such a need to do so, but this dream is getting rougher every time that I have it. So, if I can avoid having it unnecessarily then I need to find a way to stay awake.

Gym class comes around. The first of my two free periods, but one that will keep me awake. We all sit on the bleachers waiting for the class to start, when the gym teacher comes bouncing in. His beard is covered in crumbs and the track suit he's wearing is just a tad bit too small. With every move he makes the bottom of his belly bounce out of his shirt. "Alright guys." He says a little out of breath. "I don't know what to do with you all since it's the end of the year. So, how about we just play a game of dodgeball today." He looks us over. "You five on a team." He says pointing at half of the class. "And you three on a team." He points at me and two others.

"Coach Williams that's not fair." Someone says next to me.

"Life's not fair kid. Now get moving."

We all hop to our feet and get to each side of the court. Ever since I got my abilities and started training with Selene and everyone, I've tried to stay away from playing sports with humans. Aside from a little game of badminton when we played it. Maybe it won't be that much of a difference.

The coach hobbles across the gym floor placing balls along the half court line, his beat-up sneakers squeaking with his every step. "Alright. You guys ready?" He blows his whistle. Everyone rushes to the middle, except for me. An overwhelming volley of balls comes flying at us. My teammates frantically dart around preparing to dodge, while I just stand there watching them float through the air in slow motion. "Whoa." I look back over my shoulder. My teammates were moving slowly as well. If only things lasted this long when fighting Valene, or any other supernatural being.

I move to the side. As the balls go by, they go back to normal speed, and I hear someone scream behind me. "Abbott you're out." The coach yells.

My teammate rushes and grabs one the of balls and proceeds to start throwing. I grab one, target someone and chuck it at them. The ball launches so fast out of my hand that it cuts through the air with a woosh. It hits one of guys on the other team so hard that it knocks them off their feet and onto the ground. Leaving them gasping for air. *Opps.*

"Walk it off Herring. Ross this dodge ball, not baseball. Dial it back."

I was. "You got it coach." *Have I really gotten so strong?* A ball comes at me but it's so slow. I just pluck out of the air.

"You're Out Williams."

A ball flies out from behind me, and hits one of our opponents, eliminating them. "Hey Kyle if you, can act as a shield I'll pick them off from behind you."

Not a bad idea. That way I wouldn't hurt anyone with my throws. "Sounds good to me." I pass them the ball I just caught.

Another ball comes flying at us. I catch it when my teammate runs out from behind to get a better angle to throw. Before he can get the ball ready to throw, he's pelted by two balls. "Turner's out. That leaves only you Ross."

I take up a ball and underhand toss it as softly as I can. The ball clips one of them on the shoulder, knocking them out of the game. Now it's one on one.

The final person double palms two balls. "You're not winning this Kyle."

"Just throw the balls."

He throws one and I dodge it easily. The second comes in the shadow of it just as slow as all the others. I pluck it out of the air and look at them with a sly smile. The whistles blow. "Game over. Kyle's the winner."

The bell rings and we all leave the gym. Outside I find a girl staring at me her arms crossed, wearing slacks, a blouse, and white tennis-shoes. "Airca?"

She narrows her eyes before moving her straightened hair from out of her face. "Isn't you playing against humans cheating?"

"A little. Where have you been?"

"Class and helping the student council. Where have you been for the past month?"

"Going through some things."

"Is that all?"

"Yeah." She scoffs, then walks away. "Airca wait." She just keeps walking. "What's her problem?"

My phone buzzes in my pocket. Looking at the screen I get a excited and nervous all at once as I look at the notification. It was a text from Valene. 'Hey Hero.'

Finally. Okay keep it cool. Don't overwhelm her and don't overdo it. 'Hey Valene. What's up?' *Nailed it.*

'Yeah, everything's good. Are you free this weekend?'

'Yeah. Got something planned?'

'Maybe. Come over Saturday 7 A.M. Okay?'

'Yeah. Okay.'

'Good. See you then. xoxo'

A sense of relief washes over me as the knot that was my stomach unclenches. At least she's talking to me now. The clock on my phone reads 1:30 pm. My next period is a free one, so I'm just going to go home. Maybe Serena is already there making lunch.

I grab my stuff and make my way out of the school. Once I'm down the street I cut into an alley, and shadow-walk home.

Chapter 4

The week passes by in a flash. Everything at school is fine. Navigating the awkwardness of Rica is easy enough. The coldness from Airca has been off putting though and a little frustrating. No matter how often I try to get her to talk to me, she just walks away. I'll just leave her alone for a while, she'll come around, maybe. But today is the day Valene wanted to get together. I've worked out already, showered and now just waiting for 7.

The air around my room quickly becomes saturated with energy. Before me the air begins to bend and warp. *Someone is shadow-walking here, but something is wrong. It's taking too long.* After a second, a tear opens in the fabric of space sucking all the air from the room into it. Hands reach out grabbing the edges of the doorway. From out of the darkness Jason appears, a frantic look on his face and fear in his golden eyes. "Bro, help me!"

I grab his arms and start pulling. As more of his body leaves the doorway, I notice several misty hands holding onto him with a death grip. "What is that?!"

"Get them off me!" he yells.

"How?"

"Energy, blast them with energy. Command them to let go. Something!" He says struggling.

I focus energy into my throat and onto my tongue "Let Go!" I yell releasing the built-up energy in a wave. As it hits the hands, voices shriek within the darkness. They let go and we fall to the ground. Jason turns around holding his hand up. The misty hands reaching through the doorway retract back into the darkness as the opening quickly mends itself and vanishes with a pop of black smoke.

We both slump our heads trying to catch our breath. "Jason, what the heck was that?"

He rolls onto his back and starts to laugh. "The spirits that dwell in Limbo. Their so grabby."

"What?"

"I'm not that good at shadow walking. It takes me some time to you know, travel. The downside to that, it gives the spirits their time to latch onto you."

"Oh."

"Yeah, sometimes they come through with you too and then you're haunted."

I remember Mayra talking about this when she was first teaching me how to do this. *Is that what it looks like?* "Why were you coming here?"

"Well, I wanted to train with you. Since you hadn't come back because of sis. So, I thought I'd come to you. Shadow walking is the fastest way here."

"No, Zel is."

Jason looks at me so confused. "What?"

"Yeah. Zel is connected to my door. Been so for two weeks now."

He lays his head back on the floor. "That would have been so much easier."

The alarm on my nightstand turns on startling the both of us. ""Hey, hey, hey and good morning my lovelies. This is your new favorite host, DJ Alice J. The time is 7am. The sun is bright, and the day will be beautiful. Get out there and soak it in while you can. Now for those of you stuck inside, here's some tunes to wake you up. Only heard here on 98.9 WNKR, The Roc." I get up and tap the radio, turning it off.

Time for me to go. I look at Jason who is still breathing hard on the floor. "Sorry Jase, I already worked out. I'm meeting up with your sister, so I got it out of the way. Are you okay?"

"Yeah, I'm good. I'm just gonna lay here for a second."

"Take as long as you need." I walk over to my door and grab the handle. "Zel."

The door rattles, before opening to the main foyer at the Kir home. From behind me I hear Jason scoff. "That would have been so much easier!" He yells.

The door shuts and vanishes. "You're late Hero."

My hair stands on end at the sound of voice. It's nothing like the flame torn version of her but it's still enough to put me on edge. With a breath, I spin around to face her. I stare down at her feet and her white tennis shoes. "Hey Valene."

"Look at me." She orders. Slowly, my eyes track to her face, passing her legs, her short jean overalls, and purple t-shirt. Her bronze skin shines unimpeded by her long curly hair which she had pulled back into a ponytail. She watches me with her golden eyes, scanning me from head to toe. "How do I look?"

"Cute."

She smiles. "No, silly. Have I changed?"

"No. At least not yet."

"So, it's not immediate. Good." She rushes me. My stomach tenses and I step back from her, but she just keeps forward until she wraps her arms around me. "Please don't run from me. Your safe with me remember."

I hold onto her, breathing in her berry perfume before melting into her arms. "I know. I'm sorry."

She kisses me on the cheek. "I forgive you. So, are you ready?"

"Sure. Ready for what?"

She smiles. "We're going to one of my favorite places on New Birth. It was the first place I'd ever been here. Zel!"

A tall thin man, with black hair, pale white skin, and angular features, wearing a butler's uniform rises out of the floor next to us. He bows. "You summoned me my lady?"

"Is the door ready?"

"It is. This way." Zel leads us to the door that leads into the party room. A dark aura radiates out from the edges, pulsing with the same power as someone shadow-walking.

"What's with the door?" I ask.

"You'll be traveling quite the distance. Further than Shadow-walking can take you. Using a door as a portal is pretty much limitless on the distance traveled, but the time that it's open is varied.

The door flies open, and the Vacuum of Limbo takes my breath away. Valene takes my hand. "Let's go Hero, we have a lot to do and see, and only a day to do it." As we cross the threshold into the darkness, we're slung across the plane of limbo.

After about a minute of nothingness we cross the new threshold and step out of the darkness. We enter a dimly lit room with a dirt floor. My vision blurs and my stomach twists from nausea.

I fall to my hands and knees gasping for air right before hurling all over the floor. I've never been in Limbo so long to feel the effects of the realm. It's cold, the air is so thin, and everything was topsy turvy. "That was intense."

Valene sits next to me, a little out of breath herself and rubs my back. "Yeah, I know. Just breath."

My vision clears as my stomach settles. As I shift to sit back on my ankles, a pain shoots up my left arm and I nearly fall on my face. "What in the world?"

"What's wrong Hero?"

I look at my wrist to see it twisted and purple. "My wrist?!"

"Let me see." I sit up and show her. Gently, she takes and examines it. There's a huge bruise from my wrist all the way up my forearm. "Looks like something grabbed you and you forcefully slipped out of it. Damn ghosts. Luckily, it's just dislocated. I'm going to set it. Ready?" I shake my head no. "3...2...." Effortlessly she twists and snaps my wrist back into place with a loud pop.

I yell out, clenching down as hard as I can. Her hands become warm as they fill with energy and flow into my arm relieving the pain.

We sit there for about five minutes, until I can feel my hand again. "How's that Hero?"

I work it. "It's going to be stiff, but it's better. Thank you."

Valene helps to my feet and kisses me on the cheek. "You're welcome." She walks over to a wooden door. She tries to open it, but it doesn't budge. That's when she drives her fingers into the wood and rips it off its hinges, allowing the sunlight to flood in. She tosses the remains of the door to the side, before walking out. "Hero come check this out."

I follow her out and up a set steps until we reach the surface. After a moment, my eyes adjust, and I notice the field of rubble and grass that we're standing in. "Where are we?"

She points up behind me. I turn around to a huge, ruined city and the building made of pillars that sat high on the stone hill. "Wait. Is that's the Parthenon? Meaning this ruin is the acropolis." I look back to her, "We're not..."

"In the home of Gods, monsters, and heroes? Yes, we are. Welcome to Greece." She says with jazz hands.

"What?"

She takes my hand. "We have a few places to go." We shadow-walk away.

We appear in the center of another ruin. The stone that made up the broken walls and floor are bleached from the sun and worn down from the weather. "Where are we now?"

"Crete."

"As in where the labyrinth is. Is this the labyrinth?"

"Yup. Go ahead and look around."

I wander the ruins taking a couple of turns here and there until I come back to Valene. "It's a lot smaller than I thought it was."

She laughs, "This Hero, is only what Daedalus wanted the humans to see. Sure, the minotaur wandered this system, but it goes deeper. Follow me."

"Wait the Minotaur is real?"

"Hero, my best friend is a vampire. We basically fought a zombie last year. Just about anything you've ever heard of may really exist."

"That makes sense." We start walking down one of the many paths laid out. After a few turns we come to a wall with something etched into it. *A three-pronged fork? No wait a trident.* "Activate the dark sight." She says.

My eyes begin to strain and water as I focus energy into them. The color of the world fades to gray while the light of the sun dims, becoming bearable. I focus on Valene. The shimmering golden hue of her energy sitting on her skin seems to pop against the pure white wall she's standing in front of. I haven't used the dark sight in a while. This feels so weird. *I look at my hands and my energy. It's black, waving off my skin like smoke, with a tinge of blue at its edges. Compared to Valene I can see that I don't have real control of my energy. How do you fix that?*

"Hero?" Valene asks pulling me out of my thought.

I look at her. "Sorry I got distracted. What am I looking at?"

Valene points at the trident symbol on the white wall. It glows green giving me the feeling of being on the edge of the ocean. "Put your ear up to the wall and close your eyes."

I do as I am told. *There's nothing, just my own heartbeat.* Over my heart I can hear heavy breathing. It gets louder and louder, then it just stops. There's a scratching on the wall followed by a high-pitched scream. Multiple roars follow as if right there in my ear, knocking me out of the sight. I pull back. "What the heck was that?"

"The Labyrinth held more than just one monster. Alongside Minos, Poseidon – God of the sea enlisted Daedalus to build a prison to hold some of the nastier beasts the Pantheon defeated. And since Minos was on his "shit" list, he decided he wanted it here."

"Building a deadly monster prison, under a monster prison near a kingdom. What if they all escaped?"

She shrugs, "That's why you don't get on a Gods bad side."

"Noted."

Valene gently takes my left hand. "How is it. Can you use it?"

I grip her hand lightly. There's a pang of pain but it's bearable. "It's not one hundred percent but I'm fine."

"Good because we're going to do a little training."

"Here?"

"No silly. Hold on." We shadow walk.

We appear in a field of tall grass. In the distance is a huge prison-like complex made of marble and stone. There are no fences or anything. I don't think this place has been touched by people in centuries. "Where are we?"

"This is Ischyrós. One of the many hidden training facilities of the Spartans. This one was used to train the elite guard of the king."

"Whoa." We walk across the field, then through the broken gateway into the complex. Huge boulders that are my height, are scattered across the open area.

Grooves are etched into the ground from where I'm sure the trainees had to push them.

"Think you can do it?" She asks.

"I don't know. Can you?"

Valene eyes light up at the call to a challenge. She places her hand onto the huge stone. With the flick of her wrist, the stone launches across the courtyard slamming into another and turning them both to dust. "Your turn. And no energy."

"Oh okay." Infront of the stone I gauge it. This thing probably weighs a ton, a literal ton. I place a hand onto it and try to push. It doesn't budge. Placing both my hands on it I push with all I have. Still, it won't move. "This is impossible. I'm stronger but not this strong not without help."

Valene looks at me. "Try it again. This time have a little faith in yourself. Believe me. You're stronger than you think."

I start pushing and nothing. *I'm not that strong though, not yet.* I think of the conversation I had with Mayra. 'That kind of strength takes time.'

Next to me Valene has her arms crossed waiting for me to try again. "What makes you think I can do this now?"

"I don't know whether you can or not, but I've seen you do some crazy things. So, I wouldn't put it past you to be able to do this."

I look at the rock and place my hands on it. With a deep breath I push. For a minute it doesn't budge. My muscles start to burn from the strain. Tears well in my eyes, as I plant my feet and scream. My fingers drive into the stone, and it shifts forward, dragging through the dirt about a foot.

I fall back to the ground trying to catch my breath. Valene's hand touches my shoulder. "You did it Hero."

I look at her, tears streaming down my face. "Yeah. I guess I don't know my own strength."

"I know. Come on." She helps me up to my feet. But my legs feel like jelly. "I got you Hero." She says supporting me. "There's a spot inside that you can rest at."

As we enter the building, the torches burst to life illuminating the corridor. The walls are covered with depictions of beasts, like wolves, rams, bulls and even men decked out in full armor. All of them frozen in perpetual snarls. *Epic.*

We follow the path around to a dead end. To the right there's an opening leading out into a two-story facility. It's rundown, but still sturdy and sound. Along the walls, are cells with the dimensions of five-by-five feet have beds of straw and bowls in them. These must have been the barracks. "This place looks like Hell."

"It was. The soldiers would wake at the crack of dawn. Have a breakfast that consisted of bread, honey, and fruit, and then train for hours without end. Doing things that would push them beyond the limits of normal humans."

"That sounds familiar. Sounds like they trained like demons. Well at least how you guys have been training me."

"Actually Hero, the Spartans got their ideas for such a way of training from us. The demons and hell- spawn that they revered as gods."

I stop to consider what she just said. "Wait a minute. Are you telling me that the Greek Gods are demons?"

"That's right. But it's not only them. Most of the Gods, heroes, and monsters that you hear about in myths and legends from around the world were of demonic decent. Why do you think the human Light orders pushed so hard to move away from their worship and praise?"

"Wow."

"Crazy right."

"Yeah. Wait, there are still people them worship them though."

"True. But even so, they have been influenced by the Light to the point that if they were to ever find out the truth..."

"Oh, they would probably stop."

"Exactly. It's a form of control over the humans The Light implemented forever ago. A way to keep them on a leash and on their side. Now come on, I want to show you the pits." She says taking my hand.

As she leads me through the barracks, my mind is still reeling from the information she just laid on me. It brought up images of Anima; the leader of the Light sitting opposite of me on the other side a chessboard. Her motherly smile is calming even now, though I've forgotten the rest of her face. It doesn't seem like something she would do, but then again. She was the one that advised me to sacrifice a pawn. *I'm sorry Leo.*

We walk through a giant opening out into stands that encircle an arena of sand. Posts of petrified wood, the height and size of a grown men jut up from the sand. A lot of their bark had been chipped and worn away, most likely from weapons training. High above the arena, spanning the whole area, are several huge white and black cloths. They continuously weave into one another allowing sunlight to enter in a way that illuminates the whole pit.

I sit on one of the stone seats that's still intact. "I wonder if I would have been able to survive this training?"

"You've survived it so far. Be proud of that fact. Because not a lot have."

"Jeez."

"Right." Valene chuckles as she squats next to me. "And I'm so very proud of you." She says looking me in the eyes.

I chuckle as I look away a little embarrassed. "Thank y..." my breath is taken away as I look back at her. Her face blackened by flame.

"Kyle?" she asks, her voice starting to crackle.

"Thank you." She smiles reaching out to me. Before she touches me, I take her hand and put it down onto my lap. "You've changed."

"It took longer than I expected." She grabs my hand. "Come on, we need to get to our last destination." She says taking my shoulder and shadow-walks us away.

We appear, accosted by the wind. The sound of a flag flapping next to us. "Where are now?" I ask yelling over the wind in my ears.

Mt. Olympus. Get ready the gateway is near."

Gateway? A gust of wind hits us so hard that it takes us off our feet and into the air. I grip Valene's hand tight. "I got you Hero. Hang on. Here it comes."

A cyclone appears under us shooting us up into the air. A portal of light appears above us. I hang onto her for dear life as we go through it, and everything goes white.

Chapter 5

While we are rising through the light everything flips. Now instead of rising into the air, it feels like we're falling, but only for a second until we hit the ground softly. I'm holding my breath, gripping Valene's arm. "Kyle, sweetie we're okay. Open your eyes." Valene says softly, her voice still crackling.

I peek open one eye, looking at her. She is still in her burning state. A wave of fear washes over me and I freeze. "Kyle?" My mind starts to spin the longer I stare at her, and I can't take a breath. She reaches her hand towards my face, and I grip her hand, digging my nails into her skin. "It's okay Hero. It's okay." She places her hand over my eyes. "Just breath."

Energy flows from her into my skin and everything relaxes. My mind settles as I take deep breath and let her go. "I'm sorry. Everything just..."

"It's okay. That's what we're here for." She helps me to my feet.

"Where is here?"

"Look and be amazed." She removes her hand. "Welcome to the mythical home of the Pantheon. Welcome to Mount Olympus."

The sun shines brightly in the distance. Its light gleaming against a peak of stone and cloud. Atop that, reaching even further into the sky is a massive castle. The outer walls look to be made of clouds with pulsing veins of gold, silver and platinum energies running through them.

"Whoa." She takes my hand and leads me up the path of clouds that we're on. The path ends, leading to nothing. "What now?" I ask.

Valene rummages through her pockets, when she pulls out a golden lace with a coin on it. She holds it out to the space. The coin glows with a multicolored light before it shoots out. A rainbow bridge appears connecting our path to the stone path on the other side leading to the castle. "Hurry before it goes away." She drags me forward.

The moment our feet touch the bridge everything blurs around us. Within a blink of an eye, we appear in front of the castle gate. The doors are large, made of marble and etched with an elegant circular design. All the energies coursing through the clouds converges here, weaving and spiraling in the center where both the doors meet. Valene steps forward in front of them. She reaches out and runs her fingers through the energies, disrupting them.

The ground rumbles as the energy leaves the doors. They swing open. Not to the inner castle but to a small town. "What is all this?"

"The Pantheon had a lot of kids and those kids had families. This is where they lived. Not all of them lived here but a good allotment did."

Each of the houses are made from the same marble and clouds that made up most of Olympus. All of them are in pristine condition. Even after who knows how long they've been sitting here. In the center of town stands a statue of a giant man with no facial features. It's about ten feet tall, as wide as a truck and menacing. "Valene. This statue is huge. Who is it?"

"No one important. Just keep moving Hero. Pay it no mind."

"Okay."

We come to a wall at the edge of town. There is a pathway leading to a set of stairs going up. We take the first step and appear in a grassy courtyard. *All this instant movement is starting to make me nauseous.*

In the center, raised on a platform, is a tree filled with red leaves and golden apples. Around it, are stone benches and statues of humans, made of black and white stone. On the outer edges of the courtyard are empty archways, filled with darkness. "Where are we, now?"

"This is the nexus. The heart of Olympus. It can take us anywhere within the castle walls, and Hades. But we are going to the throne room."

The statues shift their gazes to one of the archways. Pointing towards our destination. *Oh, that's creepy.*

Valene takes my hand, leading me to the archway the statues were staring at. "Hero. What do I look like to you?"

I haven't looked at her directly since she snapped me out of whatever that was. Slowly, I look up to her, the moment I see her blackened flesh I lower my gaze. "Still on fire."

"Come on." She says pulling me through.

We exit into a dimly lit room, with a few torches hanging on the walls. Above us there's a trill. I look up to see a creature with red scales and bright yellow and orange eyes looking down at me, from over the edge of a huge saucer suspended from the ceiling. "Ah Valene, we're not alone."

She looks up. "It's okay Hero. That is the hearth. She's why we're here. Can we have a little light please?" the eyes seem to smile as they vanish in a fury of light and fire. The torches all around the room burst to life and a wave of warmth washes over the whole area. I can feel myself grow calm, as a sense of being at home wells up in me. "Thank you."

The room is big and circular, with three huge steps like an amphitheater. A bunch of stuff is scattered around hanging from walls, ceilings and on the floor. At the top of the steps are chairs and piles of pillows decorated in all manner of stuff: plants, weapons, art, and even skulls. Valene takes me down to the bottom of the steps. There's a pool of water about five feet wide and five feet deep, "This is it." She speaks.

"Okay, so are you going to tell me why you trekked me all the way here to Greece and to the top of Mount Olympus? I'm starting to doubt that it was just for an amazing date."

"The Hearth fire." She says pointing up to the saucer. "I was told that it has healing properties. And that maybe, it can heal you."

"Wait You did this for me?"

"Of course. I've been working on this since our talk a few weeks ago."

"How did you do all of ...this?"

"Turned in a few favors, promised some myself. Are you mad?"

I look to her, and she's looking forward making sure not to look straight at me. My hand trembles and everything starts to sway but I'm not looking away from her. "Valene, look at me." She looks at me with her hollow ember eyes and it feels like my brain is going through a blender. "Thank you. So much."

She smiles. "You're welcome, Hero." My nose starts to run and her eyes light up with worry. She grabs my face, diverting my gaze away from her. My legs give out from under me, and she catches me. Drops of blood speckle the floor. "Kyle are you okay?"

"I'm okay...I." The edges of my vision start to go dark. "I'm not..." everything goes black.

I'm weightless, floating in the darkness. There's a warmth surrounding me relieving my every ache and pain. *This is nice.*

A sound starts to ring in my ears. It gets louder and louder until it sounds like screaming. "Hero!" Valene screams in agony. There's a spark and in a show of fire and heat, flames explode to life in front me, pushing me back. The pungent smell of sulfur and ash bombards my nose as they twist and turn in on themselves until it takes shape. Forming into the flame torn Valene. She holds herself, writhing and groaning in pain. "It burns! It burns!" She looks up to me. "Kyle." She grinds out through clenched teeth." You did this! It's all your fault!" She flies at me, screaming and reaching out for my neck with her charred hands.

I can't move. My body is frozen at the sight of her. The crippling sense of fear and guilt that washes over my body twists my stomach and locks my hands. There's nothing that I can do. Except brace myself for her wrath.

Before she can grab me, a fire roars to life surrounding me, making her stop in her tracks. The colors of the rainbow dance within the flame as they expand outward, pushing Valene back. There's loud hiss. The reds and yellows of the fire surrounding me twist and meld together taking the shape of what looks like a giant salamander. Its red scales shimmer and wave up its body. Its glowing yellow eyes lock onto Valene and it hisses again. Smoke bellowing from its mouth.

Valene looks back at the creature confused but then her gaze shifts to me. Her face turns up in a rage. "You can't escape it Hero. It's inevitable."

"Just go away!" I manage to yell.

A blue light shine in the distance like a star in the night sky, drawing all our attention. Valene looks at it. She turns back towards us and smiles. "Fine. If you can't take responsibility, then someone else will. And what happens to them will be your fault." Valene spins around and takes off towards the light. They both blink out of existence. A weight lifts from my mind. Relief washes through my body and I sink deeper into the warmth of the fire.

"Kyle?" I hear Valene in my ear, her voice frantic. Water sloshes into my face, and I feel myself afloat. A hand on my back, and an arm wrapped around my waist. "Kyle, wake up. Please, wake up." She pleads.

"Valene?"

"Oh, thank the Creator. Are you okay?" I open my eyes to her looking down at me. Her hair and face are drenched. Her golden eyes glossy from the tears that welled within them. *Wait, golden?* I stare at her for a second, waiting for her to change, but nothing happens. Her skin stays perfect. Her touch is warm and not searing hot. And her eyes... "Hero, what's wrong?" She asks, her voice soft and gentle. Without the crackling sound of a hungry fire. Tears sting my eyes. I'm so relieved that all I can muster is a chuckle. "Kyle?"

"Valene, nothing's wrong. Absolutely nothing's wrong." I say excitedly. "I can look at you again. I see you."

"Really?"

I lift my left hand out of the water and touch her cheek. "Yeah, really."

She kisses my hand and looks at me with relief. "Good. Good!" She pulls me in close and squeezes me, hugging me tight. "You scared me." She says quietly into my ear.

"I'm sorry."

She takes a deep breath, before looking at me again. "Don't do it again or I'll kill you myself." She says with a smile.

"You got it."

"Come on. Let's get out of the water and dried off." She sets me up onto my feet and we make our way over to the edge of the pool. She hops out and offers her hand. I stare at it for a second and still nothing happens. Happily, I take it and she pulls me up. She walks off, heading towards one of the thrones set ups. It was thematically dark, with black, gold and purple as its color scheme. Chains sprawl on the ground around it with a weird looking collar.

She rummages through the stuff for a second until she grabs a couple of togas. One black and one purple. She tosses me the black. "Wear this while our clothes dry."

"This belongs to Hades, right? Won't he be mad if we just touch his stuff?"

"Hero, no one's here. And hasn't been for a long time. So, who cares. Now strip before you catch a cold." I do as I'm told and change into the tunic and toga. It's light and airy. Almost like I'm wearing nothing.

I look over to Valene and catch a glimpse of her changing, pulling the dress up past her waist and the Celtic knot tattoo on her back. She notices me and smiles over her shoulder. "Hey. No peeking pervert." She says playfully.

"Sorry."

"Now lay your clothes out. The hearth will have them dry in no time."

I lay my clothes out and look up to the giant saucer hanging from the ceiling. The hearth creature, the salamander looks down at me, shifting its head back and forth to get a good look at me with each eye. I wave to it. "Thank you for your help." It trills in acknowledgement and vanishes back over the edge.

I look around the throne room to the different seats, that represented each god. At the top of the steps is a lone seat. *That must be Zeus's throne. I got to check that one out.* Rushing up the steps I stop in front of it. The seat itself was made of clouds and marble like most of the structures here. At times lightning would surge through them and you could hear thunder in the distance.

"Try it out." Valene says just behind me, startling me.

"I don't know."

"Oh, come on Hero. I mean you're already wearing the clothes of the God of the underworld. Why not sit in Zeus's chair?"

A little hesitant, I spin around and take a seat. The sound of thunder is now loud in my ears. I close my eyes and my mind extends across the sky as far as I can imagine. I can sense the storms on the sea, winds that blow across the land and the people and creatures it touches. "Valene this is wild." Next to me is a golden blade, in the shape of a lightning bolt. As I take it in hand, a silent hum of energy surges through me, making the hair on my arms stand on end. *Is this really his lightning bolt? He just left it?*

I look to the other seats and see that there are weapons and clothes still sprawled everywhere. "Valene."

"Yes?"

"What happened here? The way everything is still scattered around, it looks like the Pantheon just up and left. Do you know why?"

"There were a lot of things that led to their disbanding. But the thing that sealed the deal was the defeat of the Generals. After that, they, and all the other Gods just up and vanished. No one knows why or to where. Not even their families knew."

"How do you know all of this stuff?"

"I am a history teacher Hero. I may not look it, but I like history."

"Yeah, but some of this stuff feels forbidden you know. Like not everyone would know this info."

"Oh, No they wouldn't. The reason I even have this much information is because of father."

"How so?"

"The Pantheon are my distant cousins. On father's side."

"What? Chris never mentions his family. Is that why he goes by the codename Gaia?"

"They're not on good terms. Anyone can choose the name of one of the ancients if they want, but my father is the true holder of the title – Gaia."

"What does that mean exactly? The true holder of the title?"

"I thought you had been reading up on demon society and culture?"

"I've tried, but the books are long and in *Durabi Duprima*. It's a chore trying to translate and comprehend at the same time."

"At least you're trying. Only the holder of the title can bestow it onto someone new. Most of the time they're passed down through families. Sometimes given to a worthy successor outside of it. Father just so happened to be granted the title of his family's greatest warrior and my great-grandmother."

"So, you're directly related to the Titans? That's cool."

I look down at the sword. *Wild.* I start to put it down when I notice Valene staring, with a pleased look on her face. "What?"

"Nothing. I just can't help but notice how good you look sitting on a throne." She slightly bows head. "It is an honor to be in your presence my lord Zeus."

"I'm no Zeus."

"You're right. Please forgive my insolence. I didn't mean to offend you. Lord Shadow."

My skin crawls and this feeling of power surges through me. I shake the jitters out of my hands. "Oh, that was weird."

"I just invoked your title. It can be just as powerful as your own name if used properly."

"Do you have one."

"No, not yet. I'm just plain Jane Valene."

"Please. there's nothing plain about you."

She stares at me for a minute considering something. "Valene what's up? What's with the look?" She takes a deep breath shaking away the tension that had built up in her hands. She walks up to me, takes the sword out of my hands and places it back next to the throne. "What's wrong?"

"Nothing, just stand up." She says taking my hands. Her hands are clammy as she takes mine and pulls me to my feet. "Okay." She says through a sigh.

"Valene what's going on?" She stands in front of me and pulls her toga open, just showing her sternum. "What are you doing?"

"Shhh. Just watch."

She holds her hand up. Black energy radiate from the tips of her fingers. She drives it onto her chest. Frantic I start to make a fuss, but she glares at me, stopping me. Bringing her fingers together, a golden light begins to shine between them, and the air becomes thick with her energy. With some force she pulls it away from her body. She drops to her knees, out of breath and drenched in sweat. "Valene what, what did you just do?"

"Just...listen." She takes a deep breath. "Kyle Ross, My Hero. I give you this, a piece of my very soul as proof of my promise to keep you safe. As proof of my devotion to you. As proof of my feelings for you." she says breathlessly, her hand extended to me.

Staring at the shimmering golden jewel in her hand, I get Deja vu. Wh*ere have I seen this before?*

Images of myself holding out three gems to three women come to mind. 'I've heard of these.' One of the women says. Holding the white jewel. 'A Soul drop.'

I look past her hand to her face. Valene isn't looking at me, but down to the floor, nearly holding her breath. Her shoulders tense with anticipation.

"Umm are you proposing to me?"

Her eyes shoot up, and she stares at me. Her cheeks turn a beet red. "What, no n…no."

"Then what is this?"

Valene scoffs as she stands back up. "Kyle, when I reached for you a few weeks ago. Even an hour ago, you coward away from me. I understand what you're seeing, but I thought you felt safe with me, but clearly you still have doubts. So, with this I make you a promise, that with me you will always have a safe place."

"That is what mom always said."

She holds her hand out, the soul drop glowing in her palm. "And like her, I promise." She says softly but sternly.

I don't know what to feel, or to think. When looking at her I can see her conviction and sincerity. This day has been amazing, and she did all of it to help me. "Valene." I take the soul drop from her. "I believe you and accept your promise. And I promise to be the same for you."

The soul drop melts into my hand. Like a stone tossed into a pond her energy ripples throughout me and tears well in my eyes. Normally her energy is so sharp and heavy, but this was so soft.

"Are you okay?" she asks.

"Yeah." I take her hand, pull her in close and hold her tight. "Thank you."

She wraps her arms around me. "You're welcome." We sit there for a while just holding one another. I'm sure our clothes have been dried for a while now, but we are content to just be. "Come on Hero. Let's go get some food."

"Yes please. I'm starving." We get dressed. "Do we have to go back through the castle?"

"No." She takes my hand. "We can shadow-walk anywhere from here. And I got the perfect spot. Thank you so much." She says up to the saucer. The creature peeks out and trills gleefully. "Let's go Hero."

We shadow-walk to a nice restaurant on the top of a hill with a great view of the ocean. The platter of food they brought out was amazing. This was a great day. I hope I can pay her back one day.

Chapter 6

I tap my pencil against my forehead as I stare at this stupid worksheet. I'm supposed to be studying for my finals, but I've been stuck on the same question for an hour now. It's not that I don't know how to answer it. It's just hard to concentrate, with everything that's going on around me.

Ever since my and Valene's trip to Greece last weekend my senses have been heightened more so than usual. I can hear, smell and even taste everything in this library. The snacks people are eating, the music they're listening to, and some of the conversations. The most obnoxious and distracting noise though, is the hum of the fluorescent lights above me.

I push the paper out from in front of me and lay my head down on the table. "I wish everything would just shut up."

"Aww does baby have a headache?" Page asks, putting down her phone.

"Thank goodness no. Haven't had one for a week now."

"Then what's the matter with you?"

"I'm having a hard time focusing. I can sense everyone around me, and I can't seem to turn it off like I used to."

"And it's all thanks to your girlfriend."

A big dumb smile spreads across my face at the thought of Valene. "Yeah."

"So, she really took you to Olympus? The actual home of the Greek gods. And then bathed you in special water to heal you of whatever you were going through?"

"That's the gist of it."

"I don't believe you."

"What? How don't you? I'm a whole supernatural creature myself."

"Yeah, and I have proof of that." She says motioning to me. Her face lights up. "Did you take pictures?"

"Page, I was kind of going through a psychological thing, and dying at one point, I think. Pictures were the last thing on my mind."

"See, no proof. Yeah, not real. You'll just have to take me next time."

I shake my head. "Maybe next time."

Rica slams her paper down on the table and sighs. "Guys, I'm trying to study." she interjects, sounding just as frustrated as I felt. "And I can't do that with you two yapping."

Page leans back in her chair. "Girl chill. You're already a straight A student. Even if you get a B, it's not going to hurt your G.P.A."

"Still. No one wants to hear about your demonic romp around the world."

"Speak for yourself Miss. Kinson. That cruise last year was fun, but it wasn't to a mythical place like Olympus."

Rica grumbles before she buries her face back into her papers. "We only have a few weeks left and I want to make sure I pass my finals with flying colors, and I need to focus."

Rica looks over her papers to Page, annoyed. Her eyes sweep over to me, and she takes a quick breath and kind of holds it.

Everything about her becomes tense. The air becomes sour with a pungent odor. *Valene, talked about it before but is this what fear smells like?* I've done my best to make her comfortable, but each time she sees me it's like all my work just goes out of the window. "No problem, we'll be quiet."

The smell dissipates as her body relaxes and her gaze drops back down to her papers. Page glares at me. I know exactly what she's thinking because she's said to me already. 'You don't have to take that from her.'

I put my hand up, trying to quell her annoyance. She just scoffs and picks up her packet. "Since you can't focus on your paper, help me with mine." She says scooting next to me, and we get to it.

We get through most of the packet easily. Having to focus on helping her was just what I needed to block everything else out.

I started working on a math equation for her. showing her step by step how to solve for X. "There. X equals three."

Page looks at me like I'm crazy. "I don't get it."

"Page we've gone over the rules for this equation for twenty minutes. We did four of these problems step by step. What don't you get?"

She slaps the paper from my hand. "All of it ya butt. You suck at this. Where's Airca? She said that she was going to be here. She's the best at math here." Page asks.

Rica looks at her and rolls her eyes. "Who knows. Maybe she got held up." She looks at me. "Or maybe she just doesn't want to see him."

"The last time Airca and I really exchanged words was after my gym class. Since then, she's just been giving me the cold shoulder. Has she told you guys why she hasn't wanted to talk to me?"

They both shake their heads. "Besides the whole you and Valene thing. No." Page explains.

"That can't be the only reason why? Is it?"

She shrugs her shoulders.

"Boy why don't you just talk to her?" Rica asks.

"I've tried. She just walks away."

"Well, try harder." Rica yells.

"Try harder to talk to someone who is actively trying not to talk to you."

"Yup."

"At that point I'm just pushing myself onto her."

"I mean isn't that how you demons operate? I mean that Ben guy was like that."

Page's mouth drops, as she gasps. "Rica what the hell?"

Did she just compare me to her abductor? "I'm done." I shove all my stuff into my book bag and get up from the table.

"Wait. Where are you going?" Page asks.

"I'm going home. Where I'm not going to be judged and compared to trash. Maybe I can try harder there. See ya."

I make my way through the stacks and out of the library. I get down the street before cutting into an alley and shadow-walk home.

I appear in the living room. I drop my bag onto the floor and plop down onto the couch. *What's her problem?*

Something wet and cold touches my face. I jump out of the chair and onto the floor. Looking up, I see a pair of cat eyes staring down at me. "Hello little brother." Mayra says, trying to stifle a laugh.

"Mayra!?...You scared the crap out of me."

"I'm sorry." Her body is engulfed in a red light and her form changes before my eyes, stretching and warping into a silhouette of a human woman. It falls away revealing the brown skin of her slender face and weary eyes. "Need a hand?" she asks, offering her hand.

I take it and like I weigh nothing she hoists me to my feet. "Thanks."

Mayra sits up, pulling the comforter from the back of the sofa around her long slender, yet muscular naked body. She leans back with a sigh, melting into the cushions like she hadn't felt anything soft in so long. I sit next to her. "Welcome home."

She looks at me and her eyes light up. She grabs and pulls me in close, cradling my head. "Thank you, Kyle. I missed you."

"I missed you too."

She pushes me back and looks me over. "You look different. Have you been sleeping well? Has the dream been plaguing you?"

"Not for a whole week. Valene helped me."

"Thank the Creator for her." She squints her eyes. "So, what's bothering you now?"

I groan, annoyed at the thought. "One of my friends is being a jerk towards me."

"One of the girls? How come?"

"She's afraid of me. Well not just me, but the whole demons being real thing."

"Oh, yes. I know that fear. I've had human friends turn on me because of the same situation."

"What did you do?"

"Nothing. The only thing I could do was wait and see whether they would accept me or not. Just be patient with them. If they are truly your friend they'll come around. If not, then oh well. It was time well spent."

"Right. So, where have you been all this time?"

"Traveling the world and between realms. Leo had a lot of friends. I was informing them of his death, and the day that he will be laid to rest."

"When will that be?"

"At the end of July in the Underworld. We are going to honor him in the forest of the forgotten."

"Forest of the forgotten?"

"A maze of a forest covered in a dense fog. Legends say that it was once a metropolis before the great divide and that it housed untold treasures. Countless have tried to navigate it, but none returned. Coining the name. Leo, the adventurer, the explorer and sometimes the mercenary went in. Everyone wrote him off, but he came back. His crowning achievement. So, we're going to go and send him off there."

I watch her as the smile on her face grows. I feel so gross though. *Was it my fault he was there in the first place? With that stupid chess game? What would have happened had I not sacrificed the pawn? Did I really have a choice?* 'It's okay, you tried.' I hear his voice.

"Can I come? I didn't really know him, but he was cool to me. And I want to apologize for not being able to help."

Mayra touches my face. "Of course. I'm sure he'd want you there."

"The Underworld sounds like a scary place."

"Yes, it is still very wild, and dangerous. Akin to the fantasy worlds in a lot of human books. A place filled with magic, monsters, and kingdoms."

"Sounds like I'd have to get stronger first, before we go."

Her eyes glow as I feel her gaze scan me. "You are a lot stronger than you were before I left. You'd be fine. Now, my little sister, she'd struggle a bit. She has always been a little too prissy for that realm." She says laughing. "Now, how about we order a pizza. I haven't had pizza in months."

"Sure."

"I wonder if that kid still works at that one place. He always gave me the pizza for free." She says pulling back the comforter a bit, showing her shoulders.

"No. I got it."

She laughs, covering herself back up. "Whatever you say little brother."

Chapter 7

I lay on the floor of my room at the Kir estate, watching the early morning sky on my enchanted ceiling. The sun is now just peeking over the horizon, filling the night sky with blues, purples, and oranges. Waking New Birth for the new day. But not me. I've been up for four hours now, and my body is a mixture of numb and sore. I hear Selene's voice in my ears. 'Come on Chéri. Keep up or die.'

These training sessions have been getting way more intense. Even Jason can barely keep up and he's been doing this for a full dytic. If I'm not careful, or get any stronger, I think I may die. I sit up, crossing my legs into the lotus position.

With a few deep breaths my eyes burn and the colors of the world fade to gray. With the dark sight active, I look and see the blue tinged black energy still rising off me. *I'm still giving off a lot.*

A faint golden aura appears amongst the blue. It brings my thoughts to Valene and her giving me a soul drop. A literal part of her soul. *I really must thank her somehow. Hmmm, our one-year anniversary is coming up next month. Maybe I can do something for that. But what though?*

The floor rumbles before the stuff around my room starts rattling. Waves of golden energy pulse throughout the house. It looks like Valene's, but it doesn't feel like hers. Her energy is sharp and heavy. This feels light and wild. And it's coming from the training room. *What's happening down there?* I stand and shadow-walk.

Appearing in the training room, a wave of bright energy strains my eyes, blinding me. I deactivate the sight and after a moment of adjustment, my vision returns to normal. Jason sits in the center of the room, taking deep, strained meditative breaths. With every exhale a wave of energy pulses from him hitting me like a gust of wind. "Jase?" I ask.

His eyes snap to me and his energy wavers. All at once it rushes back towards him. With a deep breath, he strains. It slows down, but he isn't fast enough. The full force of his returning energy slams into him, and he goes sliding across the floor into one of the mirrored walls, cracking it. I rush over to him, "Jason, are you okay?" I ask kneeling next to him.

He leans back onto the wall, breathing heavily and completely exhausted. "Yeah, I'm okay."

"What was that?"

"Extra training mother gave me. It's supposed to help deepen and strengthen your energy well. At least that's what she says. I don't get it, but what she says goes."

"Okay. How does this work?

"Well, you take your energy, and you flex it. Push it out of your body and off your skin. Then when it's out as far as it can go, hold it there. It sucks, because the energy just wants to come back to you, and it will keep fighting harder and harder until it does. Give it a try."

"Okay. You good though?"

He gives me a thumbs up. I walk to the center of the room. With a deep breath, I close my eyes. *Flex.* My energy blares off my skin spreading across the room. The ground beneath me starts to shake, and the mirrors rattle as my energy pulses off me.

"Okay, now hold it there."

Sweat instantly starts to pour out of me. It's hard to catch my breath as this immense pressure builds on the boundaries of my energy. I stretch my arms out to continue to hold it, but it feels like I'm being crushed. Fatigue is setting in fast. "How are you feeling, Bro?"

"This sucks." I grind out. "How do I get out of this?"

"Okay, just let it come back in before you pass out. Slowly, or you'll go flying like I did."

With another breath, my energy stops pouring from me. Like a rubber band it snaps back towards me, with all the force that it has built up. *Come on come on,* "Stop!" I say just before it can hit me. The energy stops and eases back onto my skin, relieving the strain. My legs turn to jelly, and I fall to my knee, gasping. "Man, that was intense."

"Bro, you're telling me." Jason says walking up to me.

"How did my energy feel to you?"

"It was so raw. It gave me goosebumps, and it kind of warped all the mirrors."

I look at the walls and everything is wonky in the reflections. I activate the dark sight and look at my arm. The energy radiating from me has changed. It's bluer and less black. *I'll have to remember this.* Jason helps me up. "Thanks for showing me this."

"No problem."

After a second of leaning on him the feeling in my legs return. "All right I'm good. Thanks."

"Are you sure?"

"Yeah. Hey, can I ask you something about your sister?"

His face scrunches up like a kid being forced to eat his vegetables. "What about her?"

"Well, our anniversary is coming up and I want to get her something nice. I just don't have a clue as to what."

"Oh. You could always get her something in her favorite color, which is purple."

"I know that much, but It needs to be something grand you know."

"I couldn't tell you Bro. Why don't you try talking to mom or dad?"

"Good idea."

I try to step away from him, but my legs nearly give out on me again. Jason's grip tightens on my arm as he takes most of my weight. "How about I go with you. I think mom is in the kitchen with Zel making breakfast."

"Thanks."

"We're walking though. I hate shadow-walking."

"I know."

We go through the corridor, out into the main foyer and through the door into the kitchen. Selene stands in front of the huge stove, with a bandana wrapped around her braids. "Zel, love." Zel drops silver bowls of diced veggies and meat next to her. "Merci." Jason and I walk over the huge island in the center of the room and sit in tall seats. We don't say a thing while we sit there and watch her work.

Selene has this thing about her acknowledging you first before she allows you to. She takes it very seriously. I've been slapped and punched a few times when I don't pay attention to it.

Selene takes two plates from the counter next to her, filling them up. She spins around and slides the plates in front of us. "Breakfast is served."

It was an egg scrambler with bacon, onions, peppers, and broccoli, on top a bed of sliced spinach. "Merci." The both of us say.

Her emerald eyes shine with glee as she smiles. "Thank you, Jason, for showing Kyle that training technique. I was going to show it to him during our next session."

"You're welcome mother."

"Now what can I help you with Chéri?"

I swallow the food I'd shoveled into my mouth. "I need a gift idea for my and Valene's anniversary. You wouldn't happen to know what she may want?"

Selene holds out a hand and Zel walks by placing a glass of red wine into it. "Well, I find that the best gifts are those given from the heart. Do you have any ideas yet?"

"None at all."

She takes a sip of her wine. "I can't help you Chéri. I rarely give my own husband gifts. He always says that he needs nothing, for he has everything he has ever wanted. Corny yes, but it's why I love him. Have you tried asking him?"

"He's my next stop."

"He and Valene are still training. Finish your food and head to the library."

"Yes ma'am." As we continue to eat, she explains the reasoning behind the energy training. Saying that with this, it will allow me to go beyond the strength that I've achieved so far and into the realm of superhuman. Also, the control I have over my energy will increase.

With my stomach full, my legs finally get feeling back into them. I shadow-walk from the kitchen to the library. I appear in front of the fireplace along the wall. Zel's power radiates from the flame, which tells me that they're in Chris's private training area. A place that I'm nowhere near ready to enter. They'll be in there for a while longer.

The smell of old leather, paper and parchment is strong here. There are hundreds of books, ranging from ancient to new, demon to human. A lot of the human ones are written in English, others in other languages. Most of the demon books though are written in *Durabi Duprima*: the ancient language of creation.

Learning the vocabulary and how to speak it is easy. Reading it is the difficult part. Trying to read *Durabi* is like looking into a kaleidoscope of symbols. They dance around the page, only lighting up for a second in whichever combination to catch whatever word it is that they make. I can only see about three or so words at a time. While those who are truly versed in it, can read an entire page worth of words immediately. The crazy thing is a page of *Durabi* can hold half a book of information.

I wander around the stacks on the second floor, picking books from the shelves. I have one talking about meditation in martial arts, and one on demon history which is in *Durabi*. I sit a nook tucked in between one of the bookcases. Zel appears next to me with a cup of tea. I take it without thought and continue to read. Zels presence doesn't go away, and I look over to him. "What's up?"

"You used to jump whenever I would just appear. Now look at you."

I chuckle. "I've just gotten so used to you just popping up and all."

"I just think that it's neat that you've adjusted so quickly."

"There are some things that I still struggle with."

"I'm sure you'll be fine. Is there anything else I can do for you?"

"Nope. Thank you Zel." He bows and slowly melts into the floor.

I start to read a book on meditation. An hour passes and I'm already through it. I've noticed that my reading comprehension has skyrocketed since Valene healed me. I've read over five books and my textbooks forward and back this week alone. Finals are going to be a breeze. I pretty much have everything committed to memory. Page is doomed though when it comes to math. Now, these demon books. They are on a whole other level.

Before I can start, There's a crackling noise down below. I get up, walk over to the railing, and look out to the sitting area by the fire. The flames within the fireplace roar as they reach out; the heat warping the space before it. From out of the distortion Valene appears and she's a mess. Her hair is in her face, her shirt drenched in sweat, and covered in blood. There's a wild look in her jet-black eyes while her whole-body heaves trying to catch her breath. "Val..." She appears in front me out of thin air, perched on the rail. Startled, I take a step back sucking in air, muffling a yelp.

She stares at me through the mess of hair in her face, growling. The features of her face are a little harder and monstrous. I've read about this in one of the demon books. When pushed to the brink of their mental capacities, demons will revert to a primal mindset, only running on instincts. Basically, becoming a berserker and will attack anything they perceive as a threat. "Valene, can you hear me?" She just stares, with an aggressive look. As slow as I can, I bring my hands up, palms open. "It's okay Valene. You're safe. Remember. This is a safe place."

She steps off the railing. I don't move. I barely breathe as she gets right into my face. She looks at my hand for a minute and then back to me. Slowly, she laces her taloned fingers with mine and grips my hand. "Hero." She says with a slight growl. "Safe place."

Her features soften, slowly changing back to normal. There's a popping sound out of the fireplace. "Valene." Her dad's voice radiates from the distortion.

Within a second, There's A whirlwind of emotion on her face. she spins around, yanking her hand from me. The searing pain of her talons slicing through the web of my fingers catches me off guard and I yell out. She spins back to me ready to attack when she notices the fresh blood now trickling down my hand and arm. "I'm ...sorry. " Valene struggles to say before she shadow-walks away.

Moments later Chris steps out from the distorted space. His body is tense, and his pale skin glistens in the warm light of the fire like a diamond. Blood drips from his fingertips as he works his hands. "Valene!" he yells, his voice reverberating throughout the whole library.

"You just missed her."

He looks up to me. His blue eyes are just as intense as Valene's. But where hers were filled with wild emotion, his are devoid of any. I grip the rail, preparing myself for a possible fight. Chris's face lights up with a smile. "Good. Always be ready to fight no matter who is in front of you." right before my eyes he vanishes. A hand grabs my left Wrist and lifts it in the air. "Did she do this?" Chris asks.

I snap towards him, his blank eyes focused on the wounds on my hand. "Yes." *How do they keep doing that?*

"And that's all she did?"

"Yeah."

He looks at me pleasantly surprised. "She must really care for you. I've seen her decimate whole villages while in that state. And here you are with just a couple of scratches."

"Chris, my arm. You're crushing it."

"Oh." He lets go. "Forgive me son. As far as I push her, she's starting to push me there as well. Zel."

Zel rises from the floor, next to Chris. A towel in hand. "You summoned me, Master?"

Chris takes the towel and starts wiping away the blood and sweat from his face and hands. "Where is my daughter?"

"She is currently running the estate."

"Good. She'll let off some of that steam. Take care of Kyle's hand while you're at it."

Zel walks up to me and takes my hand. He removes his glove revealing the blood red gem embedded in the palm of his right hand. The philosopher's stone. A gift from his Master that can heal almost any wound. A red-light shine from the gem on mine and the skin starts to repair itself. "Chris, what do you do to her in there?"

He stares at me for a second and smiles. "As fast as Selene says you're growing, you'll find out soon enough. But asking me about our training isn't why you're here is it? Something else is bothering you."

"Yeah. I want to do something for Valene for our anniversary. To repay her for that amazing trip, for healing me and the soul drop she gave me."

Chris places his hand on my shoulder. "My daughter is a simple kind of woman. If it comes from you, be it big or small she'll love and cherish it."

Lowering my head. "I know, but she deserves something nice."

"Well, I could tell you a couple of things that she would like but it wouldn't be from you."

"True. I just don't know where to start."

"Might I suggest asking her best friend."

"Serena?"

"No. They are good friends, but they are at odds most of the time. Simone though has been Valene's running mate since they were little."

"Really?"

"Oh yes. You see she comes to visit once a month or so. Our families have had dealings with one another since before the last war. So, if you're going to start anywhere, start with her." I sigh. "What's the matter?"

"I like Simone, but talking to her takes a little effort to keep the conversation PG."

He pats me on the back. "Have fun. I'll be in the shower if you need me" He says shadow-walking away.

"How are we looking, Zel?"

"It'll be a few minutes. Healing damage from a demon is a little more challenging than that from human means."

"While you do that. Do you know a way that I can speak with Simone? I think she's still in the underworld."

"Yes, I do believe she is. Allow me to get you a looking glass." He reaches into the pocket on the chest of his suit jacket and pulls out a giant glass marble and hands it to me. "This is a looking glass. This little trinket will allow you to connect with anyone that you've interacted with, be it here on New Birth, the Underworld..."

"And even Heaven?"

"No. Elysium has been cut off from the realms for *dytics*."

"Elysium?"

"One of the many names of the realm of light."

"Well. What about the Underworld?"

"Once upon a time, before the great divide. The demon realm was known as Gehenna. The book you were just attempting to read should speak on that history."

"Probably. It's going to take a while before I get there. Since I'm struggling to read *Durabi*. So how do I use this thing?"

"Look into it. With a clear picture in your mind of who it is that you wish to contact speak their name. It'll do the rest."

I gaze into the marble with a clear picture of Simone. Her thin frame, her pale white skin, her long blond hair, and that mischievous smile she always has as she bares her fangs at me. Clouds begin to stir within the looking glass and her image appears. "Simone Dawes."

For a second, I lose sense of myself, as I'm swept up by this things power. I open my eyes to a plain of mist. "Well, isn't this a nice surprise." I hear someone say with an old southern drawl. A thin, beautiful blond vampire appears before me, her arms crossed and that mischievous smile on her face. "I wasn't expecting to hear from you, sugar lump. To what do I owe the honor of this beseeching?"

"Sorry if I'm interrupting anything, but I need to ask you a few questions about Valene."

She looks at me with her big blue eyes. She smiles big enough to show off her fangs. "Aww let me guess. This is so you can pay her back for that little trip of yours?" I nod. "Well, ask away then. I am an open book. Just know with every turn of the page there is a price to pay. And the information about my best friend isn't cheap. Even if it's to her cute beau." she says, grabbing my nose.

"Yeah, I figured as much."

"Good. So then whatever information I give I shall set the price accordingly. Agreed?" She holds her hand out to me. *I am going to regret this.* I take her hand. She yanks me to her, wraps her free hand around the back of my neck and kisses me, hard. I pull back. "And sealed with a kiss."

"Simone why do always do that? Besides you can't suck my blood here."

She licks her fangs. "I like to think it's our tradition now. You know you like it."

I shake my head. "Anyway, so I have no clue what to get her. She took me on that trip, gave me a soul drop and I feel like I need to get her something worthy." She nods in agreement. "What would you suggest I get her?"

"A soul drop you say." She looks at me and her smile turns devilish "Hmm, how about your virginity? I feel that would be worth it." I lower my head in a sigh. "What? One's virginity is a big deal. There's a power in that innocence. It's the reason why you're just so scrumptious." She says laughing. "Speaking of which, why haven't you two..."

"Simone, focus."

She puts her hands up. "Other than that, I can't think of anything. Maybe some jewelry?"

Jewelry? I think for a second and the image of little Valene pops into my head. "Valene used to wear a medallion, right?"

"Oh, my goodness, yes. She loved that amulet with all her being. She was so distraught when Leo lost it."

"Do you think it could be found?"

She laughs, "Oh no Sugar lump, he lost that thing here in the underworld five *Dytics* ago. You've heard of the Great Divide, right?"

"I've read a little about it. It's said that the Underworld was split eons ago by the Creator for some reason. They call that event the Great Divide."

"The Great Divide is also a place. Leo was sent on an expedition there and took Valene's amulet with him. Said it would protect him from the curses that lingered there due to its make-up. And he lost it. Said that its power was drained when he entered a hidden temple. You'd be better off making one yourself."

"That's not a bad idea. Do you know who made it?"

"Your daddy made it for her when she was born. I can't tell you what it was made of, but I'm sure Sir Kir would know."

I take hold of her slender body and lift her into the air. "Thank you. You're a lifesaver."

"You're quite welcome. Now about the payment for my information." She wraps her arms around me as I put her down. "A liter of that delicious blood of yours will do. Because if you get her this, it'll be bye bye to that sweet blood of yours." My face grows hot with embarrassment. "I'll be collecting soon, so you be ready." She bites my neck. Then she shoves me away. "Later Sugar lump." She vanishes. The world around me goes black.

I blink a few times and the world around me is back to normal. I look to Zel, who is patiently waiting. Then to my hand which was completely healed. "Thanks, Zel." He bows. "Is Chris back yet?"

"I'm right here." Next to me, Chris stands fully dressed, with a bowl of scramble and an apple.

"What can you tell me about the Amulet Valene used to wear? The one Leo lost."

He laughs. "Oh, I remember that thing. Your dad crafted it for her when she was born. With my help, of course. Otherwise, he would have died trying. It was a process. You see, it was made of two metals. Imperial gold and Celestial silver."

"What are those?"

"Imperial gold is the purest and most rare form of the metal found here on New Birth. Celestial silver doesn't even exist in this realm. It comes from the realm of light."

"How in the world did you guys get your hands on that? Did you go there?"

He laughs hard, patting me on the back and winding me a little. "No son. We found it on New Birth." I look at him confused. "You see, when debris falls from the realm it's transmogrified as it enters this one into a metal. It's the hardest to find and the most dangerous for demons to handle. It can kill us. I'm still honestly amazed we were able to make it."

"I'd like to remake it for her, as my gift. To replace the one that was lost."

He looks at me skeptical, as if judging to see if I were serious. "Are you sure? It's an extremely dangerous task."

"I'm sure. She deserves it."

He smiles. "You remind me so much of your father. Only he would choose to do something so crazy for the ones he loves and believe me he did some crazy stuff for your mother, and Mayra. Alright, first things first. The materials. Both are hard to find and haven't been seen in centuries, So I'll need a little time to hunt down their locations."

"Thank you."

"No problem son. I love a challenge."

Chapter 8

Shadow-walking, I appear in an alley just down the street from my school. This week was finals week and today is the last one before I am done with high school. I don't know what I'm going to do after though. Ever since last year, choosing a college to attend hasn't really been a priority. Mainly it's just been trying to survive my training with Selene and Valene. I haven't sent any applications. Maybe I should try and get a job? I mean I technically have multiple lifetimes to figure it out now. I'll think about it after I ace this test.

I rush down the street joining the crowd of students making their way into the school. Instead of going to my homeroom I just go straight to the class that has my last final. *Once I'm done, I'll be able to leave.*

Entering the room, I feel eyes on me. Scanning the room I see Rica staring, fiddling with her cross. Next to her was Airca. She looks at me and her face instantly grows annoyed. Tough crowd.

"Hey." Page says from behind them, waving. She pats the seat next to her.

"Morning guys." I say as I approach them.

"Hey." Rica says lightly.

Airca crosses her arms and looks away from me. *Okay.*

"Come hither young man. Sit next to me." Page says, presenting the desk next to her. I walk by the others still looking at

Airca. Once I take a seat Airca turns back and starts to talk with Rica. "It's the last final. Are you excited?"

That's the first full sentence I've heard out of her mouth in a month. "So that's what you sound like? I almost thought you couldn't talk anymore." I say.

She turns around in her desk, scowling. "I can talk just fine. I just don't want to talk to you." She spins back around. "So, Rica are you excited?"

"Not really. It's the last one we'll ever have to take here, but not ever."

"True. What school are you planning on attending?"

Page raises her pencil in the air. "I plan on taking a few years off to travel the world." She says confidently.

"Really?" I ask.

Page slumps in her chair in defeat, groaning. "No. My mom wants me to go to Ohio State University in Ohio, but I'd be good just going to Roc University. Not sure what I want to major in though. Hey Rica, have you been accepted into any of your school choices yet?"

"I've gotten accepted into all of them. I'm thinking about accepting the Christian college that's known for their economic program."

Page looks at me palming her face. She looks at Rica and mouths, 'Why are you so extra?' "That's cool. What about you Airca?"

"I haven't really put in any applications. I'm thinking about just working until I decide what I want to do."

"What about you Kyle?" Page asks.

Before I can say something, the bell rings. Coach Williams hobbles in struggling to hold a big stack of papers. He lets the stack fall onto the desk. "Alright folks settle down." He says out of breath. "It's time for your test." He passes them out, setting the thick packets face down on our desks. "Now you have two hours to complete this packet. But if you finish early, you can just leave. Comprende?" He says plopping down at the teacher's desk. "Oh and no cheating. I'm looking at you Quartze." He says pointing at Page.

"Come on coach I don't need to cheat." She says blatantly winking at me.

"Sure. Your time starts...now."

We flip over the test and begin. A few minutes pass and Page already motions to get an answer out of me, but I'm already a quarter of the way through. She gives up and continues flipping through the pages.

Thirty minutes pass and I'm on the last couple of pages. These are going to be the best test scores that I've ever gotten. All thanks to this new brain of mine. Airca closes her packet and gets up. She places her test on the desk and leaves. *How did she beat me? Wait, this might be a good time to try and talk to her while I have her.*

Quickly, I jot the rest of the answers down, grab my stuff, turn in my papers, and head out the door after her. She was already halfway down the hall. "Airca wait."

She stops, with a big huff. "What do you want Kyle?"

"First off..." The lights flicker overhead. The air grows thick with a humid heat and my hair stands on end. I step closer to Airca.

"What's gotten into you?" she asks, trying to step away from me.

I take her wrist. "Something's coming."

Without any fuss she positions herself behind me. We stand completely still for a second just waiting. "Eww." She says, breaking the silence.

"What is it?"

"You stink."

"What?"

"Yeah. You smell like a wet dog." The lights flicker again. The temp rises dramatically, forming heat waves within the hall. Like a mirage shimmering into existence, a greyish- blue furred puppy appears in front of us. Covered from his black nose to the tip of his tail in soap suds. "What in the world is that?" Airca asks, pressing harder to my back.

"That's my hellhound, Smoke."

"Hellhound?"

Smoke looks to me, his little puppy face lighting up with a grin. In a full gallop he rushes to me. Airca clutches my shirt, and I can feel her tremble. "Airca, you have nothing to be afraid of, he's harmless."

"You say that, but in most of the shows I've watched, hellhounds are sent to collect on souls that have been bargained away."

"Don't believe everything that you watch on TV. Besides, he's my familiar we're in no danger." I kneel to meet him with all his wetness, and he rams into my chest. "Buddy what are you doing here, so far from the enclosure?" I ask, trying to fight him back from licking me.

Images pop into my head as he grumbles and barks. First the image of him running. Second, the color red, which he associates with anger. Third, his water bowl which associates with water. And last, the silhouette of a woman. "You're running from an angry water lady?" Smoke barks in affirmation.

"You can understand him?"

"Sort of. It's recent but he's able to show me images and I put them together. I read that it gets better as the bond between familiar and master grow, but he's still just a puppy."

"Okay. Then who's chasing him?"

The air trembles, and the lockers rattle as energy fills the hall. Airca moves in close to me pressing against my back. She's breathing hard, and her heart is racing, but I'm calm. I know exactly who this angry water Lady is.

Valene steps out of a cloud of darkness, barefoot, wearing shorts, a muscle shirt. Her hands covered in soap suds. "Now where did that little cuss go? Why would he come here?" She looks up to see me holding Smoke. "Oh, that's why. Hello Hero."

"Valene. I'm happy to see you, but you can't just shadow-walk into a public place. What if someone saw you?"

"Oh, don't worry there's no one else around. Besides most of these kids are on something, they'll just think that I'm a hallucination. Now to you." She focuses on Smoke. "You aren't getting out of a bath that easily, runt."

Smoke barks at her. The image of his water bowl upside-down on top of the woman's silhouette pops into my head. "You be nice." I tell him. "Now go on. It's a bath. It is not going to hurt you."

He grumbles. Valene steps forward to take him but stops, confused, and startled. *What is she looking at?* I look back over my shoulder to Airca making herself as small as possible.

"Has she been here the whole time?" I nod. "I didn't sense her presence."

"It's cool. It's just Airca."

Airca waves. Valene just stares at her skeptical. "It's nice to see you again."

"Likewise." Airca says softly.

Valene takes Smoke from me. "Come to the house when you're done here. I want to talk to you. Father also wishes to see you." She kisses me on the cheek.

"Okay. See you in a bit."

"See you later Airca."

"Sure will." Airca says her voice trembling.

Valene and Smoke vanish. Airca sighs, relaxing her grip on my shirt. "You, okay?" I ask.

She takes a deep breath. "That was a little scary."

"Yeah. It takes a bit to get used to. But if you must go through situations like this, don't worry. I got your back."

Airca looks at me, and her face softens. More than it has the whole school year. She sighs. "Thanks."

"So..." She turns to leave. "Wait where are you going?"

"Home. We'll talk later. Go to your girlfriend."

"But?"

"Bye Kyle." She says continuing down the hall.

"Okay, I'll just go this way." Once I'm out of the school I make my way down the street to the alley. *What in the world is her problem? Is it like what Page said? My getting with Valene so fast? I don't know.*

"It's always the same thing with you!" I hear a woman yelling out from the alley. "I try to talk to you, and you cut me off every single ..."

"You just don't understand." Says a man. He sounds so defeated and tired.

I poke my head around the corner to see a couple standing next to the back entrance to one of the buildings. She was in a black dress and the guy was wearing a black polo shirt, with jeans and boots. "Oh my God. Jacob I'm so done talking to you right now. Our therapist said that if you want us to work, you have to be present, remember?" He just stares at her and sighs. She growls, frustrated at his none answer, before storming off into the door.

After a second of just standing there with a blank face, his composure breaks as he ruffles his shaggy hair. "Our day is coming, it's our fate." He takes a deep breath before going through the door. The door slams shut with a loud bang.

Looks like everyone is having communication problems lately. My skin starts to crawl, as I feel eyes on me. I scan the alley but there's no one in sight. I shadow-walk away.

I appear just outside of the giant barn-like structure, the animal enclosure on the Kir estate. Some of the normal animals: chickens, cows, goats, sheep and horses all scatter from around me. With a deep breath I walk in. This place is cozy but once you get further in it starts to get a little more dangerous, because that's where the demon beasts of the Underworld are kept. Most of them are just as docile and domesticated as any other animal here, but some are wild and extremely dangerous. Either they're highly poisonous, man-eating or both.

Not too long after I walked through the enclosure for the first time last year, I asked Chris why he had such creatures here on Earth. He says that they were all cash cows. And that his top gainer is the *Morgal.* A Giant centipede. Its shell and poison are apparently used in a lot of demon and human medicines. Not only is this demon bug extremely dangerous, but super rare. He personally takes care of it because of its specific needs. Next is the bat which is roughly my size. Its guano is one of the richest fertilizers you can find. One bag is equal to a small truck load of normal human made fertilizer. Every other creature like them can be used to gain wealth. The hellhounds though, he always called a side project. He still hasn't said what it is though that makes them special.

As I open the door to the hellhound pen, all the black and red furred pups stop wrestling in front of their bull sized mother, Sally. They all lock their glowing red eyes on me. With open mouths and wagging tails, the pups all rush me, their fur sparking with every step. I hold my hand out and they stop at my feet. I look at Sally. With just a few steps she's in arms distance from me. The red tipped fur on her back rises, flowing like a flame, radiating heat. She bares her dagger length fangs, smoke bellowing from her mouth as she starts to pant. "Good morning girl." She gently drives her head into my chest. When she steps back, the pups bound forward, trying to climb up my leg and chew on my shoestrings. I read that with hellhounds; you should greet the Alpha of the pack before you greet the others. I'm still trying to figure out which of the pups are the Alpha but until then, I just greet Sally.

Smoke howls loudly, drawing everyone's attention. Valene scrubs him hard. "Don't give me that. You're the one that rolled in it after I had already washed you."

"Hey Valene. You wanted to talk?" I ask, walking up to her, Sally at my side. She looks at me for a second and I get a little uncomfortable. "What?"

"Is something going on between you and Airca?"

"She's been giving me the cold shoulder most of the school year. Beyond that no. Why do you ask?"

"Well, it looked to me like she still has feelings for you."

"Really? You think so?"

"You don't?"

"No. Not with the way she's been acting. The girls have said something along those lines too. But I don't see it."

"You are a bit dense sometimes, Hero."

"So, what makes you think she is still feeling me?"

"Call it intuition."

"So, you're not really sure."

"Oh, I'm sure. I just can't explain it. You're too young to get it."

"What do you mean? You're not older than me. My birthdays before yours." She looks at me with an obvious look. That's when it hits me. "Oh right. I try not to think about it, but you are **a lot** older than me."

"And have seen a lot more than you. Don't get me wrong. It's not that I don't trust you I just want you to be aware of her feelings. And maybe your own."

"What are you trying to say?"

"That you may still have feelings for her too."

"No way. I'm with you."

"True, but that doesn't change feelings. She was once someone you wanted to be with, and those feeling are hard to get over." She dowses Smoke with water. "Alright runt, get out." He hops out of the basin, shakes the water from his fur, and stretches. Steam rises off him as he uses his own heat to dry his fur the rest of the way. He gallops off to play with the rest of the pups, with Sally on his tail. Valene stands whipping her hands off on her shorts before she looks at me. "You look like you have a question?"

"Is there anyone that you still have feelings for?"

A small smile touches the corner of her mouth, but there's sadness in her eyes. "No. They died a century ago. Now, I just have you."

"Oh, I'm sorry."

She takes my hand. "I appreciate it, Hero, but that's just how life is between an immortal and a human."

I squeeze her hand. "I'll do my best to be aware."

"Thank you. Now hurry to father. He said that he had good news." I pull her in close and hold her tight. She holds me back, kind of melting into my embrace. "I'll talk to you later Hero."

"Promise?" I ask, looking into her golden eyes.

She kisses me. The energy transference takes hold of us for a split second until she pulls back. "Get going." She orders with a smile.

"Zel, can you open a door to Chris?" I ask out loud. Along the wall of the pen a door appears. "Thank you. See you in a bit."

When I get in front of the door it opens to a vortex. I step through and out the other side in the library. "There you are son. I've been waiting." Chris says sitting on the floor, his legs crossed, and his eyes closed.

"Sorry. I was talking to Valene. So, what is the word?"

"Well, I got good news and bad news."

"Bad first."

"Imperial gold hasn't been used in centuries by humans. Though there is still weaponry out there made of it. We need the unrefined ore, which hasn't turned up yet. Good news my contacts have located some of the celestial silver."

"Really?! Where?"

"Right here in the city."

"What, some crazy rich human collector of occult items has it or something? Do we have to go undercover to steal it?"

He laughs. "Not saying that that's not plausible, but no. You'll find it at the heart of the city in the Core."

The Core is where most of the crime in the city takes place. It's run/terrorized by all sorts of gangs and mobsters. "Why would something like that be there?"

"The Roc has always been a hub for demonic activity since the days before the city's creation. And many of those creatures would and still bring their wares here to sell and trade."

"In the Core though?"

"Why not? Crime is high and the authorities aren't present. Nothing could stand in the way of a literal black market. But I'm nowhere near comfortable sending you there alone." Chris doesn't really do much in the open when it comes to demons. There are just too many eyes and people still looking for the leader of Shadow's rebel faction.

"I'll be fine. I've had Selene and Valene as instructors. I can handle myself."

"Really. How about we test that."

"How?"

Chris closes his eyes and takes a deep breath. My mouth goes dry as everything goes silent. The only thing I can hear is my heart beating loudly in my ears. His eyes open with a dead stare. My stomach twists into a knot as an overwhelming pressure envelops me, filling me with dread. My skin crawls as my claws and greaves appear out of reflex and I prepare myself. I don't know what's going on, but I know for certain that if I move, he's going to kill me.

Seconds pass, but it feels like hours. I'm so tense that I can't even swallow or take a full breath. Sweat is running down my back and forehead. Everything in me is screaming to run. To get away from him. *No. Don't move.* I plant my feet. *Don't run. You can't run.*

Like he had always been standing there he appears in front of me, staring down at me. His eyes aglow. My legs start to shake, and I can feel my bladder ready to blow. Slowly, he raises his hand, bringing it to my face. Everything starts to spin, but his hand is so apparent getting closer and closer. At the last second before he can touch me, with all my strength I knock his hand away and jump back far from him.

I land readying myself. My heart pounding and my vision swimming.

Chris is frozen in complete astonishment. He looks at me and laughs, "You'll have to forgive me Kyle. I underestimated you."

As he looks away from me a weight lifts off my shoulders. I fall to my hands and knees, struggling to breathe. My claws melt away, and tears start to pour from my eyes. I fall to the ground, holding myself and sob uncontrollably. Chris walks over to me and places his hand onto my back. "It's okay son. Let it out."

"Wh...what did you do to me?" I ask between breaths.

"When your instincts and senses are so high and in tune with one another you can feel the intentions of other beings. What you just felt was my intent to kill you. And as you can see, it can be overwhelming. Debilitating. I wanted to test how well you did under that pressure before I cast you to the wolves. My boy, you far exceeded my expectations. I was sure you were going to run."

"I was but running...running from a demon or supernatural creature that has its gaze on you is bad. It is better to stand your ground, fight until you have an opening, and then retreat. Selene and Valene preach that lesson every day I have to fight them."

"Exactly. You may very well be ready to join Valene and I."

"You do this every time that you guys are training?"

"Of course. Diamonds are built under pressure."

I look at him, a smile of excitement on his face and in his sea-blue eyes. "I don't think I'm ready for that yet."

"Son, if you can handle yourself at the market, and in this situation then you're ready for the next step in your training."

I sit up and wipe away my tears and sweat. "So, this silver?" I ask, trying to change the subject from working with him.

He laughs. "Search the market. When you find it. You'll have to dull its energies. Human hands are good for that. So, I would suggest taking one of your friends."

"Why do I have to dull its energy?"

"The light realm itself is deadly to demons. So, anything from there is equally as dangerous."

I manage to get to my feet, but my legs are still wobbly. Chris takes me by the arm, bracing me until I can steady them. "Thanks. So, how do I get to the market?"

"The corner store on main. One of the doorways is there. Be warned, most of the demons there don't deal in human currency. They tend to set their own prices, depending on who you are, what they want and what you can offer."

"I already know that much."

"Good." He says slapping me on the back. "This is exciting. Good luck."

Chapter 9

I lay in my bed at the Kir's, staring up at the enchanted ceiling. The sun is shining, but it's filtered so I can look at it. My muscles are screaming. These past couple of days I've tried to push myself a little more during training and I'm starting to feel it.

I hold my hands up and watch as they tremble. They haven't stopped since Chris's little test. "That was so scary."

My phone chimes. I go to reach for it but stop short before touching it. With a deep breath I focus on my energy, drawing it in. After training my energy is kind of all over the place and affects electronics in a bad way. I've short circuited a lot of phones over the year. After a second of breathing, I finally wrangle my energy. I grab it and it doesn't spark up. *Safe.* It's a text from Page. 'Sorry I just saw that you tried to call me yesterday. What's up?'

'Page Quartze. You have been formally summoned to join me, the Master of Shadows, on a most demonic quest. Will accept this offer?' I send it. Moments later my phone rings, a picture of Page sticking her tongue out at me pops up on the screen. "Your answer madame?"

"You suck so hard."

"Can't accept?"

"I will have to decline your offer, Master of Shadows. I'm out of town right now visiting OSU."

"I thought you wanted to go to Roc U?"

"I've already accepted Roc University, but mom wanted me to look at the other school and possibly reconsider. It's a drag...Mom says hi."

"Hi Miss. Quartze."

"So, what is it that you needed me for?"

"I'm going to a supernatural market that's somewhere in the Core. I'm looking for a rare metal that is dangerous to the touch for me and I need human hands to handle it."

"That's so cool. Mom, can we go home now?" Her mother dismisses her a bit telling her to just give it a chance. "I'm stuck here." Page says with a sigh. "Did you ask anyone else?"

"Who else am I going to ask? Rica? The girl is scared of me."

"So, we just going to ignore Airca?" I'm silent. "I know, she has been hard on you, but maybe if you spend a little time together, she'll lighten up."

I groan. "I'll keep that in mind."

"Good enough. I have to go. I've lost track of mom and the tour group. Talk to you later."

She hangs up. I stare at my phone, contemplating whether I should try calling Airca or not. Before I do that let me ask if Chris can find someone to help me.

I roll out of bed and shadow-walk to the library. "Chris are you here?" there's silence. "Hey Zel, is Chris in the house?"

Zel rises from the floor, in a slight bow. "I'm afraid he is not. The Master had a few business errands to run."

"Just my luck. Thank you." He bows his head before sinking back into the floor. I pull out my phone, open my contacts and tap on her name. Her ID photo is a picture of her fast asleep. "Okay, let's give this a try." I tap the screen and it starts to ring. After a few rings it goes right over to voice mail. "Hey Airca, when you get this give me a..." My phone rings interrupting me. It's Airca. "Hello?"

"What do you want Kyle?"

"Well good morning to you too. Now I'm trying to figure out who peed in your cereal."

She takes a deep frustrated breath. "Good morning. What do you want?"

I sigh, calming myself. "Help. I need your help with something potentially dangerous."

"What is it exactly?"

I tell her the same thing that I told Page about the market and the metal. She's silent for a second. "Airca?"

"Have you tried the others?"

"Well Page at least, but she's out of town. Rica isn't fond of this whole demon thing."

"So, I was your last choice."

"I mean do you blame me. You've had a chip on your shoulder for a while now, and I don't know what your issue with me is. So, why would I come to you first?"

She falls silent. "I'll help you." she says quietly.

"Look, if you don't want to help me you don't..."

"I said I'll go with you!" she screams. "I'm already downtown. Where are we meeting?"

"Oh okay. Meet me at the Café near the tram-station."

"Okay, see you there." She hangs up.

This is going to be so much fun.

After getting dressed, I shadow-walk and appear in the alley just behind the café. As I come around the side of the building, I bump into someone. "Excuse me, I'm sorry."

They regain their composure, and then turn towards me. "It's okay I wasn't paying attention." Airca looks at me, narrowing her hazel eyes. "Kyle?"

"Oh, hey fancy meeting you here." I give her a once over. Her hair is freshly straightened. She smells like citrus. And she's wearing a nice button shirt, capri jeans and pair of brown leather sandals. "Wow, you're cute. Coming from work?"

Her face starts to turn slightly pink, but she scowls at me instead of smiling. "No, an interview. At one of the office buildings." Her face scrunches. She pulls out a handkerchief and sneezes into it. "Sorry my allergies are killing me. Now where are we going to find this stuff?"

"The Core."

She looks at me. "Are you crazy. They'll try to snatch me up in there."

"Believe me Airca they can try, but no one is going to take you from me."

Her eyes grow wide as her scowl softens. "I've never heard you talk so confidently." A smile touches the corners of her mouth. "I believe you." She rushes up to me, wrapping her arms around me.

Okay this is happening. I hug her back, which feels pretty good. *I missed this.* "Um, are we cool now? I still don't understand what I did for you to be mad at me for so long."

Airca puts her head on my shoulder, with a long-drawn-out sigh. "Nothing. Just forget about it. Can we get going?" She takes my hand. "Well lead the way."

We walk down the block in silence, hand in hand. "So, how do we get to the Core?" She asks.

"That's a good question." Most of the alley ways can lead to the Core, but it can be a bit of a maze. I've never gone myself not including being summoned by the Messenger. There are alleys that lead straight to it though.

We continue until we come to the mouth of an alley, nestled between two skyscrapers. On one of the buildings is a street sign that reads, Main St. I stop and look down the enclosed street. A tinge of fear creeps it way into my chest "Kyle, are you okay?" Airca asks, putting her hand on my arm.

"This is it. But I recognize this alley though."

"How?"

I can see it like it were yesterday. Watching the Messenger pin the young dealer to the wall and possessing him. Then walking away and disappearing into the darkness of the alley. "It's a long story. But this street is a straight shot to the Core. You ready?"

She steps closer to me, clinging onto my arm. "Yeah."

We start in. Once we step out of the sunlight, almost immediately the atmosphere changes. It becomes humid, filling with a stench of trash and other things. A sense of hopelessness lingers in the air, but everything feels normal.

Further in, beyond the buildings the alley opens to a full street. Dilapidated townhouses and apartment buildings line the block. People sit on stoops just hanging out, drinking, and talking. While others, aimlessly wander around, knocking into trash cans and cars. I'm sure the latter strung out on the popular drug in the Roc, Crystal. Airca clutches my arm, shaking a bit as a few men catcall her. I'm on high alert, but I don't sense anything truly dangerous.

Three guys walk up to us, blocking our path. One of them looking like a biker gang reject with leather boots, pants, and a vest step towards us. "Hey there kids. You guys look like your lost." Airca's grip on my arm tightens. I look at her, but instead of seeing fear in her eyes, her gaze is focused on the guy, like she was ready to fight. "No need to be afraid little lady. I just want to help you two." A big confident grin on his pale face.

"We're fine. We don't need your help." I tell him.

He laughs placing his hand onto my shoulder, looking me straight in the eye. "Come on kid everyone wandering these streets needs a little help. I just want to help you two get..." He stops talking as he stares, frozen in place.

There's a slight pull at my mind and recognize the feeling. It was the same one I felt when I was drawn into the Messenger. He's been pulled into my gaze. I snap my fingers, disrupting the connection. Startled he, back peddles so hard that falls to the ground at his friends' feet, gasping. He looks around visibly shaking, before he looks back at me. "Please don't hurt me." He screams shielding himself. His friends look at him and then to me confused as to what just happened.

"I'm not going to hurt you. But the corner store is right up the street, right?"

"Ye...yeah."

"Thanks. Come on let's keep moving." We walk by them. I hear the guy start to sob and his buddies trying to consol him, asking what happened.

"Um, Kyle what was that?"

"Locking eyes with a demon can draw you into them. Basically, you get a peek at their soul. And it can apparently drive you crazy." *Meaning I got off lucky looking into The Messengers.*

"What did he see?"

"Who knows. It might be different for every person. The way he acted he saw something that scared him."

"How come it never happens with you and us? We look you in the eyes all of time."

I think about it for a second. Serena always taught me to look others in the eyes when conversing, but most people would avert their gaze after a couple seconds. Including the girls. "No, you don't. No human does really. You think you do but not everyone looks straight into another's eyes for a long period of time. It's uncomfortable. Maybe it's just a natural defense."

"It is little uncomfortable when you stare so intently when we're talking."

"That's because you have my full...attention. My full gaze." I shudder at the thought of how it felt when Chirs set his full gaze on me. "There's still a lot that I'm learning about this stuff."

"Makes sense. I'll be careful not to look to deep then." She says gripping my arm.

We wander deeper into the core. My skin starts to crawl as a small hum of energy fills the air leading up the street. After walking another block, the energy trail ends at a dingy corner store with wood panels covering a couple of the windows that had been busted out. "Is **this** the market?" Airca asks.

A couple of kids walk out laughing, their hands filled with snacks. "I don't think so." I scan the front of the building until I come to a cardboard sign wedged into the metal bars covering the door. I recognize the symbols, and they begin to swirl. *Durabi.* I stare at the cardboard trying to decern the message.

"Kyle? Why are you staring at that piece of trash?"

"What do you see when you look at it?" I ask pointing at the cardboard.

"Um, some super illegible cursive and some random symbols. What do you see?"

"The ancient language of creation."

"The what?"

"It's called *Durabi Du Prima.*"

"Oh, okay well what does it say?"

The swirling symbols freeze for a second giving me time to read the words hidden amongst the chaos. "The door...the market...behind market? Maybe we have to go to the back?" She says, shrugging her shoulders.

I lead Airca around the store to an alley that comes to a dead-end "Maybe we missed a turn? Were we supposed to go to the back door of the corner store? That's back on the street." She says looking around.

"No, something is weird here. I can feel it." I move closer to the wall. The air around it is filled with power. I stop moving and Airca bumps into me, holding onto my arm for dear life. "It's okay Airca." She eases up a little. Now with my full attention I look at the wall. "I'm missing something." I activate the dark sight. A doorway of pulsating, green energy covers the wall. "There it is."

"There what is? What are you talking about? There's nothing there, it's just a wall."

"That's right, you can't see it." I turn to look at her and she jumps back away from me.

"Holy, y...your eyes. They're black."

"It's okay, it's just a side effect of me channeling energy." I release the sight and color returns to the world. She relaxes. "See."

"Oh...um okay. What did you see?"

I offer my hands to her. "Come here, I'll show you." She looks at them for a second before taking hesitant steps to me. She nervously chuckles placing her hands into mine. "What?"

"You've gotten a little taller."

"No, I just stand taller now."

"Oh." She steps in closer. A little too close. Her face was right in mine. "What is it that you wanted to show me?"

"Um...uh. Close your eyes." She does so, with a little eagerness in face. I place my forehead to hers. "This is going to feel a little odd." Energy swells within my body and across my skin. And I feel it touch her. She shudders and there's resistance. "Relax, breathe." I whisper. She hugs me, taking a breath. Her resistance fades and I maneuver the energy past her skin and into her eyes. "There."

She pulls back from me, surprised. "What was that?" she asks a little out of breath.

"Just a little energy. How do your eyes feel?"

She blinks a few times. "They kind of hurt. My vision won't focus."

"That's normal. Give it a second." Airca's eyes start to water as specks of black form within them. "There it goes."

She rubs her eyes and when she looks back at me, I see they've turned completely black. "I can finally see. Wait everything's gray.... whoa, except for you. You have blue smoke coming off you."

"Good it worked."

"What is this?"

"It's called the dark sight. It allows you to see the truth of some things. Like this hidden doorway." I say, motioning for her to look at the wall.

Her eyes grow so wide with surprise as she looks at the glowing door. "Where did that come from?"

I walked past her to the door. "It's probably always been here."

"So, how do we get in?"

I place my hand onto the door. Almost instantly something drives into the palm, making me pull away. The green aura around the door turns red and the door itself starts to melt away, allowing sunlight to pour through. "I guess we needed a pay a toll."

She takes my hand. "Are you okay?"

"Yeah, I'm fine. It's just a little blood. Let's go." I say, taking her hand and lead her through the door.

On the other side the sun shines bright, illuminating a huge, bustling bazaar. Vendors and booths of every kind line the street, as hordes of demons; both in their human and true forms, hell-spawn and surprisingly some humans rush between them. Airca clings tightly onto me. "Are you seeing this?"

"You'll get used to it. Just relax." I say patting her hand. "Can you still see in the dark sight?"

"No, the flash of sunlight turned it off."

"Good. The less you see here the safer you'll be. Let get going."

We walk through the crowd admiring the collection of exotic and weird things the vendors have on display. Airca pulls away from me, and I panic for a moment before I see her walking toward a table. *Oh, thank the Creator.* "Kyle, look at this." On a table, covered with a red cloth are some beautiful blue and green rings and bracelets that look like little serpent dragons. Airca picks up a piece. It shrieks and begins to wriggle and writhe, trying to escape her grasp. She yelps dropping it back onto the table. It crawls back to where it was picked up from and hisses at her. "Are these things alive?" She asks.

"Why yes they are my dear." Says someone with a nasally rasp. A creature no taller than a toddler, with green skin, a huge bulbous nose and pointed ears with hooped earrings, steps out from the shadows. It straightens its little three-piece suit and smiles with a snaggletooth under-bite, its solid yellow eyes locking onto us.

Arica jumps back into me. "What is that?"

"I am a goblin young lady. Rain the goblin at your service." The potbelly goblin vendor's eyes get wide, and its ears perk up as it sets its sight on Airca.

Hurriedly, Rain comes from behind the stand and reaches out to touch her. I grab his wrist before he can lay one claw on her. "Watch where you put your hands, if you want to keep them," I say pushing it away from her as she steps behind me.

Rain covets his wrist. He looks at me, clearly angry and grumbling. I hold my ground and stare at him with the same blank look Valene gives when she's prepared to kill me during training. Rain's ears droop and he smiles nervously. "Please forgive me. I meant no harm. It's just that, this beautiful young lady is such a fine specimen. I'll give you anything you want for her."

I look over my shoulder at her. She looks at me and I give her a slight smile. "Not for sale." She yells.

"You heard the lady." Rain Grumbles again before going back behind his table. "Would you happen to know where I could find celestial silver."

He groans in disgust. "Oh, nasty stuff. I carry none of that, too dangerous. But there is a vendor here crazy enough to carry such a rare item."

"Who?"

"Buy something and I shall reveal them to you."

"Airca, you want anything?" I ask never taking my eyes from Rain.

She walks out from around me and back to the table. She looks over the table again. "I really like that one." She says, pointing to one of the rings. It's blue with speckles of gold at the tip of its scales.

"What do you want for it?" Rain looks at Airca, drool dripping from his lips. I snap my fingers bringing his attention back to me. "One piece is not worth her, so quit trying."

Rain scoffs. "How about something of hers. A finger, her teeth, how about an eye."

Something of hers? That won't hurt her, preferably. Her hair maybe? Na, she would kill me. She starts rubbing at her eyes, and sniffling. *Oh, I know.* "You got a tissue?" Rain excitedly digs into his lapel and pulls out a silken handkerchief with an embroiled R on it. He hands it to me. "Airca, blow your nose into this."

"Umm okay." She takes it and blows into the handkerchief. She hands it back to me, soaked. And I hand it to the goblin.

He looks at me confused and a little grossed out. "What is this?"

"You said that you would take something of hers. Well, that snot is of her."

He narrows his eyes at me. He sinkers, shaking his head. "A trickster. Very well." Rain puts the handkerchief back into his lapel. "Take your jewelry girl." And she does just that, allowing the ring to crawl onto her middle finger. "Par our deal. Down the way is a little shop called The Lovers Den. Try there."

"Thanks."

"Do come again trickster. And bring your beautiful friend as well. I have more deals."

Yeah, just so you can try get something else from her. Taking Airca's hand I lead her away from Rain, his booth and through the bazaar.

At the end of the street, away from the crowd, is an old brick building. A hot pink neon sign sits in the window that reads, The Lovers Den. We enter the shop, and my nose is bombarded by incense and perfumes. Tables and shelves fill the room, adorned with crystals, books, and vials of potions. The shelf that stood out was the one behind the counter filled with porcelain dolls and little wooden puppets.

Along the path from the entrance to the counter, are two people kneeling in front of an altar, housing a golden statue. "Excuse us." Airca asks. They look at us. The guy locks eyes with me for a second. I don't sense any power from him, just a feeling of emptiness. *He's human.* "Do you guys run this shop?"

The guy gets to his feet and helps the woman next to him to hers. He has combat boots, jeans, and a button-down shirt and a gun holster on his hip. He's a hair taller than me, wider than me, with brown skin, brown eyes and a buzz cut. "No, we…"

"We're here for the couples counseling." The women, I assume his wife or girlfriend, interrupts.

The look of annoyance on his face is prevalent until he takes a few breaths. "Shay, remember what we've been working on."

She rolls her eyes at him and crosses her arms, ruffling her blouse. "Patience." She says just as annoyed as him. Beyond the sneer on her face, she's pretty. She's wearing a business casual outfit like Airca's. She's just as tall as the guy, with shoulder length curly hair, light brown eyes, and a light brown complexion.

"The owner is in the back. My name is Gene, and this is my wife, Shayla. Are you guys here for counseling too?"

Airca looks at me, scoots closer and takes my hand. "No, we're good."

I look at her, considering how this school year has been, and how she just swept it under the rug like it didn't happen. *Maybe we should be.* "No, we're here to buy something."

"Ooh and what pray tell would that be?" asks a sultry voice from the back of the store. My skin crawls as a blanket of energy fills the room, shifting the atmosphere. *A demon.* The curtain of beads in the doorway flies open as a gorgeous woman, with long silky black hair and perfect olive toned skin steps through, with a beautiful smile. Her purple and green silken shawl and dress shimmer in the light as she saunters towards us.

The couple bows their heads. She returns the bow then kneels to the statue saying a little prayer. She stands locking her bright orange eyes on us. "Hello travelers. Welcome to the Lover's Den. We have everything you would ever need or want to help you find and keep your true love. I am your hostess, Marie-Annett. How may I serve you?" She says with a bow.

I clear my throat, stepping forward in front of Airca. "I was told that I might find celestial silver here. Do you have any?"

A big smile spreads across her face. "As fate would have it young master, I do. Please follow me. Gene, Shay please continue to mediate. I will be back with you soon."

"Yes Marie." They say bowing their head.

"Kyle what's wrong?" Airca asks as we make our way toward the back."

"She's not human. She's a demon." Airca tenses. "Try not to touch anything okay?" I whisper to Airca. She nods to me, hyper focused.

We walk past the beads to the back of the shop. Pillow seats clutter the floor surrounding small tables with giant decorative hookahs on them. Silken drapes hang from the ceiling, giving me the feeling as if we were floating in the clouds. "Please sit while I fetch the silver." We take a seat as Marie moves to another room. Minutes later she walks out with a small wooden box, encrusted in jewels and gold. She sits it on the table in-front of us and I can feel the power coming off the symbols etched into it. Marie backs up a foot or two. "Please."

I look at Airca and she's just engrossed with the box. With a deep breath, I slowly open the box. The room is engulfed by light. After a second it dissipates, and I lay eyes on the silver. It was like a cluster of rocks that had melted together. Its polished surface shimmered like water in the sunlight. The atmosphere changes,

growing heavy. I fight back nausea, as I feel myself grow numb.
"Kyle, are you okay?" Airca asks.

I shut the box. The air snaps back to normal. Airca, looks at me worried. "Yeah, yeah, I'm fine now, thank you." I rub my face, and then look at Marie.

She smiles. "Is it to your liking?" Marie asks.

"Yeah. So, what's your price?" I ask.

Her gaze snaps over to Airca. She steps over the table to get to her. Marie lightly touches Airca's face. "I'll take her. Her soul seems to dance with power. Well worth my silver."

"No." I say quickly.

She looks at me up and down. With one motion her silks fall from around her shoulders, revealing her shapely body. She walks up to me. "Well then, for something so pure," She caresses the box. "How about your purity?"

Can they sense that or something? Airca's eyes grow wide and her face red. "Sorry, but no. I'm not quite comfortable with that."

Marie pouts. "Then what can you offer me for my silver?" she asks getting into my face. Her eyes grow wide with surprise. "Wait." She gets closer to me. "There's an energy about you that I hadn't noticed. You aren't human, are you?" I shake my head. "A demon? What breed are you?"

"Energy demon."

"Oh, such a rare breed." Her face lights up. "Don't move." She rushes to the front. There's some rummaging, then she comes back with three small glass vials. "Please fill these."

Airca raises an eyebrow. "With what?"

"Energy of course. I think three vials of pure energy is a fair price for the silver."

I can do that? "You got a deal. Do you know how I can do that?"

"You can feel the energy in the air can you not?" I nod. "Draw it in to yourself, condense it. Then allow it pour from you like water."

"I'll give it a try." I put my finger into one of the vials. With a deep breath, I close my eyes focusing on the energy around us and begin to draw it into my body. I visualize it pooling, and condensing. It flows through me as I direct it into my hand. From my fingertips, energy drips down taking the form of a black liquid. After a second, I open my eyes to a full vial. *It worked.* I place my fingers into the other two vials and fill them with ease. "There you go."

"Thank you very much for your business." She says corking the vials.

As Marie goes to her backroom, Airca and I sit staring at the box. I slide it over to her. "Open it and touch the silver."

"Are you sure about this? Won't you get sick again?" She asks.

"Go ahead. I'm ready this time."

I brace myself. She takes the box and slowly opens it. The air is tainted with that energy again. Everything starts to spin but I hold my composure. Airca picks it up. The moment she touches it, the energy dissipates. "It's so light, warm, and it's pulsing. It feels like what I would expect a heart to feel like."

If she only knew. "Alright, hand it over."

"Are you sure. Didn't you say that this stuff could kill you?"

"It probably would have, but now that you touched it, it should be safe. I hope." Airca holds out her hands to me, presenting the silver. Reluctantly, I pluck the silver from the palm of her hand, and nothing happens. *Thank goodness.* To my surprise and dismay, it did feel like a heart. I put it back into the box and lock it. "Come on, let's get out of here."

"Sure."

We get up from the table head to the front. Marie appears behind us. "Is that all you need? I have many other things that may serve you in your endeavors."

"That's all." I say as we keep moving.

"Then may the love of the goddess guide you."

We make our way to the front of the shop, past the couple still kneeling at the altar. I stop as the golden statue catches my eye. It looked and felt familiar. "Marie, who exactly is your goddess?"

"The goddess of love of course."

"This doesn't look like any Aphrodite I've seen, and I just got back from Greece."

"The ideals of Love are old and ever changing, and so too are the goddesses that represent it." Marie motions to the statue. "She was the first and represents love in its purest forms."

Airca looks at the statue then at the other stuff on the stand. "That doll wasn't there before." I look down at the doll she's talking about. It's an old blank faced puppet whose chest is hollowed out stuffed with string. The wood is dull and stained with what I'm sure is blood.

"They tend to move on their own." Gene says under his breath.

"Come on Airca lets get out of here." I say starting to walk away.

"Ow." I hear her say from behind me. I spin around and she's holding the doll in her left hand and looking at her index finger on her right. "It had a needle poking out of it."

"Airca, I told you not to touch anything."

"Yeah, I just wanted to get a good look at it."

"Oh, I'm sorry my dear." Marie says coming up the aisle. "This little one always has a bit of an attitude, if taken away from the goddess. Here allow me." Marie takes the doll and sets it down back on the altar. Then she looks at Airca's finger. Marie chuckles.

"What, is it bad?"

"No, my dear. It's your palm. I can see you future and know your fate."

"What do you see?"

"Love, strength, and dedication. With these three things in mind and fate by your side, you will take everything that you have ever wanted."

Airca seems all into what Marie is spouting. I look to the couple watching us. The guy; Gene shrugs his shoulders. I take her shoulder, and she jumps a bit. "Come on Airca, let's go."

"Farwell. May our paths cross in Love."

I take her hand and we head out of the store. Once outside I shadow-walk out of there.

We appear just inside Serena's, near the front door. Airca doubles over struggling to catch her breath. "Oh, right. I'm sorry I forgot to warn you."

"Oh, God. What the heck was that?"

"Teleportation. Another thing you'll get used to hanging with me."

She looks around, realizing where we are. "Can at least walk to my house? Please." I nod and then open the door for her.

We're silent the whole way to her house. I don't blame her; she's seen a lot today. In front of her house, we awkwardly stare at one another. "Airca, I really want to thank you for your help today. I couldn't have done it without you."

She smiles big, rubbing my arm. "It was my pleasure." She opens her arms for a hug.

I step in and embrace her. She sighs holding me back. She starts to rub my back with her finger. "Are you okay?"

"Yeah, it just feels a little swollen."

"I can take you to you to Valene's. She has a butler that'll fix it right up."

Airca tenses up and grumbles under her breath. "No, I don't want to go over there. I'm okay."

We stand for a minute just holding one another. Everything about her becomes apparent to me. How toned her body has become, how good she smelled, the warmth of her breath on me neck. "Thank you for the ring." She says in my ear, snapping me out of my thought.

"No problem. Look we'll hangout again okay." I say stepping back from her.

"Can we go back to the market sometime soon?"

"Airca that place is dangerous. We were lucky to get out without too much trouble."

"I get that, I want to see you be so cool and steadfast like you were. It was nice to see that side of you."

"You learn to be that way having to deal with supernatural."

"Yeah. So, can we?"

"Sure. It'll have to be sometime after graduation though?"

"Yea." She kisses me on the cheek. She goes to her door and opens it. "I'll Catch you later. Sweetie."

"I'll see you later."

She shuts the door and I shadow-walk away.

Appearing in the library, I plop down on the sofa in front of the fireplace. I lean back with a sigh and an embarrassing grin on my face. *Sweetie? What am I going to do about that girl?* "You've returned. How was your quest?" Chris says on the seat next to me.

I present him with box. "Fruitful."

He takes it from me and opens it. The energy explodes from box but it's not toxic like was before Airca had touched it. With a smile, he closes it. "Good find."

"So, now for the gold."

"No luck I'm afraid. My contacts couldn't find any."

"Well, that sucks. What exactly was it used for?"

"Binding and purification mostly. Ancient Humans worshipped it. Turned it into ceremonial garb, statues, and weaponry. What they didn't know was that the properties of the gold also gave it the ability to harm demons."

"Wait, did demons use it too?"

"Oh, all the time." He pulls his shirt up showing me one of the nastier looking scars that riddle his sculpted body. "Impearl gold burns like fire when it pierces the skin."

"Wow. How did you get that?"

"Your father and I had a stent in Egypt for a mission. We got on the bad side of some powerful beings and one of their followers got a little stab happy with an impearl gold dagger. Honestly it still aches."

I think about Zeus' sword in the throne room of Olympus. It was made of gold too. "The Pantheon had weapons of gold."

The look in his eyes grows a bit serious as he looks at me. "How do you know that?"

"Valene and I were there during our trip. I held Zeus's blade in my hand."

Chris grumbles. "That girl. I explicitly told her not to go there."

"Why?"

"Bad blood." He sighs. "That is a start though. They did say Hephaestus was proficient with all kinds of metals. Maybe he has some in his workshop."

"Sounds like I'm going back Olympus."

"Not alone. Go get some rest, we'll pick this up the morning." I get up to leave. "Oh, and son. If you see my daughter tell her she's in trouble."

Chapter 10

Jason and I sit in the center of the training room. With our eyes closed we stretch our energies as far out from ourselves as possible. Almost immediately sweat starts to pour off me and pool around my butt. I try to keep the energy at this distance but the longer I hold it the worse my body feels. With a deep breath I slowly let it in until I feel it settle back into me. "Good control Chéri. Jason my love, let it back in gently. We don't want you to break anything, again." He grunts in response. His energy kind of rushes back, but he gains control of it right before it can slam into him. "Good. You two are progressing wonderfully. Jason your control needs work, and Kyle you need to focus if you're going to increase the time that you hold that state."

"I know I'm just a bit distracted."

"He's probably... thinking about...Valene." Jason says winded.

"He's not wrong. I went to Chris a few days ago to talk about getting the gold for the rest of my gift to Valene, but he hasn't said anything to me about it since then."

"Patience is a virtue Chéri. If I know my husband, he's working diligently to help you out."

"I know. I'm just nervous about it all."

"It'll all work out. We're done for the day. Why don't you two get cleaned up. Zel and I will have breakfast ready."

"Yes ma'am." The two of us answer.

Jason and I walk through the house and take our separate ways. In my room, I remove the sweat drenched shirt and sweatpants. In the bathroom at the back of my room, my shower is already running. I place my hand in the running water and it's the perfect temperature. *Thank you Zel.* The hot water runs off me and I close my eyes, letting my mind wander. Which has been easy ever since my dip in the waters heated by the Hearth fire, but focusing and meditation has been hard. It's like I'm disconnected or something. I'm not complaining though.

I finish washing off, get dressed and make my way down to the kitchen.

Jason is already there gobbling down the plate of French toast, eggs, bacon, and fruit. My plate is waiting next to him. I sit down and look over my plate. The wonderful aroma of my food has my mouth water. *Cannot wait.* Before I pick up my fork, everything gets hazy. The smell of my food vanishes, turning into something burning. It's not flesh, *thank goodness,* but brimstone and burning hair. *What's happening?* A flurry of color floods my mind. I hear a familiar whimpering. "Smoke?"

"Kyle." someone say from a distance. The colors swirl becoming like static. The burning smell appears again, but this time I can hear smoke whining. The voice again this time loud in my ear calls to me. "Bro, wake up." Everything comes back into focus, and I turn to see Jason staring at me. "Are you okay?"

"Uh yeah. I just zoned for a second." I take a few bites of my food, but I've lost my appetite. I pass it off to Jason and without hesitating he scoots it in front of himself. "I'll see you later Jase."

"Later bro." He says with a mouth full.

I shadow-walk to the animal enclosure, appearing right into the Hellhound pin. All the hellhound pups jump, their fur flaring with sparks. "Sorry guys, didn't mean scare you." They rush me trying to climb up my leg, but I'm looking for Smoke. Over by the beds of straw that they sleep on, I see Sally curled around a sleeping Smoke and Valene standing over them. "Valene, good morning." I say walking to her.

She turns to me and her face lights up. "Good morning, Hero." A glint of power shines in her golden eyes, and in an instant she's in front of me, wrapping her arms around my neck. "What brings you here this morning? Did you miss me?"

I draw her in close and give her a quick kiss. "I haven't seen you in a couple of days. Have I? Where have you been?"

Valene sighs slumping her head onto my shoulder. "It's almost the end of the semester. I; Felicia have had a lot of papers to grade. Then there will be a conference that I'll have to attend before summer school starts. So, you might not see me for a while. I'll be at your graduation for sure though. What have you been up to? You feel a little different."

"Training mostly. Selene has been having Jason and I do this exercise to deepen our wells of power."

"I see. I think it's working. You're not putting off as much energy as you have been."

"That's good I...ah!" A flash of static cloud my vision for a second.

"Kyle, are you okay?"

"The reason that I'm here is because of Smoke. I think he called me here."

"Really?" She spins around and looks at the sleeping pup. He's been asleep the whole time I've been here. I also haven't tried to wake him yet."

I let her go and move over to Smoke. I place my hand on Sally, "Morning girl." She whines a bit before licking Smoke. He doesn't budge. "Hey little guy time to wake up." I stroke his fur and jolt of energy rushes from him, up my arm and to the base of my skull, giving me an instant headache.

Smoke pops up, looking left and right. He looks at his mother before setting eyes on me. He lunges at me driving his face into my chest, his little tail wagging away. "Good morning, buddy. Are you okay?" His head tilts to the side, followed by the image of a question mark. "Are you feeling, okay?"

He barks, and the image of a thumbs up pops up.

"Okay if you say so, go play." He licks my hand before trotting off to play with his siblings.

"Well?" Valene asks.

"Said he was fine. He didn't know what was happening."

"What about you? I noticed you hesitate when you touched him."

"He had a buildup of energy. It absorbed into me and made my head hurt, I'm fine though."

"If you say so."

A presence appears behind us. The puppies go wild, barking and wagging their tails. Zel rises out from the ground all the while being assaulted by the pups licking him all over his face. Now fully manifest he takes a handkerchief and wipes his face. "Master Kyle."

"Morning Zel. What's up?"

"The Master has summoned you."

Finally.

"What are you and father up to?"

"I'm helping him with a project. It's a bit hush hush."

"Whatever you say Hero." She says with a pout.

I take her hand, pull her to me a bit and give her a big kiss, allowing the energy transference to take hold. She pulls back and caresses my face. "I'll talk to you later okay."

"I'll be waiting, Hero."

"Oh, and before I forget. Your dad says that you're in trouble."

"For what?"

"Something about Olympus and bad blood."

She slumps her head with a sigh, "Okay thanks for the heads up."

"Sorry. Bye. Be good buddy!" I yell out to Smoke. He barks, as the image of a thumb's up pops into my mind it becomes staticky.

A door appears along the wall, and we walk through it. We walk out into one of the corridors of the library. A smile spread across Zel's angular, tan face. "What?" I ask, staring at him.

"I do believe that you and the mistress are a fine couple. I haven't seen her act in such a manor for a century now."

"A century?" *That's when her past love was alive.* "I hope to keep her that happy."

"I hope so as well. Shall we."

"Lets."

We come out to the main area of the library. Standing by the fireplace are Chris and a guy wearing jeans, Converses, a polo-shirt, and a leather satchel hanging on his hip. "Master, I have Master Kyle."

"Thank you Zel, that will be all." Zel bows and melts into the floor next to me. "Son, you remember Michael Xanthos, don't you?"

He turns around, revealing the uptight, olive-skinned demon that was almost killed by Valene last year. "Yeah, haven't seen you since Valene's birthday party."

Nervously, he runs his finger through his neatly styled hair. "One doesn't just piss off Valene and waltz right back in without a little assurance." He says, looking at Chris.

"By the name of Gaia, I promise you, my daughter will not lay a finger upon you."

"So why are you here exactly?" I ask.

"Well at the behest of Sir Kir, I am here to act as your guide back through Olympus."

"For?"

"The imperial gold Son. When you brought up the fact of Zeus's blade being made of gold. And he would allow only one person to craft him such a weapon, Hephaestus."

"Right."

"What took me so long was trying to convince someone from the Xanthos family to act as your guide."

"Why would he know the place better than Valene?"

"Because the pantheon are his relatives, and he's lived there."

"Just for a short time." Michael chides in. "And Valene doesn't know it like I do. She came to my brother, Matthew, asking about the hearth and its capabilities, and whether she could enter.

The brother that I like. "Why would she ask him for permission?"

"I'll have you know, that though he may be more unrefined than I, he is the head of our clan and holds the ability to grant such. That is the only reason why you two were safe going there."

"Oh really. Then thank him for me. I'd probably be dead if not for that." Chris pats my shoulder.

"I shall, after our excursion. Now, let us go while we still have daylight." Michael walks up to a blank wall. He holds his hand out to it. A gust of wind shoots by me, towards him. The light of fire in the fireplace dims as the air becomes saturated with water, forming a dense fog around him. It begins to swirl in front of him forming a doorway of clouds. Michael rummages in his bag and pulls out a golden coin.

He holds it up to the doorway and I feel the energy of the room shift. A rainbow of light pierces through the clouds opening wide into a door. "Move your feet, Kyle." Michael says walking into the light.

"Right behind you. Wait. How much of the gold do I need?" I ask Chris.

"Not much, about the same size as the silver should do. Also remember to get it unrefined. Refined is of no use to us. Good luck."

I walk through the doorway. On the other side, I appear in the center of the Olympian town. "Michael?"

I see him already walking through the street towards the entrance to the inner sanctum. I start rushing to catch up when something catches my eye. Something missing rather. I stop at the platform where the giant statue had been in the center of town. It was empty. My hands begin to tremble as the overwhelming feeling that I wasn't welcome washes over me. A menacing presence appears behind me. Everything in me screams for me to run, but that would be dangerous.

Focusing energy into my left hand, I spin around to attack. There's a loud boom as my backhand hits something solid. Whatever it is, wraps around my whole forearm with a vice-like grip and lifts me off the ground like a doll. I'm brought face to face with my attacker. The statue.

Its stone skin was now like leather, clammy and cold. A singular eye opens in the center of its blank face whirling around until it stops on me. It glares, and twenty more eyes open all over its head.

It lowers me down to its abdomen. Eyes now opening all over its body. All of them are a different color, whirling around looking for something. A slit appears on its abdomen, slowly opening revealing a mouth full of jagged teeth. It growls, Its breath rancid. "Oh God." I say trying not to puke.

All its eyes stop whirling, and one by one lock onto me. Its gaze sweeps over me and it sneers as it focuses on my right hand. "Demon associated with the house of Gaia." It says with a booming voice. "You are trespassing upon sacred ground and shall be dealt with accordingly." The giant lifts its free arm. All the eyes on his arm shut and brute strength begin to fill it. I summon my claw and gouge at the hand holding me, but I can't pierce its hide.

The statue rears back and I close my eyes, bracing myself to be swatted like a bug. "Argus be still." Michael yells.

The gust of wind that came off its hand takes my breath away. I open my eyes to see Argus's hand only inches from me. All of Argus's eyes are focused on Michael. They cycle through a rainbow of colors until they flash silver. "Second heir of the Xanthos family. You are welcome here."

"Then by my name, know that this man is my guest."

All of Argus's eyes shift to me. The pupils within them turn white when one giant eye opens on its chest. "Demon of the house of Gaia. State your name."

"Kyle Ross."

"Demon, look into my eye." I do as I'm told. The eye on its chest becomes glassy, to the point where I can see my reflection. The image of myself within its eye glows blue and shrinks down, becoming its pupil. The eye closes, and all the other pupils return now all blue. Argus releases my arm, dropping me. I land at its feet, noticing that it has eyes on its toes as well. "Kyle Ross, you are welcome here so long as the second heir of the Xanthos wishes it."

Michael rushes to my side. "Are you okay?"

"Besides my arm being numb I'll live." I stand and look up to the giant creature. "What is this thing?"

"Argus. One of the guardians of Olympus."

"A multi-eyed guard dog. Got it." Argus growls at me. "Thank goodness you made it in time."

"You are quite fortunate." Four of Argus's largest eyes on his chest stare at us, while the hundred others scattered across his body dart back and forth constantly surveying. "Argus. Can you take us to the forge?" Michael asks.

"The forge is off limits to those without prior permission. I cannot."

Michael reaches into his satchel and pulls out a key made of gold, tarnished with soot. "Shar, the Black Hammer, head of the Forgebourne family has granted me such."

All his eyes whirl before focusing on the key. Each of them shines in a different color before they all flicker green. "Very well. Follow me."

Argus turns around and starts walking down the path toward the sanctum entrance. Michael and I follow close behind. "That was a lot. I didn't think this encounter would have needed so much name dropping." I say to him.

"Kyle what do know about Demon culture and society?"

"I've been trying to read up on them, but the books are in *Durabi Duprima*, and I can barely comprehend it. I do know not to look a demon elder in the eyes; first and to not bad mouth someone's friend in their home...in front of them."

He gives me an annoyed side eye glare. "You're such an uncultured heathen."

"That saved your life."

"Yes, which is why we are here. A quick breakdown so you won't be so lost. High Demon society revolves around three things; the name of your family, the title in which you hold, and the power that you wield. Your name can determine whether you're high born or low, but the scale of your power and whether you hold a title will affect your social standing as well."

"Okay."

"For example. A noble with the most prestigious of family names can be no more than a worm. While on the other hand a nameless low born may be that of a sovereign."

"Worm? You called me that last year."

"It is the lowest rank of the demonic power scale. It goes Worm, Knight, Sovereign and the rarely achieved Arch. And I called you a human." He finishes with a disgusted sneer.

"Do you have a problem with humans?"

"They are unfathomably sad and weak creatures, that don't deserve our protection." He sighs. "But as my brother continuously cautions me, to give them a chance and maybe they'll surprise me." He states so unenthusiastic.

At least he's open to the idea. I'm sure there are others that would rather see humans be tortured or even eaten. "Valene and I talked about having a title. How does that effect your standing?"

"If you truly have one, then you will be instantly recognized for your prowess, because they are not given lightly."

"Do you have a title?"

He stares at me. "Yes. But it is of no concern to you." He says walking ahead of me.

"Okay. Thanks... good talk." *This is going to be a long trip.*

We get to the gateway. Argus places his giant hand onto the door. A golden light shine from between the cracks and starts to surround us. As we are fully enclosed, the ground shifts under my feet and it feels like we are propelled forward.

After a second, we come to a stop. The wall of our transport dissipates from around us and we are in a dimly lit, smoldering hot cave. Streams of lava spew from holes in the wall, emptying into several giant cauldrons along either side the walkway. "We have arrived. The entrance to the forge of Olympus." Argus says stepping aside. On the other side of the cavern are a pair of giant metal doors built into the wall.

Michael walks past Argus as I follow behind him. The cauldrons all have huge pipes coming from them, all leading towards the doors and into the wall next to it. As we walk up to the gate Michael puts his hand out stopping me. "What's the matter?" I ask.

"Don't look them in the eyes."

"Look what in the eyes?"

"Who daresss enter the forge?" Says a pair of breathy voices. From the shadows on either side of the door, two pairs of glowing green eyes appear. As I lock eyes with them the world turns a shade of green. My stomach does flips as I start to panic and I can't move. It feels as though hands have crept around my neck and were slowly squeezing the breath from me.

A hand covers my eyes. Immediately my body relaxes allowing me to catch my breath. "I told you not to look them in the eyes."

"You are trespasssing." The voices say in unison.

He removes his hand from my eyes, and I drop my gaze to their chest level. They are decked out in gleaming silver and gold armor, the relief of a face stuck in a state of fear on their chest plates. "My name is Michael, second heir of the Xanthos family. I and my guest, Kyle Ross wish to enter the forge. I have the key."

"Sisssster?" One of the creatures hiss next to me.

The two creatures circle us, inspecting us. "You may enter." They step back into the shadows and their presence vanishes.

"What in the world were they?"

"Another one of the Olympian Guardians. Gorgons."

"You mean like medusa? Aren't they supposed to turn people to stone with their gaze? And be snakes?"

Michael smiles. "You looked scared stiff too me."

"Ha ha."

"But no. Though they do tend to hiss as they talk as you heard, the whole snake thing is a misconception made by humans.

The monster known as medusa is an amalgamation of two different creatures. The gorgon and the humanoid snake creature the lamia."

"How many other things have humans gotten wrong about Greek myth?"

"Too much to talk about at the moment. Now, let's get you your gold." Michael places the key into the door. The whole cave rumbles, causing a few of the lava vents to erupt. The door shudders, before it opens, dragging across the floor. Nearly unbearable heat blasts me in the face taking my breath away, and I'm sure singing what little facial hair I have. The heat disperses, and the waves clear. Inside are Pools of molten lava being fed into by the pipes from the cauldrons. They surround a lowered platform that has a giant workbench in the middle of it. And that's it.

"Michael, this place is empty. Is this normal?"

"No. Not at all. Hephaestus was a known hoarder. There should be piles of discarded metals and works here."

"Well clearly, he didn't want people to get a hold of his stuff when pantheon had to leave. Maybe he stashed it somewhere?"

"But where?" Michael asks.

If I were a god with a hoarding problem, where would I put my stuff. It would be somewhere no one could get to it. Honestly, I would have left it all here. This place is well guarded. "Michael, how often is this place successfully broken into?"

"More than they would like to admit. Some have even made to the nexus before being taken care of."

Oh, well if that's the case then him moving his stuff isn't that crazy of an idea. I would put it somewhere no one, human nor demon would guess or dare to go. Almost like a bank or a prison. I remember the sound of something knocking on the other side of the wall back in Crete, and the fear that filled me. "Um Michael." He looks at me. "Is there an entrance to the labyrinth here?"

He looks at me in confusion. "Yeah. Why do you ask?" I motion the emptiness of the room. His eyes light up realizing where I was going with my question. "He wouldn't...he would." He finishes with a sigh. "Gorgon!" he calls out.

"Yesss second heir of Xanthos." One of the Gorgon's voices radiates from around us.

"Who was the last one to enter the labyrinth?"

"Lord Hephaestus, over twenty *dytics* ago.

"Twenty? If my math is right that's over sixteen hundred years ago."

"Yeah, around the same time the war officially ended. So, there's no telling if it'll be where he dumped it."

"Then what should we do? Should we call it and..."

"No. We are going to get that gold."

"Okay. So, what's our next move?"

Michael grumbles musing his hair to the point that he looks like his twin Matthew. "I don't know how Hephaestus got down there, but I know how we're getting down there. Come on." He says walking back out of the forge room. The doors close behind us and there's a loud latching sound. He snatches the key out of the door and puts it in his satchel. "Argus." He yells as we approach the giant.

Argus's eyes open setting on Michael. "How may I be of service second heir of Xanthos."

"I need to enter the Labyrinth." Michael says holding up his right hand. Black markings appear on it, starting from his hand and stretching to his mid-forearm. "Take us to the citadel of the moon."

Argus's eyes shine silver. "At your command."

We are enclosed in light again and teleported. It opens around us to and the first thing I see is the moon in all its glory high in the night sky. It's so close to us that you could almost touch it. In the distance, a waterfall of silver light pours from the moon into a fountain, with a statue of a naked woman holding a bow. "Where are we?" I ask.

"This is the citadel of the moon. This was the huntress Artemis's private training ground here on Olympus."

"Training?" The area is open and huge. There are no borders, just a horizon. "What kind of training?"

Michael snaps his finger. The ground heaves and a forest appear in the distance. "This place has the ability to morph and change into any terrain." *Whoa.* "This place is also part of the labyrinth. Which is why it has that ability. From here we enter and look for the gold."

"Well aright. What's stopping us?"

"The only way to get in from here. Is to go through a trail. One that I've already completed. So..."

"Okay. So, what kind of trail do I have to go through?"

"The hunt."

"What is, "The Hunt"?"

"It's my family's rite of passage. You will be sent into the labyrinth with the task of felling a great beast. In completing it you will gain the title of blooded hunter and have your name added to the legacy of Xanthos. If you return without your quarry, you will be shamed and demoted to the lowest class of hunter. Are you willing to accept and move forward?"

"Ahh I mean..."

"Don't worry, you'll have a handicap. I'll be with you and you won't be obligated to complete the task."

I take a deep breath. *For Valene.* "I agree."

"Argus. We are about to start the trail. Keep watch over the door while we are gone."

"As you command." Argus says with a bow.

Michael presents his hand. "Give me your hand." I do so. One of his fingers forms a talon like claw at its tip. He jabs it into my palm drawing blood. Then proceeds to do the same to himself.

Our blood drips onto the ground, mixing. The ground heaves and cobbled stone platform appear under our feet. Silver light erupts up out of the cracks. The light dims back into the stone and vanishes. The smell of rotting meat and stagnant water rises, and I fight the urge to gag. "Hold on." Michael says.

The stones under our feet shift, giving way to our weight. And we plummet down into the darkness of the labyrinth.

Chapter 11

The flames of the campfire dance and crackle illuminating the walls of the small cave we set up as our base of operations four days ago. It's been hell trying to juggle surviving down here and searching for the gold. There are creatures here that can kill you with nothing other than just a gaze. The tunnels constantly shift, so if you're not careful you will get lost. Then there's me not knowing what in the world to do. Thank goodness Michael is with me. With him being a hunter and a survivalist, we've gotten by. I'm positive I would've been dead a long time ago if not for him.

I pull out my phone. There's no kind of signal down here. This thing is only good for an occasional flashlight and telling me the time. A reminder notification flashes on the screen. 'Graduation ceremony this week.'

I didn't think we were going to be down here so long. We still haven't found any clue to where the gold could be. And at this rate we might be here days more. We've scoured every inch of this place. Michael has even slept out in the tunnels trying to go further out, but he's hit the wall a couple of times. With the way things are going I don't think I'm going to make it to graduation. *Sorry Serena. I know you were so excited to see me walk.*

The walls rumble, signaling the shift. Michael should be back any moment. There's a tapping just at the opening of the cave. I whistle in response. Michael wanders in wearing a hooded cloak made from a patch work of reptile skin and feathers. He plops down on the stone benches in front of the fire. He pulls back the hood and exhales. "Any luck?" I ask.

"No. I hit another wall. I did get dinner though." He tosses a bag onto the ground next to me.

"What did you get?" I ask, picking it up.

"A cockatrice and a basilisk. They were fighting each other and didn't see me coming."

"Nice." I take the bag and flip it over onto a stone slab pouring out its contents. Both carcasses fall out still writhing a bit. The cockatrice was basically a giant chicken the size of a turkey. It just had green and sometimes blue scales along its neck and feet. What makes it dangerous is the potent venom in its beak, claws, and some of its feathers.

The basilisk is just a giant venomous snake. Its scales are as hard as stone, and its venom is like acid. Michael says that it will spit its venom on its prey, and then slurp it up like milkshake.

I start the steps to begin processing them, being careful to not look them in eye or touch their fangs or claws. Apparently, both creatures have the potential to possess evil eyes. If they look you in the eye, it can effectively curse you. Petrify you, turning you to stone. Blind you. Paralyze you. Or worse case, instant death. Even dead, the curses and poisons within them are still active, and very dangerous.

"You know, I must give it you Kyle. You're a fast learner. I've only shown you the steps to cleaning them twice and you can already section and quarter two of the most dangerous creatures down here without thought."

"Well, learn or die right. So, why are there so many little creatures running around down here? I thought that this was a prison, not a bestiary."

"Some of the big bad monsters were thrown in here, but others wandered down here for shelter away from the expanding human world and made it their home."

"So, there are other ways in?"

"And out, but as you've seen this place is in constant state of change. There are ways out, but you won't find them as easily as you'll find a way in."

"And it's because of that constant moving we haven't found the gold yet." I pass him the claws, feathers, heads and skins. He extracts the venom and the eyes of the beasts, placing them in his glass containers he had in his satchel and takes the rest out of the cave. I place the meat on a stone next to the fire so they can cook.

Michael walks back in. He reaches into his satchel and pulls out a shaker full of herbs. He sprinkles it onto the meat before sitting next to me. "So, I never planned on asking but I have to know, what exactly is this gold for?"

"Valene. I need it to make something for our anniversary." He stares into the flame, and I can see his face slowly twisting up in disappointment. "You really liked her didn't you." I ask.

"Of course. She is the epitome of high demon society. She comes from a great family. She is an extremely skilled and frightening warrior. But best of all she's beautiful. Her and my pedigrees are a perfect match. We would have been the perfect couple."

"You've known her for a long time, right?" He nods. "Have you ever seen her so mad that there's no reasoning with her? It's either do what she says or get out of her way. I mean besides last year."

He freezes up touching his neck. "Never. Whenever we're all together she's normally calm, poised, and proper."

"Aren't you guys normally all together during formal events?"

"Yes."

Okay, I think I get it. "Don't take offence to this, but I don't think that you really know her, to say that you guys would be the perfect couple."

Michael's body tenses and the air about him grows menacing. "And what would you know of my feelings?"

"Nothing." I say with a sigh. "But from what you've said it sounds like you're drawn to her prestige, not her. Let me guess, you've never really seen her outside of events, or gatherings. Places where she must be the "epitome of demon society"."

He silently stares at me, going through his interactions with Valene no doubt. He turns back and looks to the flames. I tend to the meat, flipping it over and shifting them closer to the heat. Almost twenty minutes of silence go by and we're eating. "What is she really like?" He asks out of nowhere.

"Well, she's hardheaded, easily hurt, quick to anger, powerful, really scary and as kindhearted as demon can be I guess."

"How do you put up with it, her anger? How have you survived so long?"

"It takes a little patience. I also talk to her... when she wants to talk that is. And I've survived with help and a lot of luck. Her family: her mom mainly puts her in check when she's going a bit overboard because I'm not strong enough to yet. Which she takes advantage of sometimes."

"Would it not be easier to court a human?"

Airca come to mind. Followed by Valene's words about my feelings. "Yeah, definitely. I know exactly who I would've pursued, but she turned me down in a way. Then fate and a weird game of chess led me to Valene, and it feels right."

"Feels, right?" He looks around the cave. "Kyle, your feelings have us in one of the most dangerous places on New Birth. All for a gift."

I shrug my shoulders, "You're right, but I think she's worth it."

"You think sh..." He shakes his head laughing, "Kyle Ross, you are a special kind of stupid. But I respect it. Anyone who faces the possibility of death everyday deserves that much. As the humans say, perhaps I've dodged a bullet."

"Yeah well, you're welcome. Bullet, nearly killed me, but I'm good now."

Michael places his hand onto my shoulder and looks me in the eyes. "I never got the chance to properly thank you for saving my life. I am completely in your debt."

"That's why you're here right? To repay your debt. Believe me when I say this, that you've done so four times over already. You're welcome, but at the same time thank you."

I finish off my food and lay down on the pallet of cockatrice down. After a second, I drift off to sleep.

"Kyle. Kyle, wake up." I hear Michael whispering.

I open my eyes to the dim light of the embers on the ceiling of the cave. A shadow moves across it, and I hear smacking, like someone chewing with their mouth open. I try to sit up but can't. "What's going on? I can't move."

"I don't know, but neither can I."

"This is so good." Someone says with their mouth full. "It's been so long since I had a cooked meal."

"Oh, please help yourself to our only rations for the day." I say sarcastically.

"Yes, yes I shall. We all need our strength for the day to come." They say stuffing their mouth further.

I look to my right to Michael. He is struggling to move but gives up. Something long stands between us, glistening in the light just out of my peripheral. "Who are you? What do you want?" I ask looking up at the shadow.

They swallow hard. "I am fate at work, and what I want is more of this meat. Do you have any?" They ask, their voice kind of strained but light at the same time.

"A few pieces."

"Kyle?!" Michael whisper screams.

"But if I tell you where it's at, will you release us? And I mean let us go, not kill us."

It laughs. "I shall, you have my word."

"In the satchel, just above our heads. There are a few pieces of dried basilisk."

The shadows on the walls shift as they stand, then walk over to us. It was a woman, with skin as black as night and hair as white as the moon, tied into a braid that wrapped from the back, and around her neck to the front. The clothing she wore was makeshift pieces of skin like Michael's cloak but worn like old leather. She kneels next to us, proceeding to dig through Michael's bag. She's thin, almost skeletal. Like she hadn't eaten in months. "Yes!" She exclaims excitedly as she snaps a piece of the jerky off with her teeth.

She turns to walk away, and I see two things on her hip. The first was a glistening curved sword, with a jagged edge like she had been hitting rocks. Second, was a shrunken head with its mouth sown shut, held around her waist by the length of its hair. Its eyes shoot open, staring down at me as its owner walks away. Just outside of my sight she takes up something.

My body relaxes as whatever it was that held us lets go. I sit up slowly. Michael hops up to his feet. Energy rushes to his hand, forming into a bow. He takes hold of the string, and an arrow of energy appears. Just as fast as he summoned his weapon it vanishes, and her jagged blade is in his face. She continues to chew on the jerky. "You are predictable, Arrow." She says with her mouth full. "But you." She points her blade to me. "You are all over the place. It's quite interesting."

"What is it that you want?" Michael asks.

"I wish to help you. To find your gold. And in turn you two will help me." She says lowering her blade.

"Help you do what?" I ask standing.

She looks up to me with her glowing pale green eyes. She's a few inches shorter than me, but I get the sinking feeling that she is more dangerous than anything that I could ever imagine. "This is my home. It is in danger and it's all because of that man's playthings." I look at Michael who is just as confused at this whole thing as I am.

"Now go on. Just, say yes. I've seen this conversation several times now and since he's not dead," she motions to Michael, "you say yes."

What is this lady talking about seeing this conversation?
"Why come to us?"

"You are the only two able bodied demons here in the labyrinth. Of course, I would come to you."

"How did you find us?" Michael asks.

"I can see your threads." She reaches down and plucks at one of the nearly invisible threads of spider silk Michael had placed to help us get back. "Arachne silk. Far more superior than breadcrumbs. Now we have spoken long enough on the matter. Yea or nay?"

Michael and I share a look. He shakes his head no. "Do we have a choice?" I ask him.

"You always have a choice, in whatever you do young one, that is destiny. Our meeting is fate." She interjects.

Okay this is a lot. We've been down here for four days, and we haven't seen a glimmer of gold, or even a piece of Hephaestus's things. Now here's this lady talking about leading us right to it. I don't trust it, but it's our only lead. "Okay, we'll help you."

"What? Kyle this is madness. We don't even know who this woman is."

"She also could've killed us, at any moment. Yet here we are. Besides, you've hit wall after wall. We could use the help." He starts to say something but shuts his mouth. "Let us get our stuff together and..."

"No, just follow. There is no time. The path is about to open." The whole cave starts to rumble, and the entrance seals itself, which is normal. She starts to kick dirt into the fire smothering it. As the light from the flames dies, a beam of light shines out from a crack in the wall. She walks by me and up to it. "You were so close to the entrance to the deep, but as I said arrow you are predictable. So confident in your knowledge that you've overlooked the most important details."

"I don't know how you learned of my title, but if you are going to continue to refer to me by it then do so correctly." He says frustrated.

She stops and looks at him, her pale green eyes growing more intense in the darkness. "As you wish, Silver Arrow." She says with a bite to it. He just stares at her, but as she looks at me I avert my eyes, looking down to the shrunken head on her hip. She turns back to the crack and kicks it. The wall crumbs revealing a torch-lit stairway leading far down. "Follow, I shall lead you to the gold and our target." She starts down, with Michael and I follow.

For hours, we walk down the stairs in silence. I keep an eye on the woman. There's nothing too crazy about her, I mean besides the pointed teeth, the twin jagged blades on her hips and the shrunken head on her waist. The only thing that's been freaking me out is that I can't sense her. Her power nor her presence. I see that she's right here in front of me, but there's nothing.

"Kyle, this is nuts." Michael says from behind me. "I don't know what this woman is, but she's not normal."

"Yeah, I feel it too, or at least the lack thereof." From out of the wall next to her a centipede the size of a snake burrows out ready to strike at her. As if she knew it were coming, she grabs it just below the head and crushes it. Yanking the body from the wall she proceeds to greedily devour it. *Gross.* "But she's our only lead."

After another hour or so passes we finally come to the bottom of the steps. Broken pieces of golden armor riddle the floor of the stone corridor we enter. "They've been fighting again." She says.

"They?" Michael and I say at the same time.

"Follow and you shall see." She says drawing her blades. "Prepare yourselves." Michael summons his bow. With a few breaths, I focus my energy on my arms and legs. The shadowy energy that manifests solidifies turning into blackened bone claws and greaves. "Good, let's move."

As we rush through the corridor the sounds of roars, and the sound of clanging metal grow louder, echo throughout the hall. We come to an opening, leading out to a humungous cavern that stretches miles in either direction. A faux sun shines down from the ceiling onto the forest below.

"What is this place?" Michael asks, amazed.

"This Silver arrow is the entrance to the deep labyrinth. The prison of elders."

"You didn't know that this was down here?" I ask.

"No. my family has only ever been in the tunnels we were just in."

"Artemis was tasked with keeping the number of the beasts here in check. Alongside her kin she would lead hunts to take down Alpha creatures. It was when she left the task to her kin that they turned it into that little trail of yours. But you clearly lost knowledge of the deep." The lady explains.

A massive roar draws our attention down to the madness happening on the cavern's floor. Hundreds of monsters, clad in golden armor fight, ripping, and tearing at one another. "What's going on down there?" I ask.

"An affront to destiny. We must keep moving."

"I'm not going any further until you explain what's going on." Michael says standing his ground.

She stops and looks back over her shoulder to me. "I agree with him. There's a war going on down here. What exactly are we doing?"

"Just follow. You must see firsthand." She walks off to the left onto a wide ledge.

"A fine mess we're in, isn't it?" Michael says walking past me.

"You mean what a fine mess I got us into."

"I didn't say it."

At the end of the path there's a huge flight of steps leading down the wall of the cavern. Carefully we descend. The closer to the floor we get, I see streams of black, red and green liquids flow from the battlefield, pooling below us. A gust of wind rushes up the wall, bringing the putrid smell of blood and rotting flesh with it. After dealing with the Messenger this is bearable, but it's still so disgusting.

We finally reach the bottom and it's bad. Among the rocks and random trees across the area are pieces of bone and the bodies of fallen creatures. The ground starts to shake as something approaches us.

A boulder explodes as a huge horned monster charges headfirst though it and we prepare ourselves to fight. It stops just short of us breathing hard, with fresh blood and mud on the tips its horns and...*hands*? Holding itself on all fours, the beast looks at us through long shaggy hair, that partially covered its bull face. "Is that the minotaur?" I ask.

"Run." he bellows at us. From behind him another beast appears, covered from head to toe in golden armor. He turns to meet the creature, scrapping his cloven hooves across the ground preparing to charge the beast. It leaps at the minotaur screaming, its dagger length claws ready to latch onto him. Something shoots out from beside me and drives into the creature's neck within the blink of an eye, a silver arrow. The arrow explodes with concentrated energy that slices through the creature's flesh, severing its head. It lands with a thud before the minotaur.

He looks at us in slight shock, before letting out a sigh of relief. He pushes off the ground standing onto his hind legs, making him at least eight feet tall. "What are you demons here?" he asks, his voice deep and tired.

"They are with me. Minos." The lady says walking out from behind us.

At the sight of her Minos falls to one knee bowing his head to her. "My lady. You have finally returned. So, They are the help that you foretold of?"

"Yes." She places her hand under his chin raising his eyes to hers. "Of all the paths I was hoping for this one. I am happy to see you alive."

"Just barely my lady. Their craft is getting better with every wave. This last batch has been vexing." From behind him there's a clanking noise. The body of the monster launches itself from the ground at Minos. Minos swings his head around jamming his horn into its abdomen. With a quick whip of his neck the creature is flung off his horn and sent flying into the rubble of the boulder. "They don't stay down."

The body twists in unnatural ways setting itself back into its natural form. Minus its head. It rushes towards us and launches itself at us.

Michael draws back his bow. Three arrows nock themselves and are sent flying. The creature twists in the air dodging them. I launch myself forward meeting the thing in air. I bring my fists down hard between the creature's shoulders sending it plummeting to the ground. As it hits the ground the creature's body explodes, in a show of flesh, bone and gold. I land just outside of the epicenter. *Hopefully that does it.*

Michael walks up from behind me, with utter surprise on his face. "Wow, Kyle when did you get that strong?"

"Strong? No, not yet this thing was just slow."

"Nevertheless, here I was thinking you were still the weak human I saw last year. I've sorely underestimated you." He kneels and examines the body. He waves his hand over a piece of the monster that is still covered in gold. The gold lashes out trying to grab onto him. "What is this?"

"Living armor." Minos says walking up from behind us.

"There is no way, this is living armor. It's supposed to be armor, not living gold."

"As I said, their craft is getting better with every wave. We must put an end to this."

"Okay, but who is doing this and why?" I ask.

Minos snorts. "To make a long story short. A cyclops banished here by the God of the forge, has gotten a hold of his materials and began crafting, that. Now, they use the other monsters down here as playthings, even in death they are not free from their control."

"Why aren't they trying to escape?"

"Why escape from somewhere you hold all of the power?" the lady interjects.

"Point made. So, where is this cyclops."

Minos points toward the center of the cavern. "Near the river."

Michael looks in the direction. "It looked about four miles. From up top. Are there a lot of those golden zombies?"

"Most have been, dealt with. But it is only a matter of time until more arrive."

"Then let's move." Michael says, leading the way.

We make our way through the forest of trees and stalagmites. Minos walks on all fours as the lady rides on his back, gazing forward, zoned all the way out. The head on her hip bouncing with his every step. It's eyes still locked on me and a smile on its face. I speed up to catch up to Minos's face. "So, Minos, are you really "The Minotaur"?" He nods his head. "You've been down here forever, why haven't you ever tried to leave?"

"My father gave me the labyrinth, and when the Gods came to him with the idea of making it big, I reveled in it. This maybe a prison, but this is a place where no one will call me monster or try to kill me for the challenge like in the old days. This is my home."

"Our family was told that if we were to ever see you to never engage." Michael says from in front of us. "That the Labyrinth was his domain."

"I see. You are kin of Artemis. Your family's presence has been missed. The beasts here have run amuck. Though every now and then an alpha creature is missing their numbers have risen. Which is why now we are in this predicament."

"I'm sorry. We've been negligent in our duties. When I get out, I'll talk to my brother." Michael says.

"So, what of the monsters that have been imprisoned down here." I ask.

"They are in the deep. Far below us, in the prison of elders. The enchantments that hold them there are strong. I make sure of that."

"So, you serve as warden?"

"A small duty to play for the freedom my home provides."

"How did this cyclops get past you then?"

He looks at me, shaking his head in annoyance. "You ask a lot of questions." He snorts. "They were skilled, knew things about the labyrinth even I didn't. Found the forge god's things and now here we are. I've been fighting against these puppets for *dytics*. This is the closest I have ever been able to get, due to the numbers of creatures being low. They've learned not to dwell here. But in the outer passages."

"And who is she?" I asked, pointing at the lady on his back.

"My lady is a seer of paths and truths. Looking for refuge and redemption."

The air grows thick with heat and a nauseating sour smell. Michael throws his free hand out toward us. We stop moving. Michael starts waving his hand around in an S pattern and I recognize the signal. It means that there was a Basilisk close. I try to spread my senses out over the area. There's nothing. No movement besides us.

The lady hops off Minos's back. The Minotaur stands tall taking a deep breath, readying himself. My senses go wild as I feel something moving toward us from our left. Minos bellows as he takes off toward the approaching beast. Out from the trees, a gigantic serpent with gleaming black scales slithers out. Veins of gold cover its body, pulsing with its every move. The Basilisk hisses. Purple venom drips from its mouth onto the ground, killing whatever greenery it touches. "Kyle, it's an Alpha." Michael yells.

"Oh, that's a big snake."

Chapter 12

The Basilisk charges Minos as he drops to all fours and gallops towards the beast, with a grand bellow. The giant snake stops short and wipes its tail around in blur. Minos stands, bracing himself. With a loud boom, he catches it. His hooves digging into the dirt as the force of the hit pushes him back. With all his strength he manages to hold the Basilisk. "Hit it, Arrow!" He yells.

Michael draws his bow. Two golden arrows materialize, and he lets them go. They fly across the air in a streak of light and hit the Basilisk in the face. The arrows ignite, engulfing the beast in a show of light and fire.

It roars, with an ear-piercing screech. Minos tries to hold tight, but the basilisk's massive body twists and sends Minos flying. It slams its face into dirt, thrashing about trying to put out the fire. I ready myself, channeling energy into my claws making them sharper.

From the cloud of dirt, the basilisk launches at me with its mouth wide open. Its fangs dripping with noxious purple venom. Michael grabs the lady, getting her out of the way. Quickly, focusing energy into my feet I rocket to the right, barely being missed by one of its fangs. Landing, my head starts to swim. Releasing energy from my body is still hard. Even with Selene's training way too much tends to come out all at once.

The basilisk whips its head around, focusing on me. It lifts off the ground, as if preparing to strike. Poison oozes from its mouth pooling on the ground beneath it. The pools eat away at the grass with a sizzling sound. "Kyle, move!" Michael screams.

The basilisk heaves forward, opening its mouth. A huge glob of venom flies at me so fast I don't have time to move. *Oh no.*

Right before the venom can hit me, a gigantic boulder drops right in front of me. With a loud sizzle the venom hits the rock and splatters all around me. Minos runs up next to me taking hold of the huge rock. "Move boy!" he yells. His body doubles in size as his muscles fill with a wild brute strength. He lifts the gigantic boulder and throws it at the Basilisk.

The giant snake swings its tail around smashing the boulder to rubble. Minos rushes forward, bellowing loudly as he lowers his head to ram it. The snake starts to rear back to spit its venom again, but a silver arrow hits it in the snot. It explodes in a flurry of energy blades that sends it reeling back.

Minos slams into the basilisk's body driving his horns beyond its scales and into its flesh, driving it up. Two more silver arrows hit just below the Basilisks head and explodes slashing away the scales around its neck. Blood pours from its wounds, speckled with huge flakes of gold. It rears back and lobs another venom ball over my head.

I hear Michael yell behind me, but I don't take my eyes off the serpent. The Basilisk thrashes about trying to knock Minos off, but he drives forward pushing it back. The basilisk falls back, and in a blur of speed coils its body around the minotaur. Slowly it brings its head up and looks at him with pale, dead, hungry eyes. He roars in defiance. "Release me, foul serpent!" Minos demands. Its mouth unhinges spreading wide enough to devour him whole.

I have to do something. I pick up a rock. With a few breaths, some of the energy within my claws moves into the rock. With all the strength in my arm I launch it at the beast. *Please hit.* The rock hits the side of its face with a loud bang, expelling the energy within it. Pieces of scale, gold, and flesh fly everywhere. Slowly, it looks around to me, the side of its face torn all the way down to the bone.

The basilisk unravels and flings Minos across the field. He hits the ground rolling before he comes to a halt slamming into a rock. He tries to stand but falls back to the ground unconscious.

The giant snake and I lock eyes. It hisses. *Oh, I think I made it mad.* It just stares at me. *What do I do? If I move it'll come after me, but if I don't it'll just spit more venom.*

"Kyle." I hear Michael says from behind me. "On your mark."

"Gotcha. Make it rear back when you get the opening."

"Roger."

"Just be ready to fire." With a deep breath, energy rushes into my claws, manifesting into shifting darkness around my fingers. "Come at me ugly!" I scream. The basilisk rushes at me, tearing up the land as it approaches. My skin grows hot and my muscles cold as the energy grows dense and sharp. "Michael!"

An golden arrow flies by my ear and into the path of the snake. It erupts in a small torrent of fire, making it rear back out of the way. *There!* I swing my claws releasing the built-up energy. It rushes out of my fingertips taking the shape of crescent blades and launches at the beast at sonic speed. The blades hit simultaneously, ripping through the snake's damaged neck, and taking its head clean off.

Its body continues to try and fight but Micheal peppers its body with golden arrows. The ignite setting the snakes body a blaze. It falls to the ground with a thud.

I stand there for a minute, breathing hard trying to fight the fatigue from expelling all that energy. The gold melts away from the still writhing basilisk head, and it stops moving. I fall to my knees, unable to keep myself up. I try to lift my claws but they're so heavy now that I can barely stand it. Normally, I'd let them go, but not here. Not right now. "Kyle, are you okay?" Michael asks from behind me.

"Tired, but alive." He walks around me, holding his arm. "Did the Venom get you?"

"Yeah." He shows me his left arm. The skin where the venom had hit him is melted away down to the white flesh. "My arrows won't be too affective since I can't do a full draw, but I'll live." A vibrant silver and green liquid stains his wound and lips.

"What is that stuff?"

"A cure all that's hard to procure. It's strong enough to counteract any poison and some curses." His bow vanishes and he holds his good hand out to me. He helps me up.

"But what is it?"

"A mixture of different bloods. From a Unicorn and a Gorgon. It's quite disgusting."

"How did you get gorgon blood?"

"It was not easy."

"Yeah, I wouldn't believe so." Over on the other side of the field the lady tends to a stirring Minos. "Come on we should check on them." I start to walk when Michael stops next to the Basilisk.

"Kyle, you felled the great beast. You've completed my family's trial. Well done."

"Technically it was all of us."

"Very true, but the killing blow was by your hand." He walks away from me and kneels next to the back side of the giant snake head. He covers his hand with its blood, careful not to touch any of the golden flakes. He motions for me to come closer. "Your claws. Palms up." I hold them out doing my best to keep them from trembling. "Kyle Ross, you have shown great skill and strength." He says as he smears blood into both of my hands. He bloodies his other hand, then places his bloody fingers under my eyes, streaking it down my face to my neck "You have shown precision." He then places his hand onto my chest, pressing hard enough to soak my shirt through with the dark and thick crimson liquid. "And heart. Now ewith the blood of this basilisk I, Zuran, Silver arrow of the Xanthos clan mark you.

Michael lifts his hand from my chest, leaving a bloody handprint. The bloody marks begin to glow and burn. The wall of pain that hits me is staggering. It nearly makes me drop to my knees again, but I manage to catch myself. *This feels familiar. It's just like when I was getting the key from Zel. These marks are being etched onto my very soul.* Michael just watches me. With a few quick breaths, I regain some semblance of composure.

The glow starts to fade along with the pain. I take a full breath and relax. "Kyle Ross. I bestow upon you a title and rank within the Xanthos clan. For your achievement, you are now to be known as a blooded hunter of the Xanthos. May your arrow be true, and your hunt continue."

"Thank you, Mi...Thank you Silver arrow, Zuran Xanthos." I whisper. Before my eyes his human form melts away, revealing what I believe to be his true form. His demon form.

Zuran looks like he belonged in the forest. A combination of man and beast. His body is covered in grey fur with glowing silver markings etched into his skin and spread throughout his body. His eyes are like a wild beast but focused like an animal that has set its sights on prey. He smiles, his fangs still stained with silver.

He places his hand on my shoulder. "Come on we should check on the others."

Zuran's form melts away back to human, as we walk towards Minos. "Forgive me my lady. It would seem the beast was too much for me."

"Do not fret. It was not your fate to die here." He tries to stand, but instantly falls back to the ground clutching his ribs. She rests her hand on him. "Be still. Your wounds are serious."

"No, I must stop them."

He tries to rise again but can't move under her hand. "In this state, you will only serve as a hindrance. Rest, we shall handle the rest."

He looks at her, then at us. After looking over Michael, he looks at me. He furrows his brow, snorting. "Fine. You two watch over her. Or I'll kill you myself."

"Gotcha." I say with thumbs up.

"Come you two." She says walking by Michael and me. We follow close behind her as we move through the forest.

"Will he be okay there by himself? I mean aren't those golden things still out here?" I ask.

"He will be fine. He is to live out his days in peace with this path." The lady says, not skipping a beat.

"Oh okay." I say looking to Michael. He just shrugs his shoulders and keeps moving.

The further into the forest we trek, the atmosphere starts to change. The air grows hotter and stifling. The greenery is wilted, dried, and even burnt. Bleached bones of fallen monsters riddle the ground. Some were broken and speckled with gold, while others were gnawed to nothing. "We're here." The lady says stopping at the edge of a huge hole, with smoke bellowing from it.

Michael and I look over the edge. Below is a new cavern that looks like a volcano erupted and hasn't stopped.

"How do we get down there?" I ask.

"A good question, with a simple answer." She takes a step forward and vanishes over the edge. I look to Michael, panicked. He looks at me with the same face, before rushing after her.

We leap over the edge, and plummet to what I would imagine the pits of Hell would be like. The heat quickly becomes unbearable the closer to the ground we get. *How are we going to land without killing ourselves?* Further below the lady is just falling so carefree. "Here it comes!" She yells.

There's a deafening explosion. In the distance a lava vent erupts spewing ash and molten rock into the air. A wall of wind from the eruption hits us, knocking us around in every direction. With a small burst of energy, I right myself. Far below us the ground begins to twist, churn and fold in on itself. The pools and rivers of lava are swallowed up by the earth, and the heat within the air dissipates.

We quickly approach, the changing land. *There's no way for us to survive this.* The ground suddenly heaves, and a massive spout of water shoots up into the air engulfing us. I'm whipped around in the turbulent current, the roar of the water in my ears. After a few minutes the waters settle. I open my eyes to darkness. Far above me is a light. Without thinking, I swim toward it. My lungs ache trying to hold my breath and swim. I haven't been swimming since last year. Haven't wanted to deal with that stupid mermaid.

I start to swim harder, flailing a bit as panic sets in. Not about the fact that I'm so far from the surface, but that this place could be filled with monsters that I can't deal with. Mermaids or other swimming creatures could be in this water and I'm nowhere near prepared for that. A minute passes and my vision blurs as I fight to keep my breath. *Come on, make it.*

I start to focus energy into my arms and legs, but all it does is make me heavier. My claws and leg armor vanish. It helps, but the fatigue sets in hard and fast, taking my breath away. I try to swim harder, as the bubbles from my breath cloud my vision. Slowly, the light fades to black, but my arms are still moving full throttle. Until everything stops.

The pain of my lungs being forcefully filled with air wakes me. I roll over coughing up water. A hand pats my back. "Kyle, are you okay?" Michael asks.

"No, am I alive?" I ask, catching my breath.

"Yeah."

"A kiss of life, interesting." The lady says standing in front of me.

"It's called CPR." I say looking up to her. The shrunken head on her hip, is still beaming at me and smiling. Michael lifts me to my feet. "What happened, the land just started changing?"

"We are still in the labyrinth, and it is ever changing." The lady says.

"Did you know when you jumped, that the land would change like that?" I ask.

She smiles before walking away.

"Are you okay to walk?" Michael asks.

"I'm fine." I try to focus energy back into hands and legs to form my armor again, but I can't. I can't focus. I can't stop trembling.

Michael pats me on the back. "Take your time man and get your head together."

I take a deep breath. "Okay."

He keeps me shouldered as we walk after the lady on a path.

The land is so drastically different now. The air is cool, and the ground is soft. Grass and other plants grow right before our eyes around us. This place went from a hellish landscape covered in lava, to a grassy plain with random lakes scattered everywhere. The wind sweeps across the plateau heading towards us. A blistering heat hits me in the face. *I'm guessing we're close.*

In the distance, there is a huge dome structure made of blacken stone, with smoke bellowing from an opening at the top. "Prepare yourselves." The lady tells us.

Michael summons his bow. I look at my hand and visualize my claws being there, but they don't appear. I close my eyes to concentrate and can feel how sluggish the flow of my energy is throughout my body. With a deep breath, I summon all the strength, focus and energy that I can muster. My body grows a little lighter, and I can breathe easier. I open my eyes to see the black, smoke like energy flowing around my hands. They've changed, but they're not solid as they were before. Instead of becoming my hand it feels like a glove.

It doesn't take long for us to get to the massive dome. Along the side is an unguarded opening leading down under the ground. Michael rushes forward, getting ahead of the lady. He kneels at the entrance, where the soft dirt turns to stone. He sniffs the air before running his free hand along the seam of the floor. "There are traps set here. That's most likely why there are no guards. Step where I step." He says looking over his shoulder.

Step by step we make our way through the corridor toward a light at the end. He points to the odd looking and protruding rock shapes along the floor, trap triggers. After passing a complicated trip wire trap we come out to a room filled with piles of beautifully crafted statues, armor, weapons, and jewelry. "This is Hephaestus's craft." Michael says still at the ready. "This way."

After weaving through piles of magnificent works of artistry, the quality gradually starts to decline. The things in these piles were unfinished, and horrid. *The work of the prisoner no doubt.* "No, no, no." Someone screams from ahead of us. We come out from around a pile of what I think is just discarded scraps of metal to see huge area about fifteen feet below us. Two giant vats of bubbling brown liquid, sit over two lava vents, bellowing smoke on the far end of the floor.

A giant, red skinned woman, wearing a tattered toga stands before them, shaking her head and pulling at her matted green hair. "How could this have happened? The time of the land change is constant. Why was it early?" She roars, stomping on the ground so hard that it cracks. "This batch is ruined. I'll have to start over during the next change." She takes a lever in hand and pulls it. The bottom of the vats opens allowing the molten brown liquid to pour down the vent. Once empty, she shuts them and turns around toward us. Her huge singular eye focuses on the area just below where we are. *A Cyclops.*

Michael quickly puts his hand up, telling us not to move. She walks our way, picking up a giant, long handled, hammer along the way. Now under us she lifts the hammer high enough that we can see it and swings. The shock wave of it hitting the wall bounces us off our feet. The cyclops reappears, dragging a giant chunk of shimmering gold into the middle of her workspace. *There is the Imperial gold.* I get to my feet and help the lady to hers. The shrunken head sways and touches my hand. It giggles loudly.

The cyclops whips around, but we've already dropped to the ground away from the ledge.

"Who's there!" The cyclops yells looking around. She walks over to a table and grabs an orb the size of a basketball. "Arise my works and find the intruders."

There are scrapping noises all around us. Out from under the piles of her discarded scrap, golden automatons, wrapped in rotted flesh drag themselves to their feet. I prepare to fight when the lady steps in front of me drawing her jagged blades. "You two deal with her. These things have no future, there for I will handle them."

Michael grabs my arm dragging me to the edge. We jump off. As we land, a glow from behind me catches my eye. I look over my shoulder to a gapping tear in the earth, filled with gold. The cyclops pick up her hammer and places it onto her shoulder. "Why are you here, little ones?"

"We've come for the gold." Michael says to her.

"Is that all? Take as much as you wish, I have plenty."

"Not until we stop you from disrupting the peace of the labyrinth. Making the creatures fight one another against their wills is wrong." I say to her.

She chuckles, shaking her head. "Let me guess, Minos put you up to this? Well, I'll tell you the same thing that I told him. No one, nor nothing will get in the way of my work. Of gaining the attention of my LOVE!" She swings her hammer, hitting the giant clump of gold at her feet on the backside, sending it barreling toward us. We dodge to either side.

Coming out of a roll onto my feet a shadow appears over me. I look up to see the cyclops, prepared to swing her hammer from overhead down onto me. *Oh crap.*

A silver arrow slams into her eye, with a loud clang. She yells hesitating for a second. I get out of the way of the hammer before she follows through with her swing, slamming onto the ground with a deafening boom. Debris and dust kick up as I circle around her. *That sound. It was like the arrow hit metal Is her eye armored?*

She steps forward kicking the debris from her attack in Michael's direction. Then proceeds to rub her eye. *This is my chance.* I spin around and rush her, ready to attack. But before I can even get within an arm's length of her, she turns and glares at me, and everything goes dark.

I come too, as a blanket of pain washes over me. I bounce off the floor, sending me into a roll. In the confusion, I manage to get my bearings and drive my fingers into the stone floor to stop myself.

After skidding across the floor, I finally stop at the other side of her workshop. Just shy of the lava vents. Everything is spinning and everything hurts. *What hit me?* Over on the other side of the workshop the Cyclops places her foot back onto the ground, readying herself. *She kicked me? I didn't even see it. How is she so big but so fast?* She walks towards me, dragging her hammer behind her and staring daggers at me.

My body aches as I try to stand. Fighting to stay still. *Come on Kyle get up. You need to get up. Get up, get up.* With my feet finally under me I stand to face her. She's already on top of me, her hammer poised high to smash me into paste.

Her movements are slow. My hands are trembling, and my heart is pounding in my chest. I can't move. I'm so tired and in so much pain. I won't be able to dodge her.

She begins to return to normal bringing her hammer down when an explosion ignites behind her head. She staggers forward. Her hammer slams into the floor to the right of me so hard that the force throws me to the side off my feet. She swings around and looks at me when another arrow explodes right in her face.

"On your feet hunter!" Michael screams.

Thank you, Michael. I roll over onto my feet, ignoring my body and run. "Get back here!" She yells. Her steps are heavy, gaining on me with each stride.

"Kyle, to me!" Michael yells from behind the clump of gold. I look over my shoulder to see the cyclops right-on top of me preparing to swing. Focusing what little energy I had into my legs, I launch myself forward. The hammers head just misses me, but the wind of it blows me forward. I tuck and roll, get to my feet and franticly run towards Michael.

"You sure are nimble, little one. You would be a great addition to my collection."

Michael steps out from behind the gold, an arrow of shining silver light nocked. His bow drawn so far back that his arm was bleeding. He lets it fly.

It rushes over my head and there's a huge flash of light that covers the whole room. The cyclops screams and I hear the hammer hit the floor. After a second the light fades. I keep running until I get behind the gold with Michael.

"Kyle?"

"I gotta...sit...for a second." I plop down on the ground, trying to catch my breath.

"Here drink this." He says handing me a vial filled with a blue liquid.

Without thought I take and guzzle it down. Once the liquid hits my stomach, a warmth surges through me easing the pain. "What's going on?"

He peeks out above the gold. "She's still recovering."

"I can't do anything against her. She's too fast." I hold my hand up. Beyond the shifting shadow its trembling. "And I'm no good right now."

"Neither am I. We have to stop her somehow though to get out of this."

"I'm sorry, man. I got us into this."

"Kyle, focus. We don't have time for blame. We need ideas."

"Why are you asking me? You're the most experienced here."

"You jumped in front of that bullet remember?" He says with a smile.

Crud, he's right. I force myself to my feet and peek over the gold. The cyclops rubs at her eye, shouting profanities. She grabs her hammer, dragging it to her. "I'm going to squish you both when I find you."

Slowly, I drop back down doing my best not to alert her to our position. "Okay. First, we got to get that hammer away from her. Then we have to take her down."

"How?"

"I'll distract her. Then you'll hit her again with that flash bang arrow. When she's blind I'll attack her hand, make her drop the hammer and we'll go from there."

"It was moonlight, but yeah. Sounds like a plan. At least start of one. Are you good to go?"

I close my eyes and focus on the energy surrounding my hands. The wild energy solidifies into my claws. "Yeah, for the most part." I say out of breath.

"Good. Make it good."

With a deep breath I ready myself. "Okay let's go." In a sprint I round the gold and head straight for her. Her eye locks onto me as I approach. She squints, before shifting her gaze back over to the gold. She takes her hammer and swings it, dragging its head across and through the ground. I jump to the side dodging the debris kicked up. "Got you." I hear her say.

I look back over to the gold to see Michael on the ground, covered in stone debris and blood. "Michael!"

The cyclops's attention turns back to me. She swings her hammer. Putting as much power as I can spare into my legs, I launch forward just before. I roll up to my feet to ready myself, but her hammer was already coming at me, so fast. Too fast. Holding my hands out energy explodes out from them creating a wall.

The hammer slams into it with boom. The sheer force rattles me to the core, and everything starts to fade. *No.* With a sharp breath I wake up. She spins around bringing her hammer high above her head. I move the barrier up to block her again. The hammer slams onto the barrier. It feels like every muscle in my legs explodes. They give out from under me, and I fall to my knees. "No one will stop me." She says bringing her hammer high.

I close my eyes and prepare for another hit, focusing my remaining energy into the barrier, moving it above me. The cyclops screams out in pain. I open my eyes to see an arrow of silver and golden light protruding from her right shoulder. She starts to reach for it when it explodes in a flurry of fire and silver blades, knocking her off her feet. She lands so hard on the stone floor that it bounces me.

I let go of my barrier, and everything else; my claws and my leg armor vanish along with it. Overwhelming pain surges throughout my body and everything goes black.

Chapter 13

"Kyle. Kyle, wake up." I open my eyes to Michael leaning over me, breathing hard with blood dripping from his closed right eye.

"Michael? Thank the creator. "How are you still alive? You were full of holes."

He shows me the bottle of half filled with a murky green liquid in it. "Elixir of rapid healing. I'm not even twenty-five percent, but I'll live. How are you feeling?"

"I can't feel my arms and leg."

He looks at them and grimaces. "That's because they're broken" I sit up a little bit. My breath is taken away as I see bones protruding through the skin of my arms and legs. "Whoa. Calm down. I can set and heal them a bit. Here drink this."

He shoves the rapid healing elixir in my face. I drink it down in a couple of gulps. "Oh God it's horrid." There's a heat in my stomach now and I feel it spread through my body. With each breath, breathing was less of a chore.

"Okay I'm going to set your bones it's going to hurt."

"Just do it."

He grabs my leg, and I black out.

I come to screaming. My hands and legs are covered in wraps. They ache now rather than being numb. Michael was sitting next to me his bow out. "You woke faster than I thought you would. Your arms and legs. Can you move them?"

I form a fist and wiggle my toes. There's slight tinge of pain but it's bearable. "Yeah, I can. Thank goodness." I look over to him. He's got his bow in a death grip and the tips of his fingers on the bow string, ready to fire. "Why are you so tense." I ask.

"She started moving."

Feet from us the cyclops was now on her back, lying in a pool of blood, bearly breathing. Next to us, is her hammer and the remnants of her arm still holding onto it. "Thank you." I say with a sigh.

"Thank me when we're out of here."

A shadow appears over us. We both look up to the cyclops looking down at us, her face contorted with rage and her eye half-filled with blood. *When did she move?* She raises her foot. "Die!"

In mid stomp, something slams into her chest, knocking her back. She falls to the ground with a thud.

Michael and I franticly try to stand. "Be still young ones." Says the lady as she stands on the cyclops's chest. Her twin blades in hand, covered in blood and specks of gold.

The Cyclops opens her eye staring at the tiny woman. She tries to sit up but can't seem to move. She strains against an invisible force, grunting and roaring, until she stops. She glares at the lady. "Who are you?"

"Why?" The lady asks.

"Why what?"

"Why have you disrupted the peace of Labyrinth? Disrupted the fates of these creatures?"

The Cyclops laughs. "I need not to explain myself to you." Her arm blurs in a movement as she reaches for the lady.

With the flick of her wrist, the lady's blade vanishes, and the cyclops's hand is cut to pieces. The cyclops roars in pain. "No, you needn't say a word." The lady holsters one of her blades, before reaching out into the air. Delicately, she hooks her fingers around nothing.

In her palm a line of green light appears, stretching down to the cyclops's chest. She presses her fingers to it, causing it to shine bright under the tension. Gingerly she begins running her fingers along the light. A low harmonic hum, like the sound of a cello as a bow is drawn across its strings fills the area.

The notes change octaves as she strokes the light, making the beginnings of a weird song. After a second of listening colors begin to appear before my eyes. Blues, reds, and yellows swirl together mixing, turning a shade of green and taking the shape of a small, one-eyed child. It starts crying. My chest tightens with fear, as I get the feeling of not knowing where I was.

The image changes. It's years later. The kid is bigger now, running with a spear in hand. The fear quickly dissipates and is replaced by excitement and drive, like I were taking a test I needed to pass. *What is happening?*

The lady continues and the sound becomes heavy with bass. My heart starts to beat fast like it had when I stood in front of Valene for the first time. The images change to the now grown child looking at someone's back. They are muscular, covered in glowing scars and wielding a hammer. Her breathing quickens as she approaches him. Before she can place a hand onto his shoulder someone gets in her way. Another woman.

The man turns to the woman and kisses her. The image turns red, as the sound of the strings squeal making my stomach twist in rage and anguish. I cover my ears. Tears pour from my eyes, as I try to calm myself.

"You have done this for a love that wasn't even meant to be." The lady says, her voice cutting through the melody.

"Anything is possible." The cyclops grind out.

"Yes, anything is possible, but not everything is meant to be."

The cyclops roars in defiance and rage. "It was meant to be! If she hadn't gotten in my way. But she's gone now. I have a chance, but I must prove myself. That I am just as worthy to be with as she. So, I made his armor, improved it. Now, he has no choice but to notice me. To acknowledge me and my love."

"What of these creatures? Their lives, their fates have been warped, tainted, destroyed because of your obsession."

"Fate be damned. All that matters is my love."

The lady's shoulders tense as she takes a deep breath. "No. Never again." She says gripping her blade tighter. "Never will I listen to such blasphemy." She lets go the light and redraws her other blade. A pale purple light seeps from her hands and into the blades, coating them in it. "Never again will I allow that thought to consume another." She places the light in between the two jagged blades, and they resemble a pair of scissors. "Never again." She cuts through the thread of light.

A massive wave of energy explodes out across the area, taking my breath away. The Cyclops screams with unhinged agony as she thrashes about. Blood pouring from her eye, ears, nose and mouth. She struggles to breathe through her anguish, but her gasps were empty. "Fade away into the aether. Do not fight it. Embrace the end of your fate." The lady says.

The Cyclops gazes at the lady, her eye frantic and wild with fear. The lady is unfazed, just watching. Tears well up in her eye as she continues to thrash. "Please, please, please love me." The cyclops manages with what little breath she had.

The lady sighs, jumping to the ground. "Be free."

The cyclops stops moving and falls back onto the floor with a thud. Slowly, the color drains from her red skin, and her hair turns gray. The shine in her eyes fades to nothing as a final tear falls from it. Her body starts to turn to dust. Blowing away and vanish into thin air. "Be free."

"W...What just happened?" I ask, turning to Michael.

Michael falls to his knees, shifting his gaze down. "We have just witnessed a thread of life being cut by one of the sisters. The severer of fate, Atropos" He explains solemnly.

"I thought it was supposed to be quick and painless?"

"Death isn't always painless. Especially for those that have caused so much of it." Atropos says walking by us. "Rise Silver Arrow." Micheal hops to his feet as fast as possible. "Come, get your gold. Our time here is limited."

I try to stand, but I can't. Michael helps me to my feet. We slowly head towards the giant boulder of gold. I grab one of the bigger pieces that's on the floor. *Finally, we did it.* I look over to where the cyclops was. *I get that she was trying to smash me like a bug, and I know that I didn't kill her, but did she really have die like that?*

"Yes, she did." The sound of the Atropos's voice startles me, and I fumble the gold before clutching it. "You can't understand, young one. What her obsession would have led too. How many beyond the confines of the Labyrinth would have been lost." She looks at me. "Ask your question."

"I get it. You're one of the Fates, but how are you not sure that there could have been something between them?"

"Fate itself has chosen me for my ability to see the paths, the truths and cut clean those that disturb it. And I know their truths, her truths. That possible love wasn't real. Not now and not this time. It was just a sick, one-sided obsession that disrupted the lives of those around her. It needed to be stopped."

"I understand." I say looking at the gold in my hand, thinking about Valene and our relationship.

She looks at the gold and back to me. She places a hand on my shoulder. "Do not worry young one. Your actions today, and the truth of your words tomorrow will lead you to your fated."

There's a giggle. "What was that?" Michael asks.

Atropos looks down to her hip at the shrunken head, which had the creepiest grin across its stitched mouth. "Has she been smiling this whole time?"

"Your head? Yes, like a mad man since we first met. It was her giggling that gave away our position." Michael explains.

Her face grows a little grim. "It would seem that fate smiles upon you."

"Is that a good thing?" I ask.

"Not all of the time." She unties the lock of hair from around her waist, letting lose the head. "Show us what you see sister."

The head floats out of her hand. It opens its mouth and the air around it splinters like shattered glass. Hundreds of Images appear within the broken spaces. It's all so hectic that I can't keep up with what was happening in them. But of all the images, it is the ones engulfed in white fire that stand out to me. A Black sowing needle, a forest of twisted trees in a sandstorm, and yellow eyes.

More of the image's flash by in a blur, until they all turn blood red. A demented, high pitched, laugh echoes in my ears. "If I can't have you..." says a voice I don't recognize. The blood starts to pour from the shattered space, splattering on the ground and pooling at my feet. Everything around me goes black. I gasp as I feel something pierce my chest. I look down to see a dagger right in my heart. "...then no one can." And as if a hole opened beneath me, I fall and am swallowed by darkness.

The darkness shatters allowing light to shine through. Everything goes back to normal, with the head still floating above us. The head closes its mouth and drops. Atropos catches it then looks at us. "What was that?" I ask.

"The undeniable future. What did you see?"

"Death. Destruction. War." Michael says.

I look down to my chest, making sure the knife wasn't still there. "I saw a lot, but it all ended in blood and darkness." I answer.

She looks at me, her expression still grim. "Young one you will need to become strong. Stronger than you've ever thought possible if you are to survive that darkness. So, work and grow. Until your bones break. Until your mind is on the cusp of madness. And your soul is stretched beyond its limits." Her gaze shifts to Michael. "Both of you. All of you." Michael and I look at one another. Concern on his face, and I'm certain doubt in mine. The ground rumbles beneath our feet. "Come, we must go."

I hand Michael the gold and he places it in his satchel. We make our way back through the fortress and out the entrance we came through. Outside, scores of golden clad monsters lay motionless in the dirt. All of them facing toward the fortress, in pieces. *The cyclops must have summoned her whole army. And the Fate cut them all down.*

We take the path back toward the lake. With every passing second the air grows hotter. The grass that had grown when we got here was already so dry and the mud was starting to boil.

Atropos halts us. Before us is a hole so deep that you couldn't see the bottom. The sound of bustling wind echoing up. "Your way up." Atropos says.

"But that's down." I say to her.

She looks at me. "Sometimes, you have to fall before you can rise."

"Alright." Michael says.

"You're not going to question her?" I ask.

"Well, she is a Fate, and she hasn't been wrong yet." He steps forward to the edge.

I walk to the edge. My stomach tenses as I gear myself up for the leap. Atropos grabs arm, stopping me before I jump. "One more thing." I look over my shoulder to see her face stiff and her eyes serious. There's a slight tremble in her hand as her grip tightens. It reminds me of Valene when she quietly rages. "Keep your heart strong and beware the Loom, a weaver of fate."

"The Weaver of fate? Your sister?"

"Once. If all goes well, we shall meet again." She lets my arm go and I feel Michael drag me over the edge with him.

For only a moment we fall when a light appears in the distance, closing in fast. We're launched into the air of citadel of the moon. I land in patch of grass. My arms and legs seething with pain.

They're not completely healed. I manage to get my feet under me and stand. The overwhelming feeling of being watched sends a chill up my spine.

I look up to see Argus staring at me with his hundreds of eyes. They whirl around changing colors until they turn a dark shade of green and lock onto me. "Welcome back, Kyle of the Ross family. Hunter of the Xanthos family."

Michael walks up to me. "Thank you, Argus for your assistance." He says with a slight bow. "Now would you be so kind as to make a pathway for us out to New Birth."

"Wait, we should go the hearth fire. It can heal us."

"The hearth is resting. The last time it healed, drained it of most of its life force. It will not be active for another *dytic*." Argus explains.

"Oh. Then to New Birth then."

"As you wish." We are encased in an orb of light and teleported. The orb dissipates, and we are in the Olympian town. "Your gateway is here."

"Thank you, Argus." I say bowing.

He bows and walks away, to the middle of the town. We make our way through the house and into the rainbow gate. We step through and come out the other side into the dimly lit library.

"Good work Kyle." Michael says patting me on my shoulder and handing me the gold.

"Thank you so much." Michael nearly falls over, but I just barely catch him. "Zel."

Zel rises from the ground. "Welcome back master Kyle. How may I be of service?

"Heal us."

Zel takes Michael and helps him to the chair in front of the fireplace. Zel removes his glove and the red jewel in the palm of his hand gleams in the light of the fire. "This will hurt."

"If you can I'd like to keep the scar on my arm." Michael says weakly.

"As you wish." The jewel shines, its redlight blanketing Michael. Minutes pass and Zel finishes. "You are healed. I sorry to say I could not save your eye."

"I'll be fine. It'll make a fine scar to remind me of our hunt, and your induction." He stands, holding out his hand. "Till then hunter." I take his hand and shake it, even though I was still in pain myself. He walks back through the gate, and it vanishes.

I backtrack to the sofa, before my legs give out. The soft cushions of the chair cradle me as I fall into it. The soft fabric under my hands and back feels so odd, but at the same time wonderful. After sleeping on stone for almost a week this is like sitting on a cloud.

Everything turns sideways as I feel myself fall onto my side. The fatigue of this excursion hits me like a truck, making my body numb.

"Shall I master Kyle?" Zel asks, holding out his hand.

"Please." I shut my eyes, basking in the red light. Embracing how tired I am, I fade into sleep.

Chapter 14

'...become strong. Stronger than you've ever thought possible if you are to survive that darkness."

I snap awake looking up at the wooden ceiling of the training room. *How did I get on the floor? Did I pass out? What was I doing? The Nigi katas, while extending my energy. Not the best Idea but I'm sure it'll propel me forward. If it doesn't kill me.*

I sit up fighting against every muscle in my legs and arms. It's only been two days since I got back from the labyrinth and even though Zel's philosopher's stone has healed them fully the pain is still prevalent. Everything starts to spin, making me nauseas. I close my eyes for a second and breathe. The images of Fate's premonitions cloud my thoughts.

"If I can't have you no one can" The sharp pain of the dagger being driven into my chest startles me awake. I look down to see nothing there. I fight to get my feet underneath me. Once up, I set into the first form of *Nigi* forms, *Turalu* and concentrate. The energy flowing through me rises off my skin and out into the room. The mirrors along the wall rattle and warp under the pressure of my energy. "Okay."

For five long agonizing minutes, I slowly go through the kata.

I hold at the end of the form, sweat pouring off me, struggling to catch my breath. Slowly, I bring the energy back down to my skin. Once its settled, and my body relaxes and my legs waver, giving out from beneath me. I start to drop to the floor when a hand grabs my arm, keeping me up.

"Cheri, what do you think you are doing?" Selene asks, sternly. "I told you to rest."

She sets me square on to my feet, looking me in the eyes with both concern and disappointment. "I know, but I've been resting for two days now, I just can't anymore."

I try to walk away, but my legs give out. She snatches me up like a kid getting ready to throw a tantrum. "Kyle, I plan on watching you walk across that stage this afternoon so I'm going to insist that you sit down before I make you. Am I clear?"

"Yes ma'am."

I sit on the ground. She stares at me with her green eyes. "Kyle, what has you so rattled?"

"Michael and I just returned from the labyrinth. While there we ran into the sisters of Fate. Two of them at least and she showed me my future."

"What did you see?"

"A lot of things. But the ones bothering me are the blood, the knife in my chest and the darkness."

"Your death?"

"No. It didn't feel like that. It was just painful and empty. But the icing on the cake is what she said to me after. 'Become strong. Stronger than you've ever thought possible if you are to survive that darkness.' So, here I am trying to get stronger."

"Cheri, you grow stronger every day. Even just with this past month you have grown in leaps and bounds to the point where you can traverse places that most dare not set foot in." She kneels in front of me, placing her hands onto my shoulders. "You just have to be patient."

"You sound like Mayra."

"Mayra is wise and powerful. Things she gained over time. Now come on. I'm going to get you fed, clean and ready for your graduation."

She helps me to my feet. The air in front of us bends and Valene appears, dressed up in business casual attire. "Kyle, Mother."

"Ma fille, what are you doing here?"

"I was looking for Kyle. Could we have a minute?"

"Can you stand Cheri?"

"I can manage."

"I'll see you in a bit. Be nice." Selene says pointing at Valene before vanishing.

"Are you okay?" Valene asks.

"Yeah. Just pushed myself a little too hard. What's up?"

She takes my hands, as an awkward smile spreads across her face. "Hero, I have some bad news. I won't be able to make it to your graduation today."

"Why not?"

Remember those meetings I was telling you about? The ones Felica, I have to attend. Well, they start a whole week earlier than I was expecting. And today is our first meeting."

"Oh um, that sucks."

"I'm sorry Hero. I know, I promised that I'd be there but I..."

"Hey, it's okay I understand. You have to keep up with Felica's appearances."

"Yeah but..."

"Valene it's...it's okay. Do what you have to do. I'll see you later." She wraps her arms around me. "Hey I'm sweaty."

"I don't care. Are you mad?"

I look into her golden eyes. *Am I mad? I don't know.* "...No, I'm not." I give her a quick kiss.

"I'll call you okay?"

"Please do. Have fun."

She smiles caressing my face. "Have a good day Hero. I'm proud of you." She changes into Felica right before my eyes, and shadow walks away.

Okay I guess I'll go get ready.

The hours fly by, and I find myself sitting in the auditorium amongst all my peers, waiting for the ceremony to start.

My phone buzzes in my pocket. Fumbling through my robe I get ahold it. It's a mass text from Page to the group. 'I'm so board! What are we waiting for?'

'I think they said someone was running late?' I answer.

'Boo! Rica you here?'

'Yup Just sitting here waiting like everyone else.'

'Did your mom and dad show up?'

A picture of two people wearing business attire, sitting in the front row, holding a huge camera pops up. 'Yeah, they're being extra.'

'Yeah, mine too. What about you Kyle? Is your demon family here?'

I look up to the stands looking for my family. Scanning the crowd, I see Jason hoping up and down trying to get my attention. I wave back. Everyone is here. Serena, Mayra in cat from of course, Selene, Jason, and Chris. Well, almost everyone. Valene was nowhere to be seen. 'Yeah, they're here.'

'What with the long face?' I turn to see Page staring down the row at me.

'It's nothing.'

'I know what it is. Valene didn't show up.' Rica sends.

'How in world did you know that?' I ask.

'I see your Aunt/sister up in the stands, along with the rest of your demon family. But I don't see her.'

I see Page stand from her chair and starts to shimmy past everyone to me. "Oh Page no wait no. We're in front of people."

Page sits on my lap hugging me. "Sweet baby, you know I don't care. You cool?"

"Yeah, I'm okay." I sigh.

"Why didn't she come?"

"Valene's bad with time sometimes, it gets away from her. And she had some meetings that she had to attend she thought started next week, but it started today. So yeah."

"You seem mad." She says petting head.

"I'm not mad. Just Disappointed?"

"That's just a nice way of saying it." She says patting my head.

Coach Williams steps up to the up to the podium. He clears his throat fussing with his tie and adjusting his snug blazer. "Okay everyone, thank you for coming. We are about to get started so please take you seats." He says looking at Page.

"I'm going. It'll be okay big guy." Page says before going back to her seat.

"Thank you. Before we begin, we will have a word from your valedictorian, Airca Cove." He steps away from the mic, and everyone claps as Airca steps forward.

"Thank you, coach Williams. Today is a big day for all of us. It's the ending of one arc of our lives and the beginning of the next. A lot has happened over the course of these four years. We've shared adventures and traumas, made lifelong friends, and for some of us have even found love. It's my hope that fate smiles upon all of us as we venture out and find our place in the world. And build a future that we all can believe in. To us, the unmovable rock. Let's go GOLEMS!"

The crowd comes to life with cheer and applause. Airca gives a slight bow and steps over to the chairs, where the principal, vice-principal and salutatorian are sitting.

After the principal gives us her words of encouragement, they start handing out the diplomas. After about twenty minutes my name is finally called.

On the stage, I'm handed the leather-bound document. I turn around and the whole section of the auditorium where my family is sitting is filled with an obnoxious amount of cheering. Something that I honestly didn't think it would be like. *I wish my mom and dad were here to be a part of it. I wish Valene were here too.*

The rest of the ceremony went by without a hitch. Except for Coach Williams's blazer and pants ripping when he tried to pick up someone's diploma when he dropped it.

We are dismissed. Out in the hallway a cat runs up to me and climbs onto my shoulder, freaking a few people out around me. "Congratulation little brother." Mayra whispers.

"Thanks. Where are the others?"

"By the door."

As I walk over, I hear Aunt Serena squeal. She rushes over pushing past a few people to get to me. "Oh, my baby graduated." She says grabbing onto and hugging me. "I can't believe I got to see this day. I'm so proud of you sweetie."

"Thanks Serena."

"Congratulations son." Chris says holding onto Selene.

"Cheri we are all so proud of you. I know your parents would be too."

"Dad how come I haven't gone to high school?" Jason asks.

"Son you're still only twelve *dytics* and you don't know how to regulate your strength at all. You are too dangerous for human schooling."

"Oh yeah, I see that. Congratulations bro."

"Thanks. And don't worry about going to school. You got a pretty good set up. Also, you're way smarter than the kids I went to school with."

Jason smiles, and first bumps me.

"Oh, Kyle. Meet me tomorrow in the library, bright and early. We can get started on that project."

"Yes finally."

"Before all of that." Mayra interrupts. "We have a party to attend."

"Of course."

"Before we go, I need to use the bathroom. I'll be back." I give Mayra to Serena and rush off.

As I walk up to the restroom, I hear someone talking inside. Walking in, I head right over to the urinal.

"Love, I get what you're saying. Trust me, I hear you, but think about it this way. Where would you be without me. Stuck. It was fate that led us to be with one another so that I could lead you to better things. Haven't I?"

"I don't know Mark. I just feel like something is wrong. With us."

"Sweetheart you don't need to worry about anything. I will continue to do what I think is right for you, for us. Don't you want that? Have I lead you wrong yet?" He continues.

There's silence for a second, "No. I just think."

"You don't need to do any of that Love, I'll do that for the both of us. I love you. I'll talk to you later."

The person on the phone sighs with a slight growl of frustration. "I love you."

He hangs up the phone. He flushes and walks out of the stall. He freezes for a second when he notices me. "Mr. Ross."

"Mr. Jacobs." Mr. Jacobs was one of the school board committee members alongside Serena. I think he was the one she mentioned was having issues with his wife.

He walks over to the sink. "I'm sorry you had to hear all of that. Just a little trouble in paradise."

"No problem I didn't mean to intrude."

"It's okay. A little advice. When it comes to women, just go with the flow, and let fate pull the strings. Congratulation on graduating." He walks out.

I consider his words. 'Just go with the flow.' I finish up and leave the bathroom. "Hi Kyle!" Airca screams popping out from behind the door. I jump so hard that I nearly fall back to the ground, but I grab the doorframe. "Oh, big bad demon can still be scared?" Airca says with a smirk.

"Oh Airca, it's you. Yes, yes I can. What are doing here?"

"I wanted to see you and you were taking too long. Serena said you were in the bathroom. So, I came to find you."

"Thanks?" she smiles.

I get a good look at her. It's not often she wears makeup, but when she does, she always looks amazing. "What do I have something on my face? "

"No just admiring how pretty you are."

She places her hand on my chest, and steps in close to me. "Thank you."

She looks at me for a second and I get the feeling that she wants to kiss me. And I wouldn't mind it at all, especially with Valene not being here. ...*Valene.* "Your speech was good." I say stepping back a bit.

Her smile fades and she steps back, crossing her arms. "Ugh you're so annoying. So, where's your girlfriend?"

"She couldn't make it. Had things she had to do."

"You would think her boyfriend's graduation was a priority."

I sigh. "Yeah, it sucks. But it's not like she didn't want to come."

"Oh yeah, then where is she?"

"Airca you..."

She throws her hand up. "Look, it doesn't matter if she's here or not. All that matters is that I'm here with you."

"Airca you're graduating too. You have to be here."

She shoots me glare. Her eye twitches with annoyance. "You know what I mean."

"Airca what are you doing here?"

"Nothing." She says biting her right index finger, making direct eye contact with me. I feel a pull at my mind and my body gets hot. The world around us goes dark. Behind her a swell of water rises, towering high above us. A wave ready to crash down. "Air..." I stop as a massive shadow appears in the wall of water, moving closer to Airca. It vanishes behind her.

"Airca walk towards me." She just smiles, before she's yanked back into the water. "Airca!"

"What?" I hear her say.

Everything snaps back to normal. Airca is right in front of me, confused at my sudden outburst. *What the hell was that?* "Airca have you... are you okay?"

She smiles. "Of course, I am. Never better." She steps in close to me, looking me dead in the eyes again.

I look down at her nose. "Airca, you know it's not safe to look right into my eyes." *Besides I don't want to see inside you again.*

She chuckles. "So, when's our next trip to the market?" she asks, taking my arm.

I try to pull away from her, but her grip tightens. "Airca, I don't know. It's not a safe place for you."

"I know, I know but you'll be there with me. We'll be there together. I'll be fine."

"I'm going to be working with Chris for a few days. We can get together after that."

She kisses me on the cheek. "Cool." I can't help but feel my face grow warm. But I'm sure what I saw isn't a good sign. "Are you going to anyone else's party?" she asks.

"No just going to spend time with the family. You're welcome to come over."

"Tempting, but I can't. Mom is taking me and my family to a restaurant. I'll just have to wait till our market trip."

I sigh shaking my head. "Yeah."

Everyone's already made their way home, and Serena, Mayra and I just finished picking up. Slowly, I make my way up to my room, nursing the food baby I gave myself. Not only did Serena cook, but Selene and Zel too. I couldn't contain myself. Ever since I've gotten back home from the labyrinth I've been starving. But that might come from eating one meal a day there.

Opening the door, the first thing I notice is a box on the bed, with a note that read Hero.

'Dear Kyle,
You look pretty good on the throne.
Xoxo
Valene Kir'

I open the box and it's a painted portrait of me in a black toga, holding a blue blade, while sitting in on a throne made of black stone, and clouds. *Whoa.*

I take out my phone and call her. "Hey Hero." She says with Felicia's voice.

"Hey, I just got your gift. This portrait is amazing. Thank you."

"I'm happy you like it. I wanted to save it for your birthday, but then I had to miss today, and I wanted to do something nice for you. To make up for it. Are you mad?"

"I...Honestly, I was. I mean I really understand. But I was."

"We can talk about it if we need to. I have a little time before I have to get back too..."

"Hey Felicia come on." Someone says in the background.

"Give me a few minutes. Kyle?"

"Sweetheart, we'll talk later okay. Go on and do what you have to." I tell her.

She chuckles, "Sweetheart? Okay. Goodnight Hero." She hangs up.

I set the portrait on my desk and stare at it for a few minutes. A smile spread across my face. "Just go with the flow."

Chapter 15

The chiming sound of one of the alarms on my phone goes off dragging me out of my sleep. I roll over and tap it, dismissing it. I look down past the foot of my bed over to the portrait on my desk. I can't help but smile. I'm finally going to reciprocate the gifts that Valene's given me.

I roll out of bed. My body is sore from my workout yesterday morning, but everything seems to be in working order. Throwing on some shorts, a t-shirt, and a pair of shoes, I shadow walk to the Kir library. As I appear, Chris isn't in his chair. "Chris?"

"Up here son." He calls from the second floor. Up the spiral staircase I find him sitting at the table, two massive plates of food in front of him. My mouth starts to water. "Come, eat with me." I sit in the chair and dig in.

I wolf down the plate in minutes, but I'm not satisfied. "More." I yell. Zel appears with another plate, as if anticipating that I was going to want more. I'm a little more civilized with this plate, taking my time to chew and savor the food.

I look up to see Chris smiling. "Hungry?"

"I'm sorry. After all of that food I devoured last night, I thought I'd be good. I guess not."

"It's okay, son. I can tell that you're growing exponentially, and your body needs fuel. So, tell me how the trip was?" I recant everything. Argus, the battle of the labyrinth, being anointed as a hunter, the cyclops, the Fate. He just laughs. "By the Creator, I'm happy that you survived."

"Me too." I finish my plate. "Man, I missed being full."

"Been there."

"So now we have both the gold and silver, what's next?"

"Follow me." Chris stands and walks toward the stairs. I trail behind him as he descends them. We stand in front of the fireplace looking into the fire. He stomps on the ground. The fire erupts out of the cove surrounding us. Within the fireplace, a set of stairs leading down appears.

We walk for a couple minutes, and the air is starting to grow thick with heat and energy, making it hard to breathe and even harder to move. I begin to wobble. I hug the wall for a second trying to catch my breath, but Chris just keeps moving. *Suck it up Kyle.*

We continue, and the pressure worsens. By the time we get to the bottom it feels like I'm being crushed. "Son, I'm honestly surprised that you made it all of the way down here like that."

"Like what?" I manage.

"Being crushed. By your own energy."

"What?"

"The thin layer of energy that you keep on your skin, to protect yourself. Under the pressures of the natural energies in this place you're basically inside of a can that's slowly being crushed. Release it. It'll do you no good here."

I take a deep breath, and there's a snap of energy. The tension over my skin breaks, relieving the pressure I feel. Breathing becomes easier, but the air is still thick with heat and energy. "Good. Now jump a few times." I do as I'm told. It's easy enough. It does feel like there's a weight on me, but it's nothing that I can't handle. I look at him and he smiles. "Wow, you move well. Come at me." he says playfully.

"Like fight you?"

"Is there any other way? Now come on."

Selene and Valene have said those very words to me before and I would act without hesitation. But with Chris, I just don't know. I've seen what he's done to Valene, whom I can barely lay a hand on. Also, ever since that little demonstration before I went to the market, I've been way more afraid of him. My lungs burn as I take a deep breath preparing myself to go at him. But before I can move everything fades to black.

I snap awake, preparing myself for a fight. "Whoa son. Take it easy."

"What happen?"

"Well, you rushed me, threw about two punches and then you fainted."

"I got that far? Everything went dark before I took a step."

"Really?" He holds out his hand.

I take his hand and notice a sheen of glowing dust over my skin. "What is this?" I ask.

He pulls me up to my feet. "Diamond skin. A little protective barrier of mine. It'll allow you to withstand the heat and pressures down here. Until you're used to it."

"Barrier? You mean like a spell? You mean like magic?"

He groans in slight annoyance. "Humans, call it magic. It's a whole thing not many of them fully understand or want to. For us, it's more like a movement of energy and thought."

"Like shadow walking?"

"Exactly." He points at my skin. "This is just an extension me. My thought and energy made manifest."

"Could I do this?"

"You do it every day. When you strengthen your body, summon your claws, heal yourself." I sit there and take in what he just told me. *I know magic.* I look at him, a stupid smile on my face. He chuckles as he shakes his head. "Let's go. We have work to do." He walks up to a wall and places his hand on it. The room rumbles as a section of the wall the size of a door lowers. Blistering heat and Amber light pours through the doorway. Chris walks through, vanishing into the waves of heat and I walk in behind him.

We enter a cavern about the size of the library and descend smooth marble stairs with no railing. On either side of the door, two liquids pour from spouts carved into the wall. One is bright red. Lava I think. The other was a shimmering cream color. They both cascaded into their own separate motes that started from the stairs and followed the edge of the room until they met on the other side of the workplace, feeding into a giant kiln. Long tables line the edge of the workshop, with hammers, chisels and clamps neatly laid out along them. In the center is a giant slab of blackened stone atop a pedestal of black crystal.

"This place is amazing. Looks a lot better than the Cyclops's workshop."

"Of course, I built it with my own hands. No Cyclops can build better than me. It has a natural lava flow and I've been able to tap into a ley line."

"What in the world is a Ley line?"

We walk over to the edge of the workshop where the cream-colored liquid flows through its mote. "Think of a Ley line as a vein of New Birth and this its life blood. It's the purest form of energy here on this plane."

"What are we going to use it for?"

"Heating our metals. Each of them requires an astronomical amount of heat."

"Yeah. The gold needs to be at a constant and consistent temperature, so it won't seize and turn brown."

"Correct. Normal fire doesn't keep a constant temperature and for what we're making we don't have time to keep an eye on the flame. So, first before we do anything we'll be making Hell Fire."

He walks over to the kiln. Taking hold of it he slides it open over the motes. The lava and ley line energy combine. There's a loud roar as the two energies touch and a purple flame rage to life. I'm over on the other side of the workplace and even through the diamond skin barrier my skin burns. He turns and walks over to a table connected to the ley line mote that had a long handle on it. With some force he opens it. Hanging from hooks and sitting in the ley line energy are different tools, like clamps, knives and hammers. He grabs two pots from the shimmering liquid, that have been blackened by fire. "What are those?" I ask making my way over to him.

"There are four steps to this process. The first is to use these cauldrons alongside the hell fire to melt the metals down. While they're liquid we will scoop out all of impurities that float to the top. Second, we pour them into a mold and allow them to harden. Third, the metals will need to be beaten until they ring with the same frequency. This ensures that they won't react to one another when touching. Otherwise, the reaction results in a large explosion. Last, using the refined materials we'll begin to craft the amulet. This isn't too dangerous, but as the metals are being weaved their paired energies can cause violent sickness. Easy, right?" he says with a smile.

"Yeah, easy."

He places the cauldrons with the metals in them right onto the flames. Almost instantly the cauldrons glow white hot and the metals in them instantly liquefy. The gold is the first to boil. A layer of shimmering pale, yellow crystals begin to form on top. "Watch me." Chris says. He walks over to the ley line, kneels, and dunks his arms in up to his elbows. Chris takes a deep breath. His skin starts to lose its color, becoming pale and somewhat translucent. He stands and looks over his shoulder at me, his whole eye the deep color of a golden gem. Chris turns around, showing his arms covered in a pulsating green crystal.

I look up to his face and I step back a bit. It's smooth, and alien with none of his normal boyish features. He was like a living crystal. "To handle all that have been touched by the hell flame, we must be protected by the same power that has created it." He explains with his mouth never moving. His voice is calm, with the sound of splintering glass under it.

Chris turns and takes up a metal ladle. He steps up to the kiln. With the tool, he starts to skim the top of the gold, scooping out the crystals. Pieces of the green crystal begin to singe and pop, falling off from his arms as the hell flames shift. He switches hands before the last of the crystal falls and he continues to watch and skim the gold for the trash crystals of the gold. It was a second later just before the last bit of his protection fell, he scoops out the last of the crystals. He takes the ladle, and places it into the ley line. He takes a little sigh as he brushes off the remaining pieces of crystal from his skin. "Your turn son."

"Do I have to put on armor or something to do the armor" He cocks his head to the side in confusion. "I mean you went all diamond creature when you put your hands in the energy."

He chuckles. "Honestly, I get a little nervous handling this hell fire. And it doesn't help that in my human form I'm a little more sensitive to the heat. So, I changed into this form. The diamond skin you're wearing is more than enough."

I look at him reluctantly. He chuckles placing his smooth hard hand onto my shoulder. I kneel in front of the ley line and dip my hands into it. The cool energy rushes over me as I watch the green crystals begin to form on my hands and arms. I rise taking a little time to admire how much weight these things have. "The impurities of the silver should be showing any minute now." Chris says looking over to the kiln.

I take up the ladle, which too has some weight to it, and prepare to scoop. The silver starts to bubble. A foul smell starts to spread throughout the room. I step back as a black ooze begins to gather on the top of the shimmering liquid. "What is that?"

"That is the impurities the metal has picked up from being handled by human and demon hands. It longer pose a threat to our health. Even with us making it pure again, its power has still been dulled. Now hurry up and get to scooping. Make sure you pour it into the flames. There's no need to hang onto it."

With the ladle, I reach into the kiln and start scooping the black ooze. The smell reminds me of the Messengers, rotting flesh. I pour it into the flames, and it just evaporates into purple smoke. It's amazing how cool I am standing right over the flames like this. There's a popping noise and a piece of crystal protection flies off my arm. The heat quickly rises and sweat starts to form on my brow. *It's this hot only from one piece coming off? I gotta work faster.*

The silver continues to bubble, and I scoop the ooze, but the crystal armor has broken down to nothing and the heat is starting to hurt. Chris walks up behind me and takes the ladle from me, his hand covered in a fresh layer of crystal. "Go re-up on the protection before you burn yourself." Gladly I walk over the lay line and dip my arms in. It is such a relief as the cool energy washes over my skin. I stand and turn to Chris looking at me. "What, did I do something wrong."

He chuckles. "No. I just couldn't help but think of how much you remind me of your father."

"Did you guys do this a lot?"

"No, not at all. He hated coming down to my forges. The only thing he ever helped make besides those amulets, were you and your sister." We share a laugh, but it becomes silent quick. "Do you remember them?" he asks.

"Bits and pieces. Their faces, mom consoling me and dad laughing. Everything else is...red." He just stares at me waiting for me to continue. "Honestly, I hadn't thought about them until last year, when I met you and all these secrets started coming out. Then when I found out that it was the Messenger that killed them, I was so angry. I literally ripped him apart, but in the end his death wasn't even mine. It hurt. It still hurts to think about."

"I understand your pain." He scoops out some of the ooze and pours it into the flames. "Have you talked to your sisters about this?"

"No. Whenever I bring up mom or dad to Serena, she deflects. And Mayra...well she's been gone dealing with Leo's death."

"Of course. We all cope in different ways.

"How did you cope?"

He motions around. "After I found the thing that killed my friends. I came down here. Immersed myself in training. Trying to make myself stronger so to protect the rest of my family." The silver makes a plopping noise grabbing our attention. A small amount of black ooze forms on top. Carefully Chris skims it off, making sure not to take any of the silver and pours it into the flames. "Son grad those molds by your feet and place them in front of me."

I do as I'm told and grab the block molds out from the ley line and place them in front of Chris. He hands me the ladle and I place it in the ley line. Also, grabbing the clamp for the cauldrons. I started to hand it to him. "It's all yours. I have to reapply the shielding." We switch spots. "Now make sure that you have a good grip of them. And pour them slowly and evenly. Too fast or too slow will cause the metals to seize, and we'll have to start over."

With all the skill and finesse, I have in my body, I begin the process. The clamp locks around the cauldron filled with silver. As I lift it, I am surprised that it really has no weight to it. Slowly, I take the white-hot vessel from the flames and pour the molten liquid into the mold. It starts to set immediately, giving off a low glow. Chris nods approvingly. I feel the heat from the clamps beginning to burn my hands.

Through grit teeth I keep hold as the last drops of the silver set into the mold. Quickly, I drop the clamp and cauldron onto the kiln. The crystals around my hands aren't green anymore, but bright red. Chris's hands appear over mine with a cup of ley line energy and pours it over my hands. My hands are relieved as steam rises off them. New crystals grow, while the others return to their green hue.

"Son, you are just as crazy as your father. You could have just put it down. A few drops wouldn't have set us back."

"Well, this stuff is hard to find I didn't want to waste any."

He chuckles as he shakes his head. "Take a break. I'll pour the gold."

"I'm good. I don't need..."

"Sit son." He says still working.

I hop up onto the stone table and breathe. My head starts to spin as fatigue hits me. Leaning back, on my hands I close my eyes and take deep breath. "Chris, what can you tell me about my parents?"

He laughs. "A lot. Your father was low born, raised in a small village. I didn't meet him until we were in the army. But even with his upbringing he was so kind and passionate. His words moved a lot of powerful people and got us in a lot of trouble. One of the craziest things he could do was to see the potential in anyone he looked at. Told me, I was going to be a great leader one day. Look at me now."

"What about mom?"

"Your mother? She was a bit of a mystery. Your dad fell head over heels in love with her and had to have her. He went through a lot for her too, and drug me along with him. She was beautiful, regal. One look from her could either move you or break you. Hell, I've seen deities bow before her."

"Wow."

"Yeah, but she loved your father, and all of you with all that she was. Always wanted to make sure you guys were good. That you knew your home was..."

"A safe place." I say, in the same cadence mom would.

Chris starts to laugh, but the crystalline shine of his body dulls a bit. "Always son, always." He takes a deep breath. "Come on. The gold is set, and we got more work to do."

After reapplying his enhancement Chris takes both the metals from their molds. He holds them both out and I take them. The gold nearly slips out of my hand. It weighs a ton. The silver on the other hand is as light as air. I follow him over to the table and place the blocks in front of him. He runs a finger over them, scoring them into sections. The gold into five. The silver into three. Taking a knife that was in the fire, he slices the gold. Then the silver after he cleansed the blade in the fire. "Alright. We only have three chances to get this right." He slides a piece of the silver in front of me after putting the others into separate boxes at our feet. "Grab the two hammers from the ley line rack and put them in the fire."

I take the two hammers from the rack noticing that one of them was different. It has a four-spiked head instead of the normal flat head. Quickly, they turn white-hot, and I take them off the flame, to the table. He takes the one with the four-spiked head from me, leaving me with the normal one. He taps the gold and sparks fly as the stone table rings with the low, deep hum. "This is where we attune the metals." He motions towards the silver. I tap the silver. Sparks don't fly off it, but the stone table rings with the high-pitched sound of a dog whistle. "Good. You'll harden the silver by folding it in on itself and I'll soften the gold. And remember not to let them touch."

I nod. He takes the hammer and slams down hard onto gold warping it. The sound of the table booms with that deep hum, making the whole room rattle. I follow suit bringing the hammer down with full force onto the silver. It explodes like I just dropped something heavy into a pool of water, splashing everywhere. A chunk of the silver hits the gold in front of Chris. It sparks, then starts to bubble, filling with light. "Uh ho."

"Get down!" Chris yells, as he quickly steps in front of me. There's a loud cracking noise, before a big wave of heat and smoke fills the room.

A minute goes by and the ringing in my ears fades enough to hear Chris. "Kyle? Kyle, son are you okay?"

I catch my breath. "Yeah. What happened?"

He stands with a bit of a groan. "This is what happens when the metals touch before they're attuned to one another."

He turns back to the table and I see the back of his shirt was burned away revealing cracks along his crystalline back. "Are you okay?" I ask, touching him.

He chuckles. "I'm fine."

"If you say so." I walk next to him and look at the burned remanence of both gold and silver. "Why did the silver act like that? It was like hitting water."

"Celestial silver has the properties of all three states of matter: solid, liquid and gas. You just need to be gentler with it as you force it into a more solid state." He dusts the table off before placing two more pieces of the metal in front of us.

We replace our crystal protection and retrieve the hammers. I take a deep breath as I hand him his hammer. "Okay I'm ready this time."

He stares at me a second. "You're left-handed, right?" I nod. "Use your right."

"But I won't have real control of the hammer."

"True, but now you'll be aware of that. Just let the weight of the hammer do the work. Now, let's try this again."

For I don't know how long, we pound away at the gold and silver. The silver is so weird. Like Chris said it acts like every property. To the touch, it's hard, but when struck it melts and erupts with a small vent of steam. All before solidifying again, becoming harder. The sound from the table now is like the peal of a bell, long and pretty. Chris strikes the gold and It easily warps under the weight of the hammer. The sound from the table sounds just like mine. I look at him, excitement on my face. We raise our hammers. "3...2...1 and..."

We bring the hammers down onto our respective metals. They ring with the same loud pretty sound. From under my hand, the silver tries to pull away, moving toward the gold. I look over to see the gold doing the same. "They're attuned." I say excitedly.

"Yup. Now for the hard part, crafting. What are we making?"

"Well, I was just going to remake the same amulet my dad made."

He thinks for a second before shaking his head. "No, it has to be from you, not your father."

He has a point, but what could I make? I close my eyes and imagine her standing in front of me, beautiful as always. Her golden eyes and bronze skin aglow in the fire's light. Her long curly black hair flows over her shoulders and down her back. *Her back.* The Celtic knot tattoo on her back. "I want to make her something that will protect her."

"Okay an amulet. But what will the design be?"

"A Celtic knot."

He smiles. "She will love it."

"Good. Now let's get started."

Hours of grueling and tedious work pass as we weave and mend the metals together. I look at my hands which are burnt and bleeding, but it was all worth it because the amulet is beautiful. The base is imperial gold about the size of a silver dollar, shaped to be a dome with a piece that opens on top when you wave your hand over it. The piece opens. Floating in space is a Celtic knot made from weaving the silver and gold together. It continuously folds in on itself as if constantly retying itself.

We fashioned an emerald, green lace from the crystal waste that protected us from the hell flames. Chris says that they're practically indestructible, beside to hell flame.

Chris holds it up. "Does it seem done to you?" he asks, looking it over.

He passes it to me and I look over it. *Something is off about it.* "No. It's missing something." I touch my chest, feeling the weight of Valene's soul drop on my chest. "It's empty."

"You're right." He looks at me for a second before cracking a smile across his crystalline face. "How about we fill it with your life?"

"Umm, don't I need that?"

He laughs as he shakes his head. He holds out his hand. "Give it here." I place the amulet into his hand, and he flips it over onto its back. One of his fingers lengthens to a point and he begins to etch symbols into the gold around the edge until it forms a complete circle. Then he whispers something to it. The symbols begin to glow green. "All right. Put it on and let it rest on your bare chest."

I take it from him and slip the green lace over my head. As the amulet touches my skin it adheres to me, like a small suction cup. "That kind of hurts. What did you do?"

"I put a lesser enchantment on it. Residual life drain. I'm sure you've noticed, but your body is still transitioning. You're a little more than a human but not quite a full demon. So, you're still putting off as much life force as a human would. Years' worth in only days. Which is why they die so fast. So, you wear that, and it'll absorb and fill the amulet with that life. Sound good?"

"That's perfect."

"Good. Now let's clean up."

We clean the whole workshop. Wipe the tables, sweep up the green crystal remains, put all the tools back into the ley line rack, extinguish the hell flame, and close the kiln. Chris places the gold and the last piece of silver in boxes for later before we leave. Back in the training room I stop and stretch. The layer of diamond dust on my skin suddenly melts away, and I feel the heat and pressure of the room hit me, taking my breath away. I look over my shoulder to Chris staring at me. *Is this another test?* I take a deep breath of the stifling hot air and stand tall. "Come at me." He says.

Without hesitation, I turn and rush him. Within a breath, I'm in front of him ready to throw a punch. My vision wavers and I see two of him. So, I strike between them. His hand appears stopping mine. We sit there for a second, and I struggle to stay up, and conscious. He takes a step back. I move forward to strike again, but my body gives out on me. Chris catches me before I hit the ground. "Good work son. You struck less, but you're awake. Your growth is astounding."

"Thanks. Can we leave now." I ask struggling to breathe.

"Of course. Zel, a door please." A door appears in front of us. "Come on. Let's get some food, I'm hungry."

"Yeah, me too." I touch the amulet as we walk through the door. *I hope she likes it.*

Chapter 16

I lay in my bed at Serena's looking up at the ceiling, watching the shadow of the blinds move across it as the morning sun rises. *Why and how am I still up?* Apparently, Chris and I had been down in his workshop for two days straight. We came out last night and I know I'm tired, but I can't sleep. My mind is still reeling from all the intricate work on the amulet.

I sit up onto the side of the bed. The lace moves on my neck bringing my attention to the amulet. Touching it, I can feel it beginning to lightly pulse, almost like a heart. Chris said it would be a few days before I should notice anything, but it's only been a few hours.

I concentrate on my eyes willing power into them, activating the dark sight. As the world goes gray I look at the energy rising from my hands. It's bluer now than black and there's a lot less pouring from me. Is it because of the amulet or is it thanks to the exercise. *I wonder is this energy that I'm seeing is the same as someone's life force?*

I reach for my phone, deactivating the sight before I touch it. The screen turns on and I navigate to the calendar. Our true anniversary date is next week, June 10th. This little thing is going to be brimming with life by the time I give it to her.

My phone chimes as a message appears on the screen, from Airca.

'Hey good morning. You alive?'

She's up early. 'Lol, yeah, I am. What's up?'

'What are you doing today?'

'Nothing.'

'Did you and Chris finish your project yet?'

'Sure did. Just last night.'

'Oh good. Then when do you think, we can go to the market?'

'Why do you want to go back so bad?' I sit looking at the screen of my phone for minutes and nothing. 'Airca?' Minutes more and still nothing. *I guess she's ignoring me. Whatever.*

I get dressed and head outside to the back yard to train. *Last time I didn't break a sweat during my warmup. Maybe I can see what my maxes really are now.*

Minutes later I flop onto my side gasping for air, my arms and legs trembling. I roll over onto my back. *Okay, three hundred and fifty pushups, two hundred sit-ups, and a thousand squats. I really am getting stronger.*

In the distance, I hear one of the neighbors' dogs barking. And it makes me think of my blue fur ball. I haven't seen Smoke in weeks. *I wonder how's he's been.* I struggle to stand but I manage to get to my feet and then shadow walk to the animal's enclosure.

I appear just outside of the Hell hound pen. The sound of high-pitched howls fill the building. There's shuffling and the thud of massive paws on the ground. I walk into the pen. A group of the hell hound pups all rush past me, running from their mother. She stops in front me panting, her hot sulfurous breath singeing my nose hairs and the sink on my face. "Good morning to you too girl." I say patting her massive head. She continues to chase after the pups when I notice Smoke was missing from the crowd.

"Smoke? Where are you buddy?" I yell out. Smoke pops his out from the pile of hay the hounds sleep on. Lazily he drags himself out and trots over to me, but not with same enthusiasm he normally has. His head is low and his paws are dragging. He stops looking up at me. "Did I wake you?"

He yawns big, before looking at me with bags under his eye's. The image of a thumb's down pops into my head. "You haven't slept in a while, have you?" Smoke grumbles. "Come on. I could use a nap myself." I reach down to grab him. The moment I touch him, energy rushes through my arms right to the base of neck again giving me an instant headache. *Again, with this energy.*

I take him back over to the pile of hay and lay down. Almost instantly Smoke passes out while in my arms. Stroking his fur my own eyes grow heavier. When I close my eyes and I'm out too.

The sound of barking echo's in the distance. *Maybe it was the pups still running around with Sally.* I hear it again and I recognize it to be Smokes high pitched bark. I open my eyes to check whether he was still on my lap or not. Not only was he not in my lap, but I'm not even in the pen anymore. I'm sitting upright in a chair. Surrounded by nothing but what looks like a plane of static. Like looking into one of those old tv's that didn't have a signal.

"Smoke?" The barking continues growing more frantic with every second. I get up from the chair and rush out towards the sound. I've never heard him sound like that before. Even when he faced down the *Morgal* centipede, outside of its enclosure of course. He still stood his ground. This is different. This sound like he was afraid.

On the horizon, I see Smoke running in full sprint. His little bark now a closer to a high-pitched howl. "Smoke!" I yell out. His ears perk up at the sound of my voice. "This way!"

Without skipping a beat, he turns running now towards me. It takes him no time to reach me and he leaps into my arms, panting, trying to catch his breath. "What's happening boy?" He starts chattering, whining and half barking. All the while Images flood my mind. They're jumbled and covered in a layer of static and I can't make out what he's trying to franticly tell me. "Buddy, calm down. I can't understand you. What's wrong?"

He stops moving, looks me in the eyes and takes a breath. "Master, RUN!" Smoke says with the voice of a young child.

"Whoa wait a minute did you just..." Something grabs my throat, lifting off the ground. *What the in world is this?*

"MASTER!" Smoke yells. He jumps from my arms and lands on whatever this thing is. "Let him go!" He says snarling, clawing, and biting at the creature.

It drops me and I fall to the ground holding my throat. I can barely make out the silhouette of thing as it was Static too. Smoke jumps off the static creature and faces me. "Smoke what's happening?"

"You have to wake up."

"No I have to..."

"Wake up!" Smoke lunges forward, biting my hand.

His needle like puppy teeth plunging into my skin. Pain shoots up my arm. I and everything around me begins to dissolve, fading into nothing.

I wake up holding onto my hand. I look it over. There's nothing there, no blood nor bite marks. Next to me, Smoke lays fast asleep. His little body heaving with each breath. "Zel!"

Zel rises out of the floor. "You summoned me, Master Kyle."

"I need you look over Smoke. Can you tell me if something is wrong with him? Is he okay?"

Zel looks at me concerned and confused. "Of course." He takes up Smoke in his arms. Placing his right hand over Smoke, it emits a red light that covers the sleeping pup. Nothing happens. "Master Kyle, he's perfectly fine. Just asleep."

I relax wiping my face with both hands. "Oh, thank goodness."

"Master Kyle, are you okay?"

"Yeah. I just ...I just had a bad dream." My phone chimes. It's a text from Airca. "Zel, are you sure he's, okay?"

"Yes. It just looks like he hasn't been sleeping well."

"Yeah. Could you please keep an eye on him? I'm a little worried about him."

"Of course. Is there anything in particular that I should look out for?"

"I'm not sure really. Just keep me posted about his day to day."

Zel bows. "As you wish."

I pat Smoke's head, before Shadow walking back to Serena's. I plop down at the kitchen table, putting my face into my hands. "What in the world was that? That dream. All that static. That creature?" I shake away the thought. "Just a weird dream."

I take my phone out of my pocket to look at the text. 'Meet me at the entrance to the Core.'

What is this girl thinking? I rush up the stairs, hop into the shower, put on a change of clothes and shadow-walk to the alley entrance.

I appear far enough in that no one should notice me. My skin starts to crawl thinking about the Messenger. How Airca could be in the same situation if I'm too late. *Where is this girl? Did she already go in?*

A hand touches my shoulder, something was off about it. I jump away from it, spinning around ready to fight, but stop short as I see that it's a girl. This close to the core which isn't safe. Especially for a girl as pretty she is and how she's dressed. Form fitting blue jeans, a black halter top, bright green highlights in her hair and dark green make-up. She's a beacon to the creeps that wander these allies. "Miss what are you doing here?" *And why aren't you freaking out about me appearing in front of you?*

"Miss? Kyle, it's only been a couple of days. Don't you recognize me?" she asks concerned.

I look her in the eyes. They're hazel. "Uh, Airca?"

She smiles. "Hey."

"Wow you look different. Like completely different."

"Apparently. I thought I'd try something new. You like it?"

I look her up and down admiring her new look. "Yeah. You look great."

She does a little happy dance, then takes my hand. "Come on let's head on in." I don't move. Airca looks back at me. "what's the matter?"

"Did you think that we weren't going to talk about this stunt you just pulled."

She sighs, "I mean, I had hoped we weren't, but I guess we are."

"Yeah, we are...what the hell were you thinking?"

"You were taking too long, and I really wanted to come back."

"Bad enough to put yourself in danger?"

She scoffs rolling her eyes. "I wasn't in any danger."

"Airca I've seen a man get possessed in this very ally. What makes you think that you weren't in any danger?"

She stands confidently, smiles, and grips my hand. "Because I knew you'd come."

I'm flattered, but at the same time livid. "Airca...that's not a good reason to put yourself in danger."

She sighs in frustration, snatching her hand from me. "I can handle myself."

"Oh really?" I started to flex my energy, prepared to bring it down on her, to test her resolve like I had been tested. As I look at her, I remember how I reacted when Chris tested me. How distraught and destroyed I was. I relax letting go of the energy I've built up. "Look, I don't doubt that you can handle yourself, against a human. But when dealing with the supernatural, you are like a child trying to fight an adult lion. I know you remember what happened last year. And even with me here I would barely be of any help. So, I just need you to keep that in mind. Okay?"

Her face grows a bit grim as I'm sure she vividly remembers what happened with that demon guy Ben, attempting to abduct her and the others. "Okay." Airca says softly.

"Good. Why are you so hellbent on going back to the Market?"

"Because... it's a thing that I have with you. I just wanted to spend some more time with you since you've been all lovey-dovey with Valene. And I've just been trying stay out of the way."

I sigh. "Airca."

"Kyle if you feel that today isn't a good day for this then I completely understand. We can just go another time."

I stare at her going through every reason why we could postpone, but none of them are legit. I scratch my head while sighing. "We can go."

"Really?"

"Yeah. Just keep a low profile. Well as low as you can be looking like that."

She rushes me, starting her arms around me. "Yes! Let's go."

She takes my hand and starts to walk down the alley. "Airca, wait we don't need to walk remember. I've been there so we can just shadow walk. Come here."

She walks over to me, a new confidence in her step. She presses against me, slowly wrapping her arms around my neck, her face a hairs length from mine. "Is this close enough?"

A little too close. "Yeah." I grab her by the waist. "Okay ready." she nods. "Hold your breath." As she takes in her breath we vanish into the darkness, then reappear in the back of the dingy corner store.

Airca, trembles as she takes a shaky breath. "Is...is that what it feels like each time you do that?"

"Like I said, you get used it."

She lays her head on my shoulder, with a sigh. I rub her back hopefully to give her some comfort. Her head pops up and she looks at me. "Thanks."

Wow. I was a little heated, so I didn't really look at her but Man, she does look good with this make over. I feel her shift as she leans in a bit but I step away. "Come on we need to get through the gateway."

Airca just smiles at me, before turning toward the wall. "Why didn't we appear in the market?" She asks walking to the door.

I notice how much her body has changed. There was a new muscular thickness and definition in her arms and back which I hadn't noticed before. All of which her outfit shows off nicely. "Airca, have you been working out?"

She looks over her shoulder. "Kyle, are you checking me out?"

"It's not like that. I just couldn't help but notice."

"Suurrre." She flexes her arms. "On top of all the things I was doing at school I've been taking self-defense, and mixed martial art classes for the last year now. You know, since our encounter with *Ben,* last year." Arica says with such disdain.

"Yeah. Well, you look great."

"Thank you." She turns back to the wall. Her head cocks to the side as she looks at the doorway of pulsating energy that matched her theme of green. "How come I can see the door this time? I don't have that power anymore."

I walk up next to her. "Well, you've looked upon it with the dark-sight and seen the truth; that it exists there. So, now you can't un-see it." I place my hand on the door and feel prick of the toll being take. The door lights up and shimmers away to a lit doorway. Airca takes my hand and I lead us through.

On the other side, the first thing I notice is that the bazaar is nowhere near as busy as it was the last time we visited. Which isn't bad. Now we can get to more of the vendors without having to wait on others to move. As we make our way down the street we come to a fork in the pathway. There's a loud high-pitched roar that makes me, Airca and everyone around us jump. "What in the world was that?" I ask looking around.

There's another roar, bringing our attentions down to her hand. "My ring." Airca says, lifting her hand up. The living piece of jewelry slowly coils around her finger. It pokes its little head up and points to the left of the intersection. "I think it wants us to go this way."

"Hmm... okay, lead the way."

As we walk down the street, Airca intently looks forward following her ring. Which is probably for the best, because most of the vendors couldn't take their eyes off her. A couple of them were even drooling as they talked and laugh amongst themselves. One of them starts to walk out from behind their table aiming towards her. That is until they see me walking close behind her, watching them. They freak out a bit looking away or going back to what they were doing. *That's right you weirdos, she's not up for grabs.*

"Oh, hey look." I hear Airca say. My attention snaps forward. Not far ahead of us is Rain; the goblin with the three-piece suit that gave her the ring. "It's leading us there."

As we get closer, we see a guy with slick black hair, wearing loafers, jeans, a button-down shirt and a vest, walk up to Rain and lift him off the ground by the collar of his suit. "Listen half pint, it's time to pay up, or your stand will be closed down."

"Look kid. I have the money for the boss, but he and I have an understanding that I will only put what I owe in his hands." Rain explains, his nasally voice strained.

"Who do you think sent me?"

"No one. I know about you, and you're your little racket. You just want to get the money first, then skim some off the top before you hand it over. Then blame me when everything comes up short. I've heard what you've been doing. Now would you please put me down."

The guy slowly puts Rain down. Rain looks up to us and smiles. "Well, well if it isn't the trickster that duped me out of some of my merchandise. It's a pleasure to see you again."

"Rain. Is everything okay?" I ask looking at the guy.

Rain readjusts his collar. "Everything is just fine. My colleague here was just leaving."

"Oh no you little green stain. We aren't done here." The guy says stepping up to Rain.

His voice sounds familiar, but I just can't place it. I place my hand on Airca's shoulder. "Come on Airca we should..." Airca is as stiff as board. "Airca?"

"It's you. Kyle it's him."

"Kyle?" the guy says as he slowly turns to us.

His grey eyes grow wide with surprise as he looks at me and I recognize him. "Ben." I step in front of Airca preparing myself for a fight.

Rain looks between us. "You know each other?"

"Sadly." I say.

"Ben." Airca says through her teeth behind me.

Ben steps past Rain, and in front of me. "Well, if it isn't my old friend." He says with a smirk.

"I'm not your friend."

"No, but I do owe you for the last time we met." My mouth goes dry as the air becomes thick with his energy, and I feel the weight of it. He was weakened the last I had dealt with him so I was able to overpower him, but this time I can tell just how strong he really is. He takes a step towards me, and I can feel myself start to panic. He's nowhere near as strong as Valene but he's still leagues stronger than me. *But no backing down.*

As I start forward, Airca steps out from my shadow and rushes past me. With two big steps, she's in Ben's unsuspecting face, her fist locked and loaded. With all her weight behind it, she throws a wild haymaker right into his nose with a loud smack.

Jarred, Ben falls back onto the ground hard, cursing and holding his face. Airca just stands over him, her breathing fast. "We aren't afraid of you." She screams.

Do you not know what low profile means? He looks up to her in utter confusion, and rage. "The hell woman. I don't even know you." He stops and looks at her for a second. "Wait. Airca?" He takes his hands from his nose. Blood is everywhere, on his hands and vest. He glares at her. "This is the second time that you've hurt me."

"And I'll do it again. Because I'm not afraid of you."

Ben's features begin to change as he glares at her. His teeth sharpen and his eyes sink into pockets of black, an orange light ablaze within them. "You should be." he says with a menacing growl. Airca takes a big step back, but her fists are still clenched. Ben gets to his feet, and I step forward to meet him.

Between us, from a cloud of darkness a tall man in a black pinned-strip suit appears. "That will be enough." The man says calmly.

Ben's face quickly reverts to human. "Boss." He lowers his gaze. "What brings you down here?"

The man looks at me, with solid black eyes and I get a sense of him. He's an older demon. The tan skin of his hands and face are marred with scars. So, it would surprise me if he were a warrior. I lower my gaze. "I was on my way here to collect my payment from Mr. Rain, when I sensed a bloodlust in the air. And here I see you harassing costumers."

"You got it all wrong sir. They were the ones causing trouble. Look what they've done to me. I was just defending myself."

"You liar." Airca yells from behind me, pulling everyone's attention. She quickly shrinks down.

"Step forward girl." The old demon says gazing at her. "Explain yourself."

As if standing close to a fire she starts to sweat and tremble with fear. She's right to be afraid. When a supernatural being has its full focus on you, you can feel it. She takes a big gulp before taking a big breath. "He's lying. He was the one causing trouble. He was harassing Rain, trying to strong arm money from him, when we walked up. Then he tried picking a fight with us." Airca explains.

He steps up to her. Quickly, she looks down. "Rain?"

"She speaks the truth. If not for her who knows how much money would be missing now."

He kneels before her. "Your hand young miss." Hesitantly, she gives him her hand. The old demon gently takes and examines it. Pulling a handkerchief from his lapel, he wipes the blood from her knuckles. "I am sorry that my subordinate has caused you such trouble."

"It's no problem."

The man stands tall pocketing his handkerchief. Without warning energy fills the air all focused on Ben. He is slammed to the ground under the sheer force of it. "On your feet worm!" The old demon orders. Ben struggles against the torrent of energy, until he is on his feet. Blood not only pouring from his nose, but now from his eyes, ears and mouth.

The energy dissipates, giving Ben a reprieve from the torture. "Apologize to them." Ben doesn't move. He just glares at us with utter disdain, breathing hard. In a blur of movement, the old demon drives his fist deep into Ben's stomach causing him to double over. "I said apologize, worm."

"Ple...please...forgive me." he grinds out.

Airca takes a deep breath, relaxing. "Crawl under a rock and die like the worm you are."

"Airca?!" I say.

The boss laughs. "Well said human. On your feet, worm. You and I have much to discuss."

"Rain. Your payment will be postponed."

"I'll be here."

The guy places his hand onto Ben's shoulder. Ben glares at us, blood on his lips. "Know that you have made an enemy this day, Airca." They shadow-walk away.

I step up next to her and take her hand. With a sharp breath her eyes snap to me. "Breath." I say to her. Airca takes a long shaky breath before the tears begin to form in her eyes. She grabs onto me, wrapping her arms tight around my neck. "It's okay." I tell her holding her back.

"I got him." She says still shaking.

"Yeah, you sure did. Right in the nose."

"I wouldn't Have had the courage if you weren't here." She kisses me on the cheek, "Thank you."

"Are you sure you needed him?" Rain asks from behind the table. "You held your own pretty well young lady. Against a demon no less."

"It's only because I had Kyle behind me."

"If you say so. Anyway, I would like to repay you for getting rid of that nuisance. How about another piece of jewelry? Pick anything you like from the table here."

She looks over the table. The ring on her hand starts to move and wiggle until it hops off her finger. It slithers across the table to a bracelet sized creature wriggling around in excitement. "What just happened?" she asks.

"That would be your rings mate. They've missed one another."

"I'll take that." Rain picks up the two writhing pieces and hands it to Airca. Her eyes light up as she watches them embrace one another. She looks up at me, with a focused look in her eye. "Let's get some food."

"Food is that way." Rain says pointing down the road. Airca walks off and I start behind her. "Hey kid. You know, my offer still stands. I'll give you whatever you want for her."

"And like I said before, she is not for sale." I say sternly.

"Okay, fine. I won't ask again."

"Why are you so interested in her?"

A gross, sleazy smile spreads across his face. "Kid, human women are my specialty. But there's something different about her, something exquisite. I can smell it." He says tapping his bulbous nose.

"I know she's special, but at the same time she just human."

"Are you sure? I mean she did hurt a demon with her bare fist." I sit there for a second watching Airca as she gets further away.

Could she? No, somebody would have sensed it by now. Or I would felt it at least. "No, I would know. She is my best friend."

"Whatever you say kid. Hey as thanks you ever need anything, just come see me."

I nod as I run to catch up to Airca. She's still intently watching the jewelry in her hand as the ring constantly curls around the bracelet. She puts out her left pointer finger out. The ring slithers onto it. "Kyle, I want you to have this." She says offering me the bracelet.

"Airca, you just got this. And I wouldn't want to separate them."

She steps closer to me, taking my right hand. The bracelet moves from her hand onto my wrist. "As long as you're with me they will never be apart." We look at one another. This reminds me of when I was in her mind, admiring her, and wanting to kiss her. Her hand lightly pulls me closer to her. "Will you be with me?" She asks lightly, the heat of her breath on my cheek.

I step back from her. "Airca, what's gotten into you?"

She looks at me with a smile, before moving close to me again. "I told you. I'm trying something new." She caresses my face.

"Airca I..."

"Excuse me." Our attentions snap to a guy and a woman standing next to us. "Am I interrupting?"

Saved by the stranger. I push Airca away a bit. "No, not at all. How can we help you?" Airca bites her right index finger and growls under her breath.

"You were at the Lover's Den a few weeks ago, right?" He asks, directing the question to me.

"Yeah, how do you know that?" Airca asks.

"Oh right, I'm sorry. We were there too."

I look at him for a second, before it comes to me. "The couple that was praying to the statue. I remember. Gene and Shayla, right?"

"Yup that's us." He offers his hand.

I take it. "Nice to meet you guys, I'm Kyle and this is Airca."

"Nice to meet you. Hey, the girl that came with you? She got stuck by the doll, right? I just wanted to know if she's okay?"

"I'm fine." Airca says.

Both Gene and Shayla are taken aback. "You'll have to forgive me. I didn't recognize you. You look different."

"Yeah, trying a new look."

"Yeah, I see that. You look amazing."

Shayla looks at Gene and her face darkens. She quickly grabs his hand, squeezing it. He grips her hand back, and smiles at her. "Poor Shayla here, was sick as a dog after she got pricked by it. I just wanted to make sure you were okay."

"Yup, right as rain."

"That's good to here. Have you guys eaten yet? We were about to grab a bite if you would like to join us."

I look at Airca, and the look on her face is one pure annoyance. Normally, I would decline but I see that I can't be alone with her right now. "Sure, if you know a spot where the food doesn't move."

Gene laughs. "Follow me. I know a couple spots."

We eat and talk with the couple. Shayla works as a manager of a nonprofit and Gene works as a personal bodyguard, through a private security company. They were nice.

After parting ways with them, Airca and I leave the Market. I shadow-walk us back to Serena's. We appear in the kitchen. The house is empty since Serena and Mayra are out. Airca looks at me and smiles. *Nope.* I hurry her out of the house. With the way she's been acting today, I don't want her to get any more Ideas.

We walk in silence through the neighborhood. I can feel her eyes on me, but I keep my focus on moving forward.

Valene's words come to mind. 'I just want you to be aware of her feelings. And maybe your own.'

I look at Airca, who looks lost in thought as well. We've come close to kissing like four times now. Each time I've been good at staving her off, but that last time was too close. *What am I doing? Am I ignoring my own feelings? Do I still have feelings for Airca? I don't know.*

I look forward, sighing. Airca takes my hand. She looks up at me with a smile. "Kyle, are we cool?"

"Of course. Why wouldn't we be? Is everything okay?"

"It's just. Today has got me thinking about, us."

"Oh, really?"

"Yeah. I mean you know that... I still like you, right?"

"I had my suspicions."

We continue in silence, all the way to her front door. We look at one another. "Airca I..." She interrupts me, putting her lips to mine.

I freeze realizing what's happening. My hands move to her waist so that I can push her away, when I hear Mr. Jacob's advice, 'Just go with the flow.'. Instead of pushing her away I pull her in closer to me. Her hands move up my arms and onto my shoulders. She kisses me a little deeper and my lips start to tingle.

Valene's Amulet throbs, rattling my chest, before it grows hot to the point, I swear my skin was about the sizzle. I step away from her.

"What? What's the matter?" she asks.

"I don't know. Everything just got hot and painful suddenly."

"Are you okay?" she asks, holding onto and looking at me.

"I think so."

I look at her and she smiles. "So, do you wanna come in? We can pick up where we left off?"

I touch the amulet, feeling it pulse and remind me of what I went through to make it. Also, who I did it for. "No actually."

"What?"

"Airca, I'm sorry but we can't do this. I can't do this not to Valene."

"S...Sure, we can. It could be just between the two of us. She wouldn't have to know."

I stand tall. "Airca no."

She starts rubbing the tip of her right index finger with her thumb. "Kyle come on. I finally understand what I want. I want to be confident, strong, unafraid and I want to be with you." she says placing her hands onto my chest.

I take her hands from my chest. "Airca, I will always care for you, clearly, but I'm with Valene."

"You're a demon right. I'm sure you guys can have multiple women."

"It wouldn't surprise me, but that isn't me, or Valene."

Her eyes dart back and forth and become a little frantic. "Airca?" She stops and looks at me. Her face twists in anger and sadness.

"Go away." She says monotone. She walks away from me and up to her door.

"Airca, wait."

She opens the door, walks in, and turns towards me. She motions for me to come to her. I step up to the door just at the threshold. She looks me in the eyes and smiles an exaggerated smile. "Kyle Ross. You are not welcome in my home."

"What?" The barrier of the threshold slams shut right in my face. The shockwave knocked me back off my feet and onto the ground. Everything is spinning for a second until I focus on Airca still standing at the door. "Go away Kyle." She says before slamming the door shut.

I lay my head back on the ground. Covering my eyes. Trying to stop everything from spinning. *That could have gone better.* I roll over, getting to my feet and wobble my way home.

Chapter 17

The alarm on my phone goes off, followed by the annoying whine of my alarm clock. I tap them both turning them off. It has been two days since my trip to the market. Since Arica hit me with the threshold and everything is still spinning somewhat.

I grab my phone and roll over onto my stomach. There are loads of notifications, emails, and text from people I knew at school wishing me a happy birthday, but there was nothing from Arica. I texted her yesterday. I don't know why I'm looking for her to say something. I should be mad, royally so with how she hurt me, but I'm not. Well, I don't think I am. I plant my face in my pillow, grumbling. Maybe a good workout will take my mind off it.

Rolling out of bed, I throw on a pair of shorts, shoes and a T-shirt before making my way through the house and to the back yard.

After a few minutes of stretching, I take a deep breath. I push the energy within me out as far as I can manage and hold it. I feel the fatigue in my muscles already setting in and sweat on my brow. I start off slow with my warm-up now all up to two hundred. I sit on the ground trying to collect and assess myself. I'm sure I can keep going but my head is swimming.

As I stand, my body starts to fight me straining to keep the energy extended. With a finale deep breath, the energy slowly comes back within me, but it takes a little longer before I can let it go.

Finally. It rests back into my core. *That's new. Is that what it means to deepen my well? I'll have to talk to Selene about it.*

I head inside straight to the shower. As the water runs over me, I look down at the Valene's amulet. *I need to talk to her about what happened between Airca and I.* I imagine her getting angry, and ready to fight me. *Or maybe I shouldn't.* I hop out wrapping the towel around my waist and head out to my room. As I open the door, Mayra is standing there, naked as the day she was born. "Oh, Mayra you're back?" I say looking away from her.

"Oh, hello little brother."

"You are really naked right now. I take it that you're feeling better?"

She smiles halfheartedly. "I am feeling a little more comfortable in my own skin. More so than I have been."

"Did you get in contact with more of Leo's buddies?"

She nods. "And had long a conversation with them too. It helped."

"Good."

"What have you been ...up...to?" Her pupils dilate making the greenish yellow of her eyes turn black. "Ooo, what's that?" She asks pointing to my chest.

"It's an amulet that I made for Valene. For our anniversary."

At her touch the golden cover vanishes, revealing the floating ever-weaving Celtic knot. "Is that celestial silver?"

"Sure is, and imperial gold. It's to replace the one dad had made for her."

"The one...Leo lost."

"Yeah. but this one is different because it has a bit of my life in it as well." She looks at me a bit of worry on her face. "It's okay. It's just the extra bit that I put off naturally."

She nods before tapping it again, and the case closes. "It's beautiful. She will love it."

"I hope so. I know it's not a competition, but I hope it lives up to the gift she got me."

"And that was?" I tell her about the trip to Greece, our track through Olympus, my dip in the waters of the hearth fire and Valene's promise sealed with a soul drop. "A soul drop, really?"

"What? Does that mean something? I told Chris and he didn't make too much of it."

Mayra grumbles at the mention of Chris. "Of course, he wouldn't. He can barely keep his word. So, something as formal and binding as the presentation of a Soul drop is beyond him." She says, her hair starting to stand on end and tinges of red swirling in her eyes. She looks at me. With a sigh, her face softens. "Sorry."

"It's okay. I get you're still mad at him. So, it's a formality?"

"Yes, an old one at that. To give another a piece of your very soul and allowing them to make it apart of themselves. To demon kind, this is a sign of complete devotion. It's not practiced that much anymore."

"Why not?"

"Not important." She says booping me on my nose. "What is important is your answer. And that amulet is the perfect gift."

"That's a big relief that you think so."

She leans over and kisses me on the forehead. "There's no need to worry. Just give her your beautiful gift and enjoy yourselves as long as the Creator will allow." She says her voice shaky, as if fighting back tears.

I wrap my arms around her and hug her tightly. "I will. Thanks Mayra."

Mayra takes a deep breath, regaining her composure. She holds me. "No problem, little brother. Now go get dressed. Serena is making breakfast."

"You should too."

She sticks her tongue out at me. I'm quick to get dressed, throwing on some clothes. Halfway down the steps I catch the aroma of Serena's pancakes. "Serena, I'm so happy you guys are back." I say walking into the kitchen.

A young Serena pops up with a smile, but my attention is on the girl with green hair sitting at the table in front her. *Airca?* Serena runs over to me arms wide. "Hey sweetie. I missed you too." She says hugging me.

"Hey." Airca says with a little wave.

"Airca, you haven't even answered my text. What are you doing here?"

"I wanted to talk to you. But your au...sister and I started talking."

"Okay." I turn my attention to Serena who is all smiles as she hangs onto me. "I just ran into Mayra. She was in good spirits."

"Oh yes. The last few people that we located were very close to both Her and Leo. She was able to get some things off her chest. Now we just have to wait for the memorial next month."

"Memorial? Did someone die?" Airca asks.

"A very close friend of our family."

"I'm sorry to hear that."

"Thank you, dearie. It was nice to get to see the Underworld though. I've never lived there, but it's nice to visit from time to time."

"The Underworld?" Airca asks.

"Yes dear, the home realm of demons."

"Oh. Is it easy to travel back and forth?"

Serena goes over to the table, picks up a cup and starts to fill it with tea. "For the most part. You see, ages ago there were countless bridges from the underworld to New birth. I'm sorry, Earth. But as the war between the Light and demons hit one of its apexes nearly all those bridges were closed. Now we have to travel through tears in the vail."

"So whenever, Zel makes a door for the others, he's creating a tear?" I ask.

"More like connecting them. Creating a corridor from New birth, through Limbo and on to the underworld."

"That's why the gateways put off the same feeling as shadow walking."

"Exactly. Though his are more stable where most other gateways aren't and must be adjusted for the traveler's power. Anyone too powerful trying to go through one will collapse it. A natural failsafe."

"So, like in those movies, with the witches or whatever in a huge circle, with all that stuff?" I ask.

Serena walks back and hands me the cup. "That is a depiction of humans adjusting a tear."

"Wow." Airca says.

"Indeed." Serena walks over to the stove, getting ready to take the pancakes off the skillet. "There's a lot that you'll find out. Being part of this family, dearie."

Airca looks at me. My hands begin to ache, from the shock at her threshold. "I think she's catching on pretty well." I say a little more course than I intended. I head into the living room.

The TV is already on as I plop down onto the couch. The news anchor talks about things happening around the city today. A picture of an older man in a suit, with short graying hair, light blue eyes and a small smile pops up on the screen. "Deputy Mayor Juda is hosting a fund raiser for the summer youth programs of Roc city. Come down and help if you can."

He's been active a lot in the past year. I don't tend to pay attention to politics but D.M Juda has been doing such great things for the city lately, you can't help but acknowledge it.

A hand touches my shoulder. I don't turn around because I know who it is. "Kyle, can we talk?" Airca asks.

"Sure." She walks around the chair and takes a seat.

She looks at me, clearly nervous. "I'm so sorry about what I did. Are you mad?"

"You know..." I stop and take a breath. "Airca, what you did to me was dangerous. You could have killed me."

Her eyes get wide. She takes my hand. "I didn't know. I was just...I don't know what got into me."

I notice fresh scratches and band aids on them. "What happened to your hands? I didn't think that you hurt yourself when you punched Ben."

"Oh, I didn't. I just got a little carried away punching the heavy bag after our fight. Kyle, I'm really sorry. Please forgive me."

I stare at her hand, before looking up at her. There's a sincerity within her eyes. "I...I forgive you."

She takes a breath, relaxing. "Kyle, I just wanted you to hear me out you know?"

"Yeah, I heard you." She squeezes my hand, but I pull away from her. She groans.

We're silent for a while as the news report continues. Airca rubs her fingers, as she stares off into space. Most likely in deep thought about something. "Kyle." She turns towards me. "Do you love Valene?"

"Honestly, I'm getting there. I mean I really care for her, and I'm still getting to know her."

"So, you haven't said it yet?"

"No."

"Are you going to?"

"I mean at one point if we keep going the way that we are. But before that I have something that I want to give her."

"What's that?" I pull down my shirt and show her the amulet, adhering to my skin. Her eyes brighten as she looks at it. "Wow, It's beautiful. Is this the project you were talking about?"

"Yup." I tap it and opens, revealing the ever-weaving Celtic knot. "Took forever to make, but longer to get the materials. Thank you by the way."

She looks at me confused. "For what?"

I point at the amulet. "The silver, remember? I wouldn't have gotten it without your help."

"This is what that...was..." she trails off. She chuckles rubbing her hands. "What are friends, for I guess?" she says low and monotone.

I watch her, waiting for her to ask a question, but her face goes blank as she zones out. She starts to gnaw on her right index finger like she had yesterday. Slowly, her face starts to twist in disgust. "Airca?"

With a sharp breath, she snaps out of her thoughts. She turns to me with a smile. "I should go."

"You're not staying for breakfast?"

"No, I just wanted to come by, apologize and to tell you that you're always welcome in my home." She stands and I get up with her. She gives me a hug and I feel her trembling. "Oh, and happy birthday."

"Thanks. Airca you've been fidgeting with that finger something fierce. It's the same one that was pricked by that doll. Has it been bothering you?"

"What? Oh no it's been fine. It itches from time to time, but that's it. It's a reminder that fate is at work."

"If you say so."

"I'll see you later with your gift." She walks away, into the kitchen. Rubbing her hands on her legs still.

Mayra walks in with a silken dress wrapped around her thin frame. Airca stops, staring up at the tall woman. "And who might you be?" Mayra asks a little more suspiciously than I would have expected.

"Hi...I'm Airca, Kyle's friend. And you are?"

"Airca this is my oldest sister, Mayra." I say standing by the table.

"Oh, it's nice to meet you." Airca says a little weary. Mayra just stares at her, lightly sniffing the air. "Um, I should be going. I'll see you later Kyle."

Airca rushes past Mayra and out the door. Mayra walks over to the table and sits in the chair next to me. She takes my hand and places it on her head, demanding a head rub. I start to rub, and she relaxes. "Mayra. Why were you hounding Airca like that?" Serena asks, placing a plate of pancakes on the table.

She takes a deep breath, letting out a groan. "She smelled odd. Dangerous."

"Airca?" Serena and I say at the same time.

"Yes. That girl had an air about her. It was sour."

"Like the Messengers possessed?" Serena asks.

"No." I say quickly. "They weren't sour. They were rotten."

"I don't know. I couldn't put my finger on it but It was familiar. Little brother, you be weary of her. Don't let your trust for her cloud your judgement."

"Mayra I'm sure it's fine. You might just be a little on guard when it comes to humans. Especially with the way the Messenger used our parent's human friends."

"That may be true. Even so be careful. If anything happens to you and I hear that it's because of her, I will end her and her familial line."

Serena places a plate on the counter a little too hard making me jump. "Mayra, leave it. I'm sure he understands." Mayra sits back, leaning into me.

I run my finger through her hair and she starts to purr. "Don't worry Mayra, it'll be all fine and dandy." I stop and take a seat at the table. Mayra pouts at me as she starts running her own hands through her hair. "I will admit, she has been a bit off, but I've seen her go through changes like that before. Humans can change at the drop of a hat, it's normal for them." She just stares at me unfazed by my reasoning. "But I'll be careful." I finish.

"Thank you."

Serena places our plates on the table. I stuff my mouth with a fork full of pancakes.

The rest of the day passes by, and I've ended up in the living room, with Mayra asleep on my lap in car form. My phone buzzes on the armrest. I pick up to see a call from Page. "Hello?"

"HAPPY BIRTHDAY!" Yells two voices. One Page and the other Rica.

"Thanks guys. I haven't heard from you all since graduation what have you been up to?"

Page scoffs. "My mom has had me in workshops to help get scholarships and financial aid for school. Its boring but I've gotten three so far."

"That's cool. Congratulations. What about you Rica?"

She's silent for a second. "I've been busy."

"Ok, how about you not lie to one of your best friends on his birthday." Page says.

"I *have* been busy." Rica snaps.

"Doing *what?*" Page asks with the same attitude.

"Bible study."

"Okay that doesn't sound so..."

"Keep going." Page interrupts.

Rica groans in frustration. "I've been studying angelology, exorcisms, and demonology. Looking for ways to protect yourself from those like Kyle and that guy from last year. You happy?"

"Yeah, now you can stop being weird towards our friend. She has been weird right Kyle?"

"Yeah, she has, but I can't really fault her. A lot has happened."

"No, don't you stick up for her funky behavior and act like you haven't been going through a lot of things yourself."

Rica laughs. "Wait a minute we were calling to wish him a happy birthday. How did this become an intervention?" She asks.

"Oh, because this is my gift to my very demonic friend."

Rica groans loudly in frustration. "Look get off my back. I'm still wrapping my head around the whole him being a demon thing. And that they're real. And I was almost snatched up by one." She says a little fear in her voice. "I don't see how you're so accepting of this Page. How?"

"Yeah, I'm freaked out too, but I mean it is what is. It just means the world is a lot *more* than we thought. And it's a little more exciting if you ask me."

"It's just so easy for you to accept. I can't just go on accepting that my friend is soul devouring, embodiment of evil. I'm sorry Kyle, but honestly, I feel a little weird talking to you. You know how my family is, with religion."

"Rica..."

"Kyle, have you devoured a soul and are you the embodiment of evil?"

"Uh, no. And not the embodiment of evil. Darkness, but not evil."

"See same ole lovable Kyle. Just Kyle 2.Demon."

Page and I laugh, and you can even hear Rica crack a smile. "Look, Rica. Are you listening?" I ask.

"Yeah."

"I know it's a lot to take in, and to process. I've been going through the same things for a year now. I'm still learning about everything myself."

"it's just all so scary."

"Yeah. Yeah, it is. So don't force yourself or let **anyone** force you to be okay with it. Take your time. If there's anything you want to know or need to know to feel safer, just ask. I might be able to get those answers for you."

She's silent for a second. "Thank you. And I will."

"Well, that's a start. I have a question. Since you are a demon and all, do you even age like us anymore?" Page asks.

"I couldn't tell you about the next few years, but at one point, no. I'll only age one *Dytic,* every 80 years."

I hear Rica gasp. "Holy crap. So, you'll be young looking while we're decrepit. That's not fair."

I laugh like an eccentric gaudy villain. "Well, being an embodiment of evil comes with its perks."

"Oh, so funny." Rica says.

"See, I miss this. Now we're just missing Airca." Page asks.

"She was just here. Have you guys not seen her in a while?" I ask.

"Not since graduation." Page explains.

"I saw her last week." Rica answers. "Helped her dye her hair."

"She dyed her hair? Let me guess it's blue?"

"Green actually. It looks good on her." Rica explains.

"Yeah, it does. You did a good job. Was she acting different?" I ask.

"Besides dyeing her hair. Not really. Maybe a little more focused than normal. Why?"

"She has just been a bit off, since we hung out last."

Page groans. "That's because she hasn't gotten over you."

"Yeah. She told me. We had a moment, a talk, a fight...we made up? I don't know."

"Ooo that sounds like a lot. A little toxic actually." Page says.

"Page! The girl's just probably going through something."

"Yeah, well whatever. She's not here to talk so we can't help."

Rica groans. "Kyle, just be patient with her. I'm sure it'll all workout. Just be aware of her feelings."

And aware of mine. "Valene said the same thing. And I will. Thank you both for the call."

"Of course, knucklehead. We love you. Well, I love you."

Rica scoffs. "Happy birthday Kyle."

"I love you guys too. Thanks, talk to you later."

I put my phone down and scratch Mayra behind her ear. She nestles deeper into my lap, purring. The evening news comes onto the TV. The news anchor reports that the body of a woman had been found, with multiple stab wounds. They continue stating that the officials believe that it was a murder of passion and that the victim's husband, who was missing, is a prime suspect. I change the channel to a movie.

My phone buzzes again. It's a text from Valene this time. 'Come over.'

"Mayra, I gotta go."

She rolls over onto her back and paws at my hand. "I don't wanna move. You're comfortable and you pet me unlike our other sibling."

I look at her and scratch under her chin, and she melts. "Please move."

She sighs. "Fine." She rolls off my lap and onto the floor. "I'll just go throw myself at Serena."

"Love you too."

"Be safe." She says, trotting into the kitchen.

I Shadow-walk and appear in the main foyer where Valene is waiting, wearing a blouse, slacks and flats. "Hey, I didn't think I was going to see you. Aren't you still supposed to be at your meetings."

"Hero, of course I wasn't going to miss today. I already missed you graduation I'm not missing your birthday."

She hugs me and I smell her signature berry perfume but there's another lingering smell under it. "Sweetheart you reek of coffee and cigarettes."

"Sorry, I just popped in right after a seminar. It's all that the teachers drink. You know, besides alcohol. How was your day?" I tell her about breakfast and hanging out with Mayra most of the day, but I hesitate about Airca. "Kyle, what's wrong?"

"Airca and I had a moment a couple of days ago."

Valene tenses a bit, and I'm ready for her to tear into me. She takes breath. "How did it go?" She asks calmly.

I go into every detail about what happened. She just stares at me unfazed. "I'm sorry. You were right. And you have every right to be mad."

She takes deep a breath. The air grows bone chilling cold for a split second before turning back to normal. "Hero, I appreciate your honesty. At least I know that I can trust you to keep your word." She steps closer to me, wrapping her arms around my neck and putting her forehead to mine. "Let's forget about it for right now. We'll talk later."

"Are you sure?"

"Yeah. Now come on. I have something for you.

She takes my hand and leads me through the door into the dimly lit kitchen.

Zel, Selene, Jason, Chris, Serena, and even Mayra all stand around the tall wooden table, the soft light of candles atop a cake, illuminating their faces. They all start to sing, and I feel my eyes sting with tears. I haven't had this many people wishing me a happy birthday in a long time. "Thank you everyone."

"Make a wish Hero."

I look to everyone then at the cake. I wish the girls were here. Even Airca, with what's going on between us. I blow out the candles and enjoy the rest of the night.

Chapter 18

I sit on the sofa in the Kir library, trying to get through one the demon books written in *Durabi* but it's harder today than normal. The swirling words are a lot more chaotic and I'm having a hard time focusing. Maybe because I'm more worried about Smoke, than trying to read.

Over the week, since my birthday I've gone to check up on him. Each time I'd show up, he wouldn't interact with me. He'd just avoid me. Either running away, or just plain ignoring me. Zel said beyond that and his erratic sleep schedule he hadn't been showing any odd behaviors.

The air in the room shifts and a doorway of darkness appears along the wall. Valene emerges out of the darkness, looking around until she locks on to me. My chest tightens, as I feel a tinge of guilt. We still haven't talked about the whole Airca situation yet. She's been really cool though when I see her. It's starting to worry me a bit.

Valene smiles as she approaches me. "There you are Hero. What are you up to?"

"Nothing, Trying read and failing. What about you? I'm surprised that I'm seeing you here at this time of day."

"Well yesterday was the last day I had to go to these silly seminars. I'm officially free." She says sitting on my lap. She wraps her arms around my neck, giving me a peck on the cheek. "Are you busy tonight?"

"Nope. Free as a bird. What's up?"

"One of my colleagues is throwing a little party tonight in celebration of getting through these mind-numbing meetings."

"I thought they were like for teaching strategies and stuff?"

"It is, but I've technically been a teacher for about a century. To me these "strategies" are just the same regurgitated drivel that I've heard before that don't work with all the students, not even a fourth of them really. Sometimes you have to not be lazy and work with the students and find what helps them. And don't get me started with..." She stops, looking at me and takes a calming breath. "Sorry."

"No, it's okay. You never really talk about how you feel when it comes to your teaching. I always figured it was because you wanted to keep you and Felicia separate in your day to day. It's nice to see you so passionate. And as a recent high school graduate, I appreciate teachers like you."

She stares at me, a huge smile on her face. "Thank you, Hero. But what I wanted to ask was if you wanted to be my date to the party?"

"Sure, but you're Felica for this stuff?"

"Yeah. And?"

"Are you sure you'd want your alter ego, who is a college professor to be seen canoodling with a very much younger man on your arm?"

"That would be a little awkward wouldn't it." Her face brightens. "I could teach you how to shape shift a little." Her body grows hot as it begins to change in my arms. Her frame becomes less muscular and more soft and supple. Her skin complexion lightens to a caramel color, her hair shortens, and her eyes turn green. "It's not hard Hero." She says her voice a little deeper and older.

"You know this is always uncomfortable, when you do this right?"

"I know. I just think it's cute the way you squirm. What do you say? Wanna learn?"

"Um sure."

Excited, she kisses me on the cheek. I pull away from her a bit. Her kissing me while as Felicia makes me think of Airca kissing me. "Hero?" she asks confused.

"It's still a little weird to have Felicia flirt with me."

In an instant she reverts to her own human form. "Sorry."

"So, how do I do this?"

She stands in front of me like she was about to teach one of her classes. "Okay Mr. Ross. Welcome to Shapeshifting 101."

"Valene, I just got out of school." I groan.

"Shut up and listen." She continues, explaining that there are three types of shapeshifting. The first is moving back and forth between the human form and the true form.

"Wait, are demons born in a human form?"

"Most are. We don't realize our true forms until a little later in life. But those born in the true form sometimes take a human guise because it's convenient. Especially for those that are giants or monstrous. The downside to that though is that they sometimes can't completely transform. That's why you see aspects of the true form show through. Such as horns, scales and so on.

"Gotcha. I didn't know that. So, what does your true form look like?"

She smiles. "I'll show you mines if you show me yours."

Wait, what? My whole face lights up at the realization of the meaning behind her playful words. "Wait a minute. I have a demon form?"

She fights back a laugh. "Yes, Hero. You have a true form."

"Huh. You know it never crossed my mind that I would have one. I wonder what it looks like?" I look at my hands. In a burst of darkness, they change into bone claws. "Will I look like this? Covered in bone?"

Valene touches my claws. "Why are they bone?"

"It's what Shadow had when I dreamt of him."

She shakes her head. "Hero these are your weapons, and part of your armor. You can technically make them look like anyway that you will them to look. Watch." She holds out her hand. In her palm a ball of darkness swirls into existence. In an instant it transforms into the long dagger that she normally wields. "And now." The blade bends and twists until it becomes a larger and heavier short sword. "When it comes to these things you can change them at will. Your true form will be what it is when you change into it."

I dispel my claws. "Well, that's going on the list of things to figure out."

The sword vanishes. "We'll figure it out together. The second type of shapeshifting, the one you'll be learning today, is changing the features of your form, such as your height, weight, eye color and age. Like Serena had done while she was playing your aunt. Now watch. First, I'm young, and now." Valene takes a deep breath and before my eyes her body begins to change. Streaks of gray appear in her hair, while she grows shorter, and her skin becomes lose and wrinkled. "I'm old." She says with her young voice.

"Oh, that looks hard."

"It's not." She reverts to her young self in the blink of an eye. "Just place a layer of energy on your skin and with a clear picture, mold it to how you wish your form to look. Try it."

I close my eyes and focus on the energy flowing through me. It washes over my skin like the warm water of a shower. *Okay now what to change? I'm trying to look older, right? But I've never really imagined myself older. What would I look like?* I think of the oldest and most wrinkly person I've run into, but that's too old to be college professor in her late thirties. *How old was dad? He didn't look that old.* I think of the last photo that I saw of him. His smile, the way the lines on his face creased and the weariness in his eyes. A tingling sensation blankets my face. After a moment, it stops. I open my eyes to Valene smiling, her eyes wide with amazement. "What?"

"You look just like your dad." She pulls out her phone and puts the camera facing me.

"Whoa." I take the phone from her and start feeling my face, poking at the wrinkles on my brow and around my eyes. "My face is really older."

"Good job Hero. And on your first try too."

"Why don't I feel older? Serena used to complain about how her old form got to her all the time."

"That's because your sister had to act the part. You don't really change your age, just your appearance." With a breath I relax, releasing the energy on my skin. Instantly my face goes back to normal. *Thank goodness, it's not permanent.* "Now we're ready."

"Wait, what's the third type?"

"It's Felicia."

I look at her confused. "How is Felicia the third type?"

"The third type is true shapeshifting. Using your energy, you completely change, you. Your muscles, bone structure, even the way your body reacts to things. You become a whole new person."

"But aren't you still Valene when you're Felicia?"

"Technically. My soul and a piece of my mind are always me. But my body and the way she thinks, feels and reacts are Felicia."

"Doesn't it hurt to change into her?"

"It did at first, but it becomes second nature after a time."

"Isn't hard to keep that up? Having two lives?"

"I haven't had any trouble with it, and I've had her for the past two *dytics.*"

"So, you basically have a spilt personality? I don't know if that's a good or a bad thing."

"Oh hush. Now that that's done, I want to go the mall and get us a couple of new outfits. As you may have felt and seen Felicia has gained a little weight."

"She didn't look bad."

"Oh really? I felt you get a hand full." She said getting into my face.

"I did not...not on purpose."

She laughs and kisses me. She runs her hands over her waist and hips. "Thanks, but Felicia likes her snacks. Now come on let's get going." She takes my hands, pulling me to my feet and we shadow-walk.

We appear in one of the back hallways just outside one of the storage rooms of the mall. There are no cameras nor foot traffic, besides a mall-cop making rounds. So, we won't appear in front of some unsuspecting human. As we're walking through the hall Valene transforms into Felicia, as she drags me out into the mall, which is surprisingly full. The two of us hit a few clothing stores. Some of the other costumers give us odd looks in the store as the older Felicia would show off her outfits to me. It wouldn't have been too bad had she not been flirting with me so hard. She picks out a couple of outfits for me and I show them off to her. She fans herself making all kinds of cute faces, which makes me laugh and blush. We buy the clothes and move on to the next store laughing and carrying on. *This is nice.*

As we walk along the walkway near the food court, Felicia kisses me on the cheek. "You know we haven't been on a proper date in long time."

"Felicia and I have never been on a date."

"You know what I mean. I really missed hanging out with you."

"Are you talking as Valene or Felicia?"

She smiles stepping close to me, kind of pinning me up against the railing. One of her eyes turn gold while the other stays green. "Both." She edges in to kiss me.

"Kyle?"

We turn towards the source of the voice. Felicia's body tenses, as she lets out an annoyed sigh. She steps back from me. I look over to see Airca staring at us, with sunglasses on. "Airca, hey."

"Hey?" She looks at Felicia. "Who's this?"

That's right, I didn't tell Airca about Felicia, and I'm sure Valene wouldn't want it any other way. "You remember the babysitter I told you I had when I was little right?"

"The bad babysitter, yeah?"

"I've told him multiple times to stop calling me that. Felicia will do just fine" Felicia extends her hand. "It's a pleasure to meet you, Airca." she says pleasantly professional.

Airca looks at Felicia's hand for a long second before taking it. "Nice to meet you too. Kyle, can I talk to you for a second?"

"Sure. Be back in a minute."

We walk a few feet from Felicia. "So, what was that all about?" She asks. Airca sounds tired, like she hasn't slept.

"What was what all about?"

"That lady being all up in your face? She looked like she was about to kiss you." she says rubbing her hands on her sweatpants.

"What no, she was just a little excited to see me, that's all. We hadn't seen each other in while."

"Sure."

"So where have you been? I haven't heard from you since my birthday."

She smiles. "Oh nowhere. Just to work, the gym and home. I just got paid today so, I bought a few things." She steps close to me, and she smells a little like incense. "I have a gift for you, but it's not ready yet. It's going to take a little bit longer than I thought."

"Airca, you didn't have to."

"I know. You're going to love it though." She hugs me. "Um, Kyle. You do know that your ex-babysitter is a demon, right?" she whispers.

I look at her. "Yeah, I know that. How do you?"

"She has a golden mist coming off her. Like the blue smoke coming off you." *How is she seeing that?*

I take and lower the glasses from her face. Her eyes are black as night. *She has the dark sight activated. How?* "Airca how do you have the sight on?"

"I...I don't know." She hesitates. "It just started happening out of nowhere. Oh, but Kyle I have seen things, both scary and beautiful."

I take her by the arms. "Airca, be careful how react and what you say to the things that you see. Outside of the market demons and creatures like them don't like to be noticed and will target you."

"I understand. I'm not afraid though." She caresses my face. "Because I have you watching over me." She edges in a bit to try and kiss me, but I stop her. "Go home Airca. Go straight home, you hear me?"

She sighs, "I will."

I give her a quick hug. "Good and text me when you get there."

I walk away from her back over to Felicia. "I love you, Kyle!" she yells from behind me.

"I love you too Airca. Now get home." I say over my shoulder.

Now back over by Felicia, her back is turned to me, and I can see how tense she is. "Hey, sorry that took so long. Airca was just telling me something." Felicia turns around and looks at me, her lips pursed in annoyance. "What?"

"Why did it have to be her?" she asks. "We were having such a good time and she..." Felicia puts her hands together in front of her face, her eyes cycling between, green, gold, and black.

"Felicia?" She doesn't answer, she just continues to stare out into space. I place my hands on her shoulders. "Valene?" She takes a sharp breath, her eyes settling on green.

Tears well up in them as she takes deep shaky breaths. "Kyle, I'll...I'll see you tonight. Give me the bags. I'm going home."

"Felicia. Come on talk to me."

"Give me the bags!" She demands. I hand them to her. "Thank you." she says, snatching them from me. "I'll see you tonight, Hero." She starts to walk away. I reach out to touch her, but an overwhelming fear wash over me, causing me to hesitate. "We'll talk later." She says sternly, before walking away and vanishing into the crowd.

I sit down at one of the benches near the railing. I rub at my face trying to calm some of this frustration. *Airca why did you have to show up right here and now? Had it been anyone else Felicia/ Valene would still be here.* I touch the amulet on my chest, feeling its pulse. *It's so close to the true date of my and Valene's anniversary. Hopefully this doesn't dampen things.* With a deep breath, the smell of incense is still strong in my nose. *Where did Airca come from to smell like that? No store in the mall has incense burning, to smell as strong as she did. The last place I was that burned incense was, the Lover's Den. Wait, did she come from the market? What could she have been doing there by herself after I told her not to? Crap!*

I get up and make my way back through the mall to the back hallways. Shadow-walking, I appear at the entrance of the market. With the blood sacrifice, the door opens, and I step through. The bazaar is busy today, compared to the last time. People line the street looking over at the stalls and items being sold. With what little room I have, I wiggle through the crowd, heading towards the Lover's Den.

After a few minutes of struggling past a group I make it out and into a more open way. Someone bumps into me hard, and they fall to the ground. "Oh, man I'm so sorry. I wasn't paying attention." Offering my hand. On the ground is a girl no older than me.

Timidly, she looks at me out from behind long curly brown bangs in her face. Her eyes are big, brown, and shining with excitement. "No, I'm sorry. I was lost in thought." She takes my hand. The noise, and presence of the crowd seem to fade into the background, leaving just the two of us. She stands and our eyes meet. "Who are you?" she asks.

"Kyle. You?"

"Ester."

I feel a dumb smile spread across my face. "I'm Kyle." I say again.

She smiles, with a wholesome grin. Ester reaches her right hand up to my face and I notice the blood trickling from her palm. I can't help but focus on the scarlet liquid.

Something slams into my chest, winding me. The metallic taste of blood fills my mouth. I look down to see a shadowy arm reaching into my chest. The sound of heavy breathing fills the air. I follow the arm up to a shadowy figure, a giant grin across its face. Its glowing violet eyes are wide and wild with excitement. "Squirm for me." It demands. It pulls me closer, bringing us face to face. "I love it when they squirm." It says reaching for my face with its right hand.

There's a burst of golden light from my chest. The creature dissipates. Fading into the light, laughing crazily. In that moment, everything gets loud as it all comes back into focus. People walking and talking, and Ester standing before me, the look of shock in her face. *What in the world was that?* I see that I have her by the wrist. I take a deep breath and relax my grip. "I'm sorry, but your hand is bleeding."

Ester blinks, bringing her eyes back into focus. She looks at her hand confused. She laughs taking her arm back. "I didn't even notice." Ester pulls out a cloth from the pocket on her floral print sundress and wraps her hand. She looks at me innocently. "I was just told that someone would make me see red and that person would hold my heart. As fate would have it, I think...I think that's you."

The thought of that thing having its hand in my chest, makes my skin crawl. "If you don't mind me asking, where did you hear that?"

"I was told this just recently by the lady at The Lover's Den up the way." Ester steps a little closer to me. My body goes through a maelstrom of feelings all at once. Panic, excitement, confusion, and longing. My head starts spinning. That is until I feel Valene's relaxing energy radiating from the soul drop.

Before she can take another step toward me, I step away. "Sorry I'm in a bit of a hurry. I have to go."

She looks at me bewildered. "Sure... I hope we meet again."

"Anything's possible. I'm sorry. Have a good day." I wave as I hurry off down the way.

As I approach the store, I hear yelling coming from inside. Cautiously, I enter the store and bells hanging above the door ring. "Hello?" I call out.

A silhouette appears in the bead curtain leading to the back room. It opens and Marie stands there looking at me with a smile. "Oh, my it's nice to see you again young master. How may I help you?"

"Is everything okay? I heard yelling."

"Oh, everything is fine. I'm in the middle of a session, and it was an exercise that got a little intense. If you wouldn't mind waiting, I'm almost done."

"Not at all." With the slight bow of her head, she disappears back behind curtain. I walk around the store, looking at her items. There are crystals, jewelry, trinkets, and vials of liquids on tables and shelves. Out of the corner of my eye, something moves across one of the shelves along the wall. Near the end of the shelf, my eye falls onto the creepy blank faced puppet the stuck Airca hidden amongst the items.

Minutes pass as I stare at the shelf full of dolls. The sound of the bead curtain rustling catches my attention. Marie, with her arm around another woman walks through the store to the front. I recognize her. It's Shayla, Gene's wife. "Remember, when you feel like you're not being heard make him hear you." Shayla nods. Her eyes shift to me, and I wave. She gives me a weary smile before hugging Marie and leaving. "May the goddess give you strength."

"Now. Kyle, was it? How may I be of service?"

"My friend, Airca. Has she been back here since our last visit?"

"Ah yes. A few times, she said she wanted to talk about a few things." She says giving me an obvious look.

I knew it. Even after I told her how dangerous it was to come here by herself. "What did you say to her? She's been acting odd."

"You mean like herself?" She walks up to me. "My dear, all I told her to do was to take a few days to figure out what she wanted. Then when she figured that out, to live by it and fight for it. How has she been doing?"

"I think that she's figured it out. She's thrown a few punches. She's made her move."

Excitedly Marie clasps her hands together. "Oh, I am so proud of her." She looks at me, a sly smirk on her face. "And? What was the answer?"

"That I've made my choice."

The excitement drains from her face. Her eyes become distant, and her face starts to twist up. "I see." She takes a deep breath, fixing her face. "Well then, it's a shame. That girl really cares for you."

"I know and I care for her too but, she should let it go."

She stares at me for a second then crosses her arms. That sly smirk returns as she walks up to me tapping her finger on her arm. "What about you, Romeo? Have you let go of the sun?"

Is she quoting Romeo and Juliet? We just read this. What was the line after he says that to her on the balcony? "Marie, I love my friend, but she is not the sun. My sun is golden, and not green like the envious moon."

She gets tense a bit, before laughing it off. "Really? Maybe you should you take some time think about what it is that you want."

I touch the amulet on my chest. "I know who I want."

"Most people much older than you don't have a clue as to what they want, but we shall see. Is there anything else I can help you with?"

"No."

"Well then, may the rest of your day be filled with love." She says with a slight bow. She walks into the back.

As I make my way to door, there's shuffling behind me at the counter. *The doll?* It was still on the shelf, but it feels like it's focused on me now. I look at the shelf filled with dolls, and they all seem to be focused on me as well. *Yeah, it's time to go.* I turn to leave when a sharp pain shoots up the back of my neck, like I'd been stung by something. I check, but there was nothing there not even a bump. I look back over my shoulder and the doll hasn't moved. I leave out of the store as fast as possible.

As the open air hits my face, my vision blurs and my head start to swim. My legs nearly give out from under me, but I manage to stay up grabbing onto a bench. "What in the world?" I stumble a bit as I take a seat. My eyes become so heavy that I can barely keep them open. I put my face down into my hands and take a deep breath. "I have to get home...I ...have...to..." Everything goes dark.

Chapter 19

With a shuddering breath, I come to, laying on the ground. My vision is blurry but after a second it clears and I'm staring up at the thick canopy of the trees around me. *Where am I? A forest?* The ground is hard and cold. The smell of wet grass and decaying leaves all around me.

The leaves above me rustle in the wind, allowing beams of light to shine right into my face. Fighting my stiff body, I roll over onto my side and look out into the dense wood. "I'm in a forest?" I hold my hand out. As the light shines down, it casts a shadow off my arm. "I'm not astral projecting. Then how did I get here?"

A branch snaps in the distance. Loud footsteps echo through the dense woods getting closer. Struggling against my achy body, I crawl behind one of the trees out of sight. The steps grow louder, and I can feel myself start to panic. I take a few deep breaths, trying to calm myself. The steps stop just on the other side of the tree. I'm as quiet and as still as possible. *The last time something like this happened I watched a guy get killed and possessed. I think I should leave.*

Slowly, I peek out from around the tree. A figure shrouded in a veil of flowing darkness stands there looking up to the sky. "Are you here?" The shrouded person asks, its voice light and distorted.

The ground rumbles, shaking the trees and rattling the leaves. It stops. There is dead silence, and the cloaked figure just stands there.

A torrent of wind splits the canopy allowing the sunlight to shine through. My ears begin to ring with a high-pitched squeal. It gets louder and louder until it feels like someone was racking something across my brain. I close my eyes and bare it until the squealing subsides to the sound of clapping. "What an entrance. It is an honor to finally meet you." Says the cloaked figure.

I open my eyes and look back out around the tree. Standing before the cloaked person now was a figure made of a bright red and white flame. The light coming from makes all the shadows disappear. The only darkness in its presence is the person cloaked in it. The trees all tremble, as they seem to move away from the heat coming from it. "Enough, *Asvanus.*" The fiery being says, its voice booming, deafening, and frightening. *Asvanus? That's Durabi duprima but why didn't it translate.* "Do you have what I have asked for?" It continues. Its voice rattles me. Even plugging my ears doesn't help. It's as though with its every breath I was getting closer to passing out.

The dark figure is unfazed. It chuckles in amusement. "Oh, but of course." From under the veil of darkness the figure outstretches its arm. Within their fingertips was a shimmering jewel the size of a marble. "It's all here. A map of its location, and the incantation to control it." The fiery being steps forward to take it, but the dark figure takes the jewel into its hand. "Ah-ah-ah, not so fast my friend. Before I give you this. Do you have the Information that I require?"

The fiery being grumbles with annoyance. It reaches into itself and pulls out a rolled piece of parchment. "Everything that you'll need to know about your targets. Past and present."

The dark figure reproduces the jewel, in the opposite hand. They stare intensely at one another, and then make their exchange. "It was a pleasure doing business with you." The dark figure says.

"The feeling isn't mutual."

There's a snap of the branch behind me. I duck back behind the tree, to face the source of the sound. I jump back as I come face to face with a white theater mask, that had a curious face molded onto it. "Hello mister. You aren't supposed to be here." It says with the voice of a young boy.

"You didn't come alone as agreed?" The fiery figure asks its voice laced with anger.

"Neither did you. So, don't act so high and mighty."

The fiery being grumbles. The earth beneath me trembles, and my body wavers under the pressure of its presence. I do my best to hold strong, even though my heart is beating a thousand times a minute. Still staring at me, playing with his dingy white nightgown, this kid just giggles, not paying the atmosphere any attention.

"We are done here." The fiery being bellows. In a flash of light, the overwhelming presence and heat of the fiery being vanishes.

It's silent for a bit. My hands tremble with fearful anticipation of what was to come. "Little one. Bring him to me." The dark figure orders, its voice now full and menacing.

The kid shifts his head to the side and the curios face of the mask twists up into a smile. "Hey mister let's play a game. How about tag. I'll be it first. One. Two. Three..."

Without any hesitation I'm on my feet and run as fast as I can through the wood. I know when dealing with demons you're not supposed to run, but these things are far beyond me. And there's no way I would survive an encounter with them. "Six." I hear the kid say not far behind me. "Seven..." He says even further away. "Eight...Nine..." I push energy into my legs and everything around me blurs.

I stop running after a while to catch my breath. *There should be no way for this kid to catch up with me.* Besides my heart pounding in my ears everything is silent. *I don't know how far I traveled, but hopefully it's far enough.* "Ten." The kid whispers right in my ear. I snap to the right to see the kid next to me. His tar black hand touching my arm. "Tag."

The ground under my feet gives, and I begin to sink. Frantic, I struggle against its pull, but before I know it, I'm up to my neck. The kid stands over me laughing as his mask twists up into a terrifying smile. His hollow white eyes peering out from the amused eye slits.

"Good boy." I hear the dark figure's voice. He appears behind the kid. "Raise him."

Something like tentacles wrap around me in the dirt. They lift me out of the ground until I am at eye level with the figure. Their face is hidden within the darkness, but their eyes shine through. Colors dance within them. White, red and black all swirl together until they make a hue of deep purple that I've only seen in the morning and evening light, Twilight.

Without warning the Figure grabs my face, turning it from side to side. They chuckle. "You really are going to be a thorn in my side again, aren't you boy."

Again? He turns me back to him, the color of his eyes are no longer the twilight purple but crimson red. My mouth gets dry as I recognize them, from my nightmares. "Beal?!"

"To think that we would meet so soon. I'd thought you would be dead by now, but it would seem fate smiles upon you. No matter. Your luck runs out today." The hand holding onto my face starts to glow with a pale purple light. Like the blades of the Atropos had when she cut the thread.

I start to struggle against his hold, trying to pull away, but the tentacles squeeze tighter holding me still. *What am I going to do? How can I...* out nowhere my chest tightens, making me scream out. It feels like someone was holding something hot to it making my blood boil. I look at Beal and he's looking at me with such confusion. *Was he not doing this?* I scream again as the heat spreads like wildfire through my body. Creeping to the tips of my fingers and toes, up my back and onto my neck. A shock of energy punches me in the chest. My stomach clenches and I feel the gagging sensation when you're about to vomit.

I close my eyes as everything comes up and out. Beal lets go of me, gasping. "What in the Realms?" he yells. I open my eyes to see black slime all on the ground and all over Beal. His eyes swirling with rage and disgust.

There's another surge that takes my breath away. The burning intensifies burrowing through me, and I lose feeling in my hands and feet. Beal and the kid watch in bewilderment at whatever was happening to me. As the numbness reaches up my neck my vision starts to fade, burning away at the edges. I scream as I'm engulfed and the two of them vanish like sand in the wind.

I wake up, gasping for air and staring up at the morning sky. My mouth is gross and my body stiff. The burning energy surging from my chest through my body fades and I relax. I look around to see that I was on a roof looking out over my neighborhood. My fingers are driven deep in the shingles, clenched for dear life. With a deep breath, I remove them. They're trembling and covered in blood. "Where am I? What happened? Whose blood is this?"

"Yours." Says a voice from behind me.

I turn to see Airca leaning out of the window. An amused smile on her face, but bags under her eyes. "Airca?"

"Hey"

"What's happening? I was just in a forest and I met..." I can't tell her about Beal. I don't want to say his name just in case it summons him. "How did I get here?"

"You don't remember?"

"Before the forest? All I remember is sitting on a bench and passing out." Airca climbs out of her window and walks over to me. She stands over me, before straddling and kissing me. I push her back from me. "Airca what are you doing?"

"Reminding you." She kisses me harder.

I struggle to get her off me when flashes of last night come to me.

Airca appears standing tall in front of me. She looks at me, her gaze a bit distant, but fixed on me. She takes my hands and places them on her waist. I try to let her go, but a jolt of pain from my neck causes me to seize, blurring my vision.

She's on me now, both of her hands gripping my face, while she gazes into my eyes. Slowly she inches closer. I can feel the warmth of her lips near mine.

'Kiss her. Go ahead. This is what you've wanted right? Since you were young.' says a voice right into my ear.

"Yeah. It is."

'She, is what you've always wanted.'

"For a long time."

The pain in my neck recedes allowing me to finally relax. I wrap my arms around her and she does the same. 'Just give in. Show her how much you love her. Desire her.'

"I love...I love." My chest grows hot and heavy. I can't really catch my breath.

'Who do you love?'

"I love...I love..."

A smile spreads across Airca's face as she moves in to seal the kiss. "Me, right?" she says softly.

I close my eyes in anticipation. In the darkness, Felicia, Valene stands in front of me, tears welling in her black eyes. I place my hand on my chest. The second my fingers touch the bulge adhered to my chest; a shock runs up my arm.

I open my eyes and see red. Airca has a look of worry and fear as she holds my face. 'Who do you love?' I hear the voice ask. 'ANSWER ME!' The command rings loud in my ear. The muscles of my neck tense making me snap my head back. 'Who do you love!?'

"I love...I love..." I manage. A shockwave of energy slams into my chest, taking my breath away. I stand, shoving Airca off me as It surges through my whole body, setting my skin and my insides on fire. Another shock hits me, and my legs give out. On the floor, I try to catch my breath, but I can't. My chest is so tight. Everything is hot. Sweat runs down my face, while a new heat slowly creeps from the amulet and into my chest. I feel it burrowing through me. Making its way to my neck. The pain intensifies as the heat wraps around my neck, and everything goes black.

I push her back. She smiles biting her lip. "You were...we were." I look at her. "Did we? Did anything happen?"

She sighs, her smile fading a bit. "No, nothing happened. We were about to when you freaked out and came out here. You've been sitting there frozen, for hours."

"Hours?" I look out over the neighborhood to the sun peaking over the horizon.

Her hand touches my face, startling me. They're so cold. "Come inside. Maybe now we can continue."

"Continue? Airca, no. I need to go. I was supposed to be with Valene."

She grips both sides of face hard, digging her nails into my skin. "Don't go." She says a bit frantic.

I stare into her eyes. They're still distant, but now trembling. With some force I take her hands from my face and push her off me. I try to stand but my legs are shaky. With deep breath, I manage to stay up. "I have to go."

She grabs my leg, "No please. Can't we talk?"

"Airca let me go, now." I growl, out of breath. Slowly she lets me go and sits back on the roof with A blank expression.

I look at her and sigh. "I'm sorry." I shadow-walk away.

I appear in the foyer at the Kir Manor. My head is spinning, and I'm on the verge of vomiting again. The tinny taste of blood and whatever that black stuff was is heavy in my mouth. No one is out here. It's still early, they're probably still in the training area.

With a deep breath I shadow-walk again. The moment I exit the darkness, something drives into my stomach, taking my breath and the last bit of strength I have left in my legs. I fall to my hands and knees and gasping and gagging. *What in the world just hit me?* Something hits me hard in the side, sending me sliding across the floor until I slam into one of the mirrored walls. In all the confusion, pain and the inability to breath I manage to quickly roll to my side and curl up into a ball.

In the mirror I see the reflection of my attacker. In the splintered glass I see... *Valene?* She walks towards me, her golden eyes ablaze with power. I curl tighter into a ball as I see her get right over me. "Stand up." She says with a growl." I don't move. Her energy surges making my skin crawl. "I said GET UP!" I can't help but start trembling as her energy swells. I've never felt her so raw, and angry. Even when she dealt with Michael.

"Valene...give me some space, please." I manage. In the mirror Valene's eyes squint. She takes a step back. I relax out of the ball. Using the wall as support I stand, my back to her. "Valene, what's all of this about?" I ask out of breath.

"Wha...what's all of this about?!" Her fist slams into the wall right next to me, shattering the mirror. "You ask me that after what you said to me last night? Where did you go?"

"I don't...Valene I don't remember last..."

"Where did you go last night?" She snarls.

"I...I woke up at Airca's."

I slam against the wall, the mirror cracking under me. "You disrespect me, and then run to her?" Her voice cracking.

"No that's not." She pushes me harder.

"Why shouldn't I rip you and her apart?"

"*Ast yerfek Valene. Nu trado.* (Believe me Valene. I did not betray.)" I grind out under her strength, in *Durabi.*

"How dare you. How dare you lie to me? Look me in the eye and say that." She takes my shoulder, spins me around and slams me back into the wall. "SAY IT!" Her voice resonates with power.

I look her right in the eyes. "Valene, I didn't betray you." I say out of breath.

Valene growls. Her eyes shining brighter. Before she says something, a hand touches her shoulder. "Valene, dear let him go. He speaks the truth." Selene says softly.

"Mother stay out of this. He must..."

Selene's grip on her daughter's shoulder tightens. "Let him go, before you hurt him further."

"He's not hurt, yet."

Selene yanks Valene off me and she falls to the ground. "Valene, are you so blinded by your own rage? Look at him."

Valene looks from her mother to me. Almost immediately, the rage on her face changes to shock. "Where did all that blood come from? Did I do that?"

"No, I don't really know what happened. I just woke up at Airca's like this." My legs start to shake. I slide down the wall until I'm on the ground, level with Valene. The shine of Valene's eyes dims until they become normal. They are red and puffy. Streaks of black make-up stain her cheeks. *She's been crying.*

"Kyle." Selene says kneeling next to me. "What was the last thing that you remember about yesterday?"

"After Felica and I parted ways, I went to market to figure out why Airca had gone there. Before I knew it I passed out on a bench."

"You don't remember last night?" Valene asks.

"No. The only thing that I remember is meeting B..." My stomach tenses, and I throw up so hard that it takes my breath away. Everything starts to spin, before my vison starts going dark. I hit ground unable to breath.

"Kyle! Kyle! Zel get in here hurry!" I hear Selene yell before everything goes dark.

Chapter 20

As I float through the darkness, I hear barking in the distance. The weight of my body becomes apparent, and my fingers and toes start to tingle. A combination of barking and growling is right in front of me now. I open my eyes. Everything comes into focus and Smoke stands before me, the fur on his back standing on end, black smoke bellowing from him. Beyond him standing in the vast plane of static I can see the outline of the creature he had protected me from before.

He lets out a loud squeak of bark and takes off toward the thing. The creature jumps back, just barely missing being bitten. Smoke turns, quickly to pursue like he's done countless times with his siblings. Without hesitation he jumps at the creature. It swings its arm, slamming its claw into the smoldering pup. Smoke hits the ground with a small yelp. Without skipping a beat he's back up on his feet and starts to circle, putting himself between me and it. "Leave my master alone!"

The creature says something, but it just sounds like white noise.

The smoke on his back starts to turn white and his growl lowers a few octaves. He takes off at the thing, chomping at its feet. *I have to help, somehow.* I try get myself up, but my body won't move. Smoke's eyes dart towards me as he notices me moving.

In that moment the creature kicks him hard in the side, sending him sliding out into the static world. Then Its attention turns to me. My heart is pounding in my chest as it stomps towards me. I try to move but everything is numb. Now it stands over me breathing hard from its bout with Smoke. It drops onto me and wraps its hands around my neck. It says something, but all I hear is white noise. Its grip tightens.

"Let him go!" Smoke yells. He appears on the back of the creature and bites down hard onto the side of its neck. It lets me go, shaking, fighting against Smoke's hold.

Even though I can breathe, everything starts fading. The creature manages to get Smoke off. Everything goes dark as I watch them continue to fight. *Smoke!*

"Smoke!" I yell opening my eyes. Above me is the enchanted ceiling of my room. The sun was high in the air, but it looked closer to the latter half of noon. Something shifts on the bed next to me. I sit up a little to see Smoke curled up next to me, fast asleep. "Smoke?" I place my hand on his head. He shivers as his eyes open. He looks at me, a weariness on his little puppy face. "You okay buddy?"

Smoke licks my hand. An image of a thumbs up pops into my head, but it's blurry. He gets up and hops off the bed. There's a wave of heat and Smoke's presence vanishes. "That was like, totally odd." Zel says next to me.

To my right, sitting in a chair is Zel. He's as stiff as a statue, wearing his off-day attire of board shorts, thong sandals and the vest of his suit, open showing off his chiseled body. With loud cracks, his body relaxes out of the rigidness and looks at me. "What do you mean?" I ask.

"Little dude hasn't left your side since you went down. Hadn't woken up since either."

"Wait, how long have I been down? What happened to me?"

"Well, you've gone through a bit of a ringer Master Kyle bro. Not only did Lady V like almost rip you apart, but it would seem you were like totally cursed."

"Cursed?"

"Yeah man. Like hexed to the max."

"Okay how? By what?"

"I don't know. It could have happened at any time. What's like, the last thing you remember?"

"I was in the market. Went to see someone I knew. Got stung by a bee or something on my neck. And once I sat down on a bench everything is a blank. That is until I woke up at Airca's."

"Sit up for me." I get up. Zel places his hand onto the back of my neck. I jump away from him because his hand is as cold as stone in the winter. "Sorry. My body doesn't generate heat when I'm a total stiff." He rubs his hands together, before touching me again with some warmth.

He's silent for a minute. Not taking a breath. Not moving. Just a statue. *How could this of happened? Could it of been Marie? No, she wasn't even in the room, and I didn't take anything from her. Maybe it was Ben. No. I doubt he would stoop to something so low. He'd want to fight face to face so he could gloat. Who would want to curse me?* "You find anything?" I ask.

Zel takes a sharp breath, and his body comes back to life. "Sorry Master Kyle bro not a thing. It was like completely purged from your body." He says taking his hand from my neck.

"By what?"

"It's totally all thanks to this little beauty here." He says pointing at the amulet. "Before the curse could completely settle in, the Amulet was all like **"YOU SHALL NOT PASS!"** and like totally Gandalfed it."

"Thank goodness I had it. Wait, Valene didn't see it did she?"

"Master bro Everything's totally copacetic. Lady V didn't see a thing. I'm the one that cleaned you up and everything."

"Thank you."

"No worries Master bro, I got you. Besides, Lady V hasn't come in to see you since the first day you were out."

"That's right. How long was I out for?"

"Like, two whole days. This is technically the third." *What?!*

I instantly start looking for my phone. It's on the nightstand to my left. On the screen was a notification. 'Missed appointment. June 10th Our Anniversary.'

"Crap!"

"What? What happened."

"Today's the 13th of June. Which means, our anniversary was three days ago, the 10th. When all of this went down."

"Whoa, bummer."

"Right." I place my face into my hands. "What am I going to do?" I ask through a sigh. *Wait, she didn't know the date of our anniversary. I can still salvage this.* "Zel you wouldn't happen to know of a nice restaurant I could take Valene to?"

"Master Kyle bro, I'm going to completely level with you. I don't think you should try to do anything with her just yet. Lady V, is like totally up a wall right now."

"I know. I just...I've worked so hard for this moment. I can't skip out on it now."

Zel smiles. "Bro, it's your funeral. Let's see. There is this like really awesome place in the Market she's said she's wanted to go to a few times." I rub the back of my neck. *I'm sick of that place.* "It's pretty high end though. They require reservations months in advance."

"Months?!" I flop back onto the bed. The goblin Rain comes to mind. 'If you need anything.'

"I may have a way around that. I just need to go back to the market."

"Sounds like a plan."

"Zel one more thing. Could you please continue to keep an eye on Smoke."

"You got it. If you're all good I'll take my leave now." He says standing.

"All good."

He smiles, "Far out. Peace out Master Kyle bro." He says melting into the floor.

With a deep breath I roll over to the edge of bed, get to my feet and make my way to the bathroom. I wash up, throw on some clothes and shadow-walk to Market's entrance.

I give the sacrifice and enter t. For a while I wander the bazar, looking for Rain. His stand isn't in the same place as last time. *Come on Rain how are you supposed to have frequent costumers if you move around so much?* I sit down on a bench, watching all the people walk by with bags in hand, talking to one another, paying me no mind. A chill runs down my spine. The back of my neck aches a bit as I recognize the area. *Is this the bench I sat on? What happened after this? I don't remember.* I put my face into my hands. Trying to recall something. Anything.

"Kyle?" someone asks startling me.

I look up to see Gene standing in front me, wearing jeans, a t-shirt and some work boots. "Oh, hey Gene."

"Are you okay? You look like you're going through something."

"It's nothing. Just trying to remember something. What are you doing here?"

He crosses his arms, a bit embarrassed. "I came to see Marie. For some advice."

I remember seeing his wife Shay in the Lovers Den before sitting out here. Going through some sort of scream therapy. "Are you and Shay doing okay? With the therapy and all?"

"Oh yeah, we're great. Better than we've ever been." He says confidently, but there's doubt on his face. "She's just been different lately."

"Different how?"

"A little more aggressive. I know she's been having private sessions with Marie, so I just wanted to see what they've been doing. Unfortunately, the store is closed. So, what are you doing here? Looking for advice about your friend Airca?"

"No. I'm actually here looking for a Goblin."

"You mean Rain, right? The little goblin that wears the suit?"

"Yeah. You've seen him?"

"He's right down the street on the right." He says pointing down the crowded street.

"Thank you. I've been wandering around this place for an hour looking for him. I'll catch you later."

I walk by him in the direction he pointed. Gene places his hand on my shoulder stopping me. "Hey before you go. You seem like a good kid. Are you in school still?" He asks cautiously.

"No, I just graduated high school."

"Really?! How old are you?"

"I just turned eighteen." He looks at me, surprised. "What?"

"Nothing. I just thought...Nothing." He rummages through his pockets and pulls out a business card. "Look give me a call when you're free. I'm looking for someone like you to add to our ranks at Umbra."

I take the card. In bold black text it reads, **Umbra Security**. "A job?"

"Willing to hear me out?"

"Ah sure. I'll let you know."

"Good. I'll talk to you later." He says offering his hand.

I take and firmly shake it. "Yeah."

We part ways and I make way toward Rain. At the end of the street, I come upon a small crowd gawking at the living jewelry on the stand. "Kid!" The goblin's nasally voice rings out from behind the crowd. I step up to the table. "So, what brings you back around and where's that beautiful human of yours?"

"I wanted to cash in that favor."

"Hmm, that was fast."

"Well, this is pretty important."

"What pray tell could I do for ya?"

"There's this fancy restaurant somewhere here in the market, that you need a reservation for months in advanced."

"Ah, yes. "The taste of darkness". They're so exclusive that you need a spell to even see it."

"You think you can get me a table for two?"

His big ears droop. "That one's a toughie, kid. I know the owner, but I owe him a debt and asking for something while still indebted is never a good move."

"What kind of debt?"

"A life debt."

Okay. How can I make this happen? The only thing I have worth life is this amulet. I don't have any real currency. All I have is energy. "What if I could get you the energy equivalent to your life."

He snorts, cocking his head to the side in confusion. "Energy equivalent? Are you going to harvest the soul of another goblin for me?"

"What? No. Just answer my question." Rain grumbles, his brow low in skepticism. "Compared to a human how long does a goblin live for?"

"Goblins are fairly short lived compared to the other sihde." *Sidhe?* "But Compared to humans we live three times as long."

"So, about three dytics?" I turn around and look out into the crowd and concentrate. My eyes begin to focus. Some of the color of the world fades away leaving a gray scale. Instead of fading away like normal, everyone's features become apparent and more pronounced. I see every scar, and blemish on their skin. Every emotion passing through their eyes, face, and body. Then there's the different color of the smoke like energy rising off them. *I can see the energy that comes off Valene fine, but this is new being able to see it off everyone else. I wonder if this is how Valene sees things with the sight. Alright focus.*

My eye falls onto one of the many humans in the crowd. The hole in their chest looks as though a piece of them has withered away. I touch my own chest. There is no hole, but the tips of my finger touch the warm metal of the closed amulet adhered to my skin. It too pulses with energy, but it's different; It's dense, volatile, and hot. Almost like fire.

From the energy radiating off the humans, tuffs of white smoke aimlessly float into the air before dissipating. *What's that?* I reach my hand out and try to pull at it like I would with any other energy, but it doesn't move. It's like it's locked in place. I take a deep breath and focus. Sweat starts to form on my forehead. "Move." I say under my breath, gripping the air struggling to manipulate this energy. The white smoke shifts in my direction, before it has the chance to disappear. *Gotcha.* It rushes to my hand. As it touches my fingers I can feel its weight, and the heat coming from it. Just like the energy in the amulet.

"Rain, do you have a vial?" Rain digs into one of his many bags. He hands me a sizable one. He places it on the table, and I place my right palm over the opening. Focusing on the feeling of the energy, I draw from the air and into my left palm. It surges through me like liquid fire. I fight to stop myself from trembling from the pain, as a thick shimmering white substance begins to slowly trickle from my palm into the vial. Rain watches, awe stricken as it fills.

I pull the dissipating energies from the crowd of people around the stand. Once it feels like the same amount that was in the amulet I stop channeling the energy, remove my hand from the vial and cork it. Rain picks it up, his big yellow eyes mesmerized by the ethereal shine of the liquid energy. "it's beating. Like a heart."

I'm a little out of breath. My hands won't stop shaking because they burns. "That should be about three *dytics* worth of energy. Will that be enough?"

"And then some." He looks at me, and I can see his mind turn, working something out. "Kid, do this for me one more time and anything you ask for, if it is within my power, Will be done for as long as I live. Deal?" he asks holding out his claw.

I don't think I can do that again without taking some serious damage...but. "Anything?"

"Any and everything." He says without any hesitation.

Never hurts to have connections with someone like Rain. Even if he's a creep. I take his claw and shake. "Deal. Hand me a Vial."

"No." He takes one of the hoop earrings from his ear and places it in my left hand. "Use this. Fill this up."

I start again, pulling at the white energy from the crowd. It moves a little easier this time as I channel it into the earring instead of through me. The piece of jewelry starts to glow white and burn in my palm. After a moment, it stops. "Done." I say dropping the earring. Rain catches it, giddily dancing. "Wonderful. Just wonderful."

"Happy you like it." I say looking at my hands. Both of my palms are twisted by burns from handling the energy. *I hope this heals.*

"Amazing. To be able to do this. You're amazing kid."

"It's just like channeling energy. Sort of." He looks at me a little concerned. "What?"

"No. What you're doing here is technically impossible."

"What do you mean?"

"Kid, this is life energy. It's what moves us. Keeps us breathing. It's not like what you use to cast spells or fight with. I mean you can, but it'll kill you if you run out rather than fatigue you."

"There's a difference?"

"How are you a demon and don't understand how the soul works?"

"What?! Was I just taking peoples souls?"

"No no no, that would have been easier actually." He holds up the vial. "This is the essence of being. The fire that keeps the engine running, where the soul is the actual source and the energy you use and manipulate is the heat from said fire. Are you following?"

"A little. So, in terms of a fire. The soul is the wood, the life energy is the flame itself and normal energy the heat given off it."

"Correct. Now the taking of life energy isn't unheard of. The vampire and their ilk do this through ingesting blood, flesh, and emotions which it is present in. Not in abundance, which is why they tend to gorge themselves. Others do it by siphoning the energy through a spell. Or in a demons' case, they go straight to the source by devouring souls. Making you stronger."

"So adding more wood to their fire."

Rain taps his nose. "Right on the nose. More wood, more fire, more heat."

"More souls, more life energy, more power."

"But you kid. You're reaching right into the flame and taking it. Just plucking it from the air, and putting into a bottle. It's astounding."

This sounds dangerous. If anyone found out I could do this, I would be hunted down. I look at Rain, and he smiles. "No worries kid. Only you and I will ever know of this. I swear it by the lady, Queen, and Mother of summer. Nothing about this will ever come from my lips."

I stare at him for a second considering the wording of his promise. "Or your hands. You won't write about this either."

Rain's ears drop back, as he looks at me with a dark smile. "You may seem naive, but you are a trickster."

"Takes one to know one. Do you swear?"

"I swear it on my soul. I will not speak nor write of this" The air fills with power as he finishes his vow.

He places the earring back onto his ear, shuddering. He dances, like a kid that just got candy. "So, when do you need this reservation by?"

"Tomorrow evening around seven?"

"Done. I'll make sure everything is taken care of."

"Really? Thanks Rain."

"No no no, thank you."

I leave the tent, keeping an eye on the humans in the crowd. They didn't seem fatigued, or drained. They are just as chipper as they had been Prior. *Thank the Creator.*

As I leave the Market, I pull out my cell and dial Valene. It rings and rings. To the point it's about to go to voice mail. There's a click but silence. "Hello?" I ask.

"You're awake. Thank the Creator. Are you okay?"

"Yeah, I'm fine. I've been awake for a few hours now. Are you okay?"

"Not really."

"Can we talk about it over dinner?"

"I don't think I'm up to it tonight."

"Not tonight. Tomorrow."

She's silent. "Kyle, I don't know. I'm not all the way okay yet."

"I get that. But I'd rather you try and talk to me, instead of distancing yourself from me... please."

She sighs. "Okay."

"Thank you. I'll be by to get you around six. Oh, and wear something nice."

"See you tomorrow."

"See you tomorrow, Valene." She hangs up. *Well, that went well. Hopefully tomorrow does too.*

Chapter 21

Out of the darkness of sleep the loud whine of my alarm drags me to the waking world. I tap the button turning it over to the radio. "Good morning my lovelies you've tuned into WNRK the roc. You're listening to the morning report and I'm your favorite Disk Jockey Alice J. So, guys, I got some big news. My boyfriend has finally asked me the big question. And I said yes."

"Oh, my goodness it's about time. You guys have been dating forever." Someone else says on the air.

"Right. But it was worth the wait. Hey, I know you're listening babe. I love you. We'll be back after this short break."

I turn it off the rest of the way and roll onto my back. I try imagining myself kneeling before Valene like she had to me when we were in Olympus. Promising to be with her forever. I touch the amulet. *How could I even think of Marriage when I haven't even given her this Amulet. Or even told her that I loved her. But with everything that's been happening I wonder how she feels?*

The space of the room begins to shift as energy pours into. My attention shifts to the door and there's a knock. "Come in." The door opens and Jason walks through wearing his normal workout gear. "Oh, this is way better than shadow-walking. Morning Bro."

"Morning."

"How are you feeling?"

I sit up on the side of the bed. "I'm up and running."

"Cool. She sure did a number on you."

"You were there?"

"Yeah, it was morning training."

"I didn't notice you while I was being, thrown around."

"Better you than me." He says laughing nervously.

"Yeah, you're a jerk."

Worry touches his golden eyes. He sits on the bed next to me. "Bro, are you really, okay? I'm used to seeing a lot of blood and my sister angry, but that was kind of scary. I thought you were really going to..."

I pat him on his shoulder. "Jason I'm fine. Thank you." He wraps his arms around me for a hug. "I'm fine." I say hugging him back.

He gets to his feet. "Alright enough of this sissy stuff. You good to work out?"

"Of course. Let's do it here though."

"Cool."

I throw on some clothes and we make our way downstairs. In the kitchen, Serena is at the table sipping tea. "Morning hun. Jason." She says drily.

"Serena." He says in an exaggerated mocking tone.

She glares at him, before looking back to me. "What are you two up to?"

"About to go out back for our normal routine."

Mayra struts out from the living room, wearing clothes. "You two are about to work out? Serena will join you."

Serena nearly chokes on her tea. "Wait, what?"

"I have taken notice of how sluggish you've gotten sister. And that pudge you've got growing." Serena looks down at her stomach in shock. "Come on get dressed. I'll be over seeing your training."

"This is unfair. I can out class them both with my eyes closed."

"Oh really? Kyle, tell me what are your and Jason's normal routine?"

"Well, for warm up we do pushups, sit-ups, and squats. I max-out at two hundred."

"I'm at six hundred." Jason says proudly."

"Then we spar until one of us is knocked down. All while extending our energy."

Serena looks at us her mouth open in confusion. "Oh."

"I expect you to outclass them sister. You two go on ahead we'll be right behind you."

Outside Jason and I start our warmup. Minutes later Serena and Mayra come out. Serena files in and starts with us. I finish my warmup set first, followed shortly by Jason. Serena was struggling a bit to catch her breath and to keep up. Mayra watches over from the patio, an amused smile across her face.

Jason and I face off, forcing our energy out like his mother showed us. We just stare at one another trying to figure out how to move through the strain. I manage to take a few steps forward beginning to look for openings in his guard. As he takes a step toward me, my vision starts to swirl. With a deep breath I try to focus, but I can feel my control wain. I put my hand up, forfeiting the round. I sit down on the ground, slowly drawing the energy back in. "Sorry Jason. I'm a little more tired than I thought."

He takes a deep breath. "It's cool bro. I could barely move myself."

"You two have grown exponentially. Especially you little brother. I am pleasantly surprised."

"How can... you two... do this?" Serena asks between breaths.

"We do it without energy too. Cheater." Jason says standing over her.

"What?!"

"How long has it been since you worked with the Kirs?" I ask.

Mayra crosses her arms, smiling. "Too long it would seem. You heard him sister. Release your energy and continue." Serena groans struggling to stay up. "Jason, you make sure she doesn't stop. Kyle come sit with me."

As I get to my feet my vision blurs, and the world starts to spin. I close my eyes, steady myself and take a deep breath. "Kyle?" I hear Mayra, but it's a little far away. "Are you okay?" She asks even further away.

"I'm good I just stood up too...fast." I'm not in the backyard anymore but a plain of mist. Like the world from the oculus. "Mayra? Serena? Jason!?" I call out. My voice doesn't carry far, it muffles into silence. "What's going on?"

"It worked. You're here." says a voice from behind me.

I snap around, but there's no one. "Who's there?"

"I've been waiting for so long for this to work." The voice says from behind me again. "To summon you." The voice radiates from all around me.

To summon me? Why would anyone want to summon me? Or are they trying to summon Shadow? "Well, I'm here, I guess. Now show yourself." The mist at my feet disperses in with a small gust of wind. Before me a shadowy figure appears, down on all fours. Its head hangs as it chants incoherent words. "Who are you and why have you summoned me?" I ask.

It stops and slowly raises its head. I take a step back as I see that its face is shapeless. Like it was wearing a featureless flesh mask. "I am love. And you are loved."

"Okay?" I try to step away, but my feet won't budge. The being begins to chant nonsensical words again, but each syllable is filled with so much power that it makes my skin burn with each utterance. Lines begin to etch in the ground, encircling me and forming a star within a circle, a pentagram. A nasty looking dagger with a twisted blade appears in this shadow person's hand. It pricks its finger on the tip of the blade, drawing blood. The blood drips onto the pentagram.

With a flash, etchings turn red emitting a low light. As it washes over me, every muscle in my body tightens. "What are you doing...to...me?" My mind starts to get fuzzy.

It places the knife on the ground, before producing a small vial filled with a black liquid. It pops the cork off, and carefully drips its blood into it. As the two mix is turns into a dirty green. Quickly, the being drinks the mixture. "Kyle Benjamin Ross."

At the sound of my whole name, it feels like someone just hit me over the head with a bat. My everything kind of goes topsy-turvy and I relax to the point where I start laughing. "What can I do for you?"

"I want you to be mine?"

"How?"

"I want you to love me."

I giggle uncontrollably. "You want me to love you. I have a girlfriend. I can't love you."

"You will. Kyle Benjamin Ross you will be mine."

There's a pull at my mind and I can feel words starting to form in my mouth. "I...am..."

"You will tell me what I wish to know. What will you be to me?" they ask, this time energy oozing from them and their words.

The energy rushes up my body, wrapping around my throat and tongue. "I...I am...yours." I struggle.

"That's right. You are now and forever. You will belong to no other." My heart races as the foreign energy spreads to every muscle. "Say it. You are...?"

"I... am ...yours, now...and forever."

"And you will belong to no other."

"I...I..." I struggle to stop talking, but I can't. The only thing that I manage is to laugh. "I will belong to no other."

"One more time. You are...?

The energy constricts me. Like heavy chains being draped over my shoulders and wrapped around my arms and legs. "And...and..." *Stop talking, stop talking. Don't give in to it. Don't finish.*

I look this being right in the face defiant. The being takes the dagger in its hand before getting to its feet. "Say it!" It screams pointing the dagger at me.

I'm jarred as the energy reacts to its impatience, setting my body a blaze with pain. "And I...am...you..."

There's a loud growl from behind me, catching both of our attention. The being gasps as they step back away from the edge of the circle. Clawed hands, covered in a fine black fur stretch out from behind me. One covers my mouth and the other wraps around my body holding me close. "What are you?" the being asks, It's voice trembling.

"You have no power here." The creature says from behind me. It's growling voice resonating with a harsh power. "Be GONE!" It roars.

There is a flash of light. The being screams and we are all engulfed by the blazing light.

"Wake up." The creature whispers in my ear.

"Kyle..." I hear someone call, their voice distant. "Kyle hunny, wake up."

The blinding light fades as the world comes into focus. I'm still outside. Serena stands in front of me. Her deep brown eyes riddled with worry and fear. I try to speak but my mouth is covered. I look over my shoulder to see Mayra. Her eyes are blood red and filled with rage.

Serena places her hands onto my shoulders. "Kyle. Who are you? Tell me your full name. Middle and all"

Mayra slowly lowers her hand. "My name is Kyle Benjamin Ross."

"And whom do you belong to?"

"What are you asking?"

Mayra squeezes me a little tighter. "Please little brother, just answer." Her voice sharp.

"I belong to no one. I mean besides my family." They both sigh with relief. "Now what's going on? What was that just now?"

"You stopped moving bro. You've been standing here for about five hours."

"What?! What is he talking about?" I ask Serena.

"It would seem that someone summoned you and was trying subjugate you."

"Subjugate?! You mean turn me into a servant? How?"

Mayra growls. "A binding spell, but to have that kind of influence. Not only did they know your full name, but they would've had to have something of yours. Blood, or something personal."

"It didn't take, right?"

Mayra rests her head on mine and squeezes me a little tighter. "No. I made it in time, to disrupt the ritual."

"What's stopping them from doing it again?"

"I made sure to destroy their ingredients and punish them."

"Punish?"

"They tried to take you from me. That is punishable by death, but they got away from me at the last moment."

Her fingers dig into my skin, and I feel her rage start to take hold of me. "Mayra, you're crushing me." She shivers before taking a calming breath. She releases me and I catch a breath. She places her hand on my back in apology.

"Were they part of the Messenger's entourage?" Serena asks.

"No sister, they weren't demon. I'm positive that they were human."

Serena looks at me, worry all on her face, making her look like her older self. "Your dinner with Valene. It's tonight, right? Maybe you should just reschedule."

"No, I couldn't. She's already upset with me, and you know how she can be."

"Damn that. You were just attacked and almost taken from us. She'll get over it."

There's silence among them. "Sister, let him go." Mayra says.

Serena looks at her bewildered. "After what we just witnessed, you think he'll be safe?"

"A spell like that took time. Whoever has done this won't be able to do it again anytime soon." She spins me around to face her. "Do you still wish to go?"

I look at her for a second. Her face is calm, but the red slowly seeping into the yellowish green of her eyes tells me she's furious. "Mayra, are you sure you're okay with me going?"

She closes her eyes and takes a deep breath. "Go and enjoy the time you have with her while you can little brother." She says caressing my face.

"Okay. I'm going to..." Fatigue hits me, and everything just goes dark.

With a sharp breath I wake up looking up at the ceiling of my room. The clock on my nightstand reads, five o'clock. *Crap, I got to get ready.* I roll out of bed, preparing to make a b-line to my closet to pick out my outfit. Hanging on the door is a black and silver suit with a note on it. 'Got your back hun. Have fun.' Serena.

I run to the bathroom, take a shower, brush my hair and teeth. Then get my suit on. It's been a while since I wore this and it's a little tight on my arms and shoulders, but it looks good on me still. Over my shoulder the clock reads five-fifty. *Okay, need to make a quick stop.*

I shadow-walk out of my room and appear in the Kir library in front of the Fireplace. Chris sits on the chair in front of the fireplace. "Son, I've been expecting you. Your sister called and told me what happened. Are you okay?"

"Yeah, I'm okay."

"First cursed, and then almost turned into a servant. Most would say fate is against you, but here you stand as if nothing has happened."

"I'm not dwelling on it. At least right now. If I do, I'm sure I'll have a panic attack."

He shakes his head in agreement. "If you say so. Are you ready?"

"For the most part. I just need the amulet released from me."

"All you do, with energy on the tip of your finger draw a circle around the amulet. It'll sever the link and will pop right off."

"Thanks." I follow his directions. The connection breaks and it loosens from my chest. "All right, Now I'm ready."

Chris walks over to me and looks me over. "You are looking sharp, but I think you need one more thing. Zel."

Zel appears holding a bouquet of blue and violet flowers with dark brown stems. "Here you are Master."

"Thank you Zel." He hands them to me. "There you are."

"What are these?"

"Damnations. It's her favorite flower. Only found in the Underworld. It should help."

"Thank you, guys. Zel, do you know where she's at now?"

An open doorway appears on the wall. "She awaits you in the foyer Master Kyle." I nod to Zel in appreciation. With a deep breath, I step through the doorway. As I enter the foyer, I instantly feel how energized and full of excitement it is. I can't help but laugh at how nervous I am.

"What's so funny?" Valene asks from the stairs.

"Nothing. Just laughing at myself." I turn to see her standing on the bottom staircase. *Wow.*

As she walks to me her one shoulder purple gown flows with her. The golden accents on the dress gleam in the light. She looks at me, her face unobscured, with her hair braided back into a curly ponytail. "Sweetheart, you look amazing. Purple and gold are your colors."

Her shining golden eyes narrow as if deciding how to react. She takes a long, annoyed breath, like she does with Jason when he's gotten on her nerves. "You look quite dapper yourself, Hero." *Yeah, she's upset.* "What's that behind your back?"

"Oh." I present her the bouquet of the underworld flowers. "For you."

Her face breaks into a slight smile as she takes them from me. She breathes deep, taking in the scent of the flowers. "These are really Damnations. Thank you."

"You're welcome." I say with a slight bow.

"Zel." Zel appears next to her. "Would you please place these in my room."

"My lady." He takes the flowers and ascends the stairs. At the top, he gives me a thumbs-up before vanishing.

My eyes track back to Valene. We stare at each other for a second before her smile fades, back into the annoyed look she had before. "So where are we going?"

I offer my hand to her. She takes it. "It's a surprise, but I'm sure you're going to love it."

Chapter 22

We step out of the darkness into the alleyway behind the corner store. Valene looks around skeptically. "Where are we?" she asks.

"The Core. This is an entrance to the Market." I place my hand on the wall. There's that bite to my hand and the wall fades revealing the doorway. We step through into the market. The atmosphere is calm as there aren't that many people wandering around nor many vendors open even though there's still plenty of daylight left. I look over at Valene. Her eyes are wide, shining with excitement as she looks around. "Valene, have you never been here before."

"Mother and father have spoken about this place, but no I've never come."

"Oh, well then we'll have to come back when it's a little more alive."

She side-eyes me. "Mmm. You sure you don't just want to bring Airca instead?"

We lock eyes for a moment. I let out a big sigh and smile. "I'm sure. Now come on we got somewhere to be." I take the lead as we continue through the bazaar. Everyone's eyes are on us as we walk the street. Well mostly on Valene. She is gorgeous, but unlike Airca where I had to keep an eye out for the vendors. I didn't have to with her. They would look and murmur, but the moment she looked back at them they would tense up and nearly drop to find cover behind their tables. She's not one to play with. Especially not now that she's mad. *I hope this goes well.*

It's not long until we come to Rains stand, in the same place it was yesterday. "Hey Rain."

The goblin's yellow eyes lift from his wares to me. "Ah Kid, right on time." He looks over to Valene. His eyes grow wide in astonishment. "Oh my." He says as drool dribbles out the sides of his mouth. "And who is this fine beauty?"

"My girlfriend. Valene this is Rain. Rain, Valene."

He rushes from around the table to take her hand, like he had attempted with Airca. As he gets within his arms reach of her, he stops in his tracks. The focus in his eyes wavers as the lustful expression on his face melts away to concern. Rain takes a quick step back, taking a shaky breath. "She was about to kill me." He says slightly offended.

"I've heard tales of what the fae do to humans, and of what goblins do to women. But since you're Kyle's acquaintance I would have just taken your hand if you had touched me." She says nonchalantly.

Rain clears his throat. "Well, she not as nice as your other friend."

The jewelry on the table begin to squirm and screech in panic. Valene looks at Rain with a death stare. The Goblins ears droop and he touches his earring that was imbued with life energy. I place my hand on Valene's shoulder. Her gaze snaps to me and I feel her anger direct towards me. "Rain. If you would be so kind. We're going to be a little late."

Rain takes a handkerchief from his pocket and dabs the sweat from his brow. "Ah, yes. Please follow me." He places a note on the table and leads us down the street until we come to a crumbled building. We walk through a makeshift pathway up to a lone standing wall with an open stone archway the size of a door. Rain says something under his breath and claps his hands. Symbols of light, shine to life along the edges of the stone. As light begins to pour into the opening, colorful floral patterns bloom to life within it. Spreading out until they reach the edge. The air shimmers behind it hardening into black wooden door. Rain knocks three times.

There's an unlatching sound and the door slowly opens. On the other side within a dimly lit room is a young woman, floating at least a foot off the floor. Her skin is translucent, her hair snow white and her eyes sunken so far that they look hollow. Her gaze shifts down to Rain. "Raaain." She says drawing out his name. Her voice, like a gargled whisper. *Is this lady a ghost?*

"Amila my dear, good evening. I have the special guests I spoke of."

"Yes, yes. We have been expecting you. Please, this way." She moves aside. Rain walks through the door and vanishes. "Please." Amila offers, with a slight bow. I look to Valene and offer my hand. She looks at me with a slight sneer but takes it. Her palms are a little sweaty. Even though she's so strong she's still a little nervous. Which makes me feel a little better about tonight. I lead Valene through the door.

As we step over the threshold, the image of the crumbled building shimmers away to a fully put together dining area. "Welcome esteemed guest to The Taste of Darkness."

Valene squeezes my hand. "The Taste of... Hero. Mother and Father have talked about this place. It's not only crazy expensive, but super exclusive."

"You've wanted to come here, right?"

She looks at me so plain faced, but her eyes shine with excitement. "Yeah, but how did you work this out?"

"Helped Rain out of a life debt."

She looks at me confused. "What?" She looks at Rain as he chats it up with one of the staff. "What did you do?" She asks, her voice tense.

"Don't worry. Everything is square. I'm not in anybody's debt."

"I am in his." Rain says, walking towards us. He flicks his earring and smiles.

Valene's face twists in disgust at his voice. She takes a breath calming herself, and steps closer to me. "This way please." Amila directs us. I start to walk, but Valene kind of takes the lead.

Amila leads us through the dining room, gliding across the floor. The whole ceiling is riddled with crystal chandeliers. Orbs of light dance among them, making a show of prismatic lights shine around the room. The air is thick with the smell of food, drinks, and perfumes from the other diners.

I look at Valene. Her shoulders are tense, and I can see her gaze shifting back and forth as if she were waiting for someone to attack us. I grip her hand and pull at her bit. She looks back over her shoulder at me, before slowing her pace to match mine. "Valene, relax. We're okay. I got this."

"Really?" She asks. The skepticism in her voice is so apparent.

I laugh. "Yeah, I do." I say as confidently as I can sound.

A smile touches the corner of her mouth. But as she looks at me it fades, and she looks forward. Valene lets go of my hand and takes my arm instead. Holding me close to her. "You and Airca didn't walk like this did you?"

One step forward, two steps back. "This arm has been reserved for you."

"Right. It better had been."

We get to the back of the room where an elevator is. Amila just floats through the door like it wasn't there. *I knew it. She is a ghost.* The door opens. "Please." We all pile in and Amila taps the top button on the panel. Without even a jostle the elevator dings and the door open to a stone corridor. "Follow me." Amila says floating out. We follow her until we come to a door. "This is your private room." she says opening it.

I look to Rain. "A private room?"

"Only the best for you kid."

In the room the light of the evening sun shines through the skylight, illuminating the beautifully set table in its center. Rain motions us to sit. I take the chair out for Valene. She flashes me a smile as she takes the seat. Quickly, I take mine. Amila stands by the table and pours our water. "Here at The Taste of Darkness, we serve a variety of dishes ranging from vegan to human flesh. Now, what would your preferences be?"

"Nothing human please." I say quickly.

"Very good. Might I suggest the realms special?"

"What's that?"

"It is our five-course meal, consisting of wholesome dishes from both New Birth and the Underworld."

"That sounds great. We'll take that."

"Very good. We shall leave you two as we go prepare your meal." She says with a bow and leaves.

Rain follows behind her waving his hand. The door closes, darkening the rest of the room besides where we sit. Valene looks at me. "Kyle, what is happening?"

"What do you mean?" She motions to the table. "Oh well, I wanted to do something nice for you, for us." She looks at me confused.

Realization hit her face. "Is **today** our anniversary?"

"No, sadly. It was three days ago. When everything went down."

"Oh."

"Yeah, but I still wanted to do something. So here we are. Happy anniversary."

She huffs, leaning back into the chair. "I didn't even put two and two together."

"Not surprising. You have been pretty upset with me."

"I still am."

We're silent for a while, just kind of looking at one another. Out of the darkness two people appear with trays in hand. One is a platter of bread, cheeses, and fruits. The other, I'm guessing, is our first course. Amila appears with a shimmer before us. "My friends, our first dish is a soup." The waiters place bowls on the table in front of us, filled with a thick purple liquid and chunks of white flesh floating in it. "This soup is crafted from the blood and flesh of the titan centipede, the *Morgal.*"

Looking in the bowl, I see the noxious fumes rising from it. "This isn't edible. Besides its venom, the flesh and blood are the most poisonous parts of the creature."

"Very true. That's why we have these." The waiters place small glass pitchers next to the bowls, filled with a golden liquid. Submerged in the liquid is a medley of things, mushrooms, garlic, onion, herb and even flowers. "If you would indulge me. Please, pour these into the bowls." We do as she suggests. As the two liquids meet the broth turns a light green. The nauseating fumes vanish giving way to the smell of stew. "Please dig in."

Valene eyes me just as skeptical of the dish as I am. We both take a spoon full. As the thick broth touches my tongue, I can't help but close my eyes and melt back into my chair. "This so good." I hear Valene say.

Quickly, I take another scoop making sure to get some meat. It reminds me of buttery lobster. With a deep breath I swallow. "It is. How are we not dead?"

"The second broth is made from the rendered fat of the centipede, which has natural enzymes that neutralize its poisonous nature. That, paired with the herbs and ground shell of the beast also make this a very effective medicinal dish.

"My compliments to the chef." Valene says taking another bite.

Amila bows. "We shall leave you to enjoy. We shall return with the next course." She vanishes and others disappear in the darkness.

Minutes pass before I notice that my bowl is empty. This was so good I couldn't help but inhale it. Valene is only halfway done as she daintily eats, careful not to mess up her lipstick. She looks up at me. I smile. She almost smiles at me, but she purses her lips together. "Valene, talk to me. Please."

She puts her spoon down and takes a deep breath. "Kyle just because I want to spend time with you tonight doesn't mean that I want to talk to you right now. So, let's just enjoy this before we get into anything. Okay?"

She goes back to eating her stew and I'm so confused. I don't know what to say to that. Maybe I just shouldn't say anything. Minutes pass with us in silence and Valene finally finishes her stew. Right on time Amila floats out of the darkness followed by a floating tray. She stops at the table. "I do hope that you enjoyed the stew."

"It was exquisite." Valene says.

"For your second course." Tiny bowls lift from the tray and land in front of us replacing the bowls of stew. It was a scoop of Ice cream. It's bright red with a dark green swirl through it, topped with a leaf of mint. "A berry sorbet made from the strawberries of New Birth and the nether berry of the Underworld."

"What's a nether berry?" I ask.

"Named for the region that they are found, The Nether is a mountain range closest to the Great divide. These sweet fruits only grow during the peak of the Nether winter. A winter so cold that it will freeze your very soul. And these delicious fruits can do the same. Please enjoy."

Amila floats off into the darkness. I take bite of the sorbet. Instantly I catch a brain freeze. Across the table Valene is holding her own head. "What is happening?" I ask.

"The Nether barriers must have some sort of cooling effect or something. It so cold." She says, starting to suck on her thumb.

I follow her lead. The pain subsides quickly, but I can't stop shivering. "This is close to how my brain felt when I woke up a few days ago."

"Kyle. You really don't remember do you? The party."

"No. There's nothing from the time after I left you, to the dream I had and waking up at Airca's. What happened?"

Valene sits up tall, taking a long breath. "Everything was going fine. Everyone was having a good time. But at one point during the night, you started talking about Airca. No matter what the topic of conversation it always led back to her. So, before it got any more awkward than it had already been I took you aside to talk about what was going on with you."

"How did that go?"

"How do think?"

"I got a good guess but no real clue."

She puts her face in her palms, growling in frustration. "We got into it. Started arguing. But then you started yelling at me. Telling me to get out of your way. To stop trying to trick you into to loving me, because you could you never love me the way that you love Airca."

"I didn't say that did I?"

"**Yeah**, you did. And you know what you did after that?"

"I left."

"Vanished. It wasn't until an hour later that I realized where you had gone." She looks at me. "I was going to go there and end her whole life and rip you apart. Luckily one of my friends talked me down. So, I was just going to confront you the next day."

"Yeah. Valene I'm sorry."

"I gave you the benefit of doubt because you were honest with me, but then you go to be with Airca."

"Valene, I have not lied to you. At least while I was coherent. I wouldn't leave you like that."

"But you did."

I just sit there, staring down at the table. I don't know what to say. I mean she's not wrong I did leave, but it wasn't me.

Amila appears again with a new tray. "Was the sorbet to your liking?"

"It was good, but we couldn't handle how cold it was." I explain, noticing that the scoop hadn't even started to melt. It honestly looked colder.

"Not many can. But the next dish will fill your stomachs and warm your bones. Shall I?"

"Please."

"Very well." She claps her hands, and two other ghostly waiters float out from the darkness with our plates in hand. "Your entrée and third course is a mixture of the realms. New births finest steak, seasoned to perfection with the herbs and spices of the Underworld. It is paired with a dark fruit chutney, served on a bed of risotto. Please enjoy."

She and her cohorts vanish, leaving Valene and me. We both start to eat. I cut into the steak with the knife, and it glides through it like butter. Either this knife is way too sharp, or this streak is super tender. I try the fork and split it just as easily. It's just that tender. I scoop a bit of everything onto my fork and shovel it all into my mouth. Oh, my goodness this is amazing. The dark fruit is like an apple and a pear had a sweet and tangy baby. The risotto is light and fluffy. And the seasoning on the steak just brought everything together.

I look from my plate to see if Valene was enjoying the food as much as I was. She was staring at her plate, her eyes glistening with tears. "Valene?"

She takes her napkin and dabs her eyes. "I think we should call it a night."

My stomach instantly starts doing flips as what she's said sets in. "Wait what?" She starts to get up from her chair. "Valene wait, please."

"No Kyle. This is lovely and I really appreciate all the hard work you put into making this happen. But I'm just not in the mood to really enjoy it." She says getting ready to get up.

I trip up on my words trying to think of something to say, but it's all a blank. I feel the weight of the amulet around my neck. Honestly, I forgot it was there. It pulses and I'm reminded of everything that I've gone through to make this thing. Before I know it, she was already halfway across the table. Franticly I stand in front of her. "Valene, please wait."

"Kyle, move."

"Wait, just give me a few..." She interrupts me, taking me by the collar.

"Move or I'll make you." she says her voice shaky and angry. Her eyes swirling between black and gold.

Calmly, I place my hands on her hands and grip them slightly. "Valene before you go. I have one more thing to give you."

"What is it?" she snaps.

"Sweetheart let me go. So, I can give it to you." I say calmly.

She releases me. I pull apart my tie and unbutton the top few buttons of my shirt. She puts her hand on my chest stopping me. "What are you doing?" she asks her face growing red.

I take her hand from me. "Not what you're thinking." I reach under my collar, pull green crystalline lace from around my neck and pull the golden amulet from out of my shirt. "Here."

Valene's eyes grow wide as she gasps, covering her mouth, watching the amulet sway. "That's impossible." She takes it from me letting it dangle in front of her. "This is my amulet. The one your father made for me. The one Leo lost. How did you get this?"

"There was no way I was finding your old one. I've yet to even go to the Underworld myself. So, I made you a new one."

"You made this?" I just nod my head. "Hero to make this you would have to of found..."

"Celestial silver and imperial gold." I finish. "Funny thing is. The silver was the easiest to find. I had to go to Hell and back for the gold. At least the place was hot enough to be Hell." She stares, shook. "Put it in your hand."

She places it in her palm and jumps in surprise. "It's pulsing. Like a heart."

I wave my hand over it. The golden top opens and the ever-weaving, silver and gold Celtic knot rises, giving off warm pulses of energy. "Valene, you've done a lot for me this past year. You even gave me a piece of your very soul. There's no real way to repay you for all of that. So, maybe against my better judgement, I made you this impossible thing, and filled it with a bit of my own life. And well I know this will sound corny but, I leave it in your hands. My safe place."

She looks at me, stunned. Her eyes and face are wet with tears. She waves her hand back over the amulet, closing it. She puts it on. "*Ariun, Zaru. Ast halīju tren ing to univa gyfu.*" (Thank you, Hero. I promise to cherish it now and all of eternity.) She hugs me tight, gripping the back of my jacket.

I hold her back. "I'm sorry, for what I said to you. For what I did, and how I treated you. I would never..."

"I know."

I Kiss her on the cheek. "I'll see you later?"

She leans back, looking me in the eye, smiling. She caresses my face, gently pulls me in and kisses me. Filling me with her energy. "Of course." She steps away from me and vanishes in a cloud of darkness.

I walk back to my chair, and plop down. *That went a lot better than I expected.* Amila floats out of the darkness. "I'm sorry to see her leave. I hope it was on good terms."

"Yeah, we're good."

"You have two more dishes would you like to continue?"

"Rain went through all the trouble for me. Why not. What's next?"

Chapter 23

I awake to the sun beaming through the cracks in the curtains of the living room. Right into my face. I shift out of the way falling onto my side on the couch. My stomach kind of hurts. I'm still kind of full, from dinner last night. The last two courses were almost full plates, but they were so good. I almost don't want to give Valene hers.

Serena walks in from the kitchen, wearing tights, a sports bra, and a towel over her shoulder. She sips at her tea and looks at me. "Oh, good you're awake. How are you feeling?"

"My stomach hurts."

"Aww, you ate too much didn't you fatty."

"And I'd do it again. It was so good. Do we have any antacid?"

"You don't need any of that. I'll go make you some tea."

"Oh wait, I feel so much better. I don't need..." I hold back a belch. "Need it anymore."

"Yeah. You wait right there. I'll be back in a minute."

"Nooooo!"

"Yeeeesss!" she says walking back into the kitchen. As she leaves, I grab the remote and turn on the tv. The news caster comes on talking about the happenings around The Roc. Nothing special, just deputy Mayor Juda hosting the completion of the renovations to the mall. *And I helped.* "Later this evening, more on the spreading sleeping virus."

Sleeping virus? As a commercial starts to play Serena appears, holding a saucer and teacup. "Drink up." She says handing it to me.

"Do I have to?"

She just stares at me like she used to when she was just my aunt. "Drink it you crybaby."

I sit up with a groan and take the cup. "Thanks." It doesn't smell like anything, but I know better. With a sip of the hot tea, the bitter and sour taste sends shivers up my spine, but my stomach settles like I never had an issue.

"How do you feel?"

"Like I just drank the water of a week-old sweaty sock."

"Good. That means the blend was right this round." She takes a seat on the table in front of me. "Did everything go okay at your dinner with Valene?"

"Yeah, better than I anticipated. She left a little early, but a win is a win. I don't think that she's too mad at me anymore."

"Oh good. That could have gone so many ways. I had a vision that she cut your hand so deep that you couldn't use it."

I look at my hands, there's no cut just the quarter sized smooth burns on the palms of hands where I channeled the life energy. "Well, that would have sucked. This was a way better outcome."

"Yes, this was the path I was rooting for."

"You know, you sound like somebody I met in the labyrinth. Sis, are your abilities close to that of the Fates?"

"The labyrinth?" Serena gasps. "Wait. You, you met The Fates?"

"Two of them at least. One of them lead me to the imperial gold for the amulet I made for Valene."

She lowers her head with a sigh. "Kyle, you are really going to give me grey hair. What am I going to do with you? You're just as crazy as our father."

I laugh, at her reaction. "You aren't the first person to say that."

She glares at me. I mouth that I'm sorry. She takes a deep breath. "My abilities are, but a fraction of what the Fates can do. I can see what will be; the future and some of the variant outcomes. But the Fates are able see the past, present and future in all its entirety. They can see the paths that lead to and diverge from whichever future they deem fit."

"Okay. Will you be able to do that?"

"As I grow in strength, so too will my vision. So, maybe. But what makes them truly dangerous are their individual abilities. Lachesis can see the whole of your fate. Clotho can change your fate. Then there's Atropos. Now, they can sever your very fate. Ripping you from the fabric of fates design from there on end."

The screams of the cyclops ring in my ears. "And it's not death, is it?"

"Nope. All that you are ceases to exist from that point on. No soul, no body, just nothing." She looks at me. "You've seen it haven't you? A severing?"

I nod. Then go into detail of how Michael and I got the gold. Olympus, the labyrinth, the Fate and the cyclops. She's silent for a second. "There it is. My first gray hair."

"It was the only way get the gold."

She looks at me, shaking her head. "Did they, say anything to you? Did they tell you your fate?"

"Not quite. Lachesis showed me images. A needle, a forest in a sandstorm, yellow eyes, and…" I touched my chest thinking about the knife in my chest, and the words whispered into my ear. "blood. All before a darkness." She sighs before getting up. "Wait, where are you going?"

"I'm going to get some air."

She walks into the kitchen and I follow behind her. "Is everything okay?"

She stops at the door, looking back at me over her shoulder. "I've seen those images as well and interpreted their meanings."

"What do they mean?"

"Each image represents a trial you will face. One of the heart, mind and spirit. All before facing a darkness covered in blood."

"Oh."

"Yeah."

I smile. "No worries sis. I'm sure everything will be fine."

She gives me a weak smile. "Yeah, I hope so." She starts to head outside then stops. "Also, there's a business card on the table I got out of your pants." She says going out of the patio doors.

"It's not you turn to do the laundry. What were you doing in my pants?"

She hurriedly shuts the door. I grab the card from off the table. It's the card that Gene gave to me from his company. He said that he had a job offer for me. *I'll give him a call.* I take my cell out from my pocket, type in his number. "Hello. You reached Gene."

"Hey Gene, this is Kyle."

Gene gasps a bit. "Kyle hey. I didn't think you were going to get in touch with me."

"Yeah sorry, something came up. Did you still want to talk to me about that job offer?"

"YES! I'm at the office now, but I'm free after two can we meet then?"

"Sure."

"PERFECT! How about we meet at the sky café at three?

"See you then."

He hangs up. The clock on my phone says it's seven. Plenty of time to get my day going.

I get changed and get to my workout. Mayra and Serena are already at it in the back yard. Serena was struggling a bit, but you can tell that even after a day she was getting back into a groove. So, I just do my own thing. Working on the *Nigi* stances all the while still extending my energy. That is until I notice them staring at me, smiling. Apparently, I looked like dad. Serena falls in next to me getting into the position I was in and continues alongside me.

Afterwards after getting cleaned up and dressed. We all sit down for breakfast, and I tell them about the dinner and how it went. *I wonder what Valene is up to. I have to get her food to her. That is if she wants to talk to me.* After we're done eating. I grab the boxes of food from the Fridge and shadow walk to the Kirs.

I appear in the foyer. "Master Kyle?" Zel says from behind me.

Jumping a bit, I take a quick breath. "Morning Zel."

"Good morning. How may I be of service?"

"Is Valene home?"

"Ah yes, she is currently in her room. Shall I get her for you?"

"No thanks. I'll go to her. Could you please put this in the fridge though. It's Valene's food from the restaurant. And make sure Jason doesn't eat it."

Zel takes the bag from me. "Of course." And then walks off to the kitchen.

I make my way up the stairs to the east wing where her room is. In the corridor of windows, I remember Jason stepping out of the shadows in his armor ready to fight me. *I can't believe that was just a year ago.* I come to the purple door and knock. "Valene you in there?"

"Kyle? Come in." The door opens. I step in and am bombarded by the smell of lavender and berries. It's been a while since I been here. It's a little bit different. The color schemes of purple, gold and black are the same, but a lot of the furniture is different. Valene is sitting in front of her vanity, in a too big t-shirt, working on her hair. I walk over to her and sit on her bed behind her. "Hey Hero. What up?"

"I just brought your food from last night."

"My food?"

"Yeah. There were two more courses after you left."

She looks at me in the mirror. A warm smile on her face. "You really do like me."

"Did you doubt it?"

"After what happened. A little. But I know better." She says lifting her amulet. "I'm sure you went through a lot to make this."

"You have no idea. I wouldn't have been able to make without help."

"Father I'm guessing."

"Michael and Airca too."

Her smile flips into a confused frown. "Explain."

I do just that. I tell her everything. My and Airca bartering in the Market for the silver. Michael and I surviving the labyrinth for the gold. And lastly the two days straight Chris and I spent putting it together. At one point she stopped working on her hair and turned to listen to me. Her face is stuck in shock like a kid listening to an unbelievable story. I make sure not to tell her how I helped Rain with his debt. If she knew about my being able to move Life energy and that Rain knew she would probably try and end him. "And here we are."

She looks at me sideways. One side of her hair is done and the other curly and wild. "Are you crazy?!"

"Probably as much as you look right now."

She looks in the mirror. She scoffs, turning back to me. "Hero you didn't have to do all of this."

"I know. I wanted to."

She starts to say something but bites her lip. She sighs, relaxing and touches the amulet. "Thank you, Hero. I love it."

"You're welcome."

My phone chimes. It's a text message. The screen flashes on with a message from Gene. 'Hey, I'm making my way to the café. See you there.'

"Airca?" Valene says annoyed.

"No. It's this guy I met in the Market. I am meeting up with him for a possible job opportunity."

Valene perks up. "Oh. You're going dressed like that?"

"It's nothing formal. We're meeting at the sky café downtown."

"Oh, I like that place. Please go change."

"Okay."

After stopping at my room and changing into something a little more formal, some khakis and a pollo. I shadow-walk to the alley around the corner from the café, just behind a dumpster. In no time, I get down the block to the store front where the café entrance is. A free-standing sign with an arrow pointing at an open doorway reads, 'Sky Café.'

"Kyle!" A man's voice yells from above me. I look up to Gene waving over the balcony railing.

I go through the doorway and up the stairs to the third floor of the building. It opens to a huge open area, taking up most of the floor. The air is thick with the smell of fresh coffees, teas and pastries. The wooden décor gives it the homey and comfortable aesthetic. While the windows, making up the walls gives it more of an open plan along with a nice view. "Kyle!" Gene says beckoning me from the balcony, through the sliding door windows.

Walking up to the table, Gene hops to his feet offering his hand. I take it and he excitedly shake mine. "Thank you, so much for coming."

"No problem. Sorry I'm late."

"Everything is all good man. You look good. Did you dress up for this? You didn't have to."

"My girlfriend told me to."

"Ah that makes since. How is Airca?"

"She's fine. Not my girlfriend though."

"Oh, I'm sorry. You guys just seem to vibe well. I thought you two were a thing."

"Nope. That ship sailed a while ago."

"Oh well. My bad. How about we get started. Please." He directs me to sit. We sit in silence, and I'm a bit uncomfortable. His eyes dart around as he focuses on me. *Sizing me up?* He smiles, "So, let me cut to the chase. I work for a private security company called Umbra Inc. We're new, but well established. We've been hired for event security, private security and even some high-profile jobs I can't really get into right now. But ever since I started going to the market, I've realized that we're not completely equipped for all this city has to throw at us."

"How did you even find that place?" I ask.

"Marie."

"How did you meet her?"

"A lot of the guys that we employ are ex-military, police and bounty hunters. People that tend to have trauma. It is recommended that we have a therapist/counselor on retainer. Like I said we're new and broke. Counselors are expensive. One day, about a year ago, we got an anonymous recommendation, Marie. She was more of a spiritual counselor rather than someone specializing in trauma, but her credentials checked out. She has helped a lot in keeping our guys grounded. But somehow, she found out about my marriage issues and excitedly asked me to help us out. So, I gave her a chance."

"You do know that she's not human right?" He nods. "When did you find that out?"

"Our first counseling session. She told us straight up. I didn't believe her, until she showed us. She said, 'To build a relationship there must be honesty and trust.'" He looks around, checking if anyone were listening. "To find out that supernatural creatures like goblins, vampires and demons are real. It was mind blowing. But said she could still help."

I'm shocked. From what Serena says most humans that face the supernatural tend to stay clear of it, but this guy's knee deep in it. "And you still worked with her?"

"Her methods are weird, but I've seen how she works with the guys. And a lot of them are in better places than they were when they were hired. So, I gave her a chance. And our relationship has been on the up and up."

"So, what is this about, really?"

"A job opportunity. Like I said we are not prepared for all the city has to throw at us. But, with someone like you, we could be. With you as our supernatural muscle we could expand our field of service and be ready for anything."

"What makes you think that I'm supernatural?"

Gene closes his eyes and says something under his breath. There's a shift of energy that feels familiar. He opens his eyes, and they are black as night. *He has the dark sight.* "I can see that you're more than human."

Just like Airca. "Whoa. How can you do that? Do you know magic?"

His eyes grow wide. "This would be considered magic, wouldn't it? No, I don't. Marie gave us a potion that allows us to see the truths of the world and one another. It's one of her honesty and trust exercises. It wears off after a while. So, what do you think?"

I sit there for second, just staring at him. "Um, I don't think that's a good idea."

He looks at me confused. "Why not?"

"For one, I'm not strong at all, compared to some of the beings out in the world. I'm still learning about all of this myself. Second, if you don't pay the supernatural any mind, they should ignore you, for the most part. Having me there will basically be a beacon to them. Putting you in more danger than you normally would be in."

His face grows grim as he considers my words. "That makes sense, but I'm willing to take that risk to make sure we're prepared for anything. And like I said, we're young as well and still growing. So, we would love to have someone who could grow with us and isn't as demented as others of your kind."

"What makes you think that I'm not?"

He smiles, "One, your breath. It doesn't reek of blood and rotting flesh. Second, you took my hand. You're not the first I've approached with this, but you are the first to take my hand where others just looked at it like I was handing them trash."

I think of how Michael called me a human like it was an insult. "That sounds about right. There are exceptions, but most demons don't care about the wellbeing of humans, unless they're entertainment or food."

He nods, laughing nervously. "Lastly, I saw the way you protected Airca from that guy in front of Rain's."

"You were there?" He nods. "I didn't do anything really."

"True, but if things went south, you were ready to act. I know that stance well. You're a born guardian. You would be great among our ranks." I start to reject him again, but he puts his hands up. "Please, before you say no. Just think about it. We just want to do some good and protect people."

"I'll...I'll think about." I say in sigh.

"Thank you." He says taking my hand. "It's a start."

On the table, the screen of his phone lights up with a notification. He looks down at and grimaces. "Is everything okay?"

He opens and reads the message. "Oh yeah everything is great."

"Then why the face?"

Gene touches his face unaware of his reaction. He sighs, "Shayla has been in a very clingy mood lately. I'm not complaining it's been better than it has been, but she's calling and texting every other minute. It's starting to be a little, much."

I think of Airca and the way she looked at me before I left her. How she was begging me to stay. To talk. *I wonder if she's, okay?*

Gene's phone starts to ring. And when he picks it up, the first thing you hear is yelling. "Love calm down. What's the matter?" He's silent for a second. "Okay I'll be on my way, just finishing a meeting now. Okay I love you." He hangs up and looks at me. "Thanks for coming to meet with me. Please, take some time to consider my offer. You have my number."

"I'll think about." We shake hands and he leaves.

I sit there for a second looking out over the street. Thinking about his offer. *Maybe I could do some good with them. And learn a thing or two.* I see Gene leave the building. As he makes his way down the street, there's a shift in the air that sends a chill runs up my spine. Someone has their eyes on me. I scan the room, but no one stands out. I turn back to look at Gene as he rounds the corner out of sight and the feeling vanishes. Something is watching him.

I pull my phone out and call him. "Kyle?" he asks.

"I don't know how to say this, but I think somethings watching you."

"Yeah. I've gotten that feeling lately."

"I think you should lay low."

He laughs nervously. "Look at you. Already acting like my security guard. I understand. Thanks for looking out." He hangs up.

"I better get out here too."

Chapter 24

I shadow walk to Valene's room. She's not here. "Zel"

The door to her room opens and Zel stands there. "Yes Master Kyle?"

"Where's Valene?"

The Lady is currently in the courtyard entertaining a guest. Shall I inform her that you wish to see her?"

"Please." With a bow, he vanishes.

Moments later he reappears outside the door. "She's expecting you."

"Thanks." I shadow walk into the courtyard. Valene stands next to the grand fountain, wearing a black and white sundress. Her hair is all the way out. "Hey sweetheart."

"Hi Hero." She says walking toward me. She hugs me tight. "You actually got changed. You look good. How was the meeting? Did you get the job?"

"It went well. He gave me some time to think it over."

"What was it for?"

"A specialized position at private security company. Focusing on the supernatural."

"And he was human?" I nod. She looks off, thinking about it. "Well, why not go for it?"

"But won't I bring more danger into the lives of humans? Make them a bigger target? And you know I'm not that strong, compared to the rest of the demon world."

She places her hand on my chest. "Sweetheart they're already a target. Not only by demons, but by nature and by themselves. You, being there won't do any more damage than what they've already meddled with. You might even keep some of them alive with your strength and ability. You kept me alive last year, during our battle with the Messenger and you were nowhere near as strong as you are today. Go for it."

I lean into her, lowering me head onto her shoulder. "Thanks for the pep talk."

"Of course, Hero." She caresses the back of my head.

I wrap my arms around her, hugging her tight. "Valene I..." I stop short as my chest tenses and my throat goes dry.

"Hero?" I hear Valene call from a distance. I look up from her shoulder. The world becomes grey with a white haze coating the ground. A loud rattle fills the air, drawing closer to us. There's movement from behind fountain. I hold my breath, waiting.

Something large and white falls to the ground, dispersing the haze. *What in the world?* The things arms shoot in the air and is lifted off the ground and onto its feet as if it were being pulled by strings. Like some sort of puppet. Black slime pours from its joints as it tries to reorient itself. It's head snaps towards us. The hair on the back of my neck stands on end as its blank face starts to crack into a creepy smile. Rattle noises come from its mouth, sounding like laughter. It has something in its hand. Without warning it rushes at us.

I push Valene to the side and move to intercept. My claws appear and, I grab the thing by the wrist. It drops the knife and I prepare to drive my other hand into its chest.

Something grabs my wrist stopping me. "Kyle." I hear Valene say still at a distance. A hand touches my face pulling my gaze away from the creature. Valene looks at me, her golden eyes stern and alight with power. "Kyle, let her go."

"Her?" I look back to the creature. It's not the monster puppet anymore, but a green haired, hazel eyed human. "Airca?" She stares up at me wide eyed and afraid. *What's going on here?* I let her go and back away. My eyes water and the haze vanishes, bringing color back to the courtyard. "Airca? Airca, I'm sorry. I didn't mean to."

Valene helps her to her feet. "Kyle, calm down. It's okay. Are you okay?" Valene asks Airca.

"I'm not sure." She says holding her arm.

"Come on Airca let me look at your arm." Valene leads her back around the fountain. I look down to what the creature had dropped and notice that it wasn't a knife but a shattered teacup on the ground. *What in the world was that?*

"Kyle." Valene calls out.

"I'm coming." I follow them around the fountain. There's a round, white table set up with a tea set and a platter of cookies, fruits and cheeses. "Take a seat Hero." I do as I'm told, while Valene examines Airca's arm.

What was that? That haze. It was like when I was being bound. "Kyle." Airca says. I look at her and she smiles. "Get that worried look off your face. I'm okay, alright?"

"Is she okay?" I ask Valene.

"Yea, just some bruising."

"See. Tougher than I look, remember."

I sigh. Valene walks over to me, takes my face into her hands, and looks me in the eyes. "Valene, I'm okay. I think." I tell her.

She kisses me on the forehead. "We'll talk later." She takes a seat in the chair next to me.

"So, you guys are having tea, together?" I ask looking at Valene.

Valene places her hand on my lap. "Well after you told me how you got the materials for my Amulet, I decided to thank those involved personally."

"Really? Even Michael?"

"Yes, even him. When I get to him." She says with disdain.

Airca stares down at her arm, her face blank. *Wonder what she's thinking about?* That's when I notice that her hands were already wrapped from her wrist to her knuckles. "Airca, what happened to your hands?" She just smiles. "Airca?"

Her gaze shoots up, realizing that I was talking to her. "What? Oh, my hands? Well, I uh. I went a little too hard on the punching bag during a session in self-defense class again. They're just a little raw." She looks at me, then her eyes follow up to Valene. "You never mentioned what the silver was for."

"Nobody except for two other people knew what I was doing. And I didn't want to run any risks of her finding out until I gave it to her."

"So, what you're saying is that you didn't trust me. Your supposed best friend not to talk?"

"Airca it's not like that. I just didn't want to risk it."

Her face darkens and she starts rubbing her finger. "I wasn't talking to you because of her you know. Why would I talk to her?"

Why is she making such a big deal about this now? "Because of Valene? What did she do?" She's quiet just glaring at me.

"Are going to say something or are you just gonna…" Valene places her hand on mine. I stop and take a quick breath, calming myself.

"Airca." Valene starts. "I understand how you feel. I honestly don't care for you either, but you are still Kyle's friend and I still wish to extend my gratitude for your contribution. Thank you."

Airca stares at Valene, surprise all over her face. Shook from her cordial bluntness. She laughs, leaning back into her chair "You're welcome."

Airca takes a cup from the table and sips tea. Her gaze shifts to me and I get an uneasy feeling as her eyes slowly start to narrow. *What are you about to say?*

"Valene." Airca says leaning forward. "Did your boyfriend tell you about our second date back to the Market?" *Date?* "How he protected from another demon."

"Yes. And that you started it."

"Did he tell you that he kissed me? How he held me so tight."

I'm speechless. *What is happening here? Why is she trying to antagonize her?*

I look at Valene and she is unfazed. A slight smile spreads across her face. "Of course. We talked about it and I've forgiven him." Valene leans forward, looking straight at Airca. "Now is there anything else that you want to tell me that I don't already know?"

Airca sighs. "No." We sit in awkward silence for a few minutes. She gulps her tea and stands from the table. "I think it's time that I leave."

"I think that would be for the best." Valene says sitting back.

"How did you get here anyway?" I ask.

She makes her way around the table. "Serena, shadow-walked me here. I was going to call her to take me back home but since you're here. Do you mind?"

I look to Valene. She's not looking at me but at Airca, her training shining through. To never take your eye off the enemy. "Go ahead Kyle. I don't mind, just come back when you're done."

I stand, offering my hand to Airca. She stares at it for a second before interlacing her finger with mine. "Airca please stop being extra."

She steps a little closer to me. "I thought you like it when I'm extra." She says looking me in the eye.

"Don't know where you got that idea from, but no I don't, and it's already gotten old." I say to her.

The smile on her face eases down into a frown. She grips my hand tighter, digging her nails into my hand. "Airca sto..." Before I can finish, she yanks me towards her. Prepared to kiss me.

Valene gets up between us. She pushes me back and takes Airca by the mouth. "Try it again and you'll be kissing the ground."

"Why are you always in the way!" Airca screams. She throws a wild punch and lands square on Valene's face with a loud smack. Valene lets Airca go, and she walks away. "Where do you think you are going?" Airca asks on her heels.

A wave of energy fills the courtyard, making the windows of the house rattle. Everything slows down and I see Valene spin around, blade in hand. Her eyes are pitch black and wild with rage. "Oh no." I grab Airca's shoulder, pulling her back behind me. My claws appear. I take hold of Valene's wrist, her blade inches from my face. "Valene, get a hold of yourself." I yell.

"I'll rip her apart!" She yells. Her energy spikes and chunks of my armor fly into my face as a cut appears across the top of my hand. Her free hand comes up to punch me. With a burst of energy, I knock her off me, and follow up with a kick to her stomach pushing her back a couple of feet.

She lands summoning another blade into her free hand. "Valene, please calm down." She grips her blades tighter. I feel Airca press against my back, her heart racing. Valene takes a step forward.

I would just take Airca and run but we wouldn't get far. I relax dispersing my claws and put my hands up. My right hand is on fire. Blood pours from it, running down my arm, but I don't take my eyes off her. "Valene please."

Her eyes flash gold for a second as she gasps. She looks down at her blade. Then back up at me. Her eyes swirl from black to gold as she grips her blades, fighting her urge to attack. She takes a deep breath and exhales with a growl. The dagger dissipates into smoke. "Get her out of my sight. Before I change my mind."

I take a breath. "Thank you." I turn to Airca. "We're going now."

With drunken smile on her face she puts her trembling hands onto my chest. "Whatever you want."

"Valene, I'll be back."

"You better." She says, with a menacing tone. I shadow-walk away.

We appear in Airca's room. She walks over to her bed and plops down, trying to catch her breath. I walk over to her window, looking out to the driveway. There's no car. Her mom's not home. *Good. I don't have to explain why we just appeared out of thin air.*

"Well, that was close." She says laughing nervously. "Your hand?!"

The cut is down to the white meat, and I can almost see the bone. I work my fingers, balling them into a fist. They're numb, and there's a lot of blood but everything is working properly. "I'll be fine. They'll be scar but it'll heal."

Airca walks up to me with a t-shirt and takes my hand. "How could she hurt you like that?" She asks, dabbing at the blood.

"Because she wasn't aiming for me." I shake my head with a sigh. "Airca, what the hell was that? What were you thinking?"

She looks at me with drunken eyes. She leans in a little too close to me. "I'm sorry, I don't know what came over me." She inches closer, but I put my hand on her shoulder stopping her. She looks at my hand and scoffs. "What?" she asks annoyed.

"Airca, Valene was going to kill you."

"But she didn't. She couldn't because you were there. Like always. Because you love me." Airca takes my hand from her shoulder and places it over her heart. Which is still racing. "You said so yourself."

I pull away from her. "This has got to stop."

"What do you mean?"

"Airca." My phone chimes. She steps back.

I take out my cell to a call from Gene. "Hello?"

"Kyle, oh thank God. I need your help." He says desperately.

"I'm kind of in the middle of something." I say looking at Airca.

"Please. I think Shayla's in trouble."

"What kind of trouble?"

"The supernatural kind. I don't know what to do."

I look at Airca, and sigh. "Where are you?"

"My apartment. It's a block up the street from the sky café."

"Be there in a few minutes."

"Thank you. Please hurry."

I look back to Airca and the sneer now on her face. "Was that Valene?" she asks.

"No. It was Gene. The guy we met at the market. He's in a little trouble."

"Shayla's Gene?"

"Uh, yeah. Are you and her friends or something?"

"Not really. I have talked to her a few times since we met them though."

The only time that I'd run into Gene was in the Market. I sigh. "So you admit that you have been going to the market by yourself!? Are you crazy?"

She smiles. "I am a grown woman. I don't need your permission to do what, or to go wherever I want." She steps back up to me. "Or taking what I want."

"Airca that's so dangerous. Especially with Ben lurking around there." She just stares at me, so nonchalant, like he wasn't a threat. *Okay this girl is getting on my nerves.* "What do you want?"

"You, dummy." She says reaching for me.

I take her hands. "No." She looks stunned, taken aback at my sternness. "I am with Valene. And if you can't accept that I don't think we should see one another for a while.'

She looks at me for a second motionless, breathless and in shock. Her eyes begin to water, before she lowers her head and chuckles. "So, today is our fated day?" she says just under her breath.

"What?" Suddenly, she shoves me back into the window. I catch myself on the frame but the glass shatters under my weight. "Airca, what is your problem?"

She stands there breathing heavily, her fists clenched so hard that specks of fresh blood are starting to seep through the wraps. "LEAVE!" She yells angrily.

I get myself up and knock some of the glass off my pants. "Fine. I'm out." I'm pulled into the darkness.

Chapter 25

I appear in the alley around the corner from the café, just behind a dumpster.

That little! I kick the dumpster, sending it careening across the alley and into the side of the building. *What's her problem? Shoving me like that?* I stop as I see myself in the reflection of a window. My eyes are black, and I swear I can see a streak of red swirling within them. Probably a remnant of Mayra's energy. I cover my eyes and take a deep breath. *Calm down. I don't have time for this, I have to get to Gene.* I look back to the window and my eyes are back to normal. "Okay."

I rush up the block, passing the café. "Kyle!" I hear someone yelling. Across the street, Gene waves me down.

"Gene, what's up? What's the problem?"

"I don't know...just listen to this." He pulls out his cell phone and goes to his voicemail.

"Gene." Shayla says. "Gene, please pick up. There's someone. No, **something's** here in the house. Please, please..."

The phone goes silent. "Is that it?" I ask.

"Keep listening."

In the background you can hear whispers. "Yes, for us." Shayla says answering the voices. she starts to laugh, but it changes to a scream before the call cuts out.

"I was in a meeting when she called. That was about an hour ago. I just listened to this right before I called you."

"Have you called her back?"

"Yeah. She just said come home. In that monotoned psycho killer voice." He looks at the building we're standing in front of. It's a five-story tall commercial building, that had been renovated into apartments. "I need a little back up."

"We should call the police." I suggest.

"And tell them what? My wife is hearing voices and I hear them too?"

"No. You tell them that there is an intruder in your home and your wife is in danger. That way you got back up."

"I already know that the cops aren't ready for anything like this. And that'll put more people in danger." He looks at the building, worry all over his face. He takes a deep breath. "I'll have to handle this myself. With your help." He looks at me, his eyes pleading. "Please."

Crap. This is a bad idea. I groan. "Okay, okay. I'll help you."

He sighs with relief. "Thank you. Come on."

We run into the building and get on the freight elevator in the back of the hall. He pushes the button for the fifth floor.

As we wait, Gene pulls up his shirt revealing a holster tucked in his pants. Gene draws a gun from it. I tense up. I've never seen a gun in person before. He pulls back the slide to check if it was ready, then looks at me. "Can guns hurt the supernatural?"

"I don't know exactly. Human weapons supposedly hurt, but I don't think they can kill. Then again, it may also depend on what you're going against."

"Hopefully it's the latter." The elevator comes to a halt. The doors open, and Gene points to the door at the end of the hallway. We rush through the hallway, and I sense people standing just behind the doors on each side of the walls.

Someone pokes their head out. "Gene. What's going on? There was a lot of screaming and then it just stopped. I called the cops."

"Thanks, we're about to find out. Go back inside." They pop back inside and the door latches. "Keep moving."

We reach the door. Gene hands me his keys. "Once you get it open, I'll go in first. You follow close behind and check the corners of the room to the left. If it's clear, tap me twice. Clear?"

"Yeah." *He must have been in the military or something. I've seen formations like that in movies and videos.*

I work on the lock, but the door is already unlocked. I look to Gene and give him a thumbs up. He takes a deep breath as he pushes the door open with his foot. Gene purposefully walks in, his weapon close to his body, but ready.

I follow close, just about on his heels. My heart is racing as I take a quick glance at the corners of the apartment. Nothing out of the ordinary. It's a really nice set up. A fireplace along the far wall with a huge Tv above its mantle. Bookshelves and art line the wall until you get to the sliding door, that leads to balcony. I tap him twice. Gene's shoulders relax a bit, but I feel his guard still up.

"Shay? Baby, are you okay?"

There's shuffling in the kitchen around the divider wall. "Gene, is that you?" Shayla says wearily with a slight gurgle in the throat.

There's a metallic smell in the air that I recognize because I've tasted in my mouth enough times. *Blood. Something is wrong.* Gene starts to move towards her, but I grab him. He looks back at me as I shake my head no. He looks at me concerned. "Come to me sweetie." He says, preparing himself.

Shayla peeks her head out from around the wall, with a big toothy grin on her face. Both he and I take a shuddering breath as we watch blood ooze from her eyes, nose, ears and mouth. "Shay?" he says quietly, worry laced in his voice.

She steps all the way out revealing herself to be covered in blood. "Welcome home love. I've been waiting for you. I think we need to talk." She says with an exaggerated pout.

"What's happened? We need to get you to a hospital."

"I've been thinking. About us. You know that I love you, but over the past two years, things have been a bit on edge." She takes a couple of heavy steps towards us as Gene stares blankly. "Now, I know you're working so hard for me, for us. But it feels as if something is missing."

"Can we talk about this after we get you some help?"

She grins again and rushes up to him with inhuman speed. I start to move forward when he holds his hand out, stopping me. "No, it needs to be now!"

He takes a deep breath. "Okay." He holsters his gun. "What do you need from me?"

"I need you to love me."

"Shay, I do. So much."

"Yes, I know. But not the way that I want you to."

Gene is silent. Completely bewildered at her words. I watch Shayla and the now smug look on her bloody face. "How?" Gene asks. "How do you want me to love you?"

"With all of your heart."

"Shay, you're my wife. You already have my heart."

A malicious smile spreads across her bloody face and her feature darken. Shayla's gaze moves to me and we lock eyes. Her face cracks like porcelain and falls away. My stomach tenses when I see the same broken smile of the mannequin creature I had seen earlier. "No, not yet." She says.

"Gene Move!" I say moving in between them.

Shayla brings her hand up fast and backhands me. The force knocks me off me feet and across the room. I slam into a wall, and then hit the floor. *Where in the world did all that strength come from? Is she possessed or something?* I hear Gene struggling and gasping. As fast as I can, I get my feet under me and get up.

Shayla has him pinned to the wall, by his neck. While he struggles to keep her other hand from digging into his abdomen. "Why are you fighting me? Just give me what is **mine**." She says driving her fingers into his flesh, causing him to scream out.

I summon my claws, and leap over the furniture to them. With a knife-hand, I bring my claw down into the web of her elbow, slicing through it.

She shrieks, letting Gene go. He falls to the ground with her arm still knuckle deep within him and she backs away from us. Instead of blood, a black smile oozes from her arm trailing from Gene and pooling at her feet. Shayla sobs coveting her wound. "My arm. You took my arm!" she yells, still sobbing. Her cries quickly turn to laughter as she looks at us with bloodshot eyes. "That fine, but I'm still going to take what's mine."

Gene yells out a curse, his voice strained. I look back to see the arm thrashing about, flinging the slime everywhere as it still tries to dig deeper into him. I try to grab it but keep missing as it flails about. "Hold it still." I tell him.

Gene fights to tighten his grip around the wrist, while the fingers constantly wriggle, tearing into his flesh. "Hurry up and get it!"

I get a hold of it by the forearm. Beneath its skin I can feel muscle moving but also something writhing about like worms. It yanks me forward a bit still tearing into Gene, as his grip slips. He screams, still fighting to keep the arm at bay, but there was a lot of blood now coming from his abdomen and mouth. I position myself next to him, digging my claws into the arms flesh and grip hard. The things under the skin stop moving and so does the arm. "Okay I got it. Brace yourself." With a yank, I manage to pull it out of him.

As I lift it in the air, a mass of dark strands lifts out of the slime reaching all the way to Shayla and her stump. *Is this thread?* Shayla smiles and moves her arm. The threads grow taught and the severed arm turns on me. It tries to claw at my face while wiggling ferociously to break my hold. Taking it with both hands I yank it pulling Shayla off balance. The surprise makes her waver, causing the limb to stop moving for a second. I fill my claws with energy making them sharper and bring it through the thread, Cutting it.

Shayla drops to her knees and screams. The slime starts to move as all the thread within it whips around. "I knew it. I knew you didn't love me!"

"Shayla, I do." Gene says weakly.

"No, no, nooooo.' She screams, tearing at the flesh of her face. "This was supposed to be it. This was supposed to be perfect! You've ruined our fated day!" She rushes us. I stand ready to fight.

There's a loud bang and her head snaps back. She falls to the ground just at my feet.

I turn back to Gene breathing hard, panicked as he shakily holds his gun aimed at Shayla. He drops it, gasping for air. Blood trickles from the hole in his side with his every breath. *Oh, no.* "Come on buddy we have to get you some help."

"Kyle, behind you."

I look back to Shayla, shakily trying to stand. She looks at us confused as to what was happening, a hole in the middle of her forehead "Gene? Baby what's happening?" A shadow appears outside of the door to the balcony just behind her. The mass of threads coming from her arm twitches. Shayla convulses as her eyes roll back. "It was fun while it lasted" says another voice from her mouth. "Come, Love."

Shayla's eyes roll back forward, and tears start to well up in them. "Gene." Like a ragdoll Shayla is yanked from the floor, flung through the air and pulled out through the sliding door, and over the balcony.

"Shayla." Gene yells weakly. He starts to cough up blood.

"We need to get you help." I get Gene to his feet ready to shadow-walk to the Kir manor. So Zel can heal him. *Wait, I can't. He won't be able to pass the threshold at the Kir's without a formal invite, it'll kill him. I can only take him to the hospital.* I focus my thoughts onto the main hospital. "Brace yourself. This is going to be weird." We vanish and reappear in the elevator near the emergency room. The doors open and a couple of nurses look at us in horror at us. "Help us!" I yell.

They push the code button on the panel, alerting everyone. "What happened to him?" one of them asks.

"Uhh...We were attacked. He was stabbed with something."

"His breathing is labored. I think his lung is perforated. He's bleeding out. Get him on a stretcher. He needs emergency surgery."

"I'm sorry. I'm sorry. I'm so sorry." He repeats as they get him onto the stretcher.

"We'll need to ask you a few questions." Someone says to me.

They go back to focusing on him. I step back into the elevator. I push a button and the door closes. I take a breath. *Man, that escalated. I hope he'll be okay. Maybe I can get Zel to heal him later.*

I shadow-walk back to Gene's apartment building. I appear down the street in the alley that I had passed. The cops were outside the building putting tape up. I look up to the balcony and see the streak of black going from the door and around to the other side of the building.

Oh man. What in the world is happening? What was all of that? That shadow, that voice, the thread?

'You've ruined our fated day.'

"Fated day? I've heard someone say that. A while ago. And just recently. But who said..." *Wait a minute.* So, this is our fated day.' *Airca said that.* "Oh, no." I shadow-walk to Airca's.

I appear in her room. The glass from the window is still on the floor, but Airca is nowhere. "Airca? Are you here?"

"Kyle? I'm downstairs."

I rush down the steps and into her kitchen. As I round the hallway she's sitting at the table, wearing the yellow sundress that I'd gotten for her. "Airca? Are you feeling, okay?" I ask, cautiously walking up to her.

She stands from her chair and puts her hands on my chest. "I'm fine. Are you okay? You look troubled."

"We need to get you checked out." I say taking her by the arm.

She takes hold of my shirt and spins me around. She pushes me into the wooden chair and sits on my lap. "Why the rush?"

"Airca you..." She kisses me. I push her back. "Stop what are you... doing?" My mouth starts to tingle as the room spins. My body grows heavy, and I can barely breathe. "What have you... done to me?" I ask struggling to catch my breath.

She caresses my face. "Don't you worry, it's just a paralysis potion."

"A potion, when how?"

She points to her lips. "Didn't notice the lipstick, did you?"

I take a labored breath, "Where?"

"I went back to see Marie. I told her about what happened between us and my feelings for you." She puts the finger that was pricked by the doll in my face. It was stained with the same black slime that was oozing from Shayla. "Marie told me that the prick from that doll would guide me to that which I desired. Just to let it and I would know our fated day. And I'm sure today is that day. But since you can't see that we are meant to be together. I'll just have to show you." I try to say something, but my mouth doesn't work. "Now for that little, obstacle."

Obstacle? She takes my phone out of my pocket. She starts to breathe rapidly, fanning herself. Tears form as she makes herself hysterical. All while having a sinister smile on her face. After going through my phone for a second, she pushes call. "Valene! Oh, my God hurry to my place. Something's happened to Kyle. He, he stopped moving. I don't know. Please hurry." She hangs up, grabs something from off the table, and quickly walks out of sight.

Within seconds Valene appears in a flash of darkness before me, worry on her face as she franticly looks over me. "Kyle? Kyle, what happened?"

I try to warn her of the crazed Airca laying in wait, but nothing but a moan comes out of my mouth. Without my and Valene's noticing, Airca appears behind her holding a syringe. "Valene." Airca says lightly. Before Valene can turn around, Airca jams a needle into her neck. Valene quickly spins around grabbing Airca by the throat and lifting her off the ground. She takes the needle from her neck. "What is this? What have ...you...done?" Valene struggles to keep Airca up.

"Let me go!" Airca pushes Valene hard. Valene falls to the floor, unable to catch her breath. Her body shakes as she fights to stay up. "What's wrong Valene? Having a hard time?"

Valene glares at Airca, before slowly laying all the way down. Frozen in place. Airca stands over Valene, with a smug smile and then looks at me. "I'll show you Kyle. You will see. You will love only me." Unable to breathe, everything goes black as I pass out.

Chapter 26

The sound of a blaring car horn startles me awake and I suck in air. A gust of wind blows right into my face, and It's filled with smell of exhaust. I try to move, but my body is heavy, my legs are tied, and hands are bound behind my back. I open my eyes, and everything is a blur. After a few blinks the haze finally clears from my vision. On the ground under me are lines etched into the stone. The energy coming from it, the same as shadow-walking. I roll to my back, and I see the skyline of downtown Roc. "What's going on?" Airca appears over me, breathing hard. Her eyes are wild, and a wide smile spread across her face. "Airca?"

"Kyle. You're awake. You stopped breathing when we got here. I was afraid that you had..." She pauses, before she kneels next to me. "How are you feeling?"

"Confused. What did you..." I start to ask but stop when get a good look at her. Specks of crimson are on her face, and dress. She reaches out to touch me, and her hand is dripping with blood. I scoot away from her, just out of her reach. "All of that blood. What happened?"

Airca pulls her hand back and rubs at her knuckles. She laughs. "She wouldn't quit calling your name. So, I shut her up."

"Hero?" Valene say weakly from beside me.

I roll over. Valene is on her side, curled into a ball. Her legs and arms bound in ropes, with silver thread weaved throughout them. "Valene?"

She unfurls herself and looks at me. Her face is bloody, bruised and swollen. A steady flow of blood pouring from the giant gash over her eye. I look back to Airca and all I see is red. "How dare you touch her!" I strain against my restraints, filling my muscles with as much power that I can muster. They start to give.

"Calm Down!" Airca yells. She snaps her fingers. The restraints constrict around my wrists and ankles. A white-hot pain shoots up my arms and legs, sending me reeling onto my side.

"Don't get so worked up love. She's just a little less pretty. She's not dead...yet"

I look to Airca, trying to catch my breath and clam myself at the same time. "What is this Airca? Where are we?"

"This is an intervention. Where I fix everything. Look." She points out to the city. It's a pretty view and I can tell that we're high up. "This is my favorite place to come and unwind. To think. But lately I've come here to escape from having to see you so happy with her. Asking why not me?"

"How did you get us up here unnoticed?"

She places her hand on the ground rubbing at the etchings. "You learn a few things going to and from the market. Pick up a few potions. A few books. Did you know that a human can shadow walk? They just need a little energy and this circle to act as a beacon."

"Humans don't have that kind of control over energy."

She pulls out a small vial of black liquid. I instantly recognize it as the energy that I traded Marie for the silver. "All I need is a drop or two and every spell and potion that I've tried has enough power to activate."

"You got that from Marie?"

"Marie has been very helpful. She's taught me so much. Helped me through my feelings. Helped me realize that you and I..." She moves over to me, placing her bloodied hands onto each side of my face making me look her in the eyes. "Are fated to be together." She kisses me with her eyes wide open. That's when I feel something moving under the skin of her of lips and hands. Like worms...like the thread moving throughout Shayla. I pull away from her.

"Airca we need to get you some help now. You're not yourself. You're..."

She grips my face. "I, am love. And you are loved."

I remember those words. It was what the being that summoned and tried to bind me said. I look at her wrapped hands. 'I made sure to destroy their ingredients and punish them.' I recall Mayra saying. "It was you. You were the one that tried to take control of me."

"I worked so hard on that spell too. It cost a lot of blood, and energy." She laughs. "I had everything, even your whole name. You would have been mine had that thing not interrupted us. My hands haven't stopped burning since."

I'm stunned. I don't know how or what to feel or even what to say. "Why?" Valene asks. "Why are you doing this?"

Airca tenses at the sound of Valene's voice. She jumps up to her feet, walks over to Valene and kicks her hard in the stomach. "Because he was mine!" She screams. "You made me do this. It was you that took him from me." She kicks Valene again. "It was all because of you." Airca continues to kick Valene.

"Airca stop!" I yell. She stops, breathing hard. Valene gasps for air. "Airca, why are you so mad at her?"

"Because she took you from me?"

"Have you forgotten that you're the one that turned me down?"

She snaps around, bewildered. "I did no such thing. You were the one that woke up and turned me down."

"Airca, you came into my room that night before, sat on my bed and said that we should stay the way we were."

"You...you heard that?"

"Yeah. I did."

Her shoulders sag as she sighs. "I did say that, but I had changed my mind by the time I saw you awake."

"Airca that's not how that works."

She rushes me, pushing me to the ground and wraps her hands around my neck. "I **know**! You don't have to say it." Her grip tightens and I'm starting to have a little trouble breathing. "I just...I just wish I could take it back and make you love me. Make you mine."

She says looking at me, her grip steadily tightening. The thread shifts under her skin reaching just under her jaw. The edges of my vision are starting to darken. "Airca. Let go." I manage.

"Why would I? I'll never let you go. You will be mine. It's fate's design."

"He will never be yours." Valene says weakly.

The threads stop moving and her grip lessens giving me room to take a breath. "What was that?" Airca says looking forward, her face twisting up in disgust.

"Do you really think that after all of this he would choose you? You tried to force him into a contract. And I don't know if you noticed but you were just chocking him. Do you really know what you want? Do you want him? Or want to kill him?"

Airca gets up off me and stomps over to Valene. "Shut up!" She kicks Valene so hard that she goes tumbling across the ground. "What would you know? You're with him. What do you want from him?"

Valene coughs. "I want him to be strong, independent, and happy. Not only with me but with himself. I don't want to own him, like you do."

"Shut up, shut up, shut up." She runs up to Valene. Airca grabs her by the straps of her dress and lifts her off the ground. "You think you're better than me?"

"I know I'm better than you." She states and spits a glob of blood in Airca's face.

Airca's whole being shivers. She throws Valene to the ground and wipes off the blood. Airca storms off back in my direction. She's so mad that she can't hold back the tears welling in her eyes. To my dismay her tears were red with specks of black within them. *The curse is setting in.*

Airca passes me heading towards a box just outside of the circle. Once there she reaches in and pulls out a knife. The same one she had during her ritual to bind me. "I'll show you who's better."

"Airca wait." I move in her way as she stomps back to Valene, gripping the knife. "Don't do this."

"Once I get rid of the obstacle in my way, you'll be mine."

"Airca that's not how this is going to play out."

"You'll see. Just you wait." She walks around me.

"Wait. No. Stop!" I try to move again to get in her path. She snaps her fingers, and my restraints constrict. The pain knocks me to the ground. I watch as she makes her way to Valene. *How can I stop this? I can't do anything like this. What am I supposed to do?*

Airca gets to Valene, takes her by the hair and lifts off the ground to her knees. She shoves the knife to her neck. "Still got something to say?"

"Do it." Valene says defiantly.

"Airca don't!"

In a blur of movement, Airca takes the knife and drives it into Valene's abdomen. Valene fights back a scream, growling through her teeth. Airca gets right into her face. "I know this blade isn't enough to kill you. But a fall from this height might do it." Airca lets go of the blade, leaving it within Valene and proceeds to drag her towards the building's edge.

Crap, crap, what can I do? She's not listening to reason. I watch as she drags Valene closer to the edge. The knives hilt Bob's up and down with her every breath. Her face is twisted in pain as she looks at me. *Come on Kyle think of something.* In the light of the sun Valene's amulet glistens. *The amulet.*

Zel said I was under a curse and that the amulet protected me, saved me. It's the same reason why Leo took Valene's original one. To protect himself from the curses of the Divide. *I have to get Airca to touch it. Maybe it'll save her. But how?*

"Airca wait." I manage my voice cracking.

""Once I'm done."

Come on Kyle, get a grip. With a deep breath I push down all my anxiousness, fear and anger. "Airca, I love you!" I yell as loud and as confidently as possible.

She stops in her tracks. "What did you say?"

"I said that I love you. I've always loved you."

She turns back to look at me. Streaks of red staining her cheeks from her bloody tears. "You really...No, you're just trying to stop me because I have her." She says yanking at Valene.

"Airca, I mean it. From the first time I laid eyes on you, to even now. You've always been the one that I've longed for and adored. I just didn't want to admit it."

"You really mean it?"

"You know I'm not any good at lying. And I don't make promises that I can't keep. I promise that I love you."

She lets go of Valene and rushes over to me. "I knew you loved me. I knew it."

"Of course, I do. Didn't you feel it when I kissed you?"

She takes my face. "I did."

She moves in to kiss me. "Wait. Let me go. So that I can hold you."

Her eyes narrow. Her hands move from my cheek to my neck, lightly squeezing. "You won't try anything if I do, will you?"

"I promise."

Airca's face brightens up. She says something under her breath. My wrists and ankles are relieved as the magical restraints fall off me. I stand, looking at her. The thread shifts under her skin, edging further up. She hasn't noticed but blood is starting to leak from her ears, nose and mouth. I open my arms. Cautiously, she moves towards me and embraces me, burying her face into my shoulder. "See Airca, I always keep my promises."

"You do."

I look at Valene. She's managed to get to her side and calm her breathing. Through a pained expression I can tell she's trying to figure out what I'm thinking. I mouth amulet to her a couple of times. She shakes her head confused. I point to my neck and mouth again. 'Am-u-let'

Airca shifts, startling me. Her hands slide up under my shirt. "Make me a promise. Promise to always love me. Promise to be mine." Her nails dig into my back. "Promise me!" She screams.

"Airca I..."

Laughter fills the air disrupting the moment. Airca squeezes me tight. She looks over her shoulder to the source of the laughter, Valene. "What's so funny?" Airca asks in a growl.

Valene spits blood on the ground as she sits up. "Airca you just don't get it. He'll never be yours. Do you see this amulet around my neck? He made this impossible thing with his bare hands and even imbued it with his very life. That is a testament of the love we share."

Airca screams as she pushes me from her. I catch myself and prepare to rush after her. "**Kyle**," Valene emphasizes. I stop myself from pursuing Airca. "...stopped a mad cyclops, killed a basilisk, and braved the labyrinth for this, for me. Your little friendship means nothing in comparison to what we have, what we are building."

Airca walks up to Valene and grabs the knife handle, twisting it. Valene screams, doubling over. "You think this little trinket means anything? I'll show you. I'll take what you love and make it mine." Airca grabs the amulet with her right hand.

There's a flash of light. Airca convulses snapping back, struck by what I can only assume was pain. There's another flash and a white light shine within the fist, clenching the amulet. Airca's hand starts to blacken, charring from the raw power pouring out from the amulet. Within seconds, it had crept up her whole arm, crackling like a piece of wood burning in a blazing fire.

Valene is completely unconscious. Her body dangles, only being held up by the green hell-fire lace around her neck.

With strained movements Airca looks at me. Black slime pouring from her eyes, ears, nose and mouth. "Kyle, help...me!" She struggles. The White light pulses within her arm bringing her to her knees. Light fills her eyes, and I can feel the energy building within her. Airca screams, as the energy reaches its capacity. And everything goes white.

I snap awake, sitting up. Both Valene and Airca are on the ground, feet away from each other, unconscious.

I get to my feet, and rush over to them. Valene groans. *Thank the Creator.* I sit her up as gently as possible. "Valene? Are you okay?"

She opens her eyes and looks at me with a weary smile. "I'm alive." She looks down to the knife still in her. "If just barely. Will you please take this thing out of me." I take the knife, pull it out and toss it to the side. I put my hand over the wound focusing energy to it. "Thank you, Hero."

My eyes sting as tears well in them. I Can't keep my hands from trembling as my composure crumbles. The fear and panic I felt hits me hard and I can't catch my breath. I hold her close, trying not to cry. "Hey hey I'm okay. It's okay."

"I know. I..." I take a deep breath. "I know."

Airca coughs, drawing our attention. *Oh good, she's alive.* White smoke bellows from her blackened arm. Through the cracks in her skin, you can see the threads slowly burning away. "It worked. She's alive."

"How?" Valene asks.

"What do you mean? The amulet saved me from a curse. So, I thought it would do the same for her."

"You were wearing it. It had time to fight. With her being so far along, it would have destroyed the curse and burned her to ash. That light was different. Almost heav... " Valene stops talking. Her face grows dark with anger.

"What?" I look up to see Airca getting up, holding her arm.

Airca looks around confused. "Kyle? Where are we? How did we..." Her face twists up in pain. She doubles over shaking violently. She jumps to her feet like something had yanked her up off the ground. After a moment of agonized groaning, she stops and starts laughing. When she looks up, her eyes are rolled back, and a crazed grin. "I see, you've made your choice." She says but not in her own voice. It's the same voice that came out of Shayla.

I lay Valene down and get to my feet. "Airca, wake up."

She laughs before she flung into to the air. She lands on the ledge of the roof. Airca spins around to face me. "A faint cold fear thrills through my veins, That almost freezes up the heat of life." *I recognize that line. That's Shakespeare. Part of Juliet's final monologue.* She looks at me. "If I can't have you, then there is no point of living."

"Airca, wake up. Don't do this!"

"Farewell! God knows when we shall meet again. Come love."

Airca's eyes roll forward and she takes a stuttering breath. "Kyle?" She is yanked off and vanishes over the edge.

"Airca!" Without hesitation, I run to the edge and over after her. That's when I realized just how high up we were. About 30 floors up. *Not sure how I'm going to land, but first I have to get to Airca.* Below me, she's already three floors down and at this rate is going to hit the ground before I can catch her. *I need more weight.* Darkness explodes from within my body, enveloping me. It condenses and hardens, forming my armor. I force energy out of my feet propelling me toward her.

I catch up to Airca and cradle her. Time slows as my awareness peaks, giving me time to think. Landing from this height is just going to put my legs into my lungs and Airca may die from the whiplash. Down below I see a fire escape in the alley we are plummeting towards. *That's my best chance.* Time goes back to normal. Flipping right side up I drive my left claw into the stone of the building, trying to slow our descent. It's kind of working but my claws are cutting through it too easily.

After a second of falling, we're just above the alley. *Aim don't fail me now.* I push off the building towards the fire escape. I encase Airca within the darkness of my armor and we land hard. The sound of metal twisting is loud in my ears as the fire escape bends and warps underneath us. And we suddenly stop as we hit the ground hard and blackout.

I come to, in pain and my head spinning. "Oh good, pain. I'm alive." I try to sit up but as I put weight on my left hand, pain shoots up my left shoulder. "Crap is it dislocated?" I take and slowly lift my arm, until I feel slide back into place with a loud pop.

The shield I placed around Airca lowers and I check her. She has a few bruises. "Airca?" She exhales and puff of white smoke comes out of her mouth. I look down at her right arm and it's smoldering as the threads slowly burn away within it, and hopefully her.

Airca snaps awake thrashing about as she gasps for air. I wrap my arm around her trying to hold her still. "Airca, stop." In the light of one of the lamps above us I see the glint of a thread coming from Airca's chest, wriggling and writhing. I take hold of it and pull it towards me, giving slack to Airca. She stops thrashing, but I can still feel the thread pulling into the shadows of the alley. "Why don't you show yourself? Marie."

The sound of clapping echoes off the stone wall. Marie steps out of the shadows with a sly smile on her face. "What gave me away?"

"The Shakespeare mostly."

"What can I say? I love the drama of it all." She says batting her eyelashes.

"Why have you done this?"

"I was just trying to help. Poor Airca was longing for love, unable to voice it and willing to do anything to get it. A Kindred spirit."

"Why curse her?"

"I was helping. Guiding. Directing. You two made such beautiful players. But alas," Marie moves her finger. The thread in my claw pulls so hard that it cuts into my palm. Airca starts to move, trying to stand but falls back down onto me. Marie sighs. "The main player has fallen." The thread pulls from Airca's chest singed at the end. "Freed?" she says confused.

If she's freed, I need to get her out of here. I stand, cradling Airca in my arms. "Marie. We are not your puppets."

"Everyone is my puppet. My entertainment." She says menacingly, her orange eyes glowing. *Oh man, I can't sense her anymore. We need to get out of here now.* "Now shall we continue?"

"No thanks." I start to shadow-walk. As I enter the darkness, something pushes me back. Within the portal there is a wall of thread. "What in the world?"

"You really think you can escape your fate? You hero types are so predictable."

I guess I'll have to fight. I back up to the wall and lay Airca down against it. I step away from her and move to the middle of the way. Marie smiles staring at me as I move in front of her and get into a fighting stance. She laughs. "You think you can fight me?"

"Not afraid to try." I dash at her as fast as I can. Trying to get the first hit.

"Oh my. The Hero rushes into battle, but he is so focused that he doesn't notice. His enemy is one of many."

From the shadows of the alley, three others leap out. I stop, jumping back out their range as they land in front of Marie. They stand up and look at me. My stomach twists as recognize them all. First was the man from the alley that was arguing with his wife weeks ago. Then there's Mr. Jacobs. His shirt is a bloody mess. The last is Shayla, still missing her arm and hole in her forehead.

They look so unreal. Dark lines etch into the leathery, gray skin of their faces from the constant stream of black slime, that pours from their glassy eyes. Their faces are, frozen in exaggerated smiles. Chunks of flesh and muscle fall to the ground, through the blood-soaked thread that wrap and weave through their limbs. They were so decayed that the thread was the only thing really keeping them together.

Marie starts to laugh as her puppets spread out and surround me. Their movements are fluid as if they're floating. Marie raises her hands. "Now let the final act, begin."

Chapter 27

The three of them stop moving and stare at me. It's unnerving how similar this is to fighting the Messenger's possessed. "Mr. Ross." Mr. Jacobs says his voice hollow. "Don't fight it. Just let fate pull all the strings." Thread moving through his muscles pull tight as he takes a step towards me.

"Mr. Jacobs what happened? How did you end up like this?"

"As you may have heard, me and the misses have been having troubles. Marie here has been a big help with that though. But recently we had a big fight and she wanted to leave me. On our fated day no less. Things got a little out of hand and well she stabbed me in the heart. Now I can't live without that, nor could I live without her. So, I took hers." He says tapping the bloody spot on his chest.

"What?"

"Now we don't fight anymore. And she'll be with me forever. You could have that too. Just give in."

"No. Not if I'm just going to end up a psychotic meat puppet."

He chuckles. "Your lost. It's one of the most freeing experiences."

There are snapping sounds from my left. I turn to see Alley guy's arms and fingers start to lengthen, his flesh tearing at the joints.

Thread shifting where his muscles should be. "You should listen before you speak. You never know what you'll miss."

"I've heard enough."

He rushes at me, gliding across the ground. *Can't let him grab me. I have to stop him before he gets to me.* I dash into him. He swings his long arms, trying to grab me but I dip forward just under them, putting me right in front if him. With all my strength I drive my fist into his chest. He goes flying back. He hits the wall with a loud thud, and explodes into a pile of flesh, bone, and thread.

Hands hook under my arms and wrap around the back of my neck, locking me in a full nelson. I try to fight out of it but it's locked in deep. "Don't struggle Mr. Ross. Everything is going to be fine." He says lifting me off the ground.

Mr. Jacob's spins me around and Shayla, with her one arm, runs at me. "Give me your heart!" She screams.

"Let me go!" I kick my leg back with some force. My heel connects with his knee, and I feel it buckle backwards. Both of us tumble to the side, and Shayla just misses me. I wiggle free, elbowing Mr. Jacobs hard and hurry to my feet.

Shayla was already on me, her hand rigid and ready to tear into me like she had done to Gene. *Not this time.* I sidestep, dodging her strike and take hold of her arm. Using her momentum and all my strength, I swing her around and lift her over my head. For a second, I look at Mr. Jacob's on the ground as he snaps his leg back into place. Wild surprise fills his eyes as he looks up at me. Like hitting a nail with a hammer, I bring Shayla down hard onto him.

With a loud squelch, the two of them explode into a show of limbs and thread. Their bodies entangled one another to the point that I can't tell who is who.

I drop Shayla's arm, breathing hard. Disgusted. *This could have been Airca and I. One of us dead and the other suffering under the control of this monster.* I look at Marie and she smiles. "You did this to them."

"I helped them. Released them from their sorrows and set them free to experience love in its purest form."

"This isn't love or freedom. This is suffering."

"Exactly. Only through suffering and tragedy do we find love, know love, become love. I can help you too." Her orange eyes glow as she looks at me. "Just let me pull all of the strings."

I get into a fighting stance. "No."

Marie starts to laugh. "I love the fact that you think you have a choice." She runs at me, covering a lot of ground fast. She gets ready to grab me when Time slows as she reaches out for my throat. I step to side and prepare to throw a left hook to her face. As everything returns to normal Marie's eyes snap to me and she smiles. Unnerved, I throw the punch with a little more force. With a crunch, Marie's head spins right off her shoulders and flies off to the side of the alley. Her body drops with a thud and crumbles into a mess of black smile and body parts, just like the others had.

I pick up one of her arms and examine it. It's stiff to the touch almost like petrified wood, but the skin is soft like fine leather. "You were a puppet? What was her full name? Marie-Annett, Marieannet, Marionette." Then it dawns on me. "Then if you're a puppet, where is your puppeteer?"

"You jest, young master." I hear Marie say, drawing my attention to her head. The arm in my hand twitches and needles pop out of its skin piercing straight through my armor.

Frantic I toss it to the ground. That's when I notice thread emanating from her torso spreading across the ground. "It's time to go." I turn around and try to get to Airca, but my legs give out and I drop to my knees. They're numb. The numbing quickly spreads across, my body and I drop to the ground like a pile of rocks.

Out of the corner of my eye, Marie's head slowly drags across the ground, pulled by the thread. It stops in front of me with a deranged smile. Her eyes glowing. "I am no puppet." Her torso rises into air on a column of thread. "I am an avatar of love. And an architect of **Tragedy**!"

Thread erupts from her torso, shooting through the air and surging along the ground. Until it reaches her limbs and the mangled bodies of her puppet trio. Marie's head starts to float along with all the other body parts. The thread wrapped limbs and parts rattle, as they encircle her in a tornado of blood and thread.

One by one the four torsos, seven arms and the eight legs begin mashing into one another. Blood and black slime splatters onto the ground as organ, flesh and bone wrap, snap and are sown into place in a whirlwind. The heads of her players nestle into the cavities of their own ribcages. Thread bursting out every orifice until they become mounds of pulsing thread.

The long grotesque body lands with a disgusting thud. It raises up off two of its hands and thread shoots up out of its neck wrapping around Marie's head. It whips around as it is pulled to the body. With a disgusting snap her head connects with it. Her arms go slack as she falls to the ground then slithers out of sight, on a tail made from the legs, leaving a trail of blood behind her.

It's silent. *Where's she go?* She appears in front of me, getting into my face. The skin on her face hardens until cracks form around her glowing orange, glassy eyes and mouth, like porcelain as she smiles showing off her now jagged teeth. *If I could I would run. As fast as my legs would take me. I wouldn't look back. Not with this monstrosity at my heels.*

Her left eye falls out of the socket. The thread behind it twitches and it's pulled back into place. "Now let us see what my new player can do." She vanishes. I hear rattling, behind me. My vision blurs as I'm lifted to my feet. The numbness fades and I feel her threads moving under my skin and into my muscles. My body starts to move all over the place. Thrown carelessly into uncomfortable dramatic positions. I stop, out of breath and in an over exaggerated pose, straining my joints and muscles. "Such flexibility, such raw power. Where have you been all my life?"

Airca stirs, drawing both of our attention. Marie moves in front of me. Excitement all over her broken face. "Have you ever heard of Heracles?"

"What does he have to do with anything?" I ask, straining.

"So, you have. Then you know how he killed his wife and children."

"Under the influence of Hera."

"Close." Her hand moves and I turn towards Airca.

"Oh, Under Your influence?"

"At the behest of the queen of the Pantheon, Fate... I wasn't kind to him."

"You're one of the Fates?"

She slithers in front of me. "Oh, yes. I am Clotho. The weaver. The loom of and Fate. At your service." She says bowing her head.

"Beware the loom." *That's what Atropos said to me. This must have been what she was warning me about.* "Why are you doing this? Shouldn't you be with your sisters?"

At the snap of her fingers, I snap to attention. "So many questions? Are you trying to get me to monologue? Trying to distract me so that you may break free? You're no different than any of the other heroes I've dealt with." Her head spins all the way around and looks at Airca. "And like them you will know tragedy and loss by your own hand. Two of her arms move and I start to slowly walk towards Airca.

"Airca, wake up!" All she does is squirm like she normally does when I scream at her. "Airca!" I scream, now only a few feet from her. Still nothing. I kneel, my claws now over her throat. With all the energy my body can muster, I push it out against the thread. I feel it loosen and force myself to stop. "Airca Amile Cove." I say low under my breath, putting energy and will into every syllable of her name. "Wake up!" I yell. Her eyes fly open in shock as she stares at me. "**Move!**" She rolls to the side.

She shuffles to her feet and hides behind the fallen fire escape. "Kyle, what the hell are you..." She shifts her gaze to the monster slithering behind me, she stifles a scream. "Oh my God, what is that?"

"Airca run!" I command, still straining.

Marie laughs. The threads snaps back, tightening even more around my insides. The taste of blood and bile in my mouth. "Grab her!"

My arm shoots out to grab her. Airca yelps as she dodges, throwing herself to the ground. With a quick look at me she takes off down the alley. "I do love a good chase." My body lurches forward and I sprint after her. Airca slams into cans, knocking them over in my way, but I just vault over them. I'm flung into the air ahead of her. Airca doesn't notice me as I land right in front of her, until she slams into me.

She screams, and tries to run away, but I grab her digging my claws into her shoulders. Airca starts to struggle, screaming.

Clotho slithers up behind Airca. "Now let's try this again." One of her hands raise and my left hand follows suit in a knife hand, ready to pierce Airca's stomach. "The hero, now grasping his friend, prepares to end her life." She raises one of her fingers. "With one smooth motion of his claw. He eviscerates her." She says dropping it. *NO!* With all the strength in my arm I stop just shy of her abdomen.

Clotho moves around us clearly surprised at my resisting her. She moves her hand again, but I don't allow myself to move. *It burns. I can feel the thread cutting through my muscles trying to force me to move. But I'm not going to.* She cocks her head in annoyance, but just smiles cracking her face even more. "You know the problem heroes have, when it comes down to playing the role that they are given." One of her hands moves up her body, and into the chest of the torso closest to her head. She grabs something. Slowly she pulls out a too long, black needle. She licks it, coating it in black slime. Then waves it in my face before putting the tip onto my chest. "They never really put their hearts into it." She slowly drives the needle in. I scream out, trying to fight against her. My vision blurs and everything goes dark.

In the darkness, one-word rings in my ears, a name; Airca. Like a wave, all the emotions I have ever felt for her wash over me. The longing to be with her, the pain I felt when she turned me down. The most prevalent though, beginning to fill me was hate, contempt and rage. All for what she's done to me and especially for what she did to Valene. Airca's form shimmers into existence before me, still in my grasp and all I see is red.

"Yes, Kyle. You know that this is the right thing to do. After what she's done to you. Put you and your love through. She deserves to suffer, doesn't she?" I hear Clotho say in my mind.

"Yes, I should make her suffer like she made Valene." I grip her tighter, digging in my claw and preparing to eviscerate her.

Airca looks at me terrified and in pain. She tries to pull away from my grip but can't. She starts to sob, taking hold of my arm. "Kyle wake up! Please Kyle, don't do this. I'm sorry. I'm so sorry."

I lift her off the ground. "Why should I forgive you? **Why should I!**" *Why should I?*

She relaxes in my grip and grabs my arm. "Because I love you Kyle. And I'm sorry."

The burn on her arm flashes white and a wave of energy shoots up my arm and to my chest, winding me. After a second, I manage a painful breath. With every slow inhale and exhale the red slowly washes from my eyes. I see the blood from her shoulder run down her arm, staining her dress. *What am I doing?*

From behind me I feel Clotho holding onto me, breathing down my neck in anticipation. "Yes. Yes."

I look at Airca who was waiting for me to attack. *No, I can't. I won't.* My chest hurts like crazy, but the rest of my body feels light. Her grasp on me is relaxed. *I need an opening. I need to play along.* I lower Airca to the ground and force her to her knees. "Airca!" She looks down to the ground utterly terrified. "I want you to look me in the eye." She doesn't move. **"Look at me!"** She's looks up at me, trembling. "You can't **run** from your fate." I say Wide eyed. She looks at me confused before her eyes confirm that she gets the message.

Okay, think. How do we get out of this? I stopped her control last time by pushing against her thread with my energy, but that won't stop her. I need a big shock that could disrupt her control. The training I've been doing. If I just let the energy snap back into me that could be enough. I raise my hand and flex my energy, pushing all it out as far as I could. The buildings around us tremble under the Strain of my energy. "Airca, are you prepared?" Airca shudders and closes her eyes.

Clotho grips my shoulders tighter. "Yes, end her and with you I shall create such a tragedy that my love, my goddess will swoon in ecstasy."

Airca looks at Clotho with such disgust. "You monstrous hack." I feel Clotho's attention shift to Airca making her lose focus, in turn loosening her grip on the thread a little more. *It's now or never.*

I let go of the energy. It slams into me hard, creating an explosive force that knocks Airca and Clotho away from me. My blood sprays everywhere as the thread within my body is forced out through my skin. I catch myself before I fall. *Yes, I have control again.* I turn towards the giant puppet and dash to her. She thrust out her arms trying to control me again. The threads in my skin wriggle. They hurt, but they don't work. I bring my claws through her hand and up her arm, destroying it.

My body relaxes completely as her control over the threads in me completely vanishes. I can feel again, I can move, I can stop her. With one step forward my legs give out and I hit pavement. Every part of me is in pain. And my heart. *Oh god, this hurts.*

A hand grasps the back of my neck and lifts me off the ground. Clotho looks at me, rage filling her cracked face. "How dare you!" she screams. "I'll have your head!"

A brick slams into Clotho's face, taking a chunk of her skin; revealing the pulsating thread underneath. "You let him go!" Arica screams, grunting. Another brick comes and Marie dodges it. With the flick of Marie's wrist, she tosses me through the air. I crash into Airca and We land hard onto some trashcans.

"Airca, run." I rasp out. One of Marie's hands appears taking me by the throat. She lifts me back into the air.

"You ruined it. You ruined everything!" Clotho yells wrapping another hand around my neck. I can't move, I can't breathe. My vision starts fading.

There's a flash of blinding light behind me. The air grows thick with energy. Clotho wells in agony as she let's me go. I hit the ground, finally able to breathe somewhat. Airca slowly walks next to me holding a trash can lid, and a long piece of steel from the fire escape. I look up to see two more of her arms and a torso were smoldering, slowly turning to ash. *What happened? They look like they'd been cut, but by what?*

Marie quickly dislodges the pieces before they turn her to ash as well. She turns looking at Airca, her orange eyes shining with rage. "You little wretch."

"Airca?"

She looks at me. Her eyes and burned arm are ablaze with what looked like white fire. "Be still Kyle." She says her voice resonating with power. "I will handle this hack.

"I'll hack you into pieces!" Clotho clamors toward us.

I try to stand, but my body won't move. "Airca run."

The trash can lid and the steel rod glow white within her hands. As the light dies the lid and rod have transformed into a golden spear and shield. "Never run away when facing a demon." She rushes forward. They clash with Airca driving her spear into one of Marie's abdomens. The piece goes up in white fire. Clotho falls back, screaming and slamming herself on the ground. Her body explodes into pieces, separating herself from the now smoldering pile of flesh.

Clotho's bloody parts start floating. Airca readies herself behind her shield. Clotho's limbs fly at Airca slamming into her shield pushing her back. The last one, Marie's second abdomen sits there for a second. Slowly black needles protrude from the skin. It hurls itself at Airca. There's a loud bang as it hits the shield driving Airca back even further. It starts to spin, making sparks fly everywhere. Airca screams pushing it back.

The abdomen slams into a bigger trash bin. Airca switches her grip on the spear and launches it. The spear moves so fast that it looks like a beam of light. It slams into the torso, setting it on fire. Clotho screams out in blood curdling agony.

The other parts come at Airca again, all of them now covered with needles. Airca brings her hands up into a boxing guard. She takes a deep breath, and her hands begin to glow. The first of the parts rushes her, but she dips under it. The rest come in a barrage of flesh and needles. Like she'd been training her whole life rather than a year, Airca masterfully dodges them all, bobbing and weaving through them. All the while striking and obliterating a few of them, bit by bit.

Her shield starts to glow. Airca jumps dodging over one of the pieces. She lifts her shield high into the air and drops it, slamming it into ground as she lands. A shock wave of light explodes from her causing the pieces to stop and fall.

Clotho's pieces drag along the ground to her as she pulls herself together. Black slime pouring from her mouth with her labored breath. "Is that all you got?" Airca asks.

Clotho smiles, lifting the stumps where two of her remaining hands should be.

Crap. "Airca!" I yell. Before she can react, one of the hands grabs her right wrist. Even though it starts to burn away, there's a loud popping noise. Airca screams. The second hand comes from her left, but she bats it away with the shield. In the distraction, Clotho appears in front of her. Airca's shield starts to glow again with an intense light. Without hesitation, Airca throws an uppercut, driving her shield into Marie's chest. Light engulfs them both, forming an orb. After a second, the orb explodes sending the two of them flying out.

Airca slams into the wall next to me. "Airca. Are you okay? Answer me."

Airca gets up and hobbles over to me. She kneels next to me. "Whatever this is, it's going away." She places her hand on my chest and feels around, until she finds the needles head. She pulls it out. My scream is cut short by the crippling pain. "Be still." She orders placing her hand flat to my chest. Heat spreads throughout my body, alleviating the pain to a bearable level. I sit up. "Stop her." She says breathing hard. The light in her eyes dissipates, and the shield turns back into a trash can lid before she collapses next to me.

Clotho clamors out of the shadows the size of a normal person, black slime and blood oozing out her. She looks at us. Her face is pretty much gone. She hobbles towards us in a blind rage, baring her sharp and broken porcelain white teeth.

In her approach, I see that her chest is split wide open from the shield bash. Like within her face there's an ever-shifting mass of thread, but unlike the thread in her face these seem to move outward and shift with her every movement.

I force myself to stand through the pain. Clotho looks at me and screams. I sit back into the *Lokar* stance. Jagged bone extends out from her right arm. Her hobble turns into a full sprint, and she gets to me fast swinging her bone blade.

I just duck under it, but her torso twists all the way around and she backhands me knock me back to the ground. She appears over me ready to skewer me. Rolling right, I dodge it. The bone blade slams into the ground, shattering. I roll back and backhand her with my left. As her head spins, I follow through with a right haymaker so hard across her face that knocks her off feet and away from me. She skirts across the ground slamming into the wall of a building.

On my feet, my vision gets hazy, and my head starts to spin. I wipe my face and there's so much blood on my claw. *That's right. I'm still bleeding. I need to stop her, before I bleed out.*

Clotho thrashes about, flinging garbage and trash as she pulls herself back together. She stops to covet her left eye which was dangling out of the socket. The light within it dies. Probably due to the huge crack in it. Clotho growls as she rips it off, then crushes it to dust. "You have taken a piece of my soul from me. Now I will take your life!" She runs at me. This time a little more uncoordinated.

She takes wild swings at me. Flinging her arms around like whips, trying to hit or get ahold of me. I manage to dodge the deadlier attacks, while blocking the others. But as I block her, I can feel the needles penetrate my claws and arms. It hurts, but that's it. There's no numbness, nor any pull at the thread throughout my body to control me. Just the two of us, on equal footing.

Clotho growls in frustration. Her arm snaps back into place and she lunges at me, aiming to grab my neck. I step in and dip under her. With all my might, I drive my fist up into her chin. Clotho's head snaps backwards. Instead of staggering back her feet plant, as the whole of her upper body elongates, and bridges backwards. In an instant, she contorts until she reaches between her own legs and grabs mine. "Got you."

I hit the ground as she drags my feet out from under me. She pulls me through her legs, whips me over her and slams me hard onto the ground.

Gasping, trying to catch my breath she crawls on top of me. I try to push her off me, but her hands are too fast, and they quickly grip my throat. Her fingers stretch out, the sound of her joints popping in my ears as they wrap around my neck. "Take your final breath, young hero. You cannot fight fate."

I get my claws underneath the thread, but it won't cut. I claw at Clotho's face, but she just takes it, laughing at my struggle. *Let me go!* The edges of my sight grow black and it's getting hard to move. *Come on, come on, think.* Looking down past her broken face to her seeping, cracked chest, the mass of thread pulses outward with her every movement. *I saw this earlier. That must be her source. Her heart.* I grab her throat with my right claw pushing her up away from me, to get a better angle. She just cackles. *Laugh it up, you **hack**.*

With all I have, I drive my left claw into her chest and right into the threaded mass. She screams bloody murder. Frantic, her fingers wrap tighter around my neck. The thread moves under my fingers. With what strength, I have I clench my fist, grabbing as much of the thread as possible. She freezes in place, along with her fingers around my neck. *Crap.*

I roll her over onto the ground. The thread starts to move, trying to slip from my grip. Clotho's neck stretches, inching closer to me. In front of her broken face, I'm seeing stars. *Have to end this fast.* I squeeze tighter, twist and pull the bloody mess of string out from her chest. She falls back in pain, scrunching into a ball. I channel all the remaining energy in my body to my claw. Darkness starts to radiate off my arm but it's not doing anything. Her thread is actually cutting into my hand. *I can't cut her thread.*

I panic as my strength fades, and I start to sway. *What do I do?*

A hand touches my back. Airca appears next to me, her eyes shining white once again. "Be still Shadow, my love." Airca says, but not with her own voice. It's older, softer, and very familiar. "I won't let you die again. Not while my bloodline remains." From her hand a foreign energy wells up within me. A line of white fire burst to life within the darkness of my armor. It travels down my arm to the tips of my claws. Giving off the same stifling power that radiated off the celestial silver.

Clotho looks at me, confusion, and dread in her eye as the light on my claws grows brighter. I scream and with all my remaining strength pull the mass of thread out of her chest. I let go of her neck and in an arch of light and darkness, drag my claw through the thread, cutting it.

Clotho takes hard agonizing breaths, before going slack. I gasp for air, as her fingers loosen from around my neck. "Finally." I say trying to catch my breath. I look over to see Airca on the ground next to me, unconscious. What or *who was that?* Clotho's body rattles as she tries to move. "It's over Clotho. This is the end... of your little tragedy."

She looks at me, gasping. Smoke floats from her chest and mouth as the threads burn within her body. "Oh, you hero's and your cliché lines. The true tragedy has yet to befall this world and my goddess will be the one to deliver the finale line."

"Your goddess? Hera and the Pantheon are gone."

She laughs. "Hera? She betrayed me. I gave her everything, including my heart. Then she left me to suffer, when Zeus found out what I had done. No, my goddess is one of Love, honesty, and pain." Her orange eye shines its light on me and she smiles. "Oh yes. I can see it in your future. You'll be a witness, and you'll know it. **True tragedy**." She starts to laugh dramatically. The glow of her eye fades and she stops moving.

"Oh, thank the Creator."

"Yes, indeed."

I look back over my shoulder to the voice to see the thin ghostly frame of the last sister of fate standing behind me. "Lady Atropos. What are you doing here?" I ask weakly.

She walks up beside me. She stares at her fallen sitter, motionless under me. Then she looks at me with her pale green eyes. "I came for that." She says pointing at the smoldering, bloody mess of threads in my hand. "The heart of the loom."

Shakily I stand. "Take it." I drop the smoldering thread into her thin hands. "It's caused enough trouble." I say walking past her and over to Airca.

"Yes, it has, and will." I look back to her, skeptical at her words. She smiles, "Be careful young one. Your future is bright, but you will be face to face with the darkness soon enough. Hopefully, you'll be strong enough to change your fate like you've done today."

"Change my fate? I was supposed to die here?"

She looks at me still with that smile. "No, not you."

I pick up Airca, cradling her in my arms. "Safe journey home. And tell Minos I say hi." She bows her head. I shadow-walk back to the top of the building. Valene is sprawled out on the ground unconscious, with a makeshift wrap around her waist. Laying Airca next to her, I walk to the roof access door and place my bloody hand on the knob. "Zel, hear me. As bearer of the key, I command thee. Open the door to me."

The door rattles, and the metal starts to glow red. It implodes in on itself leaving a doorway of darkness. Zel steps out and then bows. "Master Kyle?"

"Help them." I say falling forward and into darkness.

Chapter 28

I open my eyes to the late sun shining through the enchanted ceiling of my room at the Kir's. I try to sit up, but I can barely feel anything. A hand halts me. "Don't move Hero, you've suffered internal damage from that thread. Any unnecessary movement could cause permanent damage."

I take her hand and kiss it. "Thank goodness. Valene, Are you okay?"

She stands next to the bed and lifts her shirt. Wrapped around her waist are fresh bandages. "I won't be able to eat solid food for a while but, I'll be fine." She says with a weak smile. "How are you doing?" she asks, gripping my hand.

"I'm good. I guess. Everything hurts, but at least I'm alive. What about Airca?"

"What about her?" Valene says coldly.

"Valene, please. Is she okay?"

She snorts. "She's alive. For now." she says crossing her arms. That's when I notice the spots of blood seeping through her bandaged hand. "Wait, what happened to your hand?"

She chuckles, looking at It. "Smoke happened."

"What? What do you mean?"

"A couple hours ago I came in to find smoke standing over you, growling."

"He was growing at me?"

"No. He was facing the door just growling. The crazy thing was he was asleep. Just standing there fast asleep."

"That's weird, I've never heard of dogs sleepwalking."

"So, I woke him up. He was confused for a second but when he saw me, he snapped. He squared up over you and lunged at me. Bit me hard. It took all I had not to end him then and there."

"What stopped you?"

"The moment he bit me, he seemed to come to his senses. Looked like he fully woke up. He apologized and left."

"That doesn't sound like him. Why would he attack you?"

"I have no idea. But he was trying to protect you and take my hand off."

Why would he want to protect me from Valene? There's a knock at the door. "Come in."

The door opens. Airca stands in the doorway, her right arm in a sling. "Kyle, you're awake. May I come on?"

"Yeah. I was just asking about you. Come on in."

Airca steps in and walks towards the bed. The air grows cold. "Stop right there, if you don't wish to die." Valene says angrily.

Airca stops in her tracks. She looks down. "Valene." I say

"No Kyle I... Valene I'm so sorry for what I've done. I've wronged you both. I wish there was a way to make it up to you."

Valene picks something from off the nightstand and throws it at Airca's feet. Airca jumps back as the dagger she used to stab Valene plunges into the floor. "You can use that on yourself."

I look at Valene sternly. She snorts, sitting on the bed next to me trying to calm down. "Airca it's, okay, you were under the influence of that monster. You had no control of yourself." Her face grows a little grim. "What's wrong?"

"I didn't have full control, no, but..."

"But What?"

Airca is silent. Looking down at the floor. "Go ahead Airca. Tell him what we talked about." Valene says.

"I meant it. Everything I said, I meant it. The thread just gave me the push I needed to say what I wanted." Airca explains.

"You, wanted to hurt us?" I ask.

"No, never. I just..." She tries to take a step forward, but stops looking at the knife, and then to Valene. "I just...wanted a chance. To be with you. By any means necessary."

The room begins to shake as Valene's energy swells. She stands, forming a dagger and points it at Airca. "*Zax mun* (Vile human), you missed your chance. Both To have him and to kill me. And You will never get that chance again."

Airca takes a step back.

"Valene." She looks at me. "Give us a minute. Please."

She looks at me confused. "What? No."

"Please."

She sighs. "Fine. But I'll be right outside." She walks to the door, never taking her eye from Airca. "I'll be right here if you need me." The door slams.

There's silence. "Come here Airca."

She slowly walks to my bedside and sits. For a few minutes, we sit in silence. "Kyle, I'm so sorry."

"I was under her control as well. I know what it was like."

"But you didn't really hurt me." She says rubbing the shoulder that I dug my claw into.

"Believe me, after what you did to Valene, I wanted to. I was going to, but something about your touch woke me up." She takes my hand. I feel a warm energy coming from her now. It makes me think of what she had done against Clotho. Displaying all that crazy power and skill. "How are you up so fast? I'm a demon and that thread did a number on me."

"I don't know. Zel said that the thread in my body had vanished, and I was healing fast. My wrist kind of hurts, but it's cool. Even the burns on my arm have almost healed. But the ones on my hands, he said they can't be healed."

"Yeah, I figured. How did the thread disappear though?"

"He thinks that it might be due to the fact I held the celestial silver when I grabbed Valene's amulet. It cleansed me instead of..."

"Killing you." *That doesn't explain her sudden ability to fight a high-level demon on equal footing or transform things into a shield and spear.* "Airca, what's the last thing that you remember in the alley?"

"Throwing a brick at her and being hit with you."

She doesn't remember. Maybe it's for the best. "You know that brick really saved my life. Thank you."

"Really? Well, you're welcome." She says with a smile. "Kyle, I'm really sorry for what I've done to you. Can you ever forgive me?"

I look at her. As much as I want to see the girl I'd grown up with and fallen for. All I see is the crazed women that nearly killed and tortured Valene. "Airca I...I can't. Not now at least."

Slowly she nods her head. "That's fair. That's fair." She says, fighting back tears. "I think I better get going. See you later?"

"Yeah, later." She gives me a hug, tears running down her face. At the door, she opens it. Valene stands there with a scowl on her face. Airca, steps to the side allowing Valene to come in before she can scoot by and walk down the hallway.

Shutting the door behind her, Valene stomps over and sits in the chair, pissed to high heaven. I sit up making her fret a little and take her hand. "Are you okay Hero?"

I take a shaky breath as tears pour from my eyes. I was this close to dying; again, nearly lost Valene and now I've lost my best friend. "No. No, I'm not."

Valene crawls into bed with me careful not to jostle me as she scoots in close. She lays me back down and holds onto me. "It's okay, Hero." For hours, we lay there as she comforted me. Until I finally close my eyes and drift off to sleep.

The sound of growling, barking, and scuffling pulls me out of my sleep. I sit up to see Smoke in the middle of floor. His teeth are bearded and the fur on his back on end and smoldering. "Stay away from my master!" He screams with a growl.

In front of him, the static creature appears. Since we're not in that static plane I can see the humanoid outline. "It's his fault." It says through the static.

Smoke growls before lunging at it. The creature swings a backhand at the blue pup and they both vanish. "Smoke?"

It's quiet. From out of the darkness of the room The static creature appears in front of me wrapping its hands around my neck. My body goes numb as it shoves me back onto the bed. The smell of ash and burning flesh bombarding my nose. In all the commotion I look over to Valene, but she hasn't budged. She's just sound asleep.

"It's your fault! It's your fault! Your fault!" It screams squeezing harder.

"Let me go." I barely manage.

In a blur of blue, Smoke appears on the creature's back. "Let him go!" Smoke yells as he bites down on its neck. It screams letting me go and they both vanish into darkness.

I sit up gasping. Valene pops up placing her hand on my chest. "Kyle? Sweetie what's wrong."

"It's Smoke. I need to go see Smoke."

"Kyle Smoke is fine. It was just..."

"No, you don't understand. Something is wrong."

There's a knock at the door. "Come in."

The door opens and it's Zel. "Master Kyle. We need to hurry to the hell hound enclosure. Something seems to be wrong with Smoke."

I try to get up but my body is on fire. Valene keeps her hand on my chest, keeping me steady. "Come on Hero." She helps me off the bed. Basically, carrying me to the door. Zel steps into the room, shuts the door and reopens it to the dimly lit enclosure.

Beyond the door you can hear barking and growling. "We have to hurry." I tell them.

We go through, entering the pen. All the hell hound pups, and Sally are in the middle of the pen, surrounding a frantic and barking Smoke.

"Zel what's happening here?" Valene asks.

"My lady I have no idea. He was asleep and a moment later woke up like this."

I let go of Valene and hobbled forward into the crowd of hounds. Tears touch my eyes as I see the state my familiar was in.

Blood trickling from his nose and mouth splatter everywhere as he barks and snaps at the air. "Kyle? What's going on?" Valene asks from behind me.

"He's fighting. He's been fighting for a while now. Trying to protect me."

"Protecting you from what?"

"You. And he's starting to lose." Valene looks at me confused.

I walk towards Smoke. "When I was healed by the waters. That nightmare version of you vanished into a blue light. Saying that it will be my fault. I think she was talking about this." I kneel in front of him. "Hey buddy."

Smoke stops, looking at me with bloodshot eyes. He shivers, and black smoke bellows off him. I slowly reach my left hand out. He looks at it, panting and swaying trying to stay up. Images of flames and the color red appear in my mind. Smoke bears his fangs and lunges at me. He latches down on my hand. "Kyle!" Valene says frantically.

I put my right hand up, stopping her. "Smoke. I know what you're seeing. I know what you've been fighting." I pull him in, and he fights me, yanking at my hand tearing into it. I grab him, pull him to me and hold onto him. He thrashes trying to get away from me. "Come on, relax. I got you." He growls louder and bits down harder cracking the bones in my hand. "Don't worry. You won't have to go through this anymore. You don't have to protect me from my curse, my nightmare. it's mine to bear." I look him in the eyes. They flash blue and I feel my mind grow heavy as an ache I haven't felt in months appears. Making me nauseous.

Smoke's bite on my hand lessens, until he lets go. He looks up to me whining apologetically. He licks the blood from my hand. "Forgive." I hear him say.

"I forgive you. How are you?"

He yawns, then lowers his head. The image of a pillow appears in my head. "Sleep."

"Go ahead." I curl him up in my lap. "Rest and thank you for shouldering it for a while." Once he puts his head down, he and the world around me fades, becoming static.

I feel the heat first in the back of my throat and on my skin before the static plane ignites in flame. "Hero?" I hear Valene say among the roar of the fire. I close my eyes. When I open them, I'm back in the enclosure, surrounded by the hounds. "Kyle, are you okay?" The familiar stench of burning flesh and ash fills the air. My nose starts to run. I wipe it away and find that it's blood. Valene moves in front of me. "Kyle answer me." She demands, her voice crackling like wood in the fire.

Hesitantly, I look up to her. A nervous chuckle escapes my mouth as I stare in horror. Valene's face is torn and blackened. Her eyes are hollow, glowing with embers. With her every breath she exhales ash into the air. "Smoke is okay now."

"What about you?" she asks caressing my face.

Ignoring the heat radiating from her hand I smile. "I'll be fine. For a little while at least."

"I'll contact Vivica right away. We'll get you help. Just give me some time."

"I know. I trust you." *I can bare this. I did it for a year. And after watching Smoke fight, I know I can too. I can take it a little longer. I won't be beaten by this nightmare.*

Acknowledgments

Thank you, Zach, for picking this story to pieces. It is all the better for it. And to those that pushed with me and for me.
Much Love!

About the Author

      Lonnie Davidson was born and raised in Columbus, Ohio. He spent summers in Pennsylvania with his father, where the two shared a love for cartoons, films both foreign and domestic, comic books, and games of every kind. Those summers sparked a vivid imagination and appreciation for stories, artistry, and the lessons hidden within them. During the school year, Lonnie's mother encouraged him to strive academically, a drive that led him to graduate at the top of his high school class and later attend Ohio University. Together, his father's inspiration and his mother's motivation gave him the balance of creativity and discipline that shaped him as both a student and storyteller.

      Although his degree wasn't in literature, Lonnie never abandoned the passion for storytelling that began in childhood notebooks filled with fantastical worlds. Today, that childlike wonder remains at the heart of his work. Through his writing, Lonnie crafts immersive tales of fantasy, mystery, and beyond—stories that explore resilience, sacrifice, and the spark of humanity that endures even in the darkest places. His goal is to build worlds with words that resonate with readers, offering both wonder and reflection.